"*Vowed in Shadows* t
intense ride with two o
—*New York Times* b

Praise for the Novels of Jessa Slade

Forged of Shadows

"Dark, dangerous, and spiced with passion, this is a well-written tale that will grab your attention from the very beginning." —Romance Reviews Today

"The wordplay is riveting and the story line is fast and action-packed." —Smexy Books

"The only thing I can say about this series is WOW! Ms. Slade brings the fight against evil from the dark and into the light. This story is so exciting and action-packed that I had a hard time putting it down. I ended up reading it in one night. I can't wait to see what comes next for this great new romantic urban fantasy series."
—Night Owl Reviews (5 stars)

"[A] heady mix of philosophy and religion ... serves as part of the framework for this excellent series and sets it apart from the pack.... Be first in line for book three, *Vowed in Shadows*." —Bitten by Books (5 tombstones)

"For readers who love J. R. Ward's Black Dagger Brotherhood, the Marked Souls series will hit the spot."
—*Romantic Times* (4 stars)

continued ...

Seduced by Shadows

"Wonderfully addictive!"
—*New York Times* bestselling author Gena Showalter

"Slade's debut presents a dark and dense supernatural conflict with high stakes in a world where demons and angels possess humans and use them as tools in the unending fight between heaven and hell . . . [a] rich crossover urban fantasy." —*Publishers Weekly*

"A beautiful and inventive new series start, with plenty of action and wonderful characters!"
—Errant Dreams Reviews

"A gripping, suspenseful story, with some hot romantic interactions thrown in for good measure."
—San Francisco Book Review

"*Seduced by Shadows* blew me away. . . . Slade creates a beyond-life-or-death struggle for love and redemption in a chilling, complex, and utterly believable world."
—Jeri Smith-Ready, award-winning author of
Wicked Game

Also by Jessa Slade

Forged of Shadows
Seduced by Shadows

VOWED IN SHADOWS

A NOVEL OF THE MARKED SOULS

JESSA SLADE

A SIGNET ECLIPSE BOOK

SIGNET ECLIPSE
Published by New American Library, a division of
Penguin Group (USA) Inc., 375 Hudson Street,
New York, New York 10014, USA
Penguin Group (Canada), 90 Eglinton Avenue East, Suite 700, Toronto,
Ontario M4P 2Y3, Canada (a division of Pearson Penguin Canada Inc.)
Penguin Books Ltd., 80 Strand, London WC2R 0RL, England
Penguin Ireland, 25 St. Stephen's Green, Dublin 2,
Ireland (a division of Penguin Books Ltd.)
Penguin Group (Australia), 250 Camberwell Road, Camberwell, Victoria 3124,
Australia (a division of Pearson Australia Group Pty. Ltd.)
Penguin Books India Pvt. Ltd., 11 Community Centre, Panchsheel Park,
New Delhi - 110 017, India
Penguin Group (NZ), 67 Apollo Drive, Rosedale, North Shore 0632,
New Zealand (a division of Pearson New Zealand Ltd.)
Penguin Books (South Africa) (Pty.) Ltd., 24 Sturdee Avenue,
Rosebank, Johannesburg 2196, South Africa

Penguin Books Ltd., Registered Offices:
80 Strand, London WC2R 0RL, England

First published by Signet Eclipse, an imprint of New American Library,
a division of Penguin Group (USA) Inc.

First Printing, April 2011
10   9   8   7   6   5   4   3   2   1

To whom-/whatever is in charge of dreams come true:
Hey, thanks.

ACKNOWLEDGMENTS

Each book is a new journey. Special acknowledgments go to my editor, Kerry Donovan, who brings clarity when I've lost my path, and to all the wonderful people at Signet along the long road from story to book, and also my agent, Becca Stumpf, for her unflagging enthusiasm at every step. I lift a glass half empty to the Beach Brainstorming Babes, who've never found a turn that can't be made twistier with the addition of more Kahlua. Much love to my family and Scott, who've been with me all the way.

And first, last, and always, my fervent thanks to the readers who've joined this wild ride.

Chapter I

"Hot as hell in here tonight." Nim unzipped the oversized rifle case. "Just the way we like it." She set aside the ammo box, and from the padded case, she lifted the sleek weight. "Ready to knock 'em dead?"

The boa spiraled up her arm and across her shoulders as she settled in front of the mirror. The fine mosaic of scales ran as smooth and cool as water against her sweaty nape, and Nim sighed with pleasure. "Yeah, Mobi. We need them live and squirming."

The thump of music coming from the stage made talking in the dressing room a chore, and the dancers rarely bothered. Which suited Nim fine. So she recoiled when Amber tottered over on her platform heels, bare breasts arriving easily a full second before the rest of her, and thrust her scarlet lips toward Nim's ear.

"He's here again."

Nim unlocked the ammo box and rummaged through her makeup. "Who's here?"

"That same guy." Amber snapped her gum impatiently. "Captain Hook."

"Oh. Him." Nim's hand shook. She reached past the *Viva Las Showgirls* semifinals invitation ticket and grabbed a fat eye pencil to give her traitorous fingers something to do. When she stared into the mirror, her pupils were wide with adrenaline.

She wasn't fooling Amber either. "Yeah, him," the girl sneered. "Everybody knows Captain Hook had a thing for cold-blooded reptiles. Didn't end so well for him, though. Wonder if he knows what he's getting this time."

Nim spun in her chair to face the other dancer. The boa lifted his head, and his forked tongue stroked the stagnant air.

Amber retreated a step. "Did you get colored contacts? That's a wicked purple."

When Nim simply stared at her, Amber scowled again and teetered away.

Nim turned to the mirror. After a moment's hesitation, she looked up. Her irises were the same muddy blue-green as always. Swamp-water eyes, her last ex-admirer had called them, to go with her dishwater-brown dreadlocks.

How weird that Amber's description echoed the dream she'd had a couple of nights ago. The violet eyes had belonged to a man, though. Mesmerized by his beauty, like something that should be in a museum behind glass, not exposed to a careless touch, she'd half fallen in love.

Then his irises had turned all eerie white, except for hundreds of swirling black specks, and he fucked her, his hand fisted in her dreads, until she screamed and woke herself up.

Very weird. Quitting her tranqs cold turkey had probably been against medical advice for exactly such a reason, but she didn't want the antidepressants making her fuzzy for the final round next week. She needed to be sharp if she was going to ditch this hellhole for the lights of the Vegas Strip.

She outlined her swamp-water eyes in pitch-dark

kohl. Almost right . . . She layered on purple shadow, thick and disturbing as a day-old bruise. Perfect.

When she finished her prep, she waited behind the blackout curtain, where the glaring stage lights failed to reach. Her gaze shot unerringly to the first table just beyond the stools drawn up to the counter at stage left.

Yeah, there he was again, just as he'd been all week, angled to keep the whole of the club in view, one knee drawn up with his boot heel hooked on the base of the bar stool. Like a cop. Or a thug.

He faced the stage. Staring at her? Her pulse quickened pointlessly. No way could he see her past the glare. Out in the audience, the club was too crappily lit for her to make out his features. Usually she didn't give a rat's ass—and, thanks to Mobi, she knew a lot about rats—who was out there, staring.

So his face was in shadow, and the garish gels washed out the color of his hair, but his body . . . that was on display for every girl in the place to assess.

Not too tall, judging by the length of thigh in his close-fitting jeans. Good jeans too; no rips in the knees. Nice to see some guys still bothered to dress up before going out. No one had gotten a long look at the bulge in his pants, so maybe he rolled with a fat wallet; maybe not. Certainly he hadn't spent any of it for one-on-one attention. The other girls had bitched about that all week while they tried—and failed—to poach him.

Of course, nobody bitched where he might hear. Nim studied the imposing breadth of his shoulders filling up a dark gray T-shirt. His biceps bunched across his chest where he'd folded his arms, blatantly displaying the reason no one bitched aloud.

Nim clicked her tongue. A cripple with any manners would wear a long-sleeve shirt, never mind the sticky heat of August in Chicago. But no, Captain Hook sat there with the honest-to-fuck metal hook instead of his right hand, shining front and center for the whole world to flinch from. Nice. She didn't know much about prosthetics, but considering that the Russians had ways to make fake diamonds even bling experts couldn't ID in a lineup, he might have found *something* less gruesome. Maybe he was hoping for a mercy dance.

Or maybe he liked gruesome.

She narrowed her eyes until her fake lashes crisscrossed like daggers in front of her. Sure, he didn't watch the other girls, but he hadn't tipped her out either. Even though he always came in just after she started her shift—obviously he was stalking her; maybe he'd watched her ace the qualifying rounds of the *Viva* competition and fallen secretly, madly in love—he always left before she could get out onto the floor after her set.

Well, that was going to end tonight. She could do gruesome like nobody's business, no one had ever accused her of being merciful, and she knew exactly where guys like him kept their love.

His congregation would have died—again—seeing him in a place like this.

Jonah Sterling Walker kept his arms crossed tight so he wouldn't inadvertently touch anything. He'd learned that lesson the first night at the Shimmy Shack when his elbow stuck to the tabletop. Presumably the tacky substance had been the congealed spill of some previous customer's, but whether the spill was a beverage . . . If he could've kept both feet off the floor, he would've done that too.

Unfortunately, the repentant demon seeking redemption that had hijacked his body in return for inhuman fighting skills hadn't gifted him with the power of levitation. It had stolen his life and replaced it with immortality, and shattered his soul in its battle against evil, but it failed to help him here.

From the gloom beyond the stage curtain, the woman's gaze weighed on him like lead anchors. Violet-tinted lead anchors—a sure sign that her demon, which had been circling her without her awareness for more than a week and had finally settled in three nights ago, was on the verge of its virgin ascension.

The only thing virginal about her.

The volume of the unrelenting din they called music dropped. The deejay exhorted them, "Put your hands together ... Scratch that. Put 'em in your pockets—not your front pockets, you filthy jag-offs, your back pockets—and start pulling out those Lincolns for ... our Naughty Nymphette!"

A few men hooted as told; a half dozen others sucked at their drinks as if suddenly very thirsty.

She stepped onto the stage, bare as the day she was born. Barer, since even newborns slid into the world with more body hair than that.

Jonah snapped his eyes closed. Too late. Under the harsh lights, her dusky skin glowed, sleek as the snake threaded across her outstretched arms. The shine off her shoulders, the snake's coils, and—ah, dear God in heaven—the fullness of her breasts burned on the insides of his eyelids. Unfair that she could invade his defenses with nothing more than ... nothing.

The costumes earlier in the week had been bad enough. Layers of vinyl and gauze, links of chain, strings of white lace from another century adding insult to injury. And he'd suffered injury aplenty, with every knock of his cock against the backside of his zipper.

At least the ridiculousness of the schoolgirl kneesocks, the maid's apron, and a kimono, of all things, had allowed him to steel himself—in more ways than one—against the inevitable flesh display.

He might as well see his oncoming destruction. He opened his eyes.

She glided across the floor toward him, her bare feet silent on the parquet. But she timed each footfall for every other beat of the music, so even though her approach was slow, his heartbeat quickened against his will to echo the incessant bass.

Exactly how repentant was his demon?

She moved with a liquid grace that ignored gravity and time and entropy, as if she had no care for the rules of the universe. Sweat glistened across the skin of her chest, but her arms spread, unfaltering under the forty pounds of reptile. Only her rounded hips marked the cadence.

After the gyrations and jiggling of the others and the gleeful flinging of G-strings, her prolonged tension tightened every nerve in the room. Where was the teasing smile? The bustier and the stockings? Here were the tits and ass they had come for, and yet this was not their fantasy. This was too raw, too wild.

Jonah stiffened against the sharp twist inside him of the demon reacting to the first whiff of menace.

Her dreads slid across her breasts, hiding, then revealing her dark areolas, and the blunt ropes lashed the upper curve of her buttocks. Achingly slowly, she raised her arms, and the snake eased from her shoulders to spiral across her torso. The scales in shades from chocolate to sand rippled down her body. Its blunt diamond head poised for a moment like an earthy jewel centered above her navel, then continued lower.

Her hands tracked its descent, easing over her breasts, lingering at the flare of her hips. She tipped her head back, throat exposed, and her dreads swung loose as the snake coiled down her thighs.

It pooled at her feet like a shed skin. Unfettered, she stood exposed, her taut curves the same tawny brown as the middling tones of the scales, an illusion of snake to woman. Hell on the herpetological half shell.

Jonah's pulse ricocheted through his body, tearing ragged holes in his calm, and he realized he hadn't taken a breath in too long. When he finally did, it sounded like a gasp.

In the middle of the stage, the lights were aimed at her with such salacious focus that not a single shadow remained, not the faintest female mystery was left to the imagination. And yet he knew he wasn't seeing all of her. The purple smudges around her eyes seemed to suck down the light, but her gaze fixed on him, still and predatory behind the unnatural thicket of her lashes.

The demon was rising in her, and it called to him, teased him to reach out.

His fingers twitched in anticipation, and he clenched his fists.

Fist. His missing hand burned as if he held it out toward open flame. Rather like he was doing with the remains of his soul by coming to her now.

The djinni that had taken his hand six months ago had taken with it his belief that their fight for good would prevail. To tip the balance in favor of his shaken faith, he was willing to do anything.

He stared at the Nymphette.

Anything.

The beat of the music stumbled from one song to the next, and she knelt to retrieve the snake, but instead of beginning her next dance, she crossed toward him and stepped out onto the bar that surrounded the stage. Another step and she was standing on a bar stool. The gawkers rumbled, a sound somewhere between approval and consternation at the break in their routine.

The three-legged stool wobbled. At his table, Jonah planted both feet on the floor, half rising to catch her, and rocked his own chair with his haste. But she crouched, one hand steady on the bar, the other on the snake, and slipped to the floor to continue toward him, as if she hadn't noticed the near fall.

Dimly, he heard the deejay squawk for the next dancer, the Nymphette having naughtily abandoned the stage. Though her hands busily rearranged the snake across her shoulders, her violet-tinged gaze never left his.

He'd been stalked before, but this made every hair on his body prickle in alarm.

She glided up to him, right between his legs. He leaned back, arms still crossed, thankful the height of the stool gave him a vantage point to look down at her.

She didn't touch him, but the heat of her naked body radiated through his jeans and sank into his thighs. "You want a dance, Cap'n?"

Her low voice hummed through his bones. The scent of the snake—a sharp, loamy tang—made him shudder.

"Assuming you can swing it." Her gaze angled down to his crotch. "The price, I mean."

She had no idea what this was costing him. "In private, if you'd oblige." His voice sounded hoarse to his own ears.

The league's leader had explained what would happen, in a conversation as excruciatingly embarrassing as that heard by any bride on her wedding night. Not that Jonah wanted to compare this moment in any way to his wedding night.

The sacrilege tightened his fist another notch, and the rage-curdled tension brought his demon screaming from his depths. The demon's power rebounded through his body, but it recoiled from the brimstone-scorched scar tissue that had been his weapon hand. Surely even her nascent demon would sense the danger, the thwarted violence, and she would withdraw.

Instead, she canted her head forward, a dare. "VIP lap dance? Well, look at you, coming on strong now."

He stood abruptly. "Yes, that's me. Coming strong." He took her arm.

The long-forgotten sensation of soft flesh beneath his fingers swept him in a hot tide, and his pulse raced ahead of the demon's seething temper like spindrift on the crest of a killer wave. His breath tumbled through his chest.

She jerked away. "Don't touch," she hissed.

"It's a strip club." But when the snake hissed too, he let her go—the better to restrain the rampant wickedness inside him.

"And I'm stripped, in case you hadn't noticed. No touching."

"Ludicrous," he muttered. He waved her toward the hall that led to the private rooms he'd scouted earlier.

She eased around him. "You paid eight bucks for a Power Slug. You'd know ludicrous." She nodded to the bartender, who popped the tab on a small aluminum can and slid it across the countertop toward them. "Have another. I get a percentage of the bar."

Jonah took the energy drink as they passed. In the hallway, the pounding music dulled to a merely irritating headache. The AC pushed the stale odors of cigarettes and damp cardboard boxes, but did little in the way of cooling. "Are you always so . . . honest with your patrons?"

"Not on the first date. But you and me, we've been dancing around this thing for a week now. Time for flattering lies is long past."

"A week is a long time?"

"You owe me for all those hungry stares. All that looking and no paying is giving Mobi a complex."

"Moby? Ah, the snake. Curious choice of names. The obsession angle works, but I can't picture you dancing with a white whale around your shoulders."

In the gloomy hall, her eyes glimmered with only human reflections. "Mobi as in Möbius strip, going round and around, always ending up back in the same place."

The brooding tenor of her words struck him deep.

Before he could speak, she ducked behind a curtain. He followed her into the closet. The VIP lounge lacked any features that might have identified it as important or a lounge. A wooden chair faced into the corner, as if it had been pushed hastily awry. He yanked the shabby red curtain closed.

She spun the chair toward him. "The only Mopey Dick I expect to see here is yours. And I can make that all better."

Jonah took a pull off the Slug. The sweeteners and caffeine buzzed through him as his demon-boosted metabolism dealt with the chemical brew. At least the task distracted the creature of evil inside him from its impotent seething.

He wished he hadn't thought "impotent" just now.

Nim plucked the can from his hand and tossed it aside. The spilled liquid fizzed. Under the lone lightbulb, her small smile was hard enough to dash hearts upon, were any careless enough to somehow find their way to this place. "So, tell me what you want, Cap'n."

Jonah sat and crossed his arms. He needed her demon ascendant before he made his move. She wouldn't believe his story otherwise. "Dance for me, Nymphette."

Physical stress triggered the demon's rise. Dangerous, but necessary, since the newly possessed needed to find a way to balance the demon within them. Males traditionally drank and fought their way through the other-realm emanations coursing through their bodies. He'd been told it worked differently with the females. Just as well, since his balance was shot.

"Call me Nim." Her voice turned husky, not with the demon, just a generic come-on. She swayed closer. "Nymphette is such a mouthful. And maybe you want me to save my mouth for . . . other things. Right, Cap'n?"

"Don't call me Captain."

Her fake tarantula lashes narrowed at his brusque tone, but she didn't speak. She sidled toward his chair and slowly sank to her knees between his legs. Her gaze rested straight ahead, and his flesh, already strung tight, lifted like a marionette. Her mouth—that wide, generous mouth—was such a short distance from his zipper. He ached all over at her closeness, his erection straining toward her, his jaw locked hard against giving in.

She unwrapped the snake from her shoulders and laid it over his feet. The weight of the beast as it wound around his ankles was surprisingly heavy and hot through the leather of his boots. He couldn't stifle a grunt of dismay.

Nim grinned, a crooked chink in her seductress armor that revealed the first hint of honest emotion he'd seen: amusement, at his expense. "Don't want you sneaking away early, like you've been doing all week."

"Hadn't planned on it." Anyway, not until her demon was firmly anchored in her soul and she'd been drawn into the league as its newest possessed fighter.

She rose, so close between his thighs that he felt the passage of air, faintly scented with patchouli. But she never touched him. The way she used her body was sinful, but he had to admit, she kept it as brutally honed as any warrior maintained his weapons. A demon could choose worse than to take such a dwelling.

Within the confines of his spread knees, she turned and set her back to him. She ran her hands up her torso, over her shoulders, and through her dreadlocks. With a single twist, she bound her hair into a thick knot at her crown.

She leaned to one side, and he couldn't stop his gaze from following the sinuous curve of her spine, down between the points of her shoulder blades to the twin dimples framing her tailbone. His hand twitched to test whether his spread fingers would span the distance.

Just as well it was the missing hand.

She glanced over her shoulder. "No touching."

"So you said." He hadn't given himself away. Couldn't, considering his maiming. But she obviously didn't think that would stop him.

Her fog-on-the-water gaze traced him. "You aren't here with flesh on the mind. No lusting man could have lasted that whole week. Definitely couldn't last now." She straddled his knee, again without touching him, and dipped low in a slow-motion grind that never quite brushed his jeans. "You're so strong. Crazy strong." Her voice was a purr. "Is that because of the ring?"

His left hand, tucked against his ribs, clenched against his will, but the gold band on his third finger was too worn to bite into his flesh. "No. Not because of the ring."

She tilted her hips and smoothed one hand over her haunch to ride above the shadowed cleft between her buttocks. Where he'd wanted to put his hand. "Because of the hook?"

The metal tip drove into his biceps as he drew even tighter into himself. How could she ask so casually? "Aren't you supposed to be dancing?"

She bent backward, an impossible contortion without making contact. And yet she managed to keep even her hair suspended above his lap, teasing but not touching. She stared at him from her inverted pose. "You're supposed to be pulling something out."

"You said no touching. Presumably that also means myself."

"Your wallet is exempt from the no-touching rule."

He sighed, aggrieved, and uncrossed his arm to shift to one hip and reach for his back pocket. "At least this is on an expense account."

"All business. I like that in a man. We're practically soul mates."

Anger, cold and jagged, wrenched like the hook through his chest, dragging the demon to the surface. "Don't say that."

"Bosom buddies, then." She turned again to straddle his other leg, facing him. Her arms, crossed in a low X across her belly, pushed her breasts into tempting handfuls. Another supple writhe brought her down low, so low and close her nipples would've grazed his lips. If not for her oft-stated no-touching rule, of course.

"You have no idea how close we'll be," he said.

He'd meant to sound as flirtatious as any of her customers, but a faint hint of alarm crinkled her brow. When he opened his billfold, though, the wary look in her eyes evaporated with a spark of simple avarice. He wouldn't bother making mental bets about the weakness in her soul that had made her vulnerable to possession.

"Let's see, then. Shall we?" She edged closer and propped her foot on the chair seat between his legs. "I bet that big, shiny hook scares the good girls away, doesn't it? Well, not me. I don't easily scare."

"Because you're a bad girl."

"Just like you wanted." Her bare toes grazed his crotch, such a glancing touch it might have been an accident, except he suspected she didn't make such mistakes. She fancied herself fully in control of the situation. Of him.

His body didn't exactly disabuse her of the notion. The surge in his jeans kindled a flare of victory in her eyes. As if this was a battle she planned to win.

No way for her to know she'd already lost.

Pity chewed at his defensive anger. "Ah, Nim. Was there no one who cared to turn you from this path?"

Her eyes widened, and a streak of violet shot across the whites. "Shit. You're one of those? Come to save me from myself?"

"No." His voice was scarcely more than a whisper. "I couldn't dream of saving you." Maybe once, he'd believed himself the man for such a task. Not anymore.

"Good, because I like what I do." Her lashes fluttered like a Venus flytrap closing on unsuspecting prey. "And I can tell you like it too."

The league had no idea what it was getting. But demons—even the repentant teshuva that fought against the darkness—never cared much for harmony. Their quest for redemption would be found through obliteration. "I still don't condone selling your soul for money."

"Very good money." She bent her knee, lowering herself toward him, the V of her breasts one deep breath away from swallowing his wallet. "And it's just a body. Don't you think it's worth that wad?"

He twitched the wallet away. "You don't even care that much about the money."

"Not true," she protested.

"You do it because you like when men ache."

"Oh yeah, I ache all over. For you." She flexed so that her shin hovered above his chest, her naked body stretched nearly parallel to his. "Just returning the favor, lover."

"Did you ache when you marked yourself with these?" He touched his fingertip to the first in a row of circular scars marching up the inside of her thigh.

She recoiled with a snarl. "Don't. Touch."

Behind her back, he reached up, and, with his hook flattened between her shoulder blades, he dragged her down to his chest.

She squawked as she sprawled over him in a tangle of long limbs and a thrust of bare breast. Her first ungraceful move of the week.

He cupped his palm to her cheek, fingers against the curve of her skull, thumb pressed under her jaw, firm but not unnecessarily cruel. "You put too much faith in your body." He was relieved at his conversational tone. "Control the head and you control the body." Control was good, yes.

Unable to regain her balance without testing his grip on her pressure point, she glared into his eyes from inches away. The purple flare spiraled from her irises into the blacks of her pupils, bright enough to dazzle him. He knew her vision was shifting into hunter mode.

An irate breath flared her nostrils. "Which head?"

She slammed her fist toward the fly of his jeans.

If she hadn't all but announced her intentions—and if he hadn't already been thinking about that part of his anatomy—she might have landed the punch. But he was already twisting away, so her knuckles caught the point of his hip instead.

She yelped, not loud enough to carry over the bump-and-grind music. He'd already confirmed that the security cameras covered only the doors and the cash register, and the bouncer had willingly taken two hundred-dollar bills with nothing more than a wink and a man-to-man nod.

More important, the isolation that had made her susceptible to the demon and now her unconscious reliance on its powers would keep her from calling out for help.

However, the rising demon also made her harder to handle. He twisted again when she braced one foot between them on the chair seat and reared back, nearly overturning them. He stood, still clasping her close. With the weight of his body, he pinned her to the wall while he awkwardly adjusted his one-handed grip.

Since the hook, he hadn't held anyone he didn't want to hurt.

And this wasn't exactly a grappling hold he could practice on his fellow fighters. "I don't want to hurt you," he said aloud, but the demonic growl in his voice made that hard even for him to believe.

Nim's irises flared to a more violent purple in response, and she jackknifed against the wall, angling and weakening his hold. Obviously she wasn't interested in what he had to say.

Come to think of it, neither was he.

"Dance for me, Nim." This time, he let the demonic double-lows ripple through his voice. He let her go and dropped into the chair. "Make me want it."

She landed in a crouch, one hand braced on the ground between her feet. But she didn't run.

She could no more escape than he could. No matter how much he hated the wicked thrill flowing through him, the pulsing, stiff flesh behind his fly pointing the way.

His long, slow descent into hell had brought him here. But the dark twist inside him promised that now he might actually enjoy it.

CHAPTER 2

Nim couldn't stop her feverish shivers. What was happening to her? She'd stepped off the stage, knowing exactly what she was after—and the number of dollar signs that entailed—and he'd taken her plans away from her, one-handed.

And now he held it out again. Not the wallet, which he'd tucked safely into his pocket. But the memories . . . those he'd yanked out of her with a single, fleeting touch against her scarred thigh.

She'd shove the past down his throat.

What else could she do? Nothing. She had nothing else. So she danced, no holds barred.

The already tiny room shrank to the circle of his thighs. His heat thawed the chill that had invaded her, as if the perpetually struggling AC had decided to turn August into Arctic. Her tightened nipples sent a pang all the way through her body, and when she ran her hands over her breasts—same as she always did when the moment came to rock the crowd—her knees almost buckled and she moaned for real, a breathy sound too soft and weak for the stage.

Oh, this was not good at all.

It was too good. His blue eyes raked her with a sensation more intimate than any touch. God, who was he that he could do this to her? No man should be able to touch her. She'd made sure of that. Now everything she knew was breaking down, all the certainties she'd lived with. Ugly, they might have been, but they were hers, simple and constant.

And all the while, he watched her as if waiting for her to finish breaking.

Fuck that. He thought he could confuse her, mess with her head and from there control her body? Well, she'd seen—*felt*—that he wasn't so calm and cool as he pretended. And if there was one thing she still knew, it was manipulating the body.

She slithered over him, as close as Mobi twined around her during a dance. His eyes widened in momentary shock. She might have laughed, but her breath was gone as her thighs scraped over his jeans and her nipples dragged on the soft cotton of his T-shirt. She reveled in his heat and rubbed the length of him.

When the chair wobbled, he put his arm around her. His hand landed on her ass, and she felt his chest heave under her as he gasped. He released her at once, so she rocked the chair again. The hook where his hand should have been thudded into the wall as he steadied them.

"Nim," he warned.

She sank her fingers into the blond waves of his hair. Somehow, in the nasty little room with its one lightbulb, his hair managed to shine like sunlit gold. No man had ever offered her gold.

"You wanted this," she reminded him. "'Dance,' you said."

"I haven't paid yet."

"You will."

"Is that a threat?" Those cold blue eyes glinted at her with a touch of purple.

She hesitated, remembering her dream of glowing eyes and Amber's strange observation. A wayward stage light? Did it matter when he was waiting for her answer? Every possible reply seemed like empty banter.

So she kissed him.

She pressed her mouth to his and sucked his lower lip between her teeth. She nibbled, gently at first, then meaner, while her fingers cradled his head.

Or held him fast, depending on the perspective. She felt him straining, with nowhere to go except to sink against the chair. Why he didn't just throw her off, she didn't know. She was strong from years of pole work, but she didn't kid herself that she could truly restrain him. Her feelings should be hurt that he was so obviously not enjoying his enjoyment. But she felt too good with the hot bulk of him between her legs, the fine silk of his hair tickling her fingers.

The AC chill prickled over her spine. "I'm cold," she whispered against his mouth. "Hold me."

"It's the demon," he murmured. "Don't let it take you."

"You can take me. If you want." Was that her voice—so needy?

"Not my demon. Yours."

She hardly cared to make sense of his rambling. Something about demons, but she'd heard that nonsense before from the religious wack jobs who occasionally picketed outside the club when they weren't contemplating their navels or the end of the world, whichever came first. He'd already promised not to try to save her.

His body, hard against hers, was made for sin. His big shoulders supported the weight of her elbows as she cradled his head. She tasted the sugar from the drink on his tongue. Between her knees, his lean hips jerked once, and she laughed into his mouth.

"Tell me you didn't just come," she said.

"You need to come with me."

"I will." She couldn't silence the moan. "I will."

"No, come with me after."

After what? she meant to ask aloud, but her body was shuddering over him, caught in the grip of something more unnerving than the hook he'd braced below her breast, holding her upright as her vision grayed.

"Look at me," he demanded. "Don't let it take you."

But she wanted to. It felt so easy, a blissful slide into nothingness that even a burning match pressed to her flesh wouldn't illuminate.

"Nim?" His hand cupped her cheek, not the bully-boy grip he'd used earlier, but tenderly. That hurt worse than the cold sinking through her bare skin. "Nim, look at me." His voice thickened.

She blinked into his violet eyes. "Did you spike the drink?"

"No. You are feeling the last stages of your demonic possession."

"Oh, God," she groaned. Not in a good way.

"No," he repeated patiently. "Demon. It is rising in you. Like the bane demon is within me."

Something was rising in him, all right, right under her hand. An aroused crazy man with a hook had her in his clutches—in his clutch, she supposed—and she was losing consciousness, probably drugged, never mind what he said, because, really, even a crazy man wouldn't *admit* he'd poisoned his evening's entertainment. Bane, he'd said. Men had always been the bane of her existence. Her thoughts did the cornered-rat thing, constricted by the darkness closing in around her.

"This will be hard for you to believe." The crazy man's voice, low and urgent in her ear, cut a path through the threatening oblivion, like a tantalizing way out. "That dream you had the other night?"

How had he known about that? Obviously, he'd been lurking around the club for the past week. Had he followed her home that night? Had he seen her touch herself in her sleep? Her face burned under his palm.

"A demon came to you then," he said. "You let it into your soul. I know you didn't understand, but your penance trigger—a weakness in your soul—made you uniquely vulnerable to one particular demon. It has anchored itself within you, and it is rising to take its place. Now, if you come out the other side alive, you will take your place with us. With me." His voice deepened another notch, the insistence throbbing in her with an irresistible allure.

"Who?" she gasped. She meant to ask "Who *are* you?" but the question sputtered out. *Come out alive?*

"Your demon called to mine, and now you will be one of the talyan—a possessed warrior, like me—with a teshuva demon lodged in your soul." His words sank into her brain, relentless as a strip-club bass line, but twisted with strangeness. "Strength, speed, deadly fighting skills, and immortality will be given to you. And the life you knew before will be stripped away." A wry note crept into his voice, and once again he sounded more human. "Although that won't be a problem for you, will it?"

She rallied against the brutal chill that sucked the breath from her lungs. "I like my life. It's mine."

"It belongs to the league now. And in return, you will fight against evil and earn what measure of grace you may." Again, he gave her that doubtful look, which would have raised her hackles if she had any.

The cold seemed to press around her heart and close down her vision. "Do I have to give up an arm too?"

The cruelty rocked him; she felt it through his body. But he did not let her go.

Instead he kissed her back.

Well, she couldn't blame him. It was a great way to shut someone up and turn the tides. Plus, he had such a wonderful mouth. The hard, tight set of his mouth was just an illusion—no, a *lie* to distract from the curve of his full bottom lip, the delicious reddened peach tone.

A wave of pleasure overpowered the chill, and she sagged against him. The scrape of denim and cotton, the brush of the metal hook and the rough wooden chair under her shins all tingled on her naked skin with distracting intensity. But mostly she felt his mouth. Softening, slanting under hers. This time, he parted his lips, but tentatively, as if the concept had just occurred to him. The tip of his tongue traced the front edge of her teeth and retreated.

Good God, he was as shy as a virgin. How could that be, with his wedding ring?

Maybe that was why he'd come.

The warm glow centered in her chest vanquished the cold entirely. "Is this your first time?"

His blue eyes glazed. "Yes."

How sweet. How sad. And she'd dragged him in here like a lamb to slaughter. Probably ruined him forever. "I'll make it all right," she murmured.

When she eased off him, his desire-clouded eyes cleared. He clutched at her awkwardly, the hook skidding over her spine. He winced. "Don't go."

"I'm not going anywhere."

"The demon realm is all around us. I smell it."

What the hell with the demon thing? Damn, his wife had obviously done a number on him if he thought sex was demonic. How could that unknown woman have denied this sexy man? "You're smelling the Power Slug we spilled. It's probably eating through the carpet." She touched her fingertip to the swollen center of his lower lip. "Sex isn't always evil, you know."

Under her finger, his lips twitched in a reluctant smile. "Not always?"

"Not this time." Who would've guessed? She did have a merciful side after all. She wondered where she'd kept it hidden; certainly not under her clothes.

Straddling his hips, she leaned back and let her hair

down. The blunt ends of the dreads tickled her skin, and she shivered.

"Stay with me," he urged.

"Keep me here." She lifted his hand and laid it against her breast, palm centered. "Stroke me. Tease me."

"What happened to 'no touching'?"

"I lied."

His groan sent a lightning shaft of delight through her, which flared brighter when his fingers closed over her nipple.

"Oh yes." She drew out the word to a hiss. Sex might not be evil, but it didn't have to be all good either.

Still clutching his hand to her breast, she rucked up the hem of his T-shirt. He sucked in a breath that rippled down the ridged plane of his stomach. Oh, he had no reason to be shy. She danced her fingers down his fly.

"Wait." He lifted the hook and stopped. He stared at the gleaming metal, surprise loosening his tight-clenched jaw for a moment.

She'd made him forget, she realized.

Before the hurt could flood in—and she knew it would; oh, how well she knew—she unzipped him. A briefs man, of course. Why make her job easy? Well, she'd teased Mobi out of tighter hideaways.

"Nim." His hand slipped down between her breasts toward her navel, as if he might be going for the block again at his crotch. So she lifted her hips and let his knuckles bump her smoothly waxed mound.

The breath exploded out of him.

While he was distracted, she eased her fingers past his waistband. His erection surged, hot and ready, into her hand, the first bead of moisture damp on her skin.

The rest of him was only a half beat behind. He clamped the hook behind her back and dragged her down so she sprawled across his chest. His mouth captured hers with a fury that bore no relation to the naïve, neglected man she'd imagined.

When she tried to sit up, to keep some measure of control, he angled his hand between them to find her slick heat. She gasped. Not naïve at all. With his thumb on the white-hot point of her desire, he slid a finger into her, then two. She bucked her hips against him and cried out. He chuckled into her mouth, a dark sound that made her suddenly believe in devils.

He'd played her, one-handed, the bastard. He knew exactly what to do, and he did it pitilessly. He stroked, he teased, just as she'd asked. He kissed his way down her neck. She had a split second to think about standing up, slapping his face, and screaming for a bouncer, but then his lips fastened on her nipple.

As if he'd completed some previously unwired circuit in her body, every nerve came alive, lit her up like a damned Christmas tree in August. She let her head tip back, let the rush of sensation fill her and overflow.

She clenched her thighs around him, the yearning threatening to break her apart unless she gave him what he wanted, what he was taking from her with each caress of his strong fingers. She didn't want to give it to him—he was practically stealing. But her will was weak, and her body betrayed her; it wanted and would not be denied.

What had he said about her soul?

"Come now," he whispered. His words blew soft and cool across a tight-budded nipple.

She convulsed against his hand and what was left of her vision went black.

Sweat beaded at his temple, and Jonah closed his eyes as Nim's pleasure throbbed around his fingers, the pulse doubled and redoubled by the demon's energies.

When the leader of the Chicago talyan had explained, haltingly, how sex would ensure the human body stayed balanced in this realm, he'd actually blushed. To see the tall, rangy Irishman blush while the blade-bearing beauty at his side snickered had been unnerving.

Liam Niall had spent almost two centuries bashing monsters to bits with his huge war hammer, but the appearance of little Jilly Chan had changed everything. And Jilly had been only the second female to take on a teshuva demon. The first, Sera Littlejohn, had broken all the rules they'd known. It was she who had initially noticed Jonah's restlessness and identified it.

He'd been pacing the rooftop of their warehouse sanctuary, driven by an agitation he couldn't pinpoint, hoping the noon sun bouncing off the flat tar would fry him into oblivion. Sera had cornered him, her mate, Archer, behind her. "When's the last time you slept?"

Jonah deflected the cool assessment of her hazel gaze with a one-shouldered shrug. "We've been busy."

"Right," Sera drawled. "Unusually intense demonic activity, weird nightly light shows, plus PMS-ing male talya. What could it possibly mean?"

Jonah stiffened. "Excuse me."

"Pre-mating shakes. I just made it up." Sera waved her hand toward the skyline. "We know how this works now. Sort of. She's out there somewhere. Go find her."

"Who?" Jonah had asked.

Archer—a big, brooding man with whom Jonah had tangled in the past—looked at him with something disturbingly like compassion in his bronze eyes. "The woman of your nightmares."

Sera just laughed, but Jonah's heart shrank.

He'd given up his life, his soul, his peace to the mistake that had made him a pawn of the devil. He'd given his pain, his suffering, his hand. He'd kept one small piece of who he'd been, one tiny, untouched sliver of his past that no one had thought to ask for, no one had wanted.

And now he had been very much touched.

Nim took a deep, shuddering breath that lifted her

from him. She looked into his eyes and he caught a glimpse of the fading violet fire. "I guess now I'll have to pay you."

"The price has already been paid." He trailed his hand down her thigh where the demon's mark had risen. The dark traceries emphasized the smooth skin over toned muscle. His body screamed for release. He ignored it.

She stumbled off his lap. "What the fuck?" Under the sparse lighting, the old burn scars across her inner thigh showed only as a faded pearl sheen when she tilted her leg. She swiped at the black lines that eddied around the faint remnants of her penance trigger. "Did you Sharpie me when I wasn't looking?"

"While I have a certain dexterity with the hook, I could not have drawn those marks with it," he said. "And my other hand was occupied."

She shot him a furious glare. "I don't do tattoos."

He'd noticed. No tattoos or piercings, along with the no body hair. As if she'd been wiped clean. Not anymore. "It's called a *reven*. It marks the demon's presence in your soul, and acts as a tether between it and you, between you and the demon realm."

"What are you on?" Unease—and anger at being uneasy—tightened her mouth.

To his surprise, Jonah decided he preferred that faintly mocking smile, wide and easy on her generous mouth, instead of this fear. Not that he blamed her. And not that he had any choice about frightening her.

He could have chosen to ignore the fleeting thought that he liked her lips under his best of all. His immoral handling of her had been vital, according to the new rules the league was fumbling through with its unforeseen female colleagues. He'd done what was necessary, and no one could ask for more. "I'm sorry. There's no easy way to explain. Not in this day and age, not in this country."

She planted one hand on her hip. "Oh? Since when

is crazy talk ever okay?" Then she glanced down at the *reven* that curled up toward her hip bone, and her hand sprang away.

Despite the vulnerability she must be feeling, her hands never fluttered forward to shield her feminine curves. Once, he would have always worn a jacket in public, something he could have offered a woman in a moment like this.

Well, never a moment quite like this. He thought it best to bite back his smile. And he'd be wise not to take off his T-shirt for her. What might start as a feeble attempt at old-fashioned gallantry could quickly become a more ancient ritual if the unabated strain in his jeans was any warning.

"I wish you had something to cover yourself," he said. "Besides the snake. It's difficult to talk to you when you are unclothed."

A flush rose under her dusky skin. "You guys aren't usually here to talk."

He wondered how mere conversation could bother her more than her nakedness. Perhaps he could use her body to make her understand.

"You fear I'm an enemy," he started.

"I'm no idiot," she retorted. "If I was afraid of you, I'd scream. But I'm not, so I didn't."

"Oh, you're afraid. Feel how you face me. On the balls of your feet, your body angled to present the narrowest target. Instinctively, you would fight me. That is the demon, rising to take on its opponent. Feel how your right hand flexes. What weapon do you imagine there?"

He stepped toward her and, since she had no clothes, was treated to the sight of every muscle tightening down her limbs, across her belly. When he brought his gaze to hers, the violet flickers made him nod. "Do you feel it rising in you when you call on it, even unwittingly?"

"I have no idea what you're talking about." Her voice wavered.

"You're uncomfortable around men, which is why you seek to control us on this most primitive level." He took in her state of undress with a sweep of his hand. "And yet now, you're afraid, but you don't call out. You believe, deep inside, that you could take me." He tilted his head, studying the waves of violet in her irises. "The demon inside you may have repented, but it retains some bad traits: violence, cunning, arrogance."

"Worst of all, a delight in confusing people," she snapped.

He nodded. "Always that."

She stalked around him in a tight circle, and he held himself still, though his skin prickled with awareness. She stopped in his peripheral vision to retrieve the snake from behind the chair and wrap it around her shoulders, letting the loops of its coils drape over her breasts. From the way she shifted from foot to foot, he knew she sensed the changes wrought in her. He'd succeeded in making her doubt her doubts.

When he didn't turn to face her, she held her position, gaze intent on him. The sweep of her focus was like a breath on his skin and passed over him from wallet to hook and back to his face.

"Where is your *reven*?" She stumbled over the word.

Still not looking at her, he reached over his shoulder to grab the back of his T-shirt and wrenched it over his head. Hadn't he told himself that wasn't a good idea? He left the T-shirt binding his biceps in front of his chest. Better the constriction than fumbling to get the hook through the armhole again.

She gasped and leaned forward. "Oh, my God. I can see through your skin."

She reached out, hesitated a moment; then her fingers slid over his skin, cool and slow, from the knob at the back of his neck down his spine and around his ribs. "But it's not muscle and bone in there. It's . . ."

A tremor sprang up in the wake of her hand. "It's nothing. The void. A glimpse into the demon realm."

"It's just a trick," she said. Then her voice softened. "But it is kind of beautiful."

He turned his head sharply to stare at her, but she was entranced by the black lines of the *reven* that spilled like wild swirls of india ink down his neck and over his shoulder, shot with threads of violet and the eerie translucence where his flesh thinned with demonic emanations. Other-realm energies glimmered in the mark, not evident to human vision without a lurking demon presence.

"Mine doesn't do that," she noted.

"It will when your demon is sufficiently aroused."

She peered up at him. "And your demon is aroused." Her touch skimmed lower, toward the waist of his jeans, and the glint in her eye wasn't purple at all.

"It responds to any threat," he said.

Her lips quirked. "How am I a threat?"

"You're not. I am."

"Ah. What are you fighting in yourself?"

"I'm not the one who strips myself bare for strangers." His voice was harsh.

She withdrew her hand—but slowly, showing him she wasn't fazed by his flare of temper. "You've been coming all week. Obviously, you wanted—still want— something from me. But why waste time on this elaborate setup? You could just pay me, you know." Her fingers curled tight. "Unless you want something kinky. I don't do kinky. And no sex. No more sex."

"I'm not vice," he said as he yanked the shirt over his head. He tucked the hem savagely into his jeans and almost groaned when his fingertips skimmed the upward-straining tip of his penis. Vice, indeed.

"Sure." She didn't sound convinced. "If you want me to do some private dance where you pretend I'm damned with a demon and you try to save me—"

"I can't save you. I'm damned too, possessed just like you."

"Right, whatever. Then we'll save each other and—"

"No, we'll fight together. That's the only way we'll be redeemed."

She huffed out a sigh. "Okay, fine. It's your scenario, your three hundreds bucks, so—"

He echoed the sigh. She'd stopped believing him and was falling into her old patterns. It was easy to do—in the beginning, at least. She needed more convincing than even her own body could give her, certainly more than his words offered. "You have to come with me."

She hesitated. "I don't do outcall."

"Tack on a convenience charge."

She scowled at him. "You make it sound so mercenary."

He laughed.

Her scowl deepened. "I prefer the term 'entrepreneur' to 'mercenary.'"

"If that helps you sleep at night."

The way she bit her lip made him think it didn't help at all. He wished he hadn't teased her. What she did, what she was, had made her a fitting vessel for the demon. And her demon would give him what he needed to offset his lost arm, to let him slay a monster and patch the holes in his tattered soul. He wouldn't presume to think he could do anything for her soul.

Which made him more of a mercenary than her greedy heart could ever imagine.

CHAPTER 3

Nim dressed quicker than she'd ever undressed, ignored Amber's rude questions, flipped off the deejay who wanted his tip for one measly song, and wondered what the hell she was doing as she stepped out of the club, into the sweltering darkness where the large, taciturn Captain Hook waited for her.

"If I can't call you Captain, what's your name?"

He began walking down the sidewalk as if he had no doubt she would follow, which she did, damn him, because she was curious and she'd already let him do . . . Well, he couldn't do much more to her.

"Jonah."

"Another whale name. That's why you and Mobi get along so great."

He turned his head to stare at her. "We do?"

"Usually when I wrap Mobi around somebody's chair, he climbs up and starts getting personal. That's because I don't feed him before I dance, to keep him from puking onstage. It's nice because he's pretty good at keeping guys in the chair. But he left you alone."

"I haven't been so blessed in a long time." Jonah paused. "If he really feels that way, let me take him."

He reached for the rifle case. When Nim hesitated to release her grasp, Jonah lifted one eyebrow. "Despite my newly discovered affinity for your snake, you can be assured I won't run off with him."

After a moment, she passed the case and adjusted the strap of her camisole. "He's heavy," she warned.

"I think I can handle it."

The edge to his tone stropped her temper. "I didn't mean because of your arm. I meant because he's heavy, even for me."

"So you're questioning my manliness, not my maiming."

She held out her hand. "Give him back if you're going to be like that."

"I said I've got it."

"See, you are stealing my snake. You have no idea how much trouble it was to steal him in the first place."

The bitter set of his mouth eased. "Your lack of morals continues to astound me."

"Now who's being insulting? A chick at some ass pit where I danced a few years ago was using Mobi in her act. He was smaller then, and she was doing all these fast spins and tossing him around. He hated it, wouldn't eat, thought she smelled like stale cat all the time."

"Ah, Mobi thought she smelled like stale cat?"

"Maybe that was me. Anyway, I snagged him and we found another place to dance with better music."

"At the Shimmy Shack?" His tone edged up in disbelief.

"God, no. It was way classier. But the GM wanted to charge me girl-on-girl tip-out rates for Mobi. Sick, huh?"

"Because Mobi's a snake?"

"Because he's a *he*."

"Unconscionable."

He was teasing her again. But she could deal with mockery. She just didn't like that grim look, as if death would've been better than losing his hand. Struck a little too close to home. "I don't mind the Shimmy Shack. Sometimes it's nice having nothing tying you down."

"No doubt that attitude made you very attractive to the demon."

She pulled a face. "Are we talking about demons again?"

"My apologies. I won't bore you with the details. For now."

"Yeah. Let's wait till we get to the place. Yours, or do you have a hotel somewhere?"

Jonah stopped for a moment, so she did too. He lifted his head, eyes half-closed. The hairs stood up on her nape, and she had the creepy feeling he was listening to something she couldn't hear, the aural equivalent of that strange emptiness in his flesh around the tattoo.

A trick, she told herself, part of his little demonic fantasy.

"Can we get this over with?" At an apprehensive twitch in her leg muscles, she shifted in her wedge sandals. Maybe she should have worn sneakers. She was faster in sneakers. Although why she had the feeling she should be running . . .

Jonah turned his face one way, then the other, a furrow between his brows as if the signal he wanted wasn't coming in clear. "I don't have a home," he said absently. "I have a boat."

She bit her lower lip. "It's expensive to keep a boat." She let her voice slide up in a question.

"Yes, the *Shades of Gray* came at a high price, even though I stole her from a thief."

For some reason, the admission didn't settle the twisting of her nerves. "I wouldn't have guessed we had that much in common."

"More than I've told you." He opened his eyes wide and a glint of violet startled her. "We'll find one soon. This is a good neighborhood for them."

"Them? What one are you talking about?" Okay, she

was definitely wishing she had her sneakers now. Or at least Mobi in her hands. "I changed my mind. I am afraid." She wished she hadn't said that aloud.

But this time Jonah did turn his attention to her. "You're honest. Painfully so. I didn't expect that."

"You want honest? Okay, you're creeping me out. Give me Mobi and we'll be on our way. And by 'we,' I mean me and Mobi." *Not you.* She figured she didn't need to be that blunt. He was crazy, but not stupid.

He ignored her. "This way." And he walked off.

He had Mobi, so she couldn't just go the other direction, even with every nerve in her body screaming that she should run.

Actually, not *every* nerve. Just half of her nerves. The other half . . .

The other half, including the little hairs on the back of her neck, told her to follow him.

That couldn't be good.

He was almost a block ahead of her and moving fast. She stumbled to catch up, cursing her slutty heels. They weren't going to get her a bigger tip, as she'd hoped; they were going to tip her over.

Jonah ducked down an alley, and she sighed. Of course. A dark alley. He fantasized about demons, after all.

"Demons could live in hot tubs too, you know." She paused in the mouth of the alley and scanned the shadows. "Let's do a possessed-hot-tub scenario. It'll be all hot, just like hell. But sudsy. Jonah, damn it, where'd you go? You have my snake."

An echoing hiss from beyond a half-open door lured her deeper into the alley. "Mobi? Shit. I danced alone for years. I could do it again."

Despite her couldn't-care-less words, she crept through the doorway. There was too much broken glass to kick off her sandals. At least the cork soles were quiet.

Inside should have been all black, the brick walls broken only by a narrow bank of clerestory windows high in the second story. But when she blinked, a glow hazed the interior, as if someone had rimed the palettes and stacked boxes with white paint and kicked on a black light. Which, she supposed, went with the demon theme. If her dreads had been any shorter, she was pretty sure those would be standing on end too. She was going to be seriously pissed if something jumped out at—

With a shriek, she spun to face the shadow-within-shadow sneaking up behind her. How she'd known it was there . . . "Jonah, you fucker—"

It wasn't Jonah.

God, it was nasty. Squat like a pile of something left on the sidewalk after the dog walker went by. Its flesh accordioned down to blunt, cloven feet, like cow hooves, except white and bulbous.

Before she could close her slackened jaw, the thing jumped at her with a squeal to match her own. She turned to run, felt the snap in her ankle, and fell headlong across the floor. Her dreads tumbled forward, blinding her.

Damn the strap for breaking now. But it wasn't the strap. Pain arrowed up her leg, shocking her vision brighter as she pushed her hair from her face. In the sudden clarity, she saw the crest of oily bristles on the creature, could almost count the teeth in its gaping mouth as it bounded over her. Those approximately one million teeth snapped with an evil whistle through the air where her head would've been if she hadn't fallen.

It whirled to face her, its rows of flabby, inflamed skin spinning a split second behind, like a zombie ballerina's dead-flesh tutu. The row of protuberant orange eyes fixed on her.

She'd gotten one sandal unstrapped, so she threw that. If the monster was going to eat anything first, it'd be the damn shoe that had tripped her up.

The thing didn't even flinch. It took one step forward,

then stopped. Which gave her a chance to throw the other shoe right in its gaping mouth. "Fucker!"

A gout of black ooze spewed from its mouth. Flecks of the noxious fluid spattered over her legs and burned worse than nail polish remover on a torn cuticle. She shrieked again and crabbed backward, dragging her ankle.

"I could do without the swearing." Jonah's head popped up over the creature's shoulder.

She screamed yet again, then realized he wasn't wearing a monster suit. He was standing behind it, his hook buried deep in its neck, which had kept the monster from coming after her.

"I could do without the screaming too, now that I think about it." The muscles in his arm stood out in stark relief as he restrained the thrashing thing.

"What the fuck?"

"Wonderful. Screaming and swearing." Despite his even tone, his face was tense with the effort, and sporadic streaks of purple lightning raged in his eyes. Though the thing was shorter than him, it was three or more times his weight, and it yanked viciously against his hold, frenzied to escape him. Obviously, it was smarter than she had been.

Nim swallowed against the sour tang of bile. "What is it?"

"It's a demon."

"I thought you said the demons were in us."

"The teshuva—the repentant demons—are. This is an impenitent demon, escaped from the demon realm to wreak havoc in this realm." He twisted the hook and another flow of black liquid gushed from the creature's throat.

She put her hand over her mouth. "Stop it."

"You want me to let it go?"

"No!"

"Do you believe in demons now?"

"Yes." Her voice sounded ragged from the screaming. When he just stared at her, she said more shrilly, "Yes. How can I not?"

"You'd be surprised what people will ignore, even when it's right in front of them."

"I believe it's bleeding on me." She recoiled from the rivulet of ooze, stinking and smoking across the floor.

"Ichor. The rot of a physically manifested demon like this feralis. I need to incapacitate it before I drain it completely." He ignored the thing's half-choked sob.

"You knew it was here."

"I baited the area yesterday. If you calm yourself—"

She hissed, and he gave her a reproving glance. "If you calm yourself and pay attention with your sharpened senses, you will notice the demon smears on the walls. I drained a dozen malice—another sort of demon—here last night and left their remnants. This feralis came poking around, hoping for an easy meal."

"And found me." Outrage warded off the sickness in her belly. "You were going to let it kill me to prove yourself."

"Don't exaggerate. I was waiting right here."

He'd wanted her to come with him just for this. "This wasn't the scenario I had in mind."

He stared at her. "No, this wasn't intended to be sexy."

At the intensity of his focus, she realized the strap of her camisole had drooped down her shoulder. She dragged it into place with a snort. "Not sexy at all."

"But you believe. Now watch and learn."

She couldn't help but watch in sick fascination as he garroted the creature. Half-decapitated, the thing sank into its own creased flesh. The black flow slowed, then ceased. "You killed it."

"No. The horde-tenebrae can't be killed. I merely incapacitated this feralis's husk, which it scavenged and stole from this realm, to keep it from killing me while I siphon its energy."

She scooted out of the way of the ichor river. "I'd say it's siphoned."

"Not of the demon's etheric emanations that energized it. See the eyeballs?"

The spidery row still glowed a furious orange. "If looks could kill . . ."

"Not looks alone. Fangs, claws, whipping tails—yes, those can kill us. We are immortal, but not indestructible."

"Immortal. Monsters." Nim shook her head. As if emptying his words could stop her spinning head from rotating right off her shoulders. Kind of like the creature sagging from his hook.

"Immortal monsters? Yes, that's us. But with this act, I win back a piece of my soul from the darkness." His gaze, almost solid indigo now, held hers, but she felt he was far away. She curled her fingers into the concrete, torn by conflicting impulses. Part of her longed to run while he was distracted. Another part demanded she step up to his side and . . .

And what exactly? She was no crime fighter. If anything, she sometimes slipped a few degrees to the wrong side of that line. With all Jonah's clear loathing of what he alleged himself to be, she wondered how he had ever done wrong enough to believe a demon wanted him.

A demon. Oh no. She was starting to think like him.

In his grasp, the feralis's orange eyes dimmed, clouded with white. She remembered her dream, the white eyes crawling with black, and she shuddered.

Jonah dropped the husk at his feet with a dull thud. The tip of the hook gleamed through the clinging gore. "Does that appall you?"

"Which part? The ooze? The reek? The fact my Louboutin sandal just fell out of a monster's slit throat?"

His jaw worked. "The part where I'm missing half my soul."

"Aren't we all?" Nim pulled her knee to her chest and clutched her ankle. She winced at the burst of pain.

After a moment, he came to her side and crouched beside her. "What's wrong?"

"Broke my ankle trying to escape your little show-and-tell." She hadn't even gotten around to feeling the pain of the knee she'd skinned or the bruise spreading across her hip. "If I'd known I'd be sliding across a concrete floor, I wouldn't have worn short-shorts."

He bumped aside her hands, gently, and probed the bones. She winced and clamped her teeth down on another scream.

He cradled her heel in one hand, his long fingers brushing her arch. "You can cry if you want. This time it's justified."

"They were all justified," she said around gritted teeth.

"None of the bones are displaced. Just wait a minute."

"And waiting is going to make a difference how? Oh, let me guess. The demon."

He nodded. "As recompense for hijacking your body, the teshuva gives you greater speed and strength, enhanced senses, and unnatural healing."

"I remember. Along with the immortality." She didn't bother hiding the snide twist in her voice.

But he just nodded again. "The demon won't, or maybe can't, deaden the pain."

"And apparently it doesn't rejuvenate limbs either."

His fingers, warm around her ankle, never tightened, but his face fell into those harsh lines that reminded her he'd just mostly lopped the head off a monster. "No," he said softly. "It gives much, but what is lost is lost forever."

"Lost . . ." His words froze her in place for a long moment. "Once again, aren't we all?"

He rose from his crouch and stared down at her. "For someone who doesn't believe in demons, you have a very bleak outlook."

"I never said I didn't believe in hell." Her gaze slid to the inert hulk collapsed in the ichor puddle. "And maybe I should blame all those late-night horror movies, but I'm starting to believe you about the rest."

He snorted. "Starting to?" He held out his left hand to her, the hook tucked unobtrusively behind him. "Let's see what else I can find to finally convince you."

"I'd really rather not. I think I'll just stay here and nurse my broken ankle, if it's all the same to you."

"The bones are strong enough to hold you now. They'll knit solid in another hour." He gave his fingers an imperious waggle.

She leaned away from him. "I thought you didn't want me screaming anymore?"

With an annoyed huff, he reached down, took hold of her arm, and lifted her to her feet without even a grunt of exertion, though she did her stubborn best to keep herself anchored to the ground. With a curse, she hopped upright on one foot.

"Just trust me," he said.

"Ha. Not a chance." But when he gave her a short tug, rather than fall on her face again—or, worse yet, stumble into the carcass—she put her foot down. And after one sharp twinge, nothing happened. "This is crazy."

His lips quirked. "Aren't we all?"

CHAPTER 4

Jonah knew he'd finally broken through Nim's resistance when she agreed numbly to return to her apartment to clean up and kicked up hardly any fuss when he didn't bother asking her address as they got into his car.

"You followed me home," was all she said as she settled into the passenger's seat, and she sounded more resigned than angry, so he neither confirmed nor denied.

Bewildered as she was, with her new demon scarcely settled and its capabilities still unknown, he didn't want to risk pushing her. Not if he didn't have to. The soothing power of a hot shower was allowable, now that she couldn't convince herself her world was still the same.

Her teshuva had already sealed over the scrapes on her knee, and the ugly bruise on her hip was fading fast. But the streaks of blood on her tawny skin remained, and the feralis had spattered ichor on her, burning holes in her already indecent shorts.

He retrieved Mobi's case from the backseat while Nim unlocked the security screen on the front door of the old brick building. Side by side, silent, they walked past the rows of mailboxes. He paused at the elevator, then had to hurry a few long steps to catch up with her when she opened the door to the stairs.

She smiled at him crookedly. "What? Are your legs broken?"

"You live on the seventh floor."

"Apparently, you haven't been watching me all that closely. I always take the stairs. Did you think taking an elevator gave me these legs?"

On cue, his gaze dropped to her legs, as if he had to make an assessment. Even streaked with blood, they were gorgeous. Slender ankles, toned calves, and *reven*-marked thighs that curved into well-rounded buttocks ... not that he could see those overflowing handfuls, even with her indecent shorts. But he remembered.

Until the day some feralis took off his head, he'd never forget.

He snapped his attention to her face. "You like to do that. Make me look at your body."

She padded up the stairs, her bare feet slapping her ire on the treads. She'd refused to put on the sandals he'd retrieved from the feralis's maw. "That's how I pay the rent."

"You do it to distract." He realized he was watching the sway of her hips, back and forth as she climbed the stairs. Distracting? Worse: mesmerizing. "You didn't like to think that I've been watching you when you weren't in charge."

She stopped so abruptly he almost collided with her. "Watching, but not closely," she reminded him.

"So you want me to watch closer. But only those parts you want me to see."

"Thanks for the analysis. Will you charge me for that, along with the orgasm?"

Though he was coming to understand her tactics, the low blow brought heat to his cheeks. "It was necessary."

"The psychoanalysis?" The wicked twinkle in her eyes dared him to disagree.

So he did. "No, the . . . orgasm." In all his years, had he ever said that word aloud? He rubbed his thumb against the base of his ring finger, ticking the band with his nail.

Suddenly, uneasily, he wondered what else he'd be forced to do. He'd wanted only a way to fight harder, to redeem himself. He hadn't quite anticipated that opening himself to another meant . . . to another person. To Nim.

She continued up the stairs. "The demon likes to fuck you over? But not be fucked."

"I'm uncomfortable with your foul language." He almost winced at how prim he sounded, how outdated.

"Oh, so it wasn't the demon that was uncomfortable with what happened between us. It was you."

"I was told the most prudent method to balance your rising demon was the . . . orgasm."

"'Prude' is right," she mumbled.

She slammed out of the stairwell and headed down the hall. He stood aside as she opened the door.

The apartment was messier than when he'd cased it previously, although the same earthy patchouli incense drifted out to tease him. He'd been surprised a stripper kept such a tidy abode. This—the magazines tangled in the folds of a blanket across the red corduroy couch, the dirty dishes piled in the sink—had been what he expected. Obviously, she'd been increasingly disturbed by the restive energies of her unbound demon.

Nice to know he hadn't been alone.

She slipped Mobi's case from his shoulder. "Okay, then. Thanks for everything. I'll call you later, yeah? Bye."

He gave her a look. Turning her back on him with an aggrieved sigh, as if that would do the trick, she went to the coffin-sized glass case against one wall and slid the snake inside. She bustled past him again to retrieve a bowl from the counter and then returned to the terrarium.

He wrinkled his nose. "Dead rat?"

"Can you think of a better use? At least this one won't morph into a monstrosity like that one you massacred." She whispered something nonsensical to the snake and placed the dish in a corner. She fussed with the water bowl before closing the lid, then slid a black sheet across most of the case.

"Praise be."

She shot him an arch glance. "That's not for your sake. Mobi doesn't like an audience when he eats. When he's done, he'll need to be left alone for a day or so."

"You dance without him?"

"Not anymore." She pointed at the framed poster above the snake's tank that showed the curves of a woman, breast to hip, body painted in tiger stripes. COMING SOON, it screamed in crimson type, *VIVA LAS SHOWGIRLS* INTRODUCES BEAUTY AND THE BEAST. "We're rehearsing for the *Showgirls* semifinals. I'll have to take a couple days off, but by the weekend, he'll be raring to go again."

By then, the Naughty Nymphette—like the rat— would be only a bad memory. She'd be fully immersed in the talyan world, never to return to her own. Jonah thought that could remain unsaid for now. "In the meantime, there are a few things we need to work out. The demon, when it came to you, might have felt like a dream or a hallucination. But did it leave you something tangible—a piece of jewelry, perhaps?"

She shrugged. "Maybe."

He struggled to keep his voice level. "Nim, this is important. I noticed you don't wear any jewelry when you dance." After Liam and Archer had explained how the women's teshuva had come to them bearing gifts of mutated metals, Jonah had made a point of checking Nim for jewelry through the week. He had looked very carefully and seen nothing.

No jewelry, anyway.

"I hocked it."

Her breezy admission snapped him back to painful reality. "What?" He took a quick step toward her, then stopped himself when she stiffened. He raked his hand through his hair. "You sold it? But you never went to a pawnshop."

"While you were staking me out, you mean? I have a neighbor who unloads stuff for me." She lifted her chin when he glared at her. "Nothing stolen. Not anymore. He gives me cold, hard cash for the cheap-ass gifts my loving customers give me. And believe me, that anklet was the cheapest-looking shit I'd ever seen."

He paced the tight confines of the room. It was that or shake her. She couldn't have known, but frustration sharpened his voice. "It was a weapon. A demonic weapon."

"It was an ugly anklet."

He coughed on a desperate laugh. "The demon should have known you well enough to at least make it shiny."

She scowled. "All I knew, I had a weird night and I woke up with some trashy jewelry lying on my floor. Could've come from anywhere." When he rolled his eyes in disbelief, she added defensively, "I have a lot of loving customers, and they tuck their gifts in a lot of places."

He held up his hand to forestall further explanation. "Which neighbor? And where does he pawn his goods?" Or evils, in this case.

"You going to chop off his head too?"

"Not before he directs me to the anklet." When was the last time he'd had to justify himself to another? The feeling chafed like the hook against his scar tissue. "I have never chopped off a human's head, and I don't plan to start. Is that answer enough?"

She crossed her arms, jaw set mulishly off-kilter.

"Nim," he said with strained patience. "If there's a demonic weapon loose in the city, don't you agree it'd be wise to find it?" With each word, his voice got louder.

"I suppose I should've asked for more money." And still she hesitated another moment. "It's Pete, down the hall in 713. But he won't answer the door for just anyone. I'll go with you."

"Clean up first. The blood on you will unnerve him more than I will." Jonah scuffed the hook along his thigh as he gave her a once-over. Just looking at her made his missing hand twitch. "After we retrieve the anklet, I suppose you have to meet the rest of the league. You should wear something . . ."

She set her arms akimbo, the tight clench of her fingers dragging the already low-slung waistband another inch past her navel. "Wear something what?"

He backpedaled mentally. "Something without ichor holes."

"Remember how you said you really liked my honesty?"

"I don't think I said that exactly."

She wrapped one long dread around the rest and tucked the edge under in a makeshift restraint and stood square to face him. "Honestly, I don't want to go anywhere else with you. I don't want to meet anyone you know. Now that I think about it—actually, I didn't even really have to think about it—I don't want to know *you*."

The scornful words grated along his nerves. "Biblically, it's a little late for that. We can't reverse this."

"Who said anything about reverse? If I really am faster and stronger, I figure I'm going to have a killer new routine worked out before the *Viva Las Showgirls* finals. I might even try fire dancing, since I'm immortal and all."

He stared at her. "You'd turn your damnation into a striptease?"

"What are you doing with it that's so much better?"

"Destroying evil." The hook dug into his leg. "Winning back my soul."

She shrugged. "That monster only attacked because you lured it in. And you only notice your soul is lost because you're still looking."

"Wrong." He all but choked on the word. Her casual denial of what had happened to her—not disbelief, just dismissal—shocked him. "Possession wasn't a choice, and neither is what you do next. The demon chose you to fight."

"I'm a lover, not a fighter." The sharp edge to her smile belied her words. "It should've asked me first."

"It did. Not in words. Still, you accepted it."

She waved one hand. "Entrapment. It'll never stand up in court."

Frustration made his temples throb. "You've already been judged and found guilty. And sentenced."

She wrinkled her lip. "By you."

"I played no part in your possession."

"Didn't you?" A merciless glint brightened her fathoms-deep eyes. "I saw you in my dream, you know. The one where you said the demon came to me. It was you I thought I was letting in." A hint of violet lurked within the glint. "Into my body."

Startled heat flashed through him. Liam had implied that both female talyan had had premonitions of their coming possession. At the same time, their partners had been driven to restlessly roam the streets, the unbound teshuva energies resonating with the demons already possessing them. The league leader had never said outright that the women had *seen* their ordained mates. Had been *tricked* by the image of the male talya meant to stand beside them.

He had been willing to lead the demon's unwitting quarry from darkness toward the light. But he would never have chosen to be the temptation that caused her downfall. When he told her she'd had no choice, he realized once again, the same had been true for him. "I'm sorry."

She tilted her head. The dreads shifted across her shoulders but never obscured her far-too-perceptive eyes. "You had no hand in it—other than the hand you had in me an hour ago—yet you're here to save me, even though you hate me. Why?"

"I don't hate—" He bit off the protest. It wasn't going to convince her. He continued, each word more clipped than the last, "When my sword hand was severed, the impairment left me out of step with my demon. I need a partner to rejoin the battle."

Her gaze ticked over him, from his boots to his face. "Maybe you just need to learn another dance."

"A tenebrae tango," he agreed. "We will fight together."

"You said there are others like us? Go fight with them."

"I have. For a very long time." Bitterness rippled through him in ragged waves, the same way the tesh-uva's thwarted energy swirled and jammed in his gnarled scars without escape. "It was for one of them, I was maimed. And now I can't . . ." The phantom muscles in his missing hand cramped, sending spasms along his *reven*. "Now I am even less than I was."

She tucked in her chin with a dubious look. "Less? Really? So you were, like, Superman before?"

"I could never fly."

"But the anklet—the demon weapon—gives you superpowers?"

"No. Without you, the anklet means nothing. But your demon is uniquely aligned with mine, in ways we can't understand."

"Can't understand?" she said, exasperated. "You mean, 'don't want.' "

"Wanting isn't a consideration."

She peered at him. "It's always a consideration. You just have it sealed up tight. Which is bad, because when that one wanting hits you—and it will—it'll be worse than if you wanted everything."

"How very . . . voracious of you. Meanwhile, I believe together we can drive the horde into hell."

"Oh, you just *want* me to be your new right hand."

Said aloud, in her mocking tone, he realized accusing her of mercenary tendencies had been unfair. Now that his perfidy was revealed, he saw no reason to conceal the worst of what he was. "You'll be the other half of my damaged soul."

CHAPTER 5

Nim let the hot shower soak away the last of her aches.
Jonah had said the demon wouldn't or couldn't purge
the pain, but parboiling disguised it well enough.

If only the water could wash away everything she'd
seen, everything he'd said.

Other half of his soul?

She leaned her head back under the spray until water
ran up her nose and she snorted.

"It's not as poetic as it sounds," he had said, with a
quickness usually reserved for monks disavowing Play-
boy TV. "Whether possession is a cause or effect of the
vulnerability in our perpetual idiopathic etheric force—
our souls—we don't know. But the result is a flaw. Not
physical, but within." He tucked the hook under his left
arm, as if he was guarding himself, and rocked to his
heels. "The etheric pattern of your demon—and what's
left of your soul—resonates with what remains of mine
and binds us. That's all."

"So we're in a spiritual three-legged race," she said.
"Tied together in the potato sack of our souls."

From the tightening of his jaw, she guessed he wasn't
a fan of summer camp games. Maybe he thought she had

cooties. Although wouldn't the demon's healing take care of that?

She touched the swirling black mark on her thigh. *Reven*, he'd called it. She scrubbed her skin until it was bright red, just in case he was quicker with a Sharpie than he'd let on. But she didn't truly expect to erase it.

Great. The one gift she couldn't pawn. She'd lost or abandoned or broken so much over the years. She couldn't believe anything—even a demon—would want to bind itself to her.

And Jonah wanted her too.

Or maybe "want" was the wrong word. He needed her.

The golden boy. Captain of the S.S. *Stuck-Up*. Even missing his right hand, his self-possession fit him as snug as fishnet stockings. Self-possession—ha. Not that he'd appreciate the fishnet comparison either; too transvestite-y, not to mention full of holes.

How it must grate on him to need someone like her.

She got out of the shower and padded into the bedroom. Buck naked.

But he was gone. The twinge of disappointment hurt more than her ankle. Well, she'd just wanted to shock him again. And he wanted her to wear something nice to meet his friends. Fuck him.

The other half of his soul? That was what he needed from her? It seemed so crazy. But after all that had happened, how could she keep denying? Saying no had never done her any good. But there had to be something in this for her.

And she didn't need another reluctant half soul. Thanks, anyway.

She rummaged through her closet for an outfit worse than the shorts and found a denim micromini and fitted white baby-doll tee. No bra. For the sake of city ordinances, she slipped on a black lace thong. From the bottom of the closet, she dragged out a pair of black high-top Vans and laced them. Tight. Like, get-the-fuck-out-of-town-in-a-hurry tight.

She was a slut, but not a stupid slut.

She checked that Mobi had eaten his dinner, then went to the window to stare down at the dark street. Maybe she should run now. Whatever tie bound her to Jonah might not break, but she'd see how far it could stretch.

Or did she just want to see if he would chase her?

A tremor went through her, and she could have kicked herself with her own speedy sneakers. Whatever had driven that wildness in the Shimmy Shack's private room had been a one-shot deal, he'd said, a way for her and her demon to get to know each other better. Jonah had kept himself as separate as he could through the whole ordeal, even with his body raging to get in on the action. He was one of those disapproving types who wouldn't be swayed by a bit of swaying flesh.

What? And she wanted him to be?

She *was* a stupid slut. With a sharp twist, she tied her damp dreads up with a heavy, fleeing-monsters-proof band, and stomped across her apartment.

Jonah was in the hall when she opened the door.

Damn, she'd hoped her imagination had overfig-mented how fine he was. No such luck. And she didn't even do golden boys.

How old had he been when the demon froze him? She guessed not as old as his eyes and his lips, set on stern, implied. Wasn't gold supposedly a soft metal?

Maybe not if it was molded over stone.

His gaze raked her once, and his expression tightened from primal king mask of gold to pure lemon sucking. "Going somewhere?"

At least he wasn't going to rant on the clothes. She supposed a fighter who wanted to stay alive—and keep the rest of his limbs—knew to choose his battles more carefully. "You went to Pete's without me?"

"Thought I'd get it out of the way."

"Does he still have his head?"

"But not the anklet. He gave me the pawnshop address. Let's go."

When he took her elbow, she was grateful for her no-skid soles. And the sudden burst of power that let her yank from his grasp. Good demon. She just wished it could kill the shiver of sensual delight at his touch. Apparently, demons didn't offer protection from pain or pleasure. "Don't manhandle me."

His jaw worked. "You didn't mind before."

"I was possessed."

"You still are."

"Not by you." She crossed her arms over her chest. No sense letting him see the perky nipples belying her manhandling complaints. "I'm not the one to be anybody's right hand or half a soul."

His expression was utterly blank. "What I've lost is collateral damage. Our eternal mission is to do what we can against the demon realm, the tenebraeternum."

She started down the hallway, leaving him to follow or not. Though she didn't question he would. A girl couldn't get so lucky. "I'm sure you think you mean well. Aside from almost getting me eaten by a monster, of course. But, really, from what I've seen, I think the world is perfectly fine falling into darkness, with or without you. So call me crazy—and considering that I'm still talking to you, I very well might be—but I don't see any point in joining your little crusade."

He was a silent shadow on her heels down the stairs and onto the street. "You'd let evil win?"

She stopped abruptly under a streetlight to face him. "You already think I'm evil, don't you?"

He took a few steps past her but didn't turn. "I told you, the teshuva are repentant."

"I'm not talking about the demon. I mean me. I saw the way you looked at me while I was dancing. It wasn't lust. It wasn't even a gay guy's no-pussy-for-me-thanks attitude. You hated it. Hated me."

"No. Not hate."

She took a step toward him. "Look at me when you deny it."

He turned slowly. He must have washed up at her sink before he left the apartment, because the black gore was gone and the hook glimmered under the streetlight with clear warning.

Too bad she'd never heeded warnings.

"We don't have time for this," he growled.

"We're immortal," she reminded him.

"But most of the people in this city aren't."

She stared at him. "Who are you fighting for, Jonah? The city? You?" She held her hands out and waggled her fingers like she was casting a spell. "The woo-woo powers of good?"

"What do you care?" Purple lights flared across his irises.

"I don't." She was pissing him off. Good. Maybe he'd answer something straight for once. "But if you can't tell me why you and that bane demon of yours are fighting, I'm wondering why you care either."

"Because it was the last promise I made to my wife."

The words burst out of him like the ichor that had gushed from the throat-slashed feralis.

She took an inadvertent step back, but still she felt the burn, melting toward the core of her as the black blood had sizzled through her skin.

"You are married," she said flatly. "I asked you about the ring." And she hadn't really cared about the answer. Not then, she hadn't.

"My wife is dead. She died more than eighty years ago."

Nim's irritation guttered. "Eighty . . ."

"I watched her grow old while I didn't, and she died holding my hand." He stared down at the hook. "She told me God had given me a gift, and made me promise I would use it for his glory."

Nim blinked. "God sent a demon to possess you? That's fucked-up." She shook her head. "Sorry; didn't mean your wife." Although, obviously, she was. What a burden to put on someone.

Despite the warmth of the night, she clutched herself tighter. She didn't have much experience with faithful men. But she could see how a man of faith might indulge a few moral quandaries about fingering a stripper into a mind-blowing orgasm, even for the sake of what remained of her soul. Tricky.

No wonder he hated her.

But she hadn't made any promises to anyone. Just as no one had ever promised anything to her. And after hearing his story, she rather thought she'd prefer to keep it that way.

"There's the pawnshop," she said instead.

Jonah gave her a sharp glance but obviously he didn't want to tell any more of his story either.

The shop—in a strip mall between a bail-bond agent and a liquor store—was dark, the security grille pulled down over the windows.

She rubbed her eyes. "I never even thought about it being so late."

"I did. We'll go around back."

"You can't break in," she objected. But he ignored her and headed for the alley. She hurried to catch up. "Not another dark alley."

"Let your demon up and it won't be so dark."

That knowledge wasn't making her feel any better about the enterprise. "I've never been to jail before."

"You won't go now either." He stopped at the alley-side metal door to the shop. "Besides, no human prison could hold you."

"How does your boss feel about B and E?"

"Liam understands expediency."

"God's name is Liam? I thought he'd be Italian, at least."

He fiddled with the doorknob. "What? Liam is the leader of the Chicago talyan. He wasn't a carpenter, but a blacksmith." The door clicked. "He taught me all locks have a weakness."

He slipped inside, and she swore to herself and followed.

The low-wattage security lighting barely picked out the shelves of digital cameras and computer-game consoles, locked racks of guns and electric guitars, and the counter display cases of wristwatches, diamond rings, and gold chains. Nim blinked and then blinked again. A strange, nacreous glow was smeared across the countertops, the walls and ceiling, even the floor. She hopped across one streak. "Who spilled the glow-in-the-dark paint?

"Malice sign. Malice are lesser tenebrae—small, incorporeal demons that draw sustenance from greed, despair, indifference. This is a significant presence, although I should've guessed they'd swarm in a place like this."

He headed for the cashier's station, where the most valuable pieces would be kept close at hand.

"It won't be there." Nim edged farther down the counter toward the cheap crystal. "I'm telling you, it looked like junk."

"Not such junk that your neighbor wasn't able to unload it here. What does it look like?"

"A dull silver chain, too long to be a bracelet, too short to be a necklace. The links were rough-shaped, not consistent, as if it was handmade. And there was one metal bead strung on it, a hollow tube about an inch long, etched with a design." She touched the top of her thigh above the *reven*. "Random patterns, like this."

Jonah leaned over the case. "I don't see anything like that."

"Not here either." She straightened. "I can't believe they'd lock it up for the night."

"Seems unlikely," he agreed, "since they leave these charming cubic zirconia out."

She sidled up beside him. "Sign says diamonds."

"My demon says fake."

She snorted. "And you told me it wasn't good for anything anymore."

He huffed out an answering breath, then turned a slow circle, his eyes half-closed. "It's hard for me to feel anything past the malice sign. If only . . ." He slapped his hand down on the counter in frustration, and she jumped. "There's nothing demonic here besides us. How could they have sold the anklet so quickly if it's as ugly as you say?"

"Don't leave fingerprints," she cautioned over her pounding heart.

"I'm not in any human record books. Not anymore."

He strode away from her toward the alley door where they'd entered, and she hurried to follow. Just her luck to get caught holding the bag. Not that they had a bag. She squelched a tremor of guilt. She hadn't known what the anklet was when she sold it to Pete.

Jonah stopped at the office door and kicked it in. The jamb splintered from the brutality of the blow.

She jumped again. "I thought you knew all the weaknesses of locks."

"This one's weakness was that it was set in plywood." He disappeared within, and the indirect glow of a light spilled onto the floor.

Hesitantly, she stuck her head in the doorway. He was flipping through a receipt book on the desk, the curve of the hook scanning down each page. He grunted and the hook stopped.

"You found it?"

"This is a receipt when Pete brought in his haul, including one silver chain." The hook bit into the paper and he flicked the book away, his jaw tight. "But there's no outgoing sales ticket. So where is the anklet?"

Nim backed away and he followed a moment later, carrying a VHS tape.

"The security tape?"

He gave a curt nod. "In case *you* are in the system." His stare weighed on her until she squirmed.

"I made sure not to touch anything," she said defensively.

"And with any luck, maybe there's something on the tape to show what they did with the anklet."

So he hadn't been trying to save her from a misdemeanor burglary. "And then we'll hunt them down?"

"Undoubtedly, we'll be able to buy it back with appropriate incentive."

"Head lopping?"

"Cold, hard cash—your favorite kind—is tidier. They won't know what they have, so they'll have no reason to resist." His eyes glittered.

If anyone would know about cold, hard, and irresistible . . . She followed him out.

"What have we here?"

Corvus Valerius dangled the coarse chain between his fingers. To his human eyes—at least the one that focused—the chain looked like nothing more than a timeworn silver veneer over some base metal. But to the djinni that infused him, the trinket twinkled with unholy power.

"I found it. Well, a swarm of darklings found it. But when I saw them all mobbing, I knew it would be something you'd like." The young man shifted uneasily from foot to foot, as if he wasn't quite sure of his welcome. Although with the youth's pants hanging baggy around his knees, Corvus wondered how quickly the boy thought he'd get away.

"Interesting." Corvus tugged the chain over his thick swordsman's hand. The links bit into his wrist. It would chafe his human flesh, but the djinni didn't care. The demon's senses expanded through him, probing at the hollow cylinder about the size of his first finger joint. When his vision blurred with the djinni's focus, the carved patterns on the bead churned inward to another dimension. The vast depth drew his attention deeper and deeper, where he would fall endlessly. . . .

His stomach heaved with a purely human reaction and he jerked involuntarily. The demon recoiled, and without his conscious effort, his hand slapped over the bead.

The youth flinched. "Are you okay? I'm sorry, I'm sorry. I'll get rid of it—"

"No. No, we like this very much. Thank you, Andre. You have proved yourself once again a valuable ally." Corvus smiled at the young man.

Judging from Andre's second flinch, though, Corvus thought perhaps he shouldn't make the effort again. Ever since that fall from his penthouse citadel, the muscles in his face didn't always respond as they should. And ever since his soul had been stolen from him, he'd had little reason to practice smiles.

But with this trinket, he'd be able to avenge both those wrongs.

Andre smoothed the nervousness from his expression. "Without you warning me to stay away from that solvo shit, it would've dissolved me for sure, and I wouldn't've even cared."

"Indeed," Corvus murmured. "It is hard to stay focused in the face of overwhelming pain. But that is what purifies and absolves us. You have risen above your pain and not dissolved into it. Which separates you from the rest."

That, and the fact that when Corvus had turned the young man toward the shadows and *shown* him what lurked there, Andre hadn't screamed and bolted. Indeed, his crowing, "I knew it!" had been singularly anticlimactic.

"Andre," Corvus said slowly. "There was a woman to whom this charming bauble belonged."

Andre frowned. "I found the little demons and the chain at a pawnshop. The owner and the guy behind the counter were both men." He hitched his pants higher. "You want me to find the woman who had it first."

Corvus nodded. The motion set his wayward eyeball rolling and upset his stomach again. "You have been an excellent soldier, Andre. It is time for you to become a centurion, to learn what we are truly fighting for. Follow the darklings' sign. They will follow the woman. Do not approach her. She will be dangerous, to you and to me. But find her."

Chapter 6

Jonah didn't want to take Nim to the @1 sanctuary.

Liam, though he had once been wholeheartedly devoted to the league, had given his heart to the second-known extant female talya, Jilly. And it had been Liam's suggestion—the coloring high in his Black Irish skin had hinted at his embarrassment—that Jonah pursue this latest female talyan in private. Jonah had been shocked that the formerly duty-bound league leader would underplay the only purpose of the mated-talyan bond: to form a stronger weapon in the battle against evil. His new priorities spoke volumes about the influence of his exceedingly rebellious woman.

Now, as Jonah drove Nim out of the predawn city, he was grateful for the distance from his league brothers.

How could he return with only half a weapon in hand? Nim, without her demon-wrought jewelry, was not the prize he'd sought. Nim, in her outrageously short skirt—when she'd bent over to scrutinize the jeweler's case at the pawnshop, the curve of her buttocks had been nearly exposed at the apex of her long legs—was perhaps too much of a prize, at least for the companionship-starved males lurking in the halls of the league's salvage warehouse.

He'd been married, and he'd lost his wife. Whatever had happened to the long-ago female talyan hinted at in league archives, he knew what the remaining men really needed to complete them.

But they'd want Nim's hell-on-heels allure even more. He'd pity them if he had room for the sentiment in all the pity he was feeling for himself.

His amoral associate cracked a yawn. "Where are we going? I'm beat."

"I want to take a look at this video. We need to find that anklet before things get out of hand." More out of hand.

"Nobody has VCRs anymore," she said. "We couldn't even have stolen one from the pawnshop. They only had DVD players."

"I know a place just enough behind the times to have what we need."

A streak of orange showed in the eastern sky, like the heating element of a toaster oven promising another broiling day, when they pulled up at the cinder-block building on the edge of the city proper.

Nim stood with the open car door between her and their destination. "A church? You brought me to a church while I'm dressed like this?"

"I was a churchgoing man." He clipped the words off; whether he was dulling them for himself or sharpening them for her, she wasn't sure. "And you dressed like that for me."

"Yeah, but I'm offending you on purpose." She clutched the doorframe. "Is this your church?"

"No. I don't belong now." And never would again. Thankfully, the reminder no longer had the power to wound him through the scars of years. He slammed his door and stalked around the front of the car.

"Right. What with being possessed by a demon. That'd probably freak 'em out."

"Most, undoubtedly. But Nanette knows what we are. She is the wife of the pastor here, and is host to an angelic force."

Nim's sneakers thudded on the concrete behind him as she scurried to catch up. "Angels? You didn't tell me there are angels here on Earth."

"Didn't it seem inevitable, once you knew demons existed?"

"Just because brussels sprouts are healthy doesn't mean they're tasty."

He stopped in his tracks. "What?"

"There are all sorts of bad things with no corresponding good."

He shook his head and continued on. "Why do you insist on dwelling on the evil?"

"Being good is too hard. Doesn't leave any room for failure. Speaking of failure, why'd you forget to tell me there're good guys—real good guys, not good guys by comparison—in this fight?"

"I didn't forget. It's just not relevant. They aren't like us. They move in the human realm and live fragile, mortal, human lives. Most of the angelic forces don't see fit to acknowledge our efforts. To them, a demon once, a demon forever."

"But the first devil was a fallen angel, right? Or do the angels think once you've fallen you can't get up?"

"There's some question whether they might not be right." He unlocked the double front door with a key from his ring and held it open for Nim.

She regarded him suspiciously. "If demons are bad news, why did this Nanette chick give you a key to her place? And does her husband know?"

"Since when does a stripper care about a betrayed spouse?"

Nim stalked past him into the vestibule. "I don't. I'll just feel even less guilty now that I know you're lying too."

"Nanette is protecting her husband from knowledge that would destroy his world."

"He's a preacher, for God's sake. He should already believe in good and evil."

"She wants him to keep believing that good has a chance."

"How nice for him that somebody cares enough to lie."

The lobby beyond was dark. Jonah's vision flickered like a failing old television between black snow and grainy image as the demon swelled and short-circuited, struggling with its tricks in his broken body.

"Nanette has seen that the battle doesn't always go to the righteous," he said. "Sometimes strategy, guile, and luck win the day. She wants the powers of light to have every possible advantage."

"So they have us, the wayward powers of darkness?" Her voice wavered, and he knew she was having as much difficulty as he adjusting her sight. But at least one day she would find her way through the demon's conflicting energies.

Cruelly, he didn't turn on the light in the hallway, and only led her deeper into the church. "She hosts the weakest of angelic forces, and yet if more people were like her—kind, caring, loving—there'd be no room in this realm for demons."

Nim followed close behind him and stumbled on the stairs leading downward, but he couldn't escape her comment. "Between Nanette and your wife, you'd have quite the virtuous harem."

He stopped abruptly at the bottom of the stairs, and she smacked into him.

She didn't reach out to steady herself, but the scent of her warm skin wreathed him in the lingering hint of incense.

"You're trying to offend me again," he said. "Is it jealousy? My wife is dead. Nanette is married to a man she adores. They cannot come between what you and I will be to each other."

She recoiled. "We're nothing to each other. Except maybe thorns in each other's sides."

"Then the ache will help us remember why we are here." When he faced her, her expanded pupils were shot with violet sparks.

"That's just sick," she hissed.

He leaned toward her and thumped the hook into the wall at her eye level. "This," he said. "This is what we are to each other. Missing pieces that will never again be unbroken. But in the striving, we will atone."

She slapped her palm against the wall just above the hook and canted forward to get in his face. "I am not your phantom hand."

"A phantom would be quieter." He stalked away from her, unlocked the storage room, and shoved open the door. This time, he turned on the light.

Behind him, Nim sucked in another breath.

"Come on," he said. "I'm sure Nanette has a VCR here with all this other junk."

"Junk?" Nim crept the last few steps to the doorway.

He stepped in amid the half dozen people standing motionless around the stacked plastic chairs and folding tables, a rolling car with a slide projector, and a teetering pile of cardboard boxes labeled CHRISTMAS DECORATIONS. None of the people moved to avoid him, spoke, or even blinked at the change of light. A misty haze hung in the air.

Nim lingered in the doorway, her fingers pressed bloodlessly against the jamb. "Who are they?"

"No one. Not anymore. Their souls have been stripped by a *desolator numinis*, a rare demonic weapon. Similar to the one you apparently sold for—what?—fifty bucks."

"Ten," she whispered. "I told you, it looked like … junk."

"The *desolator numinis* was reengineered into a street drug called solvo and spread through the city."

"But solvo disappeared months ago. One of the girls at the club, her boyfriend was a dealer. She was complaining because as the source dried up, he got twitchy and weird, and then he . . ."

"Disappeared too?" Jonah rifled through one of the shelves. "These soulless haints have a bad habit of forgetting. Everything. In their blank states, they can be overwritten by free-roaming demons. Many were destroyed last winter in a pitched battle. The league survived the conflict. Mostly. Nanette collects the haint remnants."

"And stuffs them in basements?"

"For a few days. See that flickering haze? Thanks to the teshuva, you are seeing what remains of their souls. Some of the soulflies find their way to the body. We keep the haints nearby until the dust settles."

"What happens to them?"

"Jilly knows an old Chinese witch who draws the solvo out of them, as much as she can. We hope that lets some of the soul wisps in and gives them some measure of redemption. Then we take them out to the country, where they'll wait. Maybe for the end of days."

"Oh, I've heard that line before. 'Sorry, Johnny. We can't keep the dog anymore, so we sent him to live in the country.' Meanwhile, Spot ends up at the pound. Or in a bag in the river."

"We can't afford to let the authorities find the haints," Jonah said. "Imagine the havoc of discovering zombies exist. The haints can't drown, can't really die, since their souls aren't attached."

"Well, they still aren't junk," Nim said hotly.

Jonah turned from the shelves to study her.

She shifted uneasily. "I don't really care. But I'm just saying, you don't get to judge somebody like that. Even if they don't have a soul."

He shrugged. "I didn't say *they* were junk." He held up the VCR, cables dangling. "I found what we need."

She was silent as he hooked up the VCR to a television in the conference room and slid the tape in. He stood in front of the set with his finger on the button and rewound past the images of the two of them hovering over the display cases, past the clerk closing up shop for the night, past a couple kids with a stack of video-game cartridges. A few more unlikely figures sped past the camera. Jonah paused when the clerk opened the jewelry case for a woman, but she walked out empty-handed.

Nim shifted as the tape whirred. "I don't think we're going to— Wait. Go back. I mean forward." She edged up beside him. Her bare arm brushed his as she put her finger on the screen. "That guy. Did you see him take that funny step? I avoided that spot because of the malice sign on the floor."

"Most people don't see etheric emanations." He leaned away from her, crossing the hook over his body, where it wouldn't accidentally touch her.

"He saw it."

Jonah grunted. "It doesn't show up on regular recording equipment."

"I remember stepping over it. Freeze-frame where the clerk pulls out the tray."

"Those were just watches."

"Look. When the clerk gets the second tray . . ."

"Did the guy just reach into the case?"

"It's hard to see from this angle. But I think that's who has my anklet. How nice that he stole it. We can take it back, guilt free."

She jostled his arm and shot him a wide, wicked grin.

"Now," she said, "how do we find him?"

CHAPTER 7

"'Wait in the car,' he says. 'I won't be long,' he says. And since when do I believe anything a man tells me?"

Down the far end of the street, morning sun glared off the blank windows of the warehouse where Jonah had disappeared.

"Nobody'd leave a dog in a car on a day like today," she grumbled.

There'd been some truck traffic earlier, but that had ended after the first fleet wave. A few dark, older-model sedans had ghosted past before that and disappeared down the alley that led behind the row of buildings.

Which, now that she thought about it, was kind of peculiar.

She drummed her fingers on the dashboard, the charcoal plastic—as nondescript as the cars that had passed—already hot under her hand. The problem with running around at night was that it was easy to forget the sunglasses. She squinted and concentrated this time. "Turn down the glare, demon."

Nothing. Maybe the unholy powers of darkness worked only at night.

Much like the dour vehicles returning to this particular roost.

She got out of the car.

Jonah had said there were people here who might be able to help track down the man on the tape. Now she was thinking it was people like them. People he didn't want her to meet.

Well, fuck that. What had he said about nothing getting between them? Nothing except his pride, apparently.

She gave her shirt a tug and marched toward the warehouse.

"At-One Salvage," she murmured as she ran her finger over the palm-sized sign above a pass-card reader. The sign was so small, just big enough for the logo—@1. No wonder business sucked.

Although if their business really was fighting evil, maybe business was booming.

She'd told herself no more alleys, but she followed the path the small fleet of cars had taken behind the buildings. The cars were parked in a cramped, fenced lot topped with barbed wire. The rolling gate was padlocked.

"What? No welcome mat?"

She prowled the perimeter, came around the edge of a Dumpster, and stopped abruptly at the sight of a large—very large—man lounging on the other side of the fence where a docking bay door was half-open.

He was wearing the sunglasses she wished she had—impenetrable, wraparound, probably better trade-in value than any of the crap cars in the lot around him. Smoke curled from his lips, and the smell of cloves drifted toward her. Under that was the smell of something much worse.

She blinked and caught a glimpse of glow-in-the-dark spatter on his boots before the sunny glare made her narrow her eyes again.

Without removing the clove cigarette, he rumbled, "You lost, little girl?"

Ah, he was one of those. "You the bouncer?"

Thick leather gauntlets embraced both his forearms. Metal blades emerged from under the layers of black gore—ichor—and glinted in the sun when he finally plucked out the cigarette. "You did most of the bouncing on the walk over here."

Dull heat burned in her cheeks. Sunburn from standing out here talking to this asshole. Deliberately, she put one hand on her cocked hip, her knee thrust out. The effect was somewhat diminished by the sneakers, and she wished she'd worn her work heels. That always did the trick with bouncer types. "Jonah's looking for me. Let me in."

"Somehow, I'm doubting the pray-and-slay missionary man is really looking at you. Might just set his eyeballs aflame if he did."

"That why you're wearing those pimp-daddy shades?"

"Sugar, I'd known you were coming, I woulda worn my SPF forty-five."

She smiled at him. He smiled back. She rolled her shoulder. "So, you gonna let me in?"

"Not a chance."

She ground her teeth. "Jonah will be pissed." Pray and slay, indeed. Did missionaries get pissed?

"That, sugar, is exactly what I'm hoping."

Probably they only got mad at sinners, though. Just her luck. "Damn it."

"That too."

"Did I say 'asshole' aloud yet?"

"Not yet."

"Consider it done." She yanked her skirt down and stepped out of the little puddle of denim around her ankles.

The man straightened abruptly. "Uh."

Once again, her slutty wardrobe instincts weren't

helping her out any. She walked to the fence, jammed her sneaker toes into the chain-link and hefted herself up. She tossed the skirt over the barbed wire and chinned the top of the fence.

The man tossed his cig down. "Okay, just wait a minute, now."

She didn't. The denim was tough enough to protect her hands, but not quite wide enough—she had a nicely toned dancer's ass, after all—to spare her thighs as she clambered over the barbs. She hissed at the sting, wavered a moment, balanced with one foot on either side of the fence.

Big hands yanked her from her perch.

"Asshole," she said.

"Crazy bitch." The man plunked her on her feet, not gently.

"Ecco, what are you doing out here?" Ducking under the docking bay door, Jonah appeared. "Nim?"

"Whoa," said the man, gripping her. "Who turned up the AC?"

She yanked free of his hands still on her hips. The Chicago August morning was suddenly cooler. Maybe it was her extra-bare flesh. Or maybe just that bare flesh with Jonah's chilly gaze on it.

She tugged her skirt off the barbed wire and swore under her breath when she heard the rip. "I got tired of sitting in the car."

"You left her in the car?" The man behind her—No wonder his name is Ecco, she thought with annoyance—laughed. "You thought that would save her from us?"

"No." Nim leaned over to step into her skirt, and heard the sharp intake of breath from both men. She rolled her eyes before facing them. "He thought he was saving you from me."

Ecco looked over his shoulder at Jonah, who said nothing.

She stuck her finger through the tear in the front of

her skirt, right over the strap of her black thong. "Great. Why don't you just have a front doorbell?"

"Why didn't you wait for me as I asked?"

"You didn't ask," Nim said. "You told."

"Ooh, bad move," Ecco said. "I bet that didn't work with your woman even a hundred years ago."

Nim tightened every muscle in her body, like she was about to do an inverted lift against the pole, and punched the big man in his biceps. He yelped and jumped away from her.

"Good demon," she murmured. She fixed Ecco with a hard eye. "Asshole. Don't compare me to other women."

He rubbed his arm. "I guess not."

Jonah's lips twitched, but she couldn't tell if he was about to laugh or yell at her. She didn't want to know. "Are you done here?"

He gave a curt nod. "Liam has the video. He'll print from it and make copies for the other talyan. They'll start the hunt tonight."

"Good for them. Meanwhile, I was thinking. While I was waiting in the car." She glared at him, in case he thought the punch had been for his benefit. "I think we should go back to the pawnshop."

"But the anklet is gone. The man who took it won't return for a refund."

"Maybe not. But those malice might. You said before that the bad demons sniff one another out, looking for a free meal."

Ecco nodded. "That's why bad seems to always get worse."

"So," Nim said, "let's find out where the worse is going."

Ecco clapped his hands together once. "I love malice. I'm in."

"No." Jonah jumped down from the docking bay. The thud of his boots sounded louder than they should have, and Nim lifted her eyebrows. "You were out all night."

"So were you," Ecco reminded him. "Only working

half as hard as me, of course." He lifted both hands and the gauntlets flashed as bright as his teeth. "But still."

Nim cocked her fist and headed toward him again. He angled his forearm to block her, and the embedded razors glinted.

"Nim," Jonah said warningly. "Ecco, don't be an . . ."

They both turned to look at him, and he rubbed his hand down his face. "It has been a long night. Ecco, go away." He strode forward. "Nim, we're leaving. If you can keep your clothes on."

"Now who's being an—" She huffed out a breath as he grabbed her hand. He whirled her into his embrace like an angry Astaire on demon 'roid rage. Then he spun them toward the padlocked gate. "But—"

His kick snapped the chain, and he frog-marched her out.

She scrambled to keep her sneakers under her but managed to wave to Ecco standing in the broken gate. "Bye."

"Welcome to the party, thrall." The big man raised one hand in answer.

"He didn't flip me off," she said in wonderment.

"You made a friend." Jonah's voice was sour.

"Is that why you wouldn't let me come in with you?"

"I didn't think I'd be so long. Liam had . . . questions."

"About what?"

He shrugged.

"How I lost the anklet," Nim guessed. "You told him how I was too dumb to know it was my demon inheritance."

"Of course not. As leader of the league, he knows better than most how little we know. He would never blame you for your ignorance."

She wasn't sure she appreciated the "ignorance" part. "But you blame me."

"I blame myself. As soon as we identified you as the teshuva's target, I should have been with you."

Like he'd had to be there for his wife, who'd died anyway.

Nim wasn't sure she liked being considered needy any more than ignorant. "Well, we're here now," she said at last.

"So we are." At the car, he held the passenger's door for her.

Maybe there were some parts of needy she could get used to. She slipped into the seat, and he closed the door gently behind her. She propped her feet up on the dashboard to keep her wire-scratched thighs off the scorching vinyl seats while he walked around the front of the car.

He was upset; she could tell by the hard edge of his jaw. And still he moved with a strict, almost painstaking efficiency. No screaming. No wild gesticulating. In a way, he was even scarier than some raging drunk. Because when the explosion came, she knew, it'd be bigger for having been held in so long.

When he got into the car, she asked, "Why did Ecco call me thrall?"

"It's a classification of teshuva. Like my bane demon." He sat for a moment, the hook on the gear shaft. Then he finally looked over at her. "For once, I think he's right."

His assessing stare, with one dubious wrinkle between his brows, as if she hadn't even lost her soul correctly, raised her hackles. "What's that supposed to mean?"

"The class of teshuva determines its . . . proclivities. 'Thrall' is an old word for 'slave.' And you were assuredly that."

Now her blood pressure rose too. Except the angry pulse at the corners of her eyes didn't have her seeing red, but violet. "Maybe he meant *en*thrall, as in 'enslaving others.'"

"Perhaps. All demons specialize in temptation, but thrall demons are especially . . . tempting."

The insulting pauses hadn't changed, nor had the doubtful set of his expression, and yet something in his gaze sharpened, focused on her. This time, the shiver was goose bumps that swept inward across her skin and tightened her breasts and belly.

"Could've been worse." She pitched her voice toward husky. "I could've used my shirt to get over the barbed wire."

"Did you hurt yourself?"

She cocked one knee toward him to reveal the inside of her thigh. The bright red scratches over the black lines of the *reven* were already fading. "Getting better. Good demon."

His gaze fixed on her leg, and the shivers spiraled deeper to her core. Definitely enthralled.

She let her knee fall a little farther open to bump his thigh. Certain advantages to the bench seats on old crap cars.

Instead of tracking inward toward her thong as she intended, his eyes narrowed. "Don't put too much faith in it," he warned. He started the car and clacked the hook against the wheel for emphasis.

"You'd know," she said. When he slanted her a glance, she clarified—only fishing a very little bit—"I mean, you'd know because you were a missionary man, not because the demon let you down and lost your arm."

But if he heard the question in her voice about the missionary part, he saw no need to enlighten her, unlike most missionaries. "*I* lost my arm." He shook his head. "No, I didn't lose it. I knew exactly where it was. Trapped under a sheet of broken glass. I could have let Liam's woman die, burned up in a brimstone fire, but I left my arm in the inferno instead."

Nim crossed her arms. "Yet another woman in your life."

"Liam's woman, I said."

She snorted. "I suppose he has both his hands."

"Last I checked. Although he's juggling league business so fast, sometimes it's hard to tell."

"His immortal managerial life must be so very hard."

Jonah gave her another indecipherable look, then U-turned out of the parking space. "Interesting thought you had about the malice. If they'd gathered in such numbers so quickly after the appearance of a demonic artifact, they must have been already primed on you. An unbound demon acts as an attractive nuisance to the tenebrae, which we tried to mitigate with the energy sinks we placed around your apartment and the club." He drove out of the warehouse district and toward her neighborhood. "In retrospect, perhaps I was unfair."

"Which time?" Nim examined her nails.

"There was far too much demon sign at the club. I assumed with as much negative energy as the place had, demonic emanations were inevitable."

"So strippers are automatically evil? Gee, thanks."

"Actually, the arts usually confer a certain protective effect against the tenebrae. The art specifically, not the artist. I don't know that there has been any research into whether . . . burlesque counts as art, so far as demons are concerned."

Nim snorted. "I'm a stripper, not a dancer anyway. But naughty isn't necessarily evil."

"Says the Naughty Nymphette?" He lifted his eyebrows in pointed disbelief.

"It's just a stage name."

"You mean your parents didn't choose it for you? Your talent wasn't obvious from birth?"

She gave him a long stare. "I like you better when you are silent and morose."

"As do I. Being with you brings out new facets of my personality."

"Lucky me." But she wondered at the second spurt of warmth that went through her. Not embarrassment this time, but satisfaction. Corrupting a missionary man must earn extra points for a demon. "My parents named me Elaine, after the Lady of the Lake in the Merlin stories. I thought Elaine was boring; I liked the other versions better: Viviane, Niniane, Nivian, Nyneve, Nimue. I tried them all."

"Already with the stage names," he murmured. "Why did you settle on Nimue?"

She shrugged. "That's who I was when my parents split up. I was fifteen. After the divorce, I saw my dad at the end-of-the-school-year talent show and then never again."

"You were the best ballerina," Jonah guessed. "His abandonment ruined your chance at Juilliard."

"I writhed around and lip-synched to Alanis Morissette. Sort of like ballet."

His lips curled in amusement. "So you were destined for this career path?"

"Demonic possession, you mean?"

The wry twist of his mouth flatlined at the reminder. "Of course. Your penance trigger made any other path irrelevant."

She wished she hadn't been so flip. Without that teasing lightness, the handsome lines of his face went stone-cold. "He left because his best friend, the guy in the lakeside cottage next to ours, had sex with me every summer from the time I was twelve."

Jonah's hand tightened on the wheel until the plastic squeaked. "You were raped."

"Shit. Who hasn't been?"

"Nim . . ."

She kept talking. Better to talk than to hear what he might say. "He didn't hurt me. I was a very mature twelve and did an exceedingly sultry performance of the lady emerging from the lake, wet T-shirt, pirouette, and everything."

"I'm sorry," Jonah said softly.

Damn it, those were the words she hadn't wanted to hear ever again. As if she cared about sorry. "A hundred years ago, when you were saving South America or Mongolia or wherever, what age did those girls lose their virginity?"

"It was Congo," he said. "And that's really not the point."

She fingered one dread that had fallen over her shoulder. "Maybe there, if we weren't so proper and civilized, my father could have stayed afterward, or at least looked me in the eye. Maybe when Mr. God-I-can't-stop-myself-I-need-you-so-much saw me getting ice cream at the bait shop, he wouldn't have pretended I was invisible, which made me all the more determined to attract him the next time. Maybe my mom wouldn't have acted like it never happened and told me to keep quiet."

"No one could accuse you of being invisible or quiet when you dance." His bland tone told her exactly how little he thought of her half-assed attempt—actually full, bare-assed—at sublimation.

She bristled. Easy for him to be self-righteous. Any idiot could tell, when he was at his most quiet and still, that was when he was most dangerous. "I dance so no one can doubt that it's mine. This body is mine. No one else's. No matter how much they pay, I choose."

"Except this time," he murmured. "With the demon."

A chill crackled up her already stiff spine. But he was wrong. She hadn't handed her admittedly cockeyed principles to the demon. She'd given in to the man.

With a nonchalant shrug, she reminded him, "You said I said yes. Maybe I didn't quite understand, but I said yes."

"Does that give you comfort?"

"Does it make you nervous that, yes, it does?"

"I wouldn't presume to judge."

Funny, she heard all sorts of judgment in his tone. "Who wants to go through life feeling guilty, especially if you're immortal?"

He looked ahead. "Who indeed?"

"Oh, right. A missionary man. I guess I'd rather be a slut, then."

"A tease," he corrected. "Since you don't actually give anything away for free, appearances very much to the contrary."

"Wow, you've found a way to make me worse than a whore. I thought you said we should try to look at the bright side of our situation."

He tapped the hook on the steering wheel. "I find solace in knowing God has abandoned me," he said. "Since I've fallen as far as I may, now I can fight, no holds barred."

"How very inspirational."

"At least things can't get any worse."

He pulled up outside the Shimmy Shack.

Under the harsh morning sun, the red-painted concrete blocks looked particularly worn and pitted. A half dozen cars dotted the parking lot, their hoods gleaming like cockroaches caught by the sudden kitchen light.

"Must've been a rough night," Nim said. "Usually only one or two drunks get their keys confiscated. The cleaning crew will be pissed. Taking the keys always means somebody puked."

"The janitor shows up right before the cook comes to prep for the lunch crowd, right?" Jonah asked. "That'll give us some time."

He got out of the car, and she did the same, not waiting for him to come to her door. No sense playing the lady when they were parked at the sleazy club where she took off her clothes for money. She followed Jonah to the door. "What are we looking for?"

"A trail, from where you were to wherever the anklet has gone."

"Then wouldn't the pawnshop have been a better place to start?"

"We were there already and nothing jumped out at us."

"I like it when things don't jump out at me. Especially not things with teeth."

The lock yielded under his fingers. "I'm hoping whatever—whoever—took the anklet was lurking here first. If they'd be so kind as to leave some sign for us to follow . . ."

He opened the door and a sewer stench rolled out.

She recoiled. "Ugh. Damn, the janitor is gonna quit this time."

"Nim," Jonah said softly. "Stay here."

"What? Why?" She curled her finger through the rear belt loop of his jeans and stumbled behind him. Where the frayed ends of his *reven* peeked above his T-shirt collar, the black lines sparked faintly violet, visible even in daylight. "What's wrong?"

"Don't you smell it?"

She hesitated. "Vomit. Shit. The toilet probably backed up again."

"Unless they all got sick on rotten eggs, there's demon in that mix."

As soon as he said it, a whiff of sulfur curdled in her nostrils. "Oh, that's not good," she whispered. But when he moved forward, she followed.

He raised an eyebrow, but didn't comment.

Swiftly, he led the way down the hall toward the bar. The doors to both bathrooms stood ajar and he nudged them wider. Paper towels littered the floor, but nothing worse.

They continued forward. The strobe lights of the stage reached down the hall and flickered on the walls. Nim's ears ached with the dull press of silence. She'd never heard the place silent.

Jonah stepped over the VIP red curtain lying on the ground.

The stench thickened. The rank stink made her hold

her breath, then gasp, then cough. She tried to hold her breath again when Jonah glared at her.

But she couldn't repress her small cry as they stepped past the bar into the main room.

Slaughter.

That was the smell. The people from the cars outside hadn't left. They just hadn't been found yet.

Jonah left her gripping the bar as he crouched beside one huddled mass, avoiding the shining slick on the floor that gleamed purple and blue and yellow in the rotating lights. He kept his head up, scanning the room, and never touched the body. She knew it must be a corpse. Could anything else lie that still?

Nim locked her gaze on Jonah, tried to concentrate only on the *reven* that glimmered calm and cool just above his collar. But when he moved away from her, to the next body, the streaky black-light glow of her demon's vision leapt into focus. Her rising pulse hammered through her veins, and she gulped down a panicky breath.

A dozen—no, more—crumpled shapes littered the room. How many cars were still parked outside? She couldn't even remember, but considering that last-call Shimmy Shack customers weren't the carpooling type, there hadn't been enough vehicles to account for all the bodies.

Then she realized. These weren't bodies. Just pieces. A sleeve. A pant leg. A man's leather shoe. Torn and discarded like old costumes.

She hurried after Jonah when he circled the room toward the deejay booth and clicked off the stage lights. Under the remaining incandescent white room lights, the Technicolor spill across the floor was simply red.

And in the center of the room was a bare leg, a woman's leg, curved and strong and pale. With a ragged end of muscle, sinew, and bone.

The burn in Nim's throat wasn't breath this time.

She whirled away, stomach heaving, but the red crimson scarlet bloody fucking *lake* of blood was all around her, and there was nowhere to go. She wrapped her arms around herself to banish the freeze that turned her insides to a snow cone, though the AC wasn't working any better now than it usually did.

At least her insides were still inside her. Although if she looked at that leg again, she might not be able to claim that dubious distinction.

They finished their circuit at the front door. "They locked up when they left," Jonah said.

She jumped when he spoke at normal volume. "What ..." She cleared her throat when the word came out in a croak. "What happened here?"

"Ferales happened."

"Like the thing you introduced me to."

"That was nothing. A lone feralis won't go after a crowd. But for the last year, they've started hunting in packs, more recently with malice and salambes mixed in. And there's only one master demon we know who commands the lesser tenebrae like this."

He was talking to himself now, because she wasn't listening at all. She could only think. ... "This is because of me."

"Yes. They wanted you."

"But why?" The word rose in a choked wail from her churning stomach.

"For the same reason I do. Because you are a powerful weapon in this war."

"But they already have the anklet."

"A weapon without a trigger."

She was about to explode from the sickness in her stomach and the scream tightening her throat. She definitely didn't need another trigger besides his dispassion. "How can you be so cold?"

"Because I've seen worse."

She flinched.

"No, that's not quite true," he mused. "This is the

first time the tenebrae have been so blatant. These were frustrated, unhappy men, but they weren't solvo addicts or otherwise unusually vulnerable to the darkness. This shouldn't have happened."

"Of course it shouldn't have," Nim hissed. "They only wanted a dance."

His gaze flickered violet toward her. "Don't delude yourself. They wanted more." He turned a slow circle, pausing at each quadrant of his rotation, as if memorizing the scene. "I meant, under the terms of engagement we've been following, this shouldn't have happened. Our enemy keeps to the darkness, always has." He pointed his hook at the front door. "No tenebrae locks up after itself. And no brain-dead solvo addict would think to do it either. A human, in full possession of his faculties, was leading this attack."

"The one on the security video, who stole the anklet."

Jonah shrugged. "Let's hope so. Otherwise, there are more forces arrayed against us than ever before."

Jonah kept a close eye on Nim as they left the club. She'd paused at the naked, blood-streaked leg. She hadn't broken down; the demon was working to guard her body from all threats, even if the threat was coming from inside.

Because she must be thinking, it could as easily have been her.

She didn't yet understand; her fate would have been—could still be—much worse.

As he locked the door, Nim stared out into the sun.

"Shouldn't we call someone?" Her voice was dull.

"The cleaning crew will be here soon. They'll call the police." He didn't think this was the time to tell her that to protect the human realm, the league had been known to make incriminating evidence disappear. But they wouldn't have the chance, not this time. He'd have to call Liam and prepare the league leader for possible blowback.

He'd noted that the cameras inside the club had been ripped from the walls, more evidence of a human associate overseeing the tech-ignorant tenebraé. But much worse had been left behind. . . . Although people would unwittingly go through all sorts of mental contortions to deny the existence of demonic forces in their midst, such cruel devastation as what they'd seen in the club would be hard to believe. Or disbelieve.

He gave her arm a nudge to get her moving across the parking lot.

"It's not survivor's guilt," she said, apropos of nothing except what he knew was circling in her head. He knew because he'd felt it himself. "I didn't even like Amber very much. She was a terrible dancer. And she never returned my mascara."

"But she didn't deserve that."

"Right." Nim took a gasping breath. Almost a sob. "Nobody deserves that."

He opened the car door for her and, with the bulk of his body, pressed her forward. "Just like you don't deserve this," he prompted gently.

She braced one hand on the door and the other on the frame, as if to hold her place. The metal creaked under her grip. "I'm alive. Forever, apparently."

"Focus that anger. But not on me."

"Isn't that what Darth Vader told Luke?"

"We aren't the dark side," he said. "Only shadowed."

For a long moment, she stared at him. Then she got into the car and sat with her hands tucked between her knees, shoulders hunched.

As he walked around to the driver's side, he racked his brain for the words of comfort she so clearly needed. Bad enough to theoretically lose her old life to the demon inside her, but to have seen that old life brutalized must be devastating. Uneasily, he remembered how his wife's inevitable aging, their retreat deeper into the forest so that none might question his endless youth, had eaten at him. If that had happened all at once, he would have been as torn apart as the men inside the Shimmy Shack.

"Nim," he said as he climbed into his seat.

She turned to him. "I want to destroy them. Like you did that show-and-tell monster. I want to rip them into pieces so small we won't even find their eyeballs to watch the dark creep in."

Her voice was even. In the flat haze of the climbing sun, no hint of the demon's violet flickered. She sat perfectly still, and yet he felt every muscle in his body tighten. She wasn't asking permission. She wanted direction; she wanted to be unleashed.

And he'd wanted a weapon, he reminded himself. An uneasy chill followed the line of his *reven* down his back as his demon roused to the threat of her, the promise.

The most dangerous weapons were seldom safe.

The rattle of a jackhammer on concrete broke the moment. His gaze slid away from hers to focus on the construction crew gathered near the intersection. A flagger guided the single lane of traffic around the orange cones. The orderly progression, so unlike the teshuva's frenzied energy through his damaged body, made him wonder. . . . "How did the tenebrae leave?"

She shook her head. "No one in the club—not even the bouncer—had a chance of stopping them."

"I mean afterward. They got out without leaving a streak of ether, and a pack of blood-crazed ferales isn't easy to move through the streets."

Nim rubbed her temple. "Chicken Bob's car was in the lot. He always stops in on his way to work, right before the club closes, so it must have been five thirty or so."

"Chicken Bob?" Jonah asked. "Never mind. The sun is up before six these days, so that wasn't much time to get the ferales out of there."

After a moment, Nim said, "Both doors were locked

from inside. Unless this demon wrangler you're talking about took a key from one of the bodies . . ."

"They never left the club," Jonah finished. He looked at the detour signs that blocked off an open sewer grate. "What if the building is above the old Chicago Tunnel Company passageways?" He frowned. "The league tries to stay out of there. Just too much opportunity for trouble, and we can find enough of that aboveground."

"If that's where the bastard with my anklet went, that's where we're going." She fumbled for the door handle.

He reached across his body to grab her arm. "Not here. The place will be crawling with cops soon, and they'll want answers we can't give them."

"I want answers," Nim spit out.

"We want a map," he said. "And backup."

"Why don't we—?"

"Because I can't." There was no demon in his voice, but she flinched.

He drove away from the scene of the crime. She slumped in her seat while he called Liam from his cell— although she gave him a sidelong glance as he steered with his knees. The league leader answered groggily, and Jonah heard Jilly in the background, complaining. They'd been out all night, subduing the tenebrae riled up for the last week by Nim's unbound demon. But when he told them of the massacre, they fell silent.

"Wait for us," Jilly said, her voice muffled.

"Wait for us," Liam echoed. "We'll call you with the closest access to the tunnel system and meet you there. Not everyone's home today, but I'll call in as many as I can."

Jonah agreed and hung up.

"What are we supposed to do in the meantime?" Nim asked, obviously having taken advantage of her demon-amplified hearing. "Drive around in circles?"

"We'll get breakfast."

She stared at him. She'd washed away the dark makeup at her apartment, but that just made the bruises of shock and weariness more visible. "Breakfast?"

"The morning meal. And it is still morning." Despite all that had happened.

"I can't eat after . . ."

"After what? Death? Murder? Demonic possession? If you wait for peace and quiet, you'll starve."

She averted her red-rimmed eyes to gaze out the window until he pulled up outside the hole-in-the-wall restaurant, and reached over to touch her arm. A pang of regret pierced him when she started, as if she'd forgotten where she was.

He wanted the poised, brazen dancer back. The teshuva would erase that external evidence of her distress, but inside she would still hurt. And like the demon, he had no cure for that. "Have some coffee, at least. It's been a long night, and the teshuva's first ascension takes more out of you than you might guess."

She trailed him to the entrance, past a yellowed CLOSING SOON! sign. Though he held the door open for her, she paused on the threshold, nostrils flaring. The familiar, sweet scent of corn porridge hit him, and then a wafting hint of lanolin pomade.

"Mr. Walker, hello again." The woman behind the U-shaped counter opened her hands, her smile as white as the oxford that kept its points despite the contrasting shine of exertion on her dark skin. Her gaze shifted to Nim, and her crisp British accent overtook the long, native vowels. "A booth today? And then your usual?"

"We'll take a menu, Ms. Mbengue, thank you." He gestured for Nim to go ahead.

She didn't go to the booth. Instead she chose a table pushed up against the padded bench along the side wall. Her wary gaze made the rounds, taking in the half dozen diners, the worn but clean linoleum counters, the plastic pastry case of sugared peanuts. After her experiences so far, Jonah thought her teshuva must be running close to the surface, amped up on lurking threats with nowhere to strike. When would the meltdown hit?

Ms. Mbengue returned with menus. Nim slouched behind the laminated shield. "Can I get a coffee, please? Extra cream and sugar?"

The woman nodded. "Cardamom chai, Mr. Walker?"

"Please." When she'd gone, he said to Nim, "I can recommend any of the house specialties."

"Ooh, she's a gourmet chef as well as an impeccable laundress? Plus she has amazing skin. Another of your accomplished women." Nim plucked at her tight T-shirt where a rusty stain streaked the white cotton over her navel. Dried blood.

He gave her a reproving look. "Ms. Mbengue is no chef, just a refugee who pulled herself from the brink after her children were killed in some unreported Congolese massacre and she was left for dead. And for the last year, her landlord has been threatening to condemn this block, which would leave me no place for breakfast."

Nim slumped lower in her seat. "Life sucks. Where's a demon slayer when you need one?"

"Demons weren't responsible. Just men." When she didn't look up from contemplating her shirt, he suggested, "Go wash your hands and find your spine so you can sit up straight. I'll order for us."

She pushed to her feet, jolting the table a few inches toward him, and headed for the restrooms. Not quite stomping, which was hard to do in sneakers. At least the doldrums had been chased from her sea-change eyes.

He followed a moment later, to make sure she didn't slip out the back. From the eddies of negative energy, he knew she hadn't.

He lathered up his hand and hook, and returned to the table just as Ms. Mbengue brought the flowered china on a tray. Without a single rattle of cup on saucer, she transferred the items to the table. "There you are, Mr. Walker. Now, what will you have?"

"Second thoughts?" He rubbed his forehead.

"Ah, but you must have first thoughts first. Which, perhaps, has not been the case here."

"Probably not. Meanwhile, two bowls of ugali and we'll share the kikwanga."

She straightened as if to leave, but hesitated. "If I may suggest . . ."

He looked at the menu, wondering if he had missed something. "Please do."

"Your young lady."

His missing hand twitched. "Ah."

"In her eyes, I see things. The sorts of things that chased me from my home and wake me up in the night when I think I have finally forgotten. I do not know whether to warn her. Or you."

"Thank you for your concern," he said gravely. "It is not misplaced."

Her gaze searched his face. "Not all wars happen on the outside. I know this. Breakfast will be up in a moment."

Jonah watched her walk away. At least the eternal supernatural war raging under her nose rarely erupted into the horrors he'd seen this morning. Would she want to help him if she knew he was proving as useless in this battle as his sermons had been in her country?

Ah, but now he had his weapon.

Nim returned with the front of her T-shirt soaked where she'd obviously tried to scrub out the blood. The stain, though fainter, remained, and now the thin white cotton—already fitted against her skin—was nearly transparent. He sighed and reminded himself that he'd decided earlier that her lack of a brassiere was the least of his problems.

Maybe he needed to reevaluate his many, many problems.

CHAPTER 8

Nim focused on adding as much cream and sugar to her coffee as possible without overflowing the pretty cup, until Ms. Mbengue brought their meal.

The woman studied the debris of empty packets and little plastic containers. "If you need anything—"

"Thank you." As Ms. Mbengue departed, Jonah took the round bread, his hook neatly pinning the loaf to the board, and sliced off the end. "This will go easier if your belly isn't growling along with your demon."

"Is that what you told your African kids?"

He put down the knife and gave her his patented reproving look. "Sometimes we didn't have that luxury."

She stared at her plate. "What is it?"

"Grits and flat bread. Every culture has some version. Just like they all have some variation on the war between good and evil."

"Why not tell them the truth?"

"And make them face what you faced this morning?"

"But the cleaning crew, then the police, they're going to face it anyway. Only they won't know what's going on."

"And do you feel better knowing?"

"But I don't want to be the only one who knows." She finally drank her coffee, all of it, in one long gulp, as if she could wash down the rest of the words bubbling up.

He lowered his chin, eyes half-closed, and she thought he was saying grace. "No one believed you when you were raped, but this time you are not alone."

Shit. Had she been that obvious? She pulled her bowl closer and took a few bites, rather than meet his gaze.

He kept his voice low, knowing she'd hear—thanks to the teshuva—even if she didn't want to listen. "Our task, with the demons' help, is to fight evil and win our salvation. Everything else falls away."

She put her spoon down, rattling the bowl. "Why did the demon even pick me? I never wanted to be saved."

"The teshuva are never interested in restful souls."

"Why'd the demon pick you? You had it all. A loving wife. A mission in life. Your God."

It was his turn to put his spoon down, though more gently. His jaw worked for a moment, as if he didn't want to speak but couldn't curb his defense. "Yes, we were missionaries serving in Africa. A life of service was what we'd chosen."

She was in the service industry too. She might have tweaked him about it, but the bleakness in his voice took the fun out of torturing him. "You just didn't know that your life would be so long."

"Or that hers would pass so quickly in comparison." His thumb smoothed over the gold band around his ring finger, a tiny, endless circle, like a nun counting a solitary bead on a rosary. "We were supposed to be together, teaching others our joy in God, digging wells, building schools, planting maize. Instead . . ."

Joy? She tried to picture a joyful Jonah, that full lower lip curved in a simple smile, eyes bright not with demon lights but with laughter.

When he didn't continue, she asked softly, "What

happened? How did a man of God end up with a demon lodged in his soul?"

He rubbed his neck where the demon mark spread in a black-rayed starburst just above his collar. "I was bitten by a spider."

"A spider brought you down?"

"Would you be more impressed if I told you it was a tarantula?"

"No, since a tarantula bite won't kill you." When he gave her a surprised look, she shrugged. "I did research on exotic pets when I got Mobi. A tarantula bite can make you ill, but it won't kill you."

"I was helping the men clear a forest plot and I didn't want to stop. There had been some . . . jesting the white men could not work as hard in the jungle, that we were suited only for women's labor. I wanted to prove them wrong."

"Oh, that's why this story doesn't end well," she said. "Pride is so not a virtue."

"Not that you've even a passing acquaintance with the concept," he grumbled.

She set one fingertip in the notch of her upper lip and flashed him her me-so-innocent eyes. "Which? Pride or virtue? Never mind. Go on."

"I was nauseated and dizzy. Which is how I cut myself on the machete."

"Luckily, that convinced you to go home." At his rueful expression, she sighed. "Or not."

"By the time we returned to the village the next day, I was feverish. My wife recognized the signs of blood poisoning right away."

"I'm surprised you admitted any weakness."

"I might have resisted," he admitted. "Until I was completely out of my head, anyway. It was a long fight. At one point, I was on the verge of giving up. It was too hard to keep drawing another breath. But she saved my life."

Nim tucked her hands between her knees. "She loved you."

"That last night, before my fever broke, she told me I had sworn to love her, protect her, to keep the faith with her, and I could not do that if I died. That I would be betraying our vows."

Nim knew the burn scars on her legs were all but gone, thanks to the demon, but she swore she felt the ache of them where her knuckles pressed. That vow sounded sort of like love. It also sounded like a selfish, impossible command.

Jonah must have felt her weighing the contradiction, because he straightened abruptly. "She was right. I'd made a vow. I kept it."

Suddenly, Nim understood. "That's when the demon possessed you."

"That was my penance trigger, the weak spot in my soul the demon exploited. It tricked me with the promise I'd be with her till the end. I didn't understand she wouldn't be with me. That was my bane, my curse."

They both stared down at their breakfast.

Finally he said, "You see now why I am committed to this fight?"

She looked up. That was why he had told her the story? "How many times can you make the same promise?" *To a dead woman*, she didn't add.

He met her gaze. "Forever. Just as the demon promised."

Perhaps Ms. Mbengue had felt the tension, because she whisked over with a carafe in either hand. "More coffee, ma'am? More chai, Mr. Walker?"

Jonah shook his head. When Nim pushed her saucer closer to the edge of the table, Ms. Mbengue said, "I'll bring extra cream and sugar."

"Don't bother," Nim said. "I'll drink it black now."

Jonah's phone rang. Ms. Mbengue drifted away politely. Nim picked up her spoon and pricked her ears.

A brusque voice came thinly across the line. "It's Archer. There's an access to the tunnel system that will put us ahead of the police when they get to the club. Hopefully, we'll be able to pick up the tenebrae imprints." He rattled off an address and disconnected.

"Drug dealers get calls like that," Nim noted. "Hit men too. And cheating husbands."

"Friends of yours?"

She gave him a smile, all teeth. "Just business."

"So is this." He stood to pull out his wallet and tucked a few bills under his cup.

She gulped the last of her coffee. "You left a good tip, right?" When he gave her a hard look, she shrugged. "Just asking. Since you never tipped me."

"Almost twenty percent," he said stiffly.

"Okay, then. It was just me." She stalked ahead of him.

They drove back toward the club, then angled away a half dozen streets toward the given address. Nim twisted her hands in her lap. "Whatever is down in the tunnels could go any direction."

Jonah shook his head. "It's a maze, but it's a maze with maps."

"I'm so sure monsters follow maps," she snapped.

"Except the ones that can bash through walls." He parked in a row behind three nondescript dark sedans. "There's Liam's car."

"Do you all drive such boring cars?"

"Fighting evil doesn't pay as well as stripping." He got out.

By the time he crossed to her side of the car, she'd already popped out and was staring at the four-story office building with its multicolored signs for a real estate office, a chiropractor, a CPA. "The doorway to hell is here?"

"No, the doorway to last century's freight-tunnel system is here. The door to hell has better signage."

He led the way inside and found the stairwell. The stairs leading up were smooth concrete. The stairs going down were metal grate with no hand railing.

At the lowest level, a voice called out Jonah's name.

They followed the echoes. In the corner of the basement, a metal door stood ajar. Pitch-blackness filled the open rectangle. Nim sighed. Of course there was a lower level.

"Looks like a doorway to hell to me," she muttered.

A light stabbed out through the darkness. "In here."

Jonah strode ahead. Nim tried to force her Vans to move, but they seemed stuck on the rough concrete floor.

He paused. "You coming?"

"I've always made it a policy not to run into dark basements half-dressed, chasing eerie voices." She held up one hand. "Don't remind me that I picked the outfit."

"That's Sera. She's not eerie. At least when she's not mad."

"And when she is?"

"Then Archer has to deal with her. But since he's usually the one who makes her mad, that's his problem. Come on." He held out his hand.

She didn't want to take it. And didn't want to look like she didn't want to. He might get the wrong impression. Like she didn't want to touch him. Which she didn't, but not because she didn't want to, but because she wanted to touch him too much. No touching. That was the rule, which had been working great.

And here she was, standing in a dark basement, half-dressed, with a bunch of demon-possessed psychos waiting for her. She sucked at following even her own rules.

She put her hand in Jonah's. His palm rasped across hers, and he led her over the threshold.

As her vision adjusted, the shadows on the other side lightened, like someone had boosted the contrast on a grainy scan. If only she could Photoshop herself out of the picture.

Five people waited, including the big man—Ecco—she'd met earlier and two other men, almost as large. The two women tucked among the men looked small and slight even though one was relatively tall and the other decidedly curvy.

Jonah huffed out a breath. "This is all you brought?"

All? Among them, Nim counted a recurved axe, a hammer big enough to knock a basketball like a golf ball, three long-bladed knives, and Ecco's multipronged gauntlets. Jonah, with his simple hook, looked seriously underdressed. She knew that feeling well and edged closer to him.

"I sent a second team under Lex's command, with Haji tracking, to the nearest exit," Hammer Man said. "But the tenebrae have several hours' head start, if they finished their butchery around dawn. Likely, this is nothing more than a scouting mission."

The curvy woman propped her hand on the low-slung hip of her black cargo pants. "And honestly? We didn't have many talyan to choose from. One whiff of estrogen and you alpha males go racing for your hidey-holes."

"Hey," Ecco protested. "I sniffed and didn't run."

At Nim's side, Jonah stood motionless. Whatever had freaked out the others had left him untouched.

Untouched. No wonder their demon resonance had brought them together.

"By the way, hi, I'm Sera," said the taller woman. "Here's your flashlight." In one smooth action, she pulled the light from the back pocket of her black chinos, clicked it on, and pitched it underhand. "Welcome to the bad old boys' club, Elaine."

The beam tumbled through the air, glinting off the dizzying array of blades.

Dazzled, Nim reached out to fend it off. To her surprise, the grip slapped into her palm as if her hand had known where to be. "Actually, I go by Nim in all the clubs I work. And while I love a good light show, I could do without the need for second teams and major weaponry."

"You don't need the flashlight either," said the man standing nearest Sera. Archer. Nim recognized his brusque tone from the phone call and clutched the flashlight to her chest. "And if you work anything, it's your teshuva. Master its vision along with its reflexes."

"I'm concentrating on the basics," she said. "Like sucking the juice out of bad guys."

Ecco straightened. "I think I love you." His gaze was fastened on her front, where the flashlight shone across her breasts.

Damn thin T-shirt. From now on, sports bra, she decided. In black.

She lowered the flashlight to her side and bumped it against Jonah's hook. When had he moved around her? At the clack of plastic on metal, he edged away and circled around her again in a protective prowl. It was sweet that he wanted to defend her.

Unless, of course, he was just nervous she was going to embarrass him in front of his people.

The shorter woman stepped forward. Two crescent knives glimmered in her grasp, the blade points just wider than a spread hand, but wickedly pointed. "I'm Jilly. That's Archer with Sera. Ecco, who you met already."

The tall, rangy man eased up beside her and canted the hammer over his broad shoulder. "I'm Liam."

Nim studied him. "I guess that makes you my new boss. Usually I get naked and dance at job interviews."

Ecco raised his hand, metal-studded gauntlets flashing. "I'll be the new league leader."

Jilly cut him a glance bright with violet highlights. "Over Liam's—and my—dead bodies."

Ecco blinked. "Is that how we do promotions? I

thought we drew straws." He grinned at Nim. "But if you end up looking for a side job . . ."

Liam rumbled, a low menace in the dark. "You'll get a chance to dance with the demon, Nim, if we catch up with the tenebrae who butchered your friends."

His words seemed to ignite the scarcely banked ferocity in the crew. A half dozen pairs of eyes sparked violet, and Nim's spine prickled as if someone had struck a match down the bones.

They hadn't been her friends, but she didn't correct him. Because she felt the same urge for vengeance rising in her. From the tight set of Jonah's jaw, she wondered how he justified the impulse for violence. If vengeance belonged to the Lord . . . Well, the Lord wasn't available right now, so please leave a message scrawled in black ichor.

Sera pulled a sheaf of papers from a backpack. "After the river flooded downtown, some of the tunnels were closed down or filled in. Those changes are marked. Sometimes. I doubt the tenebrae drywalled after themselves when they fled this morning, so we should have a clear path to follow." She passed around the maps. "And here's a close-up from the security tape Jonah brought us. It's the man who took Nim's anklet, the same man who might be leading this tenebrae pack." She handed that sheet to Archer.

Each talya studied it with predatory interest, eyes flaring brighter, before passing it on. Until it got to Jilly, who gasped. "I think that's Andre."

Ecco plucked it from her grasp. "Who? I thought I knew everybody who's tried to kill me before."

"He'd gotten kicked out of the homeless-youth shelter where I worked, for dealing solvo. We thought he was dead, or at least soulless. I was out looking for him the night I ran into my first feralis. And met Liam." Jilly took a step closer to the tall man and he shifted the hammer to make room for her under his arm.

How romantic. Nim cleared her throat. "Why would your kid be leading a bunch of murdering demons?"

"Let's say we go find out," Ecco said.

Finding out started with a forty-foot descent via the ladder set into the wall of the elevator shaft. The elevator car was nowhere in evidence. Liam went first, then Archer and Jilly.

As they dropped into the darkness, Sera handed Nim the backpack she'd been carrying. "Since you don't have any pockets, this might be handy."

Nim considered a few snarky comments and a few self-deprecating ones. She tucked the map and flashlight in the big main pocket and settled on "Thanks."

Sera nodded and backed out onto the ladder.

Nim started after her, but Ecco shouldered her aside. "Let me go before you," he said. "I'll catch you if you fall. Farther."

She eyed him. "You want to look up my skirt."

"Nah, I've seen it already. Remember?" He leered at her, then backpedaled as Jonah stepped between them.

Though the big talya topped Jonah by a head and a half, something about the smaller man's utter stillness made Nim put her hand on his arm. He said nothing.

"What?" Ecco grumbled. "You've seen more than me." He backed up another foot. "Fine, fine. I'll go last."

Jonah moved to the ladder.

"Will you be okay on the rungs?" Nim murmured.

"Yes." His tone was flat. As flat as the pancake he'd be if he lost his grip and plummeted to the bottom of the shaft. She berated herself for asking as he dropped out of sight.

"Even if he fell, his demon probably wouldn't let him die," Ecco said. "Unless he smashed his head into a wall or impaled himself on something on the way down."

Nim looked at him. "Everybody here has a girl except you."

He grinned. "Go figure."

"Don't step on my fingers." She swung out onto the ladder.

Under her hands, the metal reverberated with the scrape of Jonah's hook. She concentrated on placing her feet firmly on the slick, rounded rungs. Thank God she'd worn sneakers and not her high-heeled sandals.

The pack bounced against her hip, and she forced herself not to hold her breath. At least the dark meant she didn't have to look down. Not that she had a fear of heights, but if ever she were going to develop one, now seemed like a good time.

When her foot hit solid concrete, the contact jarred all the way up her spine. She hadn't realized she'd come to the bottom of the shaft, and the talyan were so quiet she hadn't known they were gathered close.

Jonah tugged her out of way as Ecco dropped the last few rungs.

Liam gave some hand gesture that made the rest nod. Strippers learned only a few hand gestures, most of them variations on "fuck." This wasn't one she knew, but she had a sneaking suspicion—depending on what they encountered in the next few minutes—it could easily become another alternative.

They stepped out of the elevator shaft and into an empty concrete corridor.

The men were able to stand upright in the center of the arched passage, though Ecco's head would've almost hit the trolley wire if it had still been hanging above them. The tracks, a couple feet apart, were perfect for tripping over, especially in the distracting black-light, disco-ball glow of the demon sign smeared across the walls.

She swallowed hard. From the map, she knew the corridor to the right ran toward the club. To the left was the murdering demons' escape route.

Though none of them had bothered bringing out their

flashlights except her, the talyan were already moving down the path to the left.

Of course they were.

Like winter wolves on one of those nature programs that always ended with the voice-over mournfully droning on and on about extinction, they loped down the corridor. Smooth, silent, and coordinated, they avoided as if by instinct the tracks that kept trying to break her other ankle.

"Let the demon choose where your foot falls," Jonah said.

"Why would I trust it?"

"Because it wants to keep you in one piece."

That was more than her customers—at least the ones who were still alive—could claim. They liked seeing just a few parts. Still, should she give in to a demon that had stolen a piece of her?

She kept the flashlight on. She remembered what had happened to Obi-Wan when he trusted in the Force and turned off his light saber while Darth Vader was still swinging. The dark side didn't bother with fair play. But she stopped watching the tracks and concentrated on the man beside her.

She'd be an idiot to trust the Shimmy Shack regulars, and even stupider to trust a demon. But strangely, it was easy to believe in Jonah. "What happens if we catch up with the demons?"

"We destroy the tenebrae and take possession of the horde leader. If it is Andre, as Jilly believes, and he took the anklet, we'll convince him to give it up."

"We don't turn him over to the cops? For justice and whatnot?"

He said nothing. Well, there were different kinds of justice, she'd learned.

The tunnel curved abruptly into pitch-blackness, except for the glow of demon sign. The talyan slowed. All of Nim's senses screamed to keep moving. Her demon must really want its jewelry.

Archer paced the curve of the tunnel. "Nim, toss me your flashlight."

"Shouldn't you master your demon's vision . . . ?" she started. His gaze flashed violet at her, and she threw the light.

He cast the oval of illumination back and forth across the floor. He paused on a section of track. Between the otherwise clean-swept and tidy rails, a lump of something stuck up.

Nim peered closer, then recoiled, bumping into Jonah. "Is that a foot?"

"Feralis leftovers," he said. "The downside of a physique cobbled together from disintegrating corpses."

Archer sent the beam down the corridor, toward Nim and Jonah. She stepped out of the way and realized she'd been standing on a black stain. The beam went behind her and she turned to follow its track. Another black puddle stained the concrete back the way they'd come.

"Ichor," Jonah said. "The stump was leaking as it traveled that direction."

"Well, we already guessed they came this way," Nim said. "And I suppose it's good news they were falling apart before they even got to the club." Not that the weakness had helped the victims there.

Sera's voice was soft, but it carried. "And where are the pieces they left on the way out?"

"Not even any blood trail from after the feast." Ecco scratched one razor tip of his gauntlet across the wall. Nim gritted her teeth at the blackboard screech. "And if cleanliness is next to godliness, there's a reason ferales are damned."

From down the corridor behind them, an answering screech echoed, thin and high. And hungry.

As one, the talyan turned to face the way they'd come.

"Who woulda thought they'd wait around below the club," Ecco said conversationally.

"Ferales hunted Sera last winter," Archer said. "Apparently, these want more than the anklet."

"They waited for me?" Nim wished her voice hadn't squeaked. No wonder her demon had wanted to keep moving.

"Now we don't have to chase them," Jonah said.

"Because they're about to be chasing us," Nim shot back. She wished her voice *had* squeaked this time, because the panic sounded worse.

"Easier to clean up down here," Archer said. "When we're done draining them, we can just leave them to rot."

Nim swallowed hard when everyone else murmured agreement. Liam's rumble cut through. "According to the map, there's an open junction just a bit farther along. Let's fall back and let them bottleneck. Don't incapacitate them too quickly; we'll need to draw them into the junction and get around behind them before Andre, if it is him, realizes he's in trouble and bolts while the ferales keep us occupied."

They retreated. Nim would've urged a little more speed, but the talyan moved with their habitual maddening grace while she was tripping on the tracks again. God, if she didn't get it together, she was going to leave a foot in the rails too.

"Don't be frightened," Jonah said. "At least, don't be unnecessarily frightened." She cast him a disbelieving glance, and he lifted one shoulder in apology. "Okay, then. Stay close and keep the screaming and swearing to a minimum. Ecco hates it when anyone screams and swears more than he does."

"Hey," Ecco said from close behind them.

Liam rocked to a halt. "Here. No cell reception, shockingly, so we can't call in the second team. Jilly, Sera, scout ahead and make sure the junction is where the map says it is. I don't want to get trapped against a locked Com Ed gate."

Jilly stiffened, and for a second, Nim thought she'd protest. But Sera touched her arm, and with a sharp nod, Jilly led the way into the darkness beyond.

The silent communication tugged sharply at Nim's chest. Despite years working with other dancers, she'd never had that sort of easy closeness. They'd been too busy screwing one another out of customers.

How nice it would be to have a friend or two at her back, friends with knives aimed outward.

She turned to face down the tunnel. The tension in the four brawny men around her pinged off her skin. "When are they coming?"

"They know we're here," Jonah said.

"No, they know *you're* here," she said. "The testosterone is like ozone in here. But it's me they want."

"They'll be cautious because of us." Liam cocked his head at a whistle from one of the women he'd sent ahead. "Too bad. As you might have deduced from the pieces falling off the ferales, it's more convenient when they're overexcited."

"Then maybe we can hurry them along." She took a deep breath and let out a shriek fit to melt concrete from the walls.

For a frozen heartbeat, she *saw* the belling wave of her cry reverberate through the corridor. As the echo faded, the walls trembled with some invisible force.

Jonah sighed.

"Yup, that did get 'em excited." Ecco took a step forward, straddling half the track. Archer joined him, and the wall of warrior felt almost impenetrable.

Almost.

CHAPTER 9

Jonah tightened his fist. The middle position—neither in the front with the fighters, nor in the rear guard—rankled, even if Nim was unarmed. As was he.

"Sorry about the scream," she whispered.

"Great idea." When she stiffened, he clarified, "It was. Your thrall demon knew it instinctively. Fear is an aphrodisiac to the tenebrae."

"I know all about aphrodisiacs," she said. "Even without the demon."

He could swear to that. For a second, he wondered why the tenebrae had responded to her so zealously. Almost as ardently as he himself, which wasn't exactly a flattering comparison. And why did he have the sneaking suspicion the demons knew the reason?

Since the musing had no immediate survival value, he cast it aside. "Don't let the fear overwhelm you when the horde overwhelms us. They'll use that energy against you when you need to use the teshuva's energy against them."

"Is this the time for a schooling?"

"None better, since you're about to get your first test."

And then the shadow was upon them.

The malice hit first, in an inky boil deeper than the tunnel's blackness. A quick handful of the incorporeal little demons squirmed past Archer and Ecco. Their solitary red eyes glared immaculate hatred. Liam stopped them with the blunt-force projection of his teshuva's power, formidable as the hammer braced across his chest.

The malice shredded with multiharmonic screams and the stench of rotting eggs. Nim coughed.

Jonah tucked the hook under his left arm. "If malice get on you, they sting like ice. Don't try to run away; you can't. Let the teshuva rise—like when you let it choose your footsteps. It will match itself to their energy and consume them. The next wave will be salambes. Like the malice, but worse. They burn if they touch. Don't try to run away from them either."

"Why'd I bother wearing sneakers?"

"The ferales, slower, will come last. You can run from them, but you've seen our preferred method."

"Seeing isn't the same as doing."

"You're about to do."

"Trial by fire?"

"And ice. And worse."

"I wish you'd stop saying 'worse.'"

So he stopped talking.

A second surge of malice welled like a black tide past Archer and Ecco. A few avoided the sweep of Liam's hammer and ricocheted off the walls. Straight toward Nim.

Jonah stepped forward.

Since he'd lost his hand six months ago, the teshuva lurked off balance in him. It had healed the wound below his elbow, though it hadn't touched the pain, but now the sinuous, twisting flow of its energy backed up in the scars of his arm with no way out. He thought he'd reconciled to all the ways the demon had betrayed him.

This time, it had left him not just less of a man, but less of a monster.

With the malice aiming at Nim, though, he'd force that damned demon to rise.

The teshuva stuttered along his nerves like a reluctant diesel engine, agonizingly slow as the malice corkscrewed toward them, streamers of oily ether staining the air behind them.

He drew himself upright, taller than he would be on his own, with the demon expanding him into dimensions that were not his. But he felt the lack, the emptiness where his hand had been, where the dance of the demon through his body faltered at the dead end. The stump itched, then ached, then blistered as the teshuva's energy bottlenecked in the scars.

The malice hesitated, skittered sideways, but darted in again. He lifted the hook like a lightning rod.

Then Nim was beside him. No, not just beside him; practically *inside* him, she was so close. She tucked herself up under his raised arm, her breasts pressed against his ribs.

When the malice arrowed in, they were both engulfed.

He'd expected the chill, even warned Nim, but the contrast with her warm body made his muscles scream. Or maybe that was her again. The thought made him grin, and he hoped no one saw the no doubt insane expression. He pulled her tight against him.

She wrapped one arm around him, holding him with a violence that flashed back to the hot confines of the Shimmy Shack VIP lounge. His flesh tightened, not with the demon, but with desire.

"Where'd they go?" Nim murmured.

The malice had vanished, as utterly gone as that long-lost moment when the Naughty Nymphette had writhed against him.

But he didn't have time to be grateful. Liam shouted as the rusting stink of salambes clogged the corridor.

A hellfire glow silhouetted Ecco and Archer. Crowding the passage beyond the men, the immense, hazy shapes of salambes advanced, their jutting scimitar teeth carving hieroglyphics in the ether. Chaotic emanations boiled ahead of them and stung Jonah's skin like a million army ants biting for bone.

Liam called for them to retreat. The ferales would be waiting behind that burning wall of salambes.

Jonah eased Nim back a few steps. "Can you give them a little more incentive?"

Her elbow nudged into his ribs. "Should I swear this time, or just scream again?"

"You seem to have a knack for this. Your call."

Her chest expanded against him as she took a breath. "Andre! You thieving spawn of a toothless whore. Come and get me!"

Jonah stilled. "Not quite what I had in mind."

"What? I have all my teeth."

"I meant the 'come and get me' part."

"Oh. Well, he doesn't stand a chance against you."

Probably she meant Ecco and Archer, even Liam, standing stoic guard. And still her trust sent a rush of primitive pleasure through him, soothing the teshuva's knotted energies. But he couldn't stop to consider the implication, since the sensation was quickly swamped by fear. Because she could so easily be wrong about their chances.

Through the glare of oncoming salambes, a half dozen ferales jockeyed for position. A clawed foot, a vastly oversized pincer, a ratty wing. It was impossible to tell where one monstrosity left off and the next began.

The air in the tunnel crackled with conflicting energies as the demons—malevolent versus repentant—struggled for dominance. Concrete dust puffed from the walls. One-on-one, a teshuva easily mastered a bad demon, but with the fluctuating waves of malice, salambes, and ferales . . . The first row of tenebrae cleared the etheric fog, and behind them was a second rank.

And "rank" was exactly the right word. The stench in the corridor backed up in his throat like sewage. A third row jostled the second, and Jonah revised the talyan chances downward.

They edged toward the open junction, not to lure the horde to their doom but merely to breathe.

Jonah turned at a chill wafting across his shoulders. Jilly and Sera had come from behind. Sera rushed past him in a swirl of air too cold and dry to be merely the fresher air of the open corridor beyond. The teshuva inside him expanded and tensed, like a cat staring at ghosts in an open room. The female talya was cracking her way into the tenebraeternum, where she could banish the lesser demons. It was a skill only the women had, focused by the artifacts left during their possession. And it was heresy, if one read the league archives in the right paranoid mind-set.

Considering the way the army of tenebrae hesitated despite their superior numbers, the league, perhaps, had reason to be paranoid.

"Go." Jilly paused next to him. Her eyes were solid amethyst, and the edges of her *reven*, visible above her décolletage, raced with answering violence. Her breath curled in an icy plume. "You can't do anything here." He stiffened, and she added, "Not when Nim doesn't have the anklet. There are too many of them, and we can't play nice, not if we want Andre."

It was Nim's turn to stiffen. Her fingers latched onto his shirt, tugging the material loose from its neat tuck. "We have to stay. It's my fault I lost the anklet."

"And I lost the boy who may have turned to this path. Who's guiltier?" Jilly stared past them. "I need to be with Liam. You have your map and light. Get out of here." She didn't promise to call later.

Jonah took Nim's hand in his. "We're gone."

Nim tugged at him. "But—"

Jilly strode past them. Without looking back, Liam

reached out to her. His tall, almost too-thin form and her short, full-bodied stance blended together. One weapon.

Jonah dragged his gaze away, almost as difficult as dragging Nim with her stumbling feet.

"We can't leave them." Her flashlight swung toward the fight, adding a strobe to the clash of talyan against ferales. "They're in trouble."

"They'll have less trouble without us." The truth churned in his stomach, a sickening counterpoint to the riled teshuva.

In a dozen strides, they emerged in the open junction. Three lines of tracks led into the darkness beyond the reach of Nim's light.

"Which way?" She fumbled for the satchel over her shoulder, where Sera had stuffed the map.

Jonah conjured up the diagrams in his mind. "The left leads toward the second team."

"We can send them back here." Suddenly, Nim was pulling him forward. "Reinforcements."

He didn't bother telling her the fight would be over—one way or another—long before they reached the next exit.

They sped down the corridor. With her mind focused on the task ahead—summoning help for the others—she moved with her natural grace plus the demon's speed. It was he, half-unbalanced, who fell a step behind. The teshuva's energy ripped through him, a warning.

"Slow down," he said.

"Take my hand." She reached for him, as Liam had reached for Jilly.

Anger flared. "I said, 'slow down.' There's something blocking the path."

She half turned. He grabbed her when she tripped and kept her from blundering right into the metal grate ahead of them, powder coated the same flat gray as the surrounding concrete and almost invisible in Nim's jouncing light.

A padlock the size of his hand dangled at eye level from the door set into the blockade. He set Nim to one side and threaded his fingers through the thin wire. "Watch your eyes."

He heaved back. The metal tore from its hinges with a rusted squeal.

She slipped through and waited for him. "Good catch. I would've grated myself like cheese."

"I don't like that the lock-off wasn't marked on the map."

"The tenebrae must've come down a different path."

He propped the gate against the wall. "There's no demon sign at all."

"Hard to make you happy."

"Hard to imagine that some tenebrae sometime hasn't used these tunnels to get around the city. The gate wouldn't stop the malice and salambes, but the ferales would've broken through."

"Why would they? Not much down here to keep them happy. Or me, for that matter. Let's go." Her whole body canted toward the promise of the exit.

He followed, drawn along because they couldn't go back.

They passed another junction, and he steered them toward where the second team would probably have come down by now. Hearing no word would be an irresistible invitation to join the fray.

Nim's flashlight dimmed. "What?"

No, it hadn't dimmed. The black-painted wall blocking their path had just swallowed the light.

"Watertight seal," Jonah said. "No wonder there's no demon sign. Even a malice couldn't squeeze through."

Nim stomped her foot. "What's the point of having a map if it's wrong?"

"Life's funny that way."

"Death, not so much," she shot back. "Can't you—?"

"Rip it open?" He touched the solid barrier. The teshuva didn't twitch. "I don't think so."

He reared back and slammed his shoulder into the wall. Flakes of concrete drifted down. He rammed the wall again. Chunks of concrete the size of his clenched fist tumbled from the curve overhead, and Nim let out a startled cry.

When he drew back again, she grabbed his arm. "Don't. The tunnel is too old to take the abuse."

He let her draw him away. His body rang painfully with the force of the blows, the teshuva slow to respond to the damage it hadn't authorized.

Everyone was disapproving these days.

"Back to the last junction," he said. "According to the map . . ." He waited while she scoffed. "According to the map, there's another exit. Farther and not as circumspect, but it's our best option now."

The junction had only one other choice, so they passed through it at a run. Their speed didn't stop him from noting the demon sign smeared on the walls. This had been the path the horde had taken to get to the club. Though he felt dizzy with the effort, he pushed the demon hard through his body to pick up the pace.

They crossed into another Y-shaped junction.

"Which way?" Nim gasped.

He hesitated. Follow the demon sign out—but into who knew what nest? Or take another turn? He led her down the smaller route, still marked with etheric traces of tenebrae, but faintly.

Unlike the other corridors, this one plunged downward. More ominously, the freight tracks ended. He tried to summon the map into his mind. This branch of the tunnel had been diagrammed, but were they passing under a street? Maybe the softer layer of soil the city had dug through to make the tunnels had shifted.

Or maybe the map had failed completely.

The corridor behind them trembled, and the scent of grave dirt breathed from cracks in the walls.

"Go," Nim gasped.

Movement was opportunity, hope, life. Which was why the teshuva in him held itself so still.

Down they went.

Here the walls had not been finished with the concrete veneer, and clods of earth pattered down. The horde wasn't visible yet, but etheric emanations flowed ahead like sulfuric wind before a hellish storm.

Nim hurried beside him. "The bad demons. They broke through your friends, didn't they?"

"It seems likely."

She mumbled something under her breath, maybe a curse.

The corridor took another dip downward, and this time the ceiling lowered. The walls in the swinging beam of Nim's flashlight showed the gouge marks of earth-moving machines. Though the hooks had been set in the ceiling to hold the electrical line, the tunnel itself had never been finished.

The light bounced off the corroded metal hooks and glimmered off something shinier on the floor. A mirror . . . No, water.

After escaping the cold of the tenebraeternum, he hadn't noticed the damp chill in the air.

Nim rocked to a halt at the edge of the standing pool. She played the beam out as far as it could go. The black surface of the water reflected the light away, and the depths of the tunnel swallowed it. "You said I shouldn't be unnecessarily scared," she mused. "How would you rate this moment?"

He considered. His leader and friends were trapped in a desperate fight somewhere behind them. And maybe ahead of them too. The forces of darkness had the advantage. He was lost—well, unfound, at least—under the city with a half-dressed woman who was about to be very wet. "I'd say there's no point screaming, since that just brings the tenebrae down faster."

"That good, huh?"

He shrugged. "Maybe it doesn't get too deep."

She snorted and waded in. She hissed as the water topped her sneakers. His boots kept out the cold bite for just another heartbeat. Under his heels, the floor was slick with a coat of mud.

By the time they reached as far as the light had, the water was up to their knees, and still the tunnel angled downward while the water rose. Nim cast the light ahead. The light bounced up in a rippling cat's eye where the ceiling of the tunnel sloped to touch the water. If the path continued, it did so only underwater.

"Crap," she said.

Under the circumstances, he thought she restrained herself admirably.

As they stood contemplating, the ripples around them stilled. Until a tremor shivered the surface like breaking glass.

"Nim," he said softly. "Turn off your light."

A wonder she didn't ask why, but just did as he asked. In the pitch-blackness, his demon strained to help him see. He wasn't asking much, and it found a few stray photons of light. A red glow, almost cheery, if he hadn't known what was coming.

"Salambes," Nim whispered. "Oh, fuck." She didn't bother turning on the light again. "So you said these demons can't morph through waterproof walls, right? Can they swim?"

"They can't dive." It didn't necessarily follow that he and Nim could.

As if she were reading his mind, or maybe just his expression, Nim said, "Out of the frying pan and into the cold, dark, possibly bottomless well. Do we have a choice?"

Once, he would have. He could have taken the tene-brae, maybe even had a chance. Or if not a chance, he could have won back at least a measure of grace.

He imagined slamming his missing hand into the wall. The nerves in the stump screamed up his arm, and the teshuva rose to the threat . . . only to be dashed back by the scarred flesh.

He couldn't risk Nim on these odds, not with his limitations.

Without waiting for his answer, she waded deeper, up to her thighs. Her *reven* sparked restlessly. She raised her hands to keep them dry, pointlessly, as the water reached her navel. The hem of her T-shirt floated up.

Jonah followed her, and the cold water wicked up his jeans, dousing any momentary—and equally pointless—flare of ardor.

When the chill reached his chest, he paused. The glow behind them was flame bright, but the salambes weren't yet in view. "I don't know how much of the tunnel is submerged," he warned.

"And here I thought you knew everything." She took a deep breath. "No chance teshuva breathe underwater, I suppose."

"I don't know that either. Never had reason to find out."

"Well, I donated my body to a demon. Might as well give it to science too."

"Don't." He wasn't sure where the word came from; it just jumped from his tongue. "Don't give yourself away."

She eyed him, violet clashing with the red gleam of the approaching horde. "Does it matter now?"

He supposed not. "The teshuva will at least help you hold your breath," he said instead. "It will keep you going longer than you could by yourself, as long as you don't choke on the need to breathe."

"I have almost no gag reflex," she said. "Ready?"

Facing each other, they each took a long, deep breath. The swell of her chest brought her breasts above the waterline. He sighed at the thrust of her nipples through her wet shirt, sucked in one last breath, and dove.

Nim didn't look back, but she knew the moment the red light of the salambes faded away. Ahead of them, only black. She doubted the flashlight was waterproof. Not like the tunnel was turning anyway. If anything, it was still going down. Which wasn't good, because that meant more water before it went up.

Her heart pounded like the biggest drum in the orchestra—loud and slow. Good demon, taking it easy. Now, if the tunnel would just turn upward . . .

Even with the demon, visibility was zero, but the fine brush of silt drifted past her tight-clenched lips. Not an encouraging sign. Dirt on the floor meant this was still the rough tunnel, not the start of the higher, finished passage. Despite her blindness, she felt the current from Jonah's body rush around her. With just one hand, he must be struggling too.

Her heart cranked up a little faster, as if the orchestra percussionist had gotten bored with the steady beat and decided to join a marching band. At Mardi Gras. Jonah would be telling her not to swear or scream. Since even one good curse would mean drowning, perhaps she'd listen to him this time.

Too bad she might not get the chance to tell him how this impromptu baptism had converted her.

She probably should have mentioned she was a terrible swimmer. She much preferred lying topless on Oak Street Beach, under the hot sun and angry glares of the girls who had the boobs but not the backbone to minimize their tan lines. Yeah, she would've liked to see his face when she mentioned that.

Now her heart had run off to join a punk band. Her arms burned from paddling, and she found herself clawing at the water. Her fingertips raked the concrete.

Concrete, not dirt. The floor was slanting up.

Still no light. But of course there wouldn't be. Unless someone were waiting for them. The dark was better, since—considering their luck so far—she could guess what'd be on the other side.

Never mind the salambes; her lungs burned, legs burned, throat burned. Water crept into her nostrils, but she did not breathe. Very good demon.

Had to be just a little farther; then she could gasp all she liked.

Her good intentions jolted out of her when something grabbed her from behind.

Chapter 10

She flailed and cracked her head on . . . on the ceiling? The floor? Every direction seemed like down.

She wanted to scream this time. Scream Jonah's name. He would be forging on ahead without her, oblivious to her capture. It would drag her away. . . .

Whatever it was didn't drag her, though, just held her, which was death enough, of course.

She reached behind her, half expecting fangs. The hook that would have held the power line for the tracks somewhere below her kicking feet had snagged between her backpack and spine. She slipped out of one strap of the backpack, but the other wrapped like a tentacle around her arm. She wrenched at it, tearing cloth and skin like she was a fish on a hook.

She couldn't help it. She let out the last of her breath.

But as the bubbles left her open mouth, a strong arm wrapped around her chest.

His hook dug under her breast, but she didn't care. Water flooded her throat, and the utter blackness sparked with stars. Odd. Or maybe not, if she were dying.

The cold touch of open air poured over her face as the water fell away, and Jonah roared her name.

He slogged through the chest-deep pool. Was he swearing? Impossible. Maybe that was just her inner voice.

Then he was running. She jounced in his arms, and suddenly all the water in her spewed out in a silty gush.

How embarrassing. Thank God it was dark except for the deep-sea-fishes gleam of the *reven* between her thighs. She didn't want him to see the blush on her cheeks, except she felt so cold, maybe blushing would be nice.

Before his boots cleared the edge of the water, he laid her out on the concrete floor.

And then his mouth covered hers.

Maybe that stupid, drowning gasp hadn't been such a bad idea after all.

His lips were as cold as hers, his first breath as desperate as her last one, but it filled her with fire.

Her heart slam-danced to the demon's pulse. She reached for Jonah, but he rolled her to her side and another lungful of water drained from her. She choked and snorted, wishing her *reven* would dim enough to not add the party lighting to her after-hours-style purge.

He touched her shoulder. "Just lie back."

There was something she'd never expected to hear from him. She coughed a few more times and then pushed against his hand. "I'm all right now." She gathered her legs under her and sat up, her palm flattened against her chest.

He peered at her. "Still water in there?"

"No. I ripped up the back of my shirt on that fucking hook. Not much left."

He sat back abruptly.

She started to snicker at his prudish recoil. Then he peeled out of his T-shirt, and she choked again instead.

How did a missionary man get abs like that? The concrete where she had bashed her head had nothing on the hardness of his obliques. Apparently, machete swing-

ing needed its own workout video. Or maybe almost a
century of demon swatting had some advantages. The
soaked cotton clung to his broad shoulders for a moment, then released with a sound like a wet kiss.

She took the shirt when he handed it to her, too
stunned to do otherwise.

"Wouldn't want you catching a chill." His gave her
that lopsided grin she was beginning to recognize.

Despite his teasing, the *reven* that half spiraled around
him from the back of his neck to the bottom of his rib
cage flared with the presence of his demon. He wasn't
nearly as cool inside as his skin temperature indicated.

She let her shredded T-shirt fall and tugged his over
her head. Her back twinged where the hook had caught
her as the shirt settled around her, several sizes too big,
but damp enough to cling. Too bad the muddy stink of
the water had washed away whatever scent he left on
his clothes.

While she wrestled with the wet cotton, he'd risen to
his feet and was staring down the corridor.

"I had the flashlight in the backpack," she said. "It's
probably not too far down."

He shook his head. "What are the chances it will still
work? Between us, we make enough light to see any
places the tunnels diverge."

"I'll have to change my stage name. Phoebe the Phos-
phorescing Floozie, maybe." She dug her fingers into her
thigh as she remembered—how had she forgotten?—
that she wouldn't need a stage name anymore. She had
more important sins to indulge.

Jonah held his hand down to her, the crooked set of
his mouth more wry than amused at her antics. Apparently, he didn't need any light to know what she was
thinking. "If you're strong enough to feel guilty, let's go."

"You mean we can outrun guilt?"

"At least we can keep it in shape." He kept her hand

for a moment, testing her balance, she thought. When he released her, his fingers were slow to slide free.

She understood his reluctance. If there was anything worse than running from monsters in the dark and getting nowhere, it was desperate kisses in the dark that didn't go anywhere either.

Chilled droplets crept down her spine, as if to rejoin the black water behind them. "We did outdive the tenebrae, though."

"Yes."

"So we're in the clear."

"No. We're very much still in the dark."

"Maybe your friends—the other talyan—were able to stop them."

"Maybe. We'll find out. If we find a way out of here."

More guilt prickled. "The map was in the backpack too."

"Like it was doing us any good."

She wasn't liking how much he sounded like her drowning voice. Maybe she hadn't been the only one to hit a low point at the tunnel's low point.

"Jonah," she said softly. "Thank you for saving me."

"The teshuva would've gotten to it. Eventually."

"Sooner was better, really."

He inclined his head. "I got a good look at the map, so don't worry—" The words must have struck him wrong, because he gave a harsh laugh. "I should stop saying that."

Man, she'd flashed her tits at him and that still hadn't brought him back from his dark place. This was why dating a missionary man would be bad for her ego. "I bet having a knack for maps was useful in the jungle."

He shrugged. "About as useful as down here. Jungles are so wild and ever changing. . . ."

She wondered at the note of pleasure that crept into his voice. "You liked it?"

"I loved it. From the first dime novel I read about the dark continent, I wanted to go."

"To convert heathens?" She couldn't resist needling him.

He laughed, more honestly this time. "To find treasure. Or a lost tribe. Or monstrous dinosaur bones. The dime novels were very explicit about what I'd find."

"Bare-breasted native girls?" She gave him a wicked smirk.

He returned a good-boy grin. "Not that explicit. Not in those days."

"Mobi could've been your sidekick. Well, in the end, you did find monsters. And a lost tribe. Of a sort."

His smile slipped. "True. A demon's finger tightened on my penance trigger, and the teshuva gave me exactly what I asked for."

She cursed herself—silently—for ruining the moment. She was so good at that. "Oh, you know the demon is a big, honking liar, taking advantage of us to make itself look better. It's no better than one of those old, fat, balding farts who shows up at the club, waving his pinky ring and a roll of twenties, but spends more time watching himself in the mirror than drooling over the dancers."

Warming to her topic—and to the barely visible return of his smile—she went on. "Maybe the teshuva is more like the frat boy who shows up hooting and hollering, but fifteen minutes later, he's puking between your platform heels. If you'd ever tried to jump backwards without warning in platform heels, you'd know what a bitch it is, and you can bet he doesn't remember to tip. And then it's just you dancing again."

"What a colorful array of customers."

"Yeah." She brooded a moment, thinking of the ones that hadn't made it out of the Shimmy Shack. What a terrible place to die. "I'm sorry I puked on you, by the way. I always hate that."

"So you said. It was just bilge water. I was already soaked with it."

She smacked her lips. "I'd actually pay eight bucks for one of those nasty energy drinks right now. Heck, I'd pay ten."

He frowned. "Do you feel all right?"

"Other than having recently drowned, you mean?" When the tense set of his body didn't change at her teasing, she gave it a little more thought. "I feel thirsty and sad and gross and stupid for losing the backpack, and cold and—"

"No teetering on the verge of insanity?"

"Uh . . ."

"Even you'd recognize it."

"What? I said 'heck' instead of 'hell,' and you think I'm losing it?" She scowled at him. "I'm feeling a little mad, but not crazy, no."

He relaxed—as much as he ever relaxed anyway. "By the clarity of your *reven* after possession, the teshuva seemed well integrated in you. But you haven't even had a chance to sleep since its ascension, and the league doesn't know enough about female talya to be sure the absence of your demon's artifact might not put you at risk."

"What? If a girl doesn't have her jewelry, she freaks out? I've heard of feeling naked without earrings, but not insane."

He slanted a glance at her. "Your ears aren't pierced."

He'd been looking at her ears? "I don't mind feeling naked."

He dragged his fingers through the waves of his hair. Somehow he'd managed to come out of the mucky pool looking like a sexy swimsuit-calendar model, all beach-tousled hair and glistening skin. Except for the soaked jeans clinging to his hips. Which would just make him a sexy jeans model.

The flush of heat through her body should have been

welcome in the cavelike chill, but she didn't want to want him. She had enough troubles without wanting things she couldn't win with a flash of flesh.

But she could make him squirm. "I have enough holes in my body without adding more voluntarily."

"What about the burns on your legs?"

She stopped as if she'd run into one of the black walls. Fucker, bringing that up.

He turned back to face her. "You just going to stand there?" His voice bounced around the curved tunnel until it seemed to come from all directions. "Refusing to get up out of your own darkness wins you no points, Nim, not even with the tenebrae."

When she didn't answer, he stalked toward her. As he approached, her *reven* pulsed brighter and the old scars ached.

He kept coming until he was right inside the circle of her arms, had she been that kind of dancer. He didn't touch her. But he didn't have to. His gaze weighed on her heavier than Mobi's coils. "Not so long ago, someone was stubbing out cigarettes in your skin. Who else hurt you, Nim?"

She lowered her eyes. Around the *reven*, her flesh seemed to fade, drifting into another realm. The small, round scars, which had been almost invisible, glimmered white as stars in the void.

Man, why had her thrall demon picked a missionary man, of all people?

She gazed up at him through her lashes, then took the last step into his space. "Speaking of languishing in your heart of darkness, how long did you stay in the jungle after your wife died?"

He half turned, as if she had struck him, and the curling lines of his demon's mark flared in answer. "Long enough to know it didn't help. But why listen to me? Between the burning and the drowning, I'm sure you have a few lives left."

"Did you just call me a pussy?"

"Would you prefer—?" He bit back the next word.

She goggled. "You were about to call me a bitch too?"

He rubbed his neck where the *reven* pulsed his anger. "How did you ever make any tips with that mouth?"

"No one asked me to use it to talk before." She thought he might pull out his wallet to shut her up.

Instead he wheeled away and started walking again. "You need to contain the fire. And the dark deeps, for that matter."

"Then quit provoking me." She stomped after him.

"Me? Provoke you?" He hesitated. "You're right. We're like a nuclear reactor—precariously balanced destruction on the verge of total annihilation. We can't melt down or we'll take the world with us."

She paced at his side in silence a moment as she thought. She wouldn't make him pay for that moment. "I wouldn't want to take out the whole world," she said finally. "Just parts of it."

His lips twitched. She was close enough to see how the ebb and flow of his *reven* had settled into rhythm with hers. "Maybe the parts with the tenebrae."

"That'd be good." And maybe, just a little bit, she'd like to melt with him.

"Would you take out the balding fat man and the frat boy? And the man who raped you?"

So he was testing her. Maybe repentance needed a booster shot. "I'm over it. I'm over the human fire extinguisher thing too. No more matches for me."

He slowed but didn't stop. "Some of the scars aren't that old."

Her fingers twitched to reach down and rub the faded wounds. "They look ancient now."

"That was the demon's doing, not yours."

Irritation quickened her steps, and she stumbled once as the beat of their matching light show faltered. Like she needed the reminder of the darkness in her. "I *did* do it. I snuffed out matches on myself. I liked the pain, okay? But I'm getting plenty of that from other sources now." She gave him a significant look.

Then wished she hadn't when he stumbled to a halt, his face stricken. "I don't understand."

She sighed and walked past him. "I suppose you haven't had much reason to read up on the adult expression of childhood sociosexual traumas. I'm textbook."

"But—" He hastened to catch up.

"There's nothing to understand," she said. "I knew it was fucked-up. And I didn't care."

"The same way you became a stripper."

"Weren't you listening when I explained about proudly owning my body?"

"That song and dance? No, I didn't listen. But I watched. And what I saw wasn't about pride or pleasure."

They came to a junction, both paths equally dark. He didn't hesitate, and she fell behind a step, her way lit by the quiet glow of the *reven* on his bare back.

"Sometimes," she admitted, "I wasn't sure who owned it. So I started putting out matches on my skin to see who jumped. It was always kind of a relief to see the scars. They meant I was still here." Her voice bounced off the hard walls and fractured. "How did that old song go? 'Nobody here but us chickens.'"

Except now, of course, there was the demon, which owned her, body and soul.

"If you burned yourself, I would flinch," he said.

She grimaced. "Do the teshuva link us that closely?"

"No."

She pondered his answer. Then why would he care?

He paused while her slowed steps brought her even with him again. "I wouldn't want to see you hurt."

Weird how he seemed to read her mind, though he said their demons weren't that close. "Why not?"

He reached out and touched her cheek. "Because."

His touch was warm, but in the fitful light of the

reven, his eyes were too shadowed to read. He lowered his hand and kept walking.

Damn, she was tired of playing catch-up. She was tempted to just sit down, maybe curl up in a ball, like Mobi sulking around a dead rat.

The corridor grew dark, and she realized her *reven* had sputtered out. And really, once she'd thought of rats in the darkness, she wasn't that eager to sit down. Fine, then. She'd stay caught up.

She brushed her fingers over her skin where he'd touched her. What kind of man could listen to her nasty stories, could look right at her scars, could argue with her—even lose—and yet still touch her so gently that even as the sensation faded, she wanted more?

Never mind teetering on the edge of insanity; she'd apparently flung herself over with a "cowabunga" for unnecessary emphasis.

She stayed on his heels, though not so close she'd have to talk anymore. Something about being with him, in the mostly dark, made her say things she didn't even like to think. Must be some confessional vibe he gave off.

"Not much farther," he said. "I know you're tired."

"I'm not." She didn't want to talk to him, but she also didn't want him to think she was weak. Besides, it was true. Her nerves were too fried for her to be tired.

In fact, after what she'd seen today, maybe she'd just never close her eyes again.

When he veered at another junction, in her distraction she collided with him. How had he gotten so warm?

"You're so cold." He wrapped his arm around her. Even the metal hook felt warm against her skin. "I shouldn't be pushing you like this. What can I do?"

"Nothing." Although his body heat was actually a good start. But that would sound weak too. "I just want to get out of here."

He released her. "I know."

She felt colder when he walked on.

A million years later, he finally said, "Here."

She looked up the shaft where he pointed, and sighed. "Do I go first and get eaten by whatever's at the top, or do I go last and get eaten by whatever's sneaking up behind us?"

"There's nothing sneaking up behind us. Remember, you drowned to get away from them."

"I notice you don't say anything about what's ahead."

"If you're climbing up, chances are you won't drown again." He tapped a metal plaque set in the concrete near where he'd stopped.

She leaned forward to reach the inscription. "We're right below Buckingham Fountain? I thought you said chances are I wouldn't drown again."

"I'm guessing we'll exit in the underground pump room. Then we just have to get out of the pump room without attracting undue attention."

She studied him. He must have felt her continuing disbelief, because he crossed his arms over his chest, the hook tucked protectively against his ribs.

She couldn't decide which would attract more attention, the hook or his chest. Either way, she in his dress-sized T-shirt wouldn't warrant a second glance. What an odd position to be in. "Right," she said at last. "No problem."

He narrowed his eyes at her, then started up. He'd angled the hook around the side rail and just slid it upward as he climbed. He was quite . . . handy with the thing, although he probably heard that all the time. Whatever weaknesses the injury had left him with, leaving her ass in the dust wasn't one of them.

The ladder was even more rickety than the one they had descended under the strip club. If this was a "secondary addition" to the map, she wondered what other odd byways snaked through the city.

Well, no. Really she didn't want to wonder all that much.

With a sigh, she wrapped her fingers around the cold metal and started hauling herself up.

She hadn't expected choirs of angels when they got to the top—what with being demon possessed and all—but running up against the bottom of Jonah's boots was a drag. "Why are you stopping?" She longed to see the sun again. Right now. She'd make a terrible vampire.

"There's a hatch. It's sealed shut."

She groaned. "No. No, I don't want to hear that. I can't. . . ." Her voice had risen, and she clamped her teeth down on the note of hysteria.

Before the note had died away, Jonah slammed his shoulder into the hatch.

Flakes of rust rained down on them. "Never mind," she said. "I can wait. We can find another way out."

Bang. She wanted to cover her ears to keep out the desperate thud of body hitting metal, cover her mouth to keep from screaming, cover her nose to keep out the wet iron that smelled of blood. Hear no evil, speak no evil . . . smell no evil? She didn't have enough hands to keep out all the evil, not if she didn't want to plunge backward to another death.

God, what a wimp.

She shouldered up beside him, gripping the ladder rungs precariously, one foot hanging off in space. "Together?"

He nodded once.

Throwing her shoulder at the barrier was trickier than he'd made it seem, and she clanged her head against it for good measure. But the hatch popped open with an unholy shriek. Just the unholy shriek of resisting metal, not the unholiness of actual unholy things.

Still no choirs of angels or even a stray beam of sunlight. Of course not, since the pump house was underground. Jonah levered himself up into the open chamber and held his hand out to her. She let him pull her up behind him. The thunder of water through the pipes around them made her wince. If the hatch they'd knocked loose had broken into one of those pipes . . .

Jonah didn't release her hand. He drew her across the large room. How could he know which way to go without even that worthless map? She didn't want to be any more impressed with him. What with saving her life and everything, pretty soon she might actually start liking him. And that never ended well for her.

At the far end of the room, light poured down another metal staircase. Finally. She tugged him impatiently forward.

"Wait," he said. "We can't go rushing out there. People will be watching." With his good hand in hers, he tucked the hook against his chest.

"I'm used to that," she said. "Don't you want to find a phone and call your friends?"

Ah, appealing to his savior complex worked. Suddenly, he was pulling her to the stairs.

At the top of the stairs, the much smaller room—a room of levers and knobs that controlled the fountain—was toasty in the sunlight. She sighed. "Safe."

"Hardly." He gestured out the low bank of windows overlooking the fountain. "We have to get past them."

As was true on any nice day—or even most crappy days—people milled around the park. "At least they don't have fangs," she objected.

"They have eyes, and this they don't need to see."

She scowled. "You're not that bad."

He frowned back. "I meant this. What we are." His hand swept over his *reven* again.

"You said they see what they want to see," she reminded him.

"After what happened at the club, I don't know how

much longer we can keep them blind, for their own good."

"Please." She let a note of whine creep in. "Let's just get out of here."

He hesitated another moment, then popped the lock on the door. Modern and well kept, it yielded easily to his brute strength. They slipped out into the bright summer afternoon, and Jonah eased the door shut.

They'd gone only a few steps when a brusque, officious voice called out, "You there."

They turned to face the park ranger striding toward them.

"Oh, great," Nim said.

"I told you," Jonah said.

"Shut up." She spun him against the wall of the control booth and kissed him.

CHAPTER 11

Jonah had a split second to realize what she intended. He'd had split seconds to make life-and-death decisions before, and yet somehow this one sneaked by him. A soft, cool, sighing sneak. The flare of heat that blazed through him had nothing to do with the August sun beating on his shoulders.

Or maybe that wasn't the sun, but the cop tapping on his shoulder. "Sir? I'm going to have to ask you to move along."

He wasn't moving, not with Nim's lithe frame pressed tight against his, one long leg thrust between his thighs. And her lips, heating now but still closed, almost sweet beneath his own.

The cop cleared his throat. "Sir?"

Nim slid away from him, a torture of friction over his skin. "Oh, I'm so sorry, Officer. We didn't hear you." She cast her eyes downward and curved one shoulder with demure bashfulness.

Jonah tried not to choke. Bashful fit her as well as his shirt did.

The park ranger frowned at them, sweaty despite his

short sleeves and more than a little annoyed. "This isn't the place for a free-for-all."

Jonah flinched when Nim grabbed his hook and clutched it to her chest. "No, sir," she said fervently. "Freedom is never free, is it?"

Jonah swore he could feel her breasts yielding against his nonexistent hand. Just one more of her breathy gasps, and the pulse raging in his elbow would probably blast the hook right off his arm.

The ranger straightened. "You're a soldier?"

Before Jonah could answer, Nim said, "Just back from the war. I mean, just."

"Well, God bless you, son."

Jonah hunched against a possible lightning strike. "He's behind me every day, sir."

After a last warning that they better not be swimming in the fountain, the ranger moved on toward a group of preteens screeching like ferales at the edge of the water.

Jonah let out a breath. "I prefer to get through my days without lying."

"It wasn't a lie," Nim said. "He just heard what he wanted to hear."

"I'm not a soldier."

"Maybe not by choice."

He squinted. She'd bought into the horrors of this new life as carelessly as she'd shrugged off the ugliness of her old. Was there no skin she couldn't slip into—or out of—on a whim?

Shame pinched in his gut. The thought was unfair. Just because he was still wrestling with his demon almost a century later was no reason to condemn her to the same fate. Although how her teshuva had called to his when they were so unsuited baffled him. "Let's find a phone and see if we won this battle or not."

Pay phones were harder to find in a cellular world, but Nim brazenly interrupted the park ranger from scolding the kids to ask where they could make a call. She sauntered to Jonah. "Give me your wallet."

"Again?" He hauled the sodden leather billfold out of his pocket.

She plucked two twenties from the interior and handed it to him with a long-suffering sigh. "For the phone call."

"Since when is a local call forty bucks?"

"The commemorative T-shirt is twenty." She dragged him across the park to the nearest vendor. "I wish the snow cones were spiked. I could use a drink."

She dickered with the vendor for a shirt and two pairs of plastic sunglasses. "Do you want the fake rhinestones or the grandpa glasses?"

"No."

"Grandpa glasses it is." She tossed him the blue-tinted wraparound shades.

He pulled the shirt over his head and tucked in the hem. "Why'd you get me a small?"

"It's not small; it's stylish. And better shows off your muscles." She plucked at the limp, stained material of her shirt. "So people won't look at me."

"Since when do you not want people to look at you?"

"Since I was branded, drowned, and smudged off the last of my eyeliner."

She'd all but invited him, so he let his gaze roam over her. With her hair in ropes and his T-shirt hanging like a gunnysack, she looked . . . wild. Terrifying in the same way he'd felt the one night he stepped into the jungle for a moment alone and realized he'd lost the path. He'd calmed his racing heart with the reminder that he'd been smart enough, at least, to bring a lamp. When he cranked up the wick, he'd been dazzled by the light of bright, twin stars shining through the impenetrable canopy.

Only to realize the stars were the cold, unblinking eyes of a night-roaming cat.

The predator hadn't been hungry, or maybe the light

had dissuaded it from attack. The twin stars had winked out and he'd been very alone. He didn't think his heart had started beating again until a voice called him from the way he had come and he stumbled back into the circle of the village, saved by his little lamp and his worried wife.

Nothing would save him this time. He tugged at the neck of his too-tight T-shirt.

She scowled at him. "The long stare ... the silent treatment ... You really know how to make a girl feel special."

He shook his head. "You are special. One of only three female talya we know of."

She sighed. "Right, one of your harem."

Unlike that long-ago leopard watching him from the jungle, she would never give up the attack. He turned and walked away. Which might invite an assault, but her nails weren't that long.

They found a pay phone across the street. He lifted the receiver. The dial tone seemed disturbingly loud, bordering on ominous.

Nim pushed her tacky sunglasses up on her head. In the daylight, her turbulent eyes had settled to clear cyan. "There's only one way to find out what happened to them." Her voice barely carried over the flat buzz.

He punched in the @1 number.

The phone didn't finish a full ring before Liam was on the line. "You're both alive?"

"Yes." Jonah watched both of Nim's fists unclench. She'd been worried no one would answer. He turned to face the wall. "You all? And the second team?"

A longer hesitation than before he'd picked up the phone. "The teshuva will earn their keep tonight," Liam said.

Jonah closed his eyes a moment. He, of all the talyan, knew how the demons' healing powers, the knitting of flesh and bone, never touched the pain. He opened his eyes again when he felt the brush of Nim's fingers against his arm. He'd dug the hook into the mortar between the bricks. A sharp tug pulled it free. He said to Liam, "Bonus points for breathing."

Nim gave him her best devil-may-care-but-what-business-is-it-of-his? smile.

Jungle cat, warrior woman, heathen, temptress. Dear God in heaven, he wanted to kiss her again.

"Take her home," Liam said. For a heartbeat, Jonah's cheeks heated; then Liam continued. "Not her apartment. Take her to the warehouse. The police will no doubt be interviewing everyone on the books at the strip club, and I'd rather work out a script with her first."

"She'd do fine on her own," Jonah said. He'd seen her in action.

"The demons prefer us on our own," Liam agreed. "But she doesn't have to be alone, because she has us now."

Jonah tried to believe that was better. He had to believe the battle was worth the cost. After all, he was almost a league poster child for fighting on, never mind the odds.

Deliberately, he scraped the hook down the wall again, leaving a furrow in the brick. "Do we have anything to show besides the scars?"

He knew Liam wouldn't bother debating the philosophy with him and, sure enough, the league leader went straight to the literal interpretation. "We have Andre. He was quite surprised to see Jilly."

Since the young punk had known her only as a street counselor, Jonah could imagine the shock of seeing the woman wielding her double knives and the demon-realm trap that was her teshuva's legacy.

"Did he have the anklet?"

Nim edged closer, head cocked as she listened in.

"No. He sold it."

"There's a market for demon artifacts?"

"Among the djinn."

Despite the shimmering August heat, Jonah's bones chilled. "Corvus."

"And Andre was supposed to bring him Nim next."

As their cab pulled up near the warehouse, Jonah finished his explanation to Nim. "And now, after two attempts to rip through the Veil that divides us from the tenebraeternum, Corvus finally has a weapon in hand. The etheric energy of his lost soul is all that stabilizes the rift in the Veil. If he reclaims his soul, using the anklet to call that energy to him, he'll loose hell on earth. Only we can stop him."

He handed money over the seat to the driver, who said, "Aw, man. You can't stop there. How does it end?"

Nim opened the door. "You'll have to read the book. Or see the movie." As the cabbie pulled away, she shook her head. "It is an incredible story. That this Blackbird guy has been possessed by an evil demon since he was a gladiator in Rome, and he wants to end demonic possession by pitting hell directly against heaven, without the intervening human pawns. . . ."

"And now he's recruiting humans to his side. Bad enough when we were fighting just demons. But at least the tenebrae can be drained and even banished. We've been struggling to keep up with the soulless haints. If we have a tide of people willing to align with unrepentant evil—"

"Not a tide," Nim interrupted. "One man. Just a boy, really."

"That's how it starts," Jonah said. At the front door, he ran his @1 pass card in front of the scanner.

"Enter the sanctum," Nim intoned. She hummed a few vaguely *Twilight Zone* notes. "There should be theme music for the movie."

"This is serious."

"As a heart attack. But I already had one of those when I drowned. I figure you'll bring me back again."

She stopped just inside the doorway. "I love what you've done with the place."

The warehouse had held architectural salvage materials before Liam made it the league's main headquarters. After their last battle with Corvus left the warehouse in pieces, they'd used the salvaged stone, tile, and glass to rebuild. The results were ... eclectic.

Nim ran her fingers over one of the pink Italian marble columns that supported a web of steel beams bracing the outer wall. "Does the fire marshal approve of siege towers?"

"He would if he'd ever seen a salambe."

She turned to him. "Where are the dungeons?" When he lifted one eyebrow, she pursed her lips. "Oh, please. You know you have one. I want to meet the punk who stole my anklet."

"You sold it," he reminded her.

"Not to Andre. He stole it from that nice pawnbroker." Her voice lowered toward the demon harmonics. "And he was coming to steal the matching piece: me."

Jonah shook his head. "What are you going to do?"

"Obviously, Andre isn't afraid of evil, not if he's hooked up with Corvus. So let's see what he thinks of repenting."

When had he developed a reckless streak? Had his good sense been severed with his arm? He'd blame Nim's bad influence, but that seemed too easy. Because the streak felt a little too good. "This way."

He led her down the stairs. "Into the basement, of course," she muttered.

Another turn of the staircase took them to the sub-basement. But the halls were lined with the best examples of what they'd saved from the salvage operations: gorgeous landscape paintings in museum-quality, gilded frames; a mosaic fresco that might have been stolen from a museum; a midcentury stained-glass panel that shimmered even in the ugly gleam of the fluorescent bulbs overhead.

"Nice torture chamber."

"I told you that art has a dampening effect on the tenebrae," he said. "And we don't torture." When she gave a disbelieving little cough, he added, "We haven't tortured."

"Kept it to yourself, have you? How martyrish."

He clenched his jaw.

She stopped in the middle of the empty hallway and turned to face him. Then she stripped out of her T-shirt.

"Nim," he gasped. He stepped closer to her, not that there was anyone around to see, not that there was any part of her to grab to stop her. Against the backdrop of the odd pieces of art, she was an oddity in a class of her own, all smooth, tight muscle and soft, curving flesh. And the silly sunglasses sparkling in her hair. The bruises from their escapades were already fading on her dusky skin, but his hand itched to soothe away the sting he knew remained.

"Torture doesn't always mean pain," she said conversationally. "At least, not in the way you're thinking of it." With her gaze fixed on his, she gave the shirt a lazy twirl around her finger.

He hurt all right, and he wasn't in the mood to parse the exact sensations. "You're going to fuck Andre into a confession?"

She gave him a coquettish gasp. "Harsh words from the missionary man. Shouldn't I do it—do him—though, for the good of the mission?"

"He's a minion of evil."

"And you were just telling me how they have their needs too. Not that I didn't already know that, probably better than you." She jerked her chin toward him. "Give me your shirt."

He recoiled, a fierce heat and panicked cold colliding in him.

"Hurry up," she said. "Before somebody catches us in this compromising position."

"How is my being half-naked too going to improve the situation?"

"Oh, please. Your precious league practically pimped you out when it sent you my way. Don't get righteous on me now. Again."

He clenched his teeth. "You bought a shirt that was too small for me because you planned to take it for yourself."

"I knew you'd faint if I tried to swap at the park." She crooked her finger. "Give it up already."

He'd taken off more shirts for this woman. . . .

As he lifted the shirt over his head, he felt her step up to him. She didn't touch, but she didn't have to. His body knew, anticipated, shivered with longing. The clench of his stomach muscles was like a sucker punch.

He gripped the shirt to keep from reaching for her, grateful that his other hand was occupied with having been severed. Because if he'd been whole, nothing would have stopped him from taking her in his arms. And when he did that, what little remained of the man he'd been would burn to dust.

She gazed up at him with shadows and hazards and mysteries oceans deep in her blue-green eyes. A man could lose himself there and not remember to mind. . . .

He straightened abruptly and yanked on her shirt—which had been his shirt but now was irrevocably hers, stained down the back with her blood where the hook in the tunnel had gaffed her and teasing him with the temple-incense scent of her skin.

She had already pulled on the BUCK YOU! T-shirt and was smoothing down the iron-on decal of Buckingham Fountain while he was still wrestling his hook through the armhole.

He glowered at her while he viciously jammed the bottom hem into his jeans.

She flaunted her Nymphette smile. "Quick wardrobe changes are a vocational skill."

He didn't answer, just led her to the end of the hall where a door stood a few inches ajar. He paused to let her change her mind, but she stiff-armed the door and sailed past him.

Despite his protestations earlier, he was mildly surprised there was no blood.

The young man—Andre—was seated in a chair centered in the middle of the room. He was not restrained, except by the prowling menace of Archer, whose teshuva flared in his eyes even under the bright fluorescents.

Ecco stood in the corner, arms crossed. The rot of decomposing husks clotted his gauntlets. Over the slow drip of ichor, his stare never left Andre.

"Where's Liam?" Jonah pitched his voice low, loath to overset the precarious tempers in the room.

Ecco answered. "Jilly jumped in between him and a feralis rush."

Jonah winced. He could guess how the league leader had felt about that. That the man had answered the phone spoke of his commitment. That he wasn't present at the interrogation told Jonah how badly Jilly must have been hurt.

Andre gripped the edge of his chair. "I told her to fucking back off. I told her the fucking monsters don't listen once I set them loose. They're crazy, out of control." He caught his breath. "She never fucking listened when I told her to back off."

Archer never stopped his restless pacing. "That's because for some fool reason, she wanted to save your fucking ass." He snarled the last two words with demon harmonics, and Andre flinched.

Jonah knew that feeling, of the teshuva burning close to the surface, threatening to overwhelm what was left of his humanity. Then only constant movement—like Archer's pacing or the concentration of battle—distracted the demon enough to keep his persona intact.

With the loss of his arm, sometimes it seemed he couldn't move or fight enough to hold himself and the demon together. That loss brought to him courtesy of this boy's master.

Still, he had survived, which had nearly not been the case for Nim.

As if sensing the spike of anger, Andre met Jonah's stare. His face paled at whatever he saw there.

As if she didn't care about the escalating threat of carnage, Nim nudged past him to approach Andre. "You're the gutter punk who stole my anklet? I thought a minion of evil would be taller."

He angled his head back insolently. "You're the stripper Blackbird sent me for? I thought you'd be . . ."

Jonah took a silent step that put him right behind Nim, directly in Andre's line of sight.

Nim waited a moment. "Naked-er?"

Archer stopped pacing, and Ecco made a noise that might have been a laugh. Or maybe a growl of the sort that preceded a fatality. Andre swallowed hard.

Without glancing back, Nim said, "Archer, Ecco, stop scaring the poor boy. He won't be able to tell me where my anklet is."

Jonah pitched his voice for her ears only. "I'm not scaring him?"

"You're the kind of scary no one notices until it's too late. So we're cool."

The young man scowled. "Why would I tell you anything?"

Nim gave a little huff. "Of course you'll tell."

Andre's gaze shuttled among the male talyan, as if he couldn't quite decide who was the biggest threat. Jonah wished he could clear up the question. But he'd let Nim play her game . . . at least until Liam came down to rip the man apart for damaging his mate.

But Nim said, very softly, "Not them, silly. Look at me."

Andre's stare snapped to her, and his eyes widened. Black pupils expanded to swallow the irises in a gulp.

Jonah felt a chill at the small of his back that he couldn't blame on the damp waistband of his jeans. He didn't think the punk was wrong about exactly where the threat lay.

Nim's voice lowered, and Andre leaned forward in his chair. "You'll tell me because that's what men do." She circled him. "They tell me things they shouldn't. Do things they shouldn't. I guess you'd call it . . . a gift."

A curse. Jonah heard the word echo, distorted, in the demon harmonics of her voice.

Andre obviously heard it too, and shuddered, but his expression was rapt. Jonah had seen that entranced, hungry look before, when the Naughty Nymphette stepped onto the stage.

The chill crept farther up his spine, even though the thin cotton of his shirt was mostly dry. That wasn't an air-conditioned subbasement breeze.

That was the tenebraeternum.

From the corner of his eye, he saw Archer stiffen. The mated talya knew what was happening. Ecco canted forward, as much under Nim's sway as the young punk.

She came to a halt in front of the boy and leaned down, her palms flattened on the fronts of her thighs. At her fingertips, the black traceries of her *reven* blazed, matching her half-lidded eyes with violet intensity. "But don't you worry about doing something you shouldn't. Because Corvus sent you to find me. Didn't he?"

"Yes."

"And didn't you find me?"

"Yes."

"Then won't you take me to my pretty demon jewelry?"

Andre's answer drifted off on a dreamy sigh, his breath visible in the plunging cold. "Yes."

"No," Jonah snapped.

"Oh yes," Nim said. "Tell me."

Archer pulled Jonah aside. "She's opening a path into the demon realm."

Jonah shrugged out from under the talya's hand. "Hard not to notice."

"Without the teshuva's artifact, she shouldn't be able to do that."

The rare note of alarm in Archer's voice almost made Jonah smile, except he was equally dismayed. "Which makes me think we don't quite understand the purpose of the demons' offerings. What if the relics don't grant the power, or even channel it? What if the jewelry is a control?"

"Like a limiter that only allows a certain amplitude of power through?" For a heartbeat, Archer looked intrigued. Then he recalled himself, brows crashing down in a scowl. "Well, we're missing hers. So you have to control her."

Jonah choked back a laugh that would have sounded desperate. "How?"

"The way you control any woman."

"Sera would have your head if she heard you."

"Both of them. And while she was busy, she wouldn't be tearing open the barrier between our realm and hell."

Jonah couldn't keep his gaze off Nim. Her soft croon spiraled up on a breath, visible in the deepening chill. She gleamed with the demon's raw power, like a jewel herself.

Archer punched his shoulder, sharp and hard. "She doesn't need another lust slave. Snap out of it and back her up."

Jonah shook his head. "I don't—"

"You'd better. There are no tenebrae here to shove back into the demon realm. Do you want her using her soul to patch the hole she rips through the Veil?" When Jonah shook his head again, trying to throw off his spellbound fascination, Archer continued relentlessly. "Do you want her to use mine? Ecco's?" He paused. "Yours?"

"Enough," Jonah growled. He wasn't sure if he spoke to Archer or Nim. Not that it mattered.

He reached out to grab her. Her skin was like dry ice, so cold it burned, fusing him to her. When he tried to pull her back, away from Andre, he felt resistance. But not in her. She bent toward him, pliant and yielding.

The resistance was in Andre. In the soul stretching from him like a fish being teased from the river. As if Jonah were the fisherman, casting Nim upon the water like a lure.

He almost let her go, at the cruel mockery of the life's work he'd once aspired to, a fisher of souls leading men from sin.

Instead, he was using sin incarnate to lure evil itself.

Because he shouldn't have been able to see Andre's soul. The teshuva had once—like their angelic and djinni kin—been privy to the warp and weft of the human soul, but they'd sacrificed the ability when they chose a third path, sanctioned by neither heaven nor hell.

They were able to see the wayward soulflies cut adrift from their haint husks, but a soul contained within its body should have been indiscernible.

Of course, Andre's soul wasn't entirely within his body anymore. And judging from the murky tatters drifting from him, she was only getting the nasty bits.

"Nim," he murmured. "Put it back. That's not a toy."

"He treated it like one," she replied. "No, worse. He valued most of his toys more than this."

"Don't judge," he warned. He didn't want to guess

what his own soul would look like, with the teshuva threaded through the shards.

"I'm not judging. I like toys too. In fact, I might just keep this one."

"It's not yours."

"Andre doesn't mind. Do you, Andre?" She gave a little tug; Jonah could feel it through her body.

Andre's soul stretched a bit more. "I don't mind."

Jonah's throat tightened. "That's something Corvus would do."

"You're trying to make me feel bad about myself, comparing me to a bad man." Nim's voice was dark, brooding. Andre whimpered. "But I never pretended this darkness wasn't here. And now you want to control it, control me."

"You're not controlling yourself. Is this how you would dance? Destroying your audience?"

He felt another tremor go through her. "He took what was mine."

"That's the thrall talking," he said. "Would you, Nim, take a man's soul?"

"I've taken their money—all their money—and their time, their sobriety, their faithfulness, their innocence. . . ." But she shivered again, as if the cold burning him had finally penetrated her focus.

"Then tell me: If that boy stubbed out a match flame on his skin, wondering if there was someone inside him who cared, who would be left to flinch if you do this?" When she didn't answer, he murmured, "You never let anyone take this part of you, not even at your worst. Give it back to him, Nim."

The moment drew out, spun brittle and sharp like the old pane of glass that had severed his hand.

Then she turned and threw herself into his arms, unmindful of the point of his hook. He gathered her gingerly and buried his fingers under the fall of her dreads.

Andre tipped forward out of his chair and thudded to

the floor. Ecco and Archer drew in ragged breaths, and Jonah realized there'd been more than one soul drawn toward her.

When he'd identified her as temptation, he hadn't known quite how deeply the charm set its hooks.

He stroked his hand down the line of her back until the shivers eased.

Ecco knelt beside Andre and flipped the young man over. The punk's eyes were open and fixed, but he took a shuddering gasp. As Ecco levered him up into the chair, he groaned a few words.

Jonah stared over Nim's bowed head at the gauntleted talya. "What did he say?"

"That Blackbird always talks about flying free." Ecco gave him a sharp grin. "And that if Nim is coming for him, he better fly faster."

Jonah took her to his room. All the talyan kept rooms at the warehouse, even if they had private retreats hidden elsewhere in the city. And while there were unoccupied rooms in the building, with plenty of salvaged furniture to scavenge, still, he took her to his room.

From the sidelong glances that slipped away as he lifted her into his arms—her face buried in his chest, her hands locked behind his head—he doubted anyone would dare challenge him for the right.

He'd had opportunity before—after a long, ichor-soaked night of tenebrae slaughter—to be grateful for Liam's foresight in retrofitting the warehouse with private baths for each room. But for the first time in a long time, his thankfulness bordered on a prayer as he awkwardly unlatched the door to his suite.

He let her feet slide to the floor but kept her tucked against his side as he cranked on the hot water in the shower.

"Please turn the light on," she said. "The dark and the water . . ."

Too much like the tunnels. He clicked on the light. Shortly after his maiming, being none to eager to see himself, he'd broken all but one bulb in the old-fashioned vanity light bar. At least the muted light was better than the blackness under the city. Or the shadows that must be coursing through her mind.

He knelt at her feet. The laces of her sneakers were stiff and grimy and resisted his fingers. He sliced through them with the tip of the hook. He tapped her ankle to let him pull off her shoe, and she lifted her foot with a passivity that was starting to alarm him. "You didn't do it," he reminded her.

"I would have," she said. "I wanted to. I was pulling his soul—his soul!—out of him. Like teasing a dollar bill out of a guy's pocket." She gripped his shoulder when he lifted her other foot. The skin above her sock was crusted with silt.

"A hundred-dollar bill, at least." He tried to keep his tone light.

"No, he gave it up as easily as a single dollar. I don't mind being a bad girl, Jonah, but I never wanted to be evil."

He looked up at her and was shocked to see tears glistening in her eyes.

Something shifted in his chest. He remembered that moment himself, in a jungle less forgiving than this one of asphalt and concrete. He and the Naughty Nymphette were more alike than she knew.

He wrapped his fingers around her ankle and gave her a gentle squeeze. "Nim, Andre was a drug dealer before he fell in with Corvus. He's one of the few humans to see a djinn-man—truly see, just like he saw the demon sign at the pawnshop—and it didn't stop him from offering his services. He was leading a horde of demons to kidnap you after he let them butcher a dozen people. After all that, do you think he held his soul in any particular regard?"

One tear escaped and tracked over her cheekbone. "Maybe he was like me, and didn't believe in it."

"But you believe now." He stood. Unable to stop himself, he reached up and thumbed away the tear. "More important, you're trying to do the right thing now that you know."

She sniffled. "The right thing? Like I just did?"

"I suppose there's a learning curve," he admitted. And apparently the league—male dominated for millennia—knew less than ever.

Her lip quivered, as if undecided between another sniffle and a smile. She echoed his touch, her fingers curving around his jaw. "Would you be so generous if it had been your soul I was stealing?"

"You can't steal my soul," he said. "You already have it."

CHAPTER 12

Nim froze despite the steam starting to drift over the top of the shower, and despite the warmth of his touch. "I didn't take your soul."

"Before we even met," he said. "I told you, your demon called to mine. That's how I found you. Because our damage, the vulnerability that opened us to the demon, resonated and made us a matched pair, one fitting into the other."

"You would not have chosen me." The words hurt to say, so she knew they must be the truth. She was just a necessary evil in his fight. And after what she'd almost done, emphasis on the "evil" part.

She let her hand drop from his face, but he caught it. "Nim? I didn't mean you'd taken my soul in cold blood. I know this is all still so strange to you. We'll figure it out together."

"Together," she echoed softly.

"Now get in the shower before we use up all the hot water. And then go to bed. You need the sleep."

She took a steadying breath. "That's not what I need."

"I can get you some dinner too. You hardly ate any breakfast...."

"Not food." She turned her hand to lace her fingers through his. With her free hand, she tugged down her bedraggled skirt. The skimpy denim snagged on her hips, then slipped free to puddle at her feet.

Now he was frozen in place. "Nim . . ."

She wrinkled her fingers in front of his shirt, over his belly, scrunching the material out of his jeans. With his only hand trapped in hers, there wasn't much he could do to stop her. Except club her with his hook, maybe, but she was sixty-forty sure it wouldn't come to that. "You know, nobody tucks in a T-shirt."

He sucked in a breath. Not to make her job easier, she guessed, so much as to avoid her touch. "A habit from the jungle," he said. "Tucking in cuffs and hems kept out the mosquitoes and botflies and leeches."

"Oh, my," she murmured as she eased his shirt higher. Her fingers tripped up the rippled muscles of his abdomen. "Sexy."

"What are you doing?" The question grated out past the breath he was still holding.

"Money, time, and the other thing I could always take from a man—his body. But at least I give up my own in return. Fair trade?"

"I have only one arm."

She blinked at him, unsure if he was serious. "Well, you're taller than me. So it works out."

"I didn't ask for this."

Didn't ask for her. "I know." He was the only man who hadn't. She knew better than to want things she couldn't have, but she wanted this man. This good man. She wanted him to want her. Because if he did, then maybe, despite what she'd almost done, what she'd done before, maybe there was good somewhere in her. "It's a bribe."

"For what?"

"I don't want to be in the water alone again."

"You won't drown in a shower. You won't die."

"Not with you in there." She let go of his hand to peel the shirt from his shoulders. She let it fall to the floor and took that moment to strip off her own.

Standing only in her black thong, she knew he'd finally give in. Not even a man with demonic strength could resist a black thong.

But when her hand went to his fly, he caught her. "Nim . . . Elaine . . ."

She put her finger over his lips to silence him. "I haven't been Elaine for a very long time. Elaine would not have survived what happened to Nimue."

"And now I have the Naughty Nymphette." His breath teased her skin.

"Not her either. She doesn't allow touching, remember?" She stroked her finger across his bottom lip. "You were right the first time. It's Nim. Nobody but Nim."

His breathing was ragged. Her own wasn't much better. What she was doing was wrong, selfishly taking advantage of a good man. Well, a good man and a repentant demon. *She* was wrong to think his goodness would rub off on her. Goodliness, like cleanliness, didn't transfer. Unlike dirt, blood, and sin, which were endlessly contagious.

But he was the one who'd said "together."

When she reached for the front of his jeans this time, he didn't resist.

In fact, parts of him were eager to be free. As she eased the zipper apart and the backs of her fingers grazed his erection through his briefs, his whole body shuddered. Feralis teeth didn't scare him, but zipper teeth would bring down any man. And bringing this man to his knees was her job.

She'd make him forget he hadn't wanted her, couldn't want her.

He kicked off his boots as she pushed down his jeans, his briefs along for the ride. Then he was naked, except for the hook. "Nim . . ."

"I figured out how to pull a soul from a body. I think I can get your arm out of this trap." She ran her fingers along the straps that cuffed the hook to his upper arm, searching out the snaps. Underneath the pad, knotted scars gnarled his flesh.

He pulled away from her, nudging the hook from her hand. "It's ugly. The birnenston where I fell sealed the wound. Hellfire saved my life and crippled me for the only purpose I had left."

"Jonah." She wasn't sure what she should say next.

He took the chance away from her. He lifted her off her feet and pushed her through the shower curtain. For a heartbeat, she thought he would leave her standing there alone, but then he was beside her.

The curtain blocked most of the lone lightbulb, and the swirling steam gave the wan light a mysterious glow. It definitely wasn't demon light, since his *reven* and hers remained quiescent.

She touched the black lines of the demon that marked his neck.

"No demon," he murmured, barely audible over the *shush* of the water. "Just Jonah for nobody but Nim." He smiled, but fleetingly. "I don't know if that will be enough anymore."

She pulled off her thong and tossed it toward the end of the tub. "I guess we'll find out. Together."

The bar of soap in his hands gave off no scent beyond clean. "Turn around," he said. "Let me see where that electrical hook got you."

She turned obediently in the circle of his arms, and lifted her dreads over her shoulder.

At the first touch of his hand, she closed her eyes. God, he was so gentle. As if she might fall apart. "It doesn't hurt."

"It's all healed." He slicked the soap down her spine until she was slippery with lather, but stopped short of her buttocks.

She leaned back into him and pulled his arm around her middle. "Let me return the favor." She rubbed her back into his chest, pleased to hear the rough hitch in his breath.

The soap joined her thong on the bottom of the tub as he twisted her in his grasp and kissed her.

That hadn't been so hard. Maybe because *he* was so hard. His erection pressed against her belly, and she felt the answering throb inside her. She wanted this, wanted him since he had teased her during the lap dance, when she was supposed to have been teasing him. He hadn't meant to, she knew.

Oh, but *now* he meant to. He sank his fingers into the muscle of her butt and pulled her closer, as if there were a closer when already not even the water droplets could find a way between their bodies.

His mouth angled over hers, almost rough with impatience, and she made a soft sound of pleasure and surprise. He broke off at once and tipped his head back into the stream with a groan.

"Jonah." She leaned forward to press her lips into his throat. Water sluiced around her mouth. She danced him in an intimate little tango to put the water at her back.

"I want you so much. I'm afraid you're going to slip away."

She decided not to remind him that this had been her idea. "I'm not going anywhere," she said against his skin.

"None of the others could hold you, and they had two hands."

With a huff, she reached up to frame his face in both hands and forced him to look at her. "Are you trying to piss me off by calling me a whore, or are you angling for my pity?"

His eyes blazed with purely masculine affront. "Neither."

"Then kiss me again."

He pulled her up against his chest, anchoring her with

his arm at the small of her back. His fingers cupped the back of her head as he brought his mouth down again. He definitely wasn't going to let her slip anywhere.

Except, maybe, here . . . She sucked in her belly to wedge her hand between their bodies and took him in a gentle grasp. He bucked against her. Just as well he had her locked in an iron hold. At his growl, she laughed against his mouth.

"Easy," she said.

"Hard," he corrected. He kicked off the water behind her and pushed aside the curtain. Then she was in his arms again. She wrapped her elbow behind his neck. Despite the slick floor, the soap somewhere underfoot, she felt oddly secure in his hold.

She tucked in her legs as he maneuvered her through the doorway. "I'm still dirty."

"I thought you didn't want to be reminded of your old life." When she huffed as if annoyed, he hugged her tight. "It's an excuse to bathe again later. After."

"Ooh, after what?" She squeaked as he tossed her onto the bed.

She hadn't gotten a good look at the room as he carried her in. And she didn't get much more of a look before he loomed over her and distracted her with his undeniable desire.

But she had the impression of dark woods and pale fabrics. She at least got a close-up of the creamy chenille spread on the neatly made poster bed when he flipped her onto her stomach and straddled her.

She strained to turn back, but he traced his fingertip down her spine and she caught her breath.

"Let me start small," he murmured.

"Too late, I think."

He chuckled, a deep, seductive sound. "I meant the small of your back. I wanted to touch you here, when you danced for me." He leaned down and his breath, then his lips, followed the path his finger had outlined. "I thought these dimples would drive me mad." His tongue dipped into one while he tickled the other. Her nerves jumped and she squirmed under him. He palmed her flat. "You said you weren't going anywhere."

"You said you don't torture."

"You said there were different kinds of pain, and you implied some of it was good."

She moaned as his hand finally slipped down the cleft between her legs, just grazing the heated core of her. "I'm a liar and a tease. Put me out of my misery."

He rolled her onto her back, and she angled one leg around him so he was captured between her thighs.

When he blinked at her, she smiled. "Just making sure you understand this is sexual banter, and that any laying on of hands better go a lot further."

He nodded, all seriousness, and she locked her ankles behind his back. He lowered himself slowly. Without his hand to brace him, he had to rest on his elbow, which left him hovering scant inches above her.

She took a deep breath, teasing her nipples against his chest. "I ache. Since the first night I saw you."

"I thought I was doing the right thing, holding back." He dipped his head and pressed a kiss between her breasts.

She held him there a moment. "Maybe you were, but the right thing isn't always possible."

When he turned his head and took her nipple into his mouth, she gasped and ran her hands over his shoulders, dug her fingers into the pad of muscle.

He reached between them and smoothed his thumb through the dampness gathering there. Up and over and down, the teasing, tightening circle of pleasure made her writhe. His mouth on her breast and his hand at her core stroked her toward a climax. Not alone this time. There'd been other men who brought her this far, but in the end, she'd always been alone.

"Now," she said. "Come inside me now."

Finally, Jonah thought hazily. It had been only a few heartbeats, and yet he worried she would never ask. With a rasping breath, he shifted his weight and guided the hot, heavy head of his erection into her. He clenched his teeth, easing in. So long it had been . . .

Her heels, clamped over his backside, drove him deeper. "Now," she demanded.

He plunged into her. His elbow slipped on the bedspread and he caught himself with his good hand. Never—even when he'd faced a charging feralis, minus his hand—had he regretted his maiming as much as now, when he wanted only to reach down, touch her cheek, tip her head back, and kiss her.

But if his loss had brought him to this moment, maybe those dark times since the teshuva had come for him and he whispered "God, why me?" had been answered: for this reason. For this . . .

Not that he had time to contemplate, not with Nim's body closing around him, legs and arms and the soft, molten core of her embracing him with a ferocity that made his heart pound. He levered himself up onto his knees and angled her hips high, stroking deeper. She clutched his hip bones and mewled, such a desperate sound he almost climaxed right then. But he clenched his teeth, tightened every muscle in his body so that he wouldn't let go, not before her.

She bucked against him, and he almost lost his precarious grip. She panted his name, and her internal muscles clenched him with an intensity that rolled his eyes back.

This was a demonic strength the other pair-bonded talya males hadn't mentioned.

For a moment, they lost the rhythm, his awkwardness and her impatience jolting them. He swore, shocking himself with his vehemence, and she laughed.

His cheeks heated. "I'm sorry."

She hushed him. "I'm flattered." She stroked her fingers down his belly to the junction of their bodies. His flesh leapt inside her, and she sighed.

Slowly, he rocked, his hips bumping the sleek muscles of her inner thighs. She watched him through half-lidded eyes and caught the tempo he set. Her dusky skin flushed with pleasure. A little faster he moved, and she matched him, beat for beat. With every stroke, her blush deepened, no demonic violet, just human delight.

Her fingers danced across his chest and fastened on his biceps, holding tight. He would not falter again. Just as well he had the stamina, the determination, the stubbornness, because he knew he did not have the art.

She did not seem to care, and if she was flattering him, he could not bring himself to care either. She murmured words without sense and touched him everywhere—the quiet marks of his *reven*, even the ugly stump—as if she would learn his body as well as she knew her own.

In sync, their pace quickened, and his breath came in bursts, when he could hold it no longer. This was what it was like to drown, in the spiraling well of his own desire.

"Come now," she whispered. "Oh, come now."

With jackknife violence, he did, and she seized around him, a possessive hold that wrenched a gasp from him along with the last of his semen and his strength.

His elbow unlocked without his command, and if he hadn't had the demon's latent strength at his disposal, he would have flattened her. Instead, he was able, barely, to angle to one side and merely drag the gnarled scar of his arm across her middle.

"Oh," he said.

Under him, her belly trembled with her heaving breath and a laugh. "Yeah."

Tacky, sweaty, slick. He wanted to lie there forever. As his body finally softened, he rolled to his back to cradle her in his arm. His good arm. He'd give that up for her.

"You don't have to worry," he said. "About pregnancy or disease, I mean."

"You said we're immortal," she reminded him. "Besides, I know you're too responsible to knock me up. You'd use the rhythm method, at least."

"Your faith terrifies me."

He didn't look down but he felt her angle her head to look up at him, as if she could see up his nose, into his brain. "I'm sure you're used to having people believe in you."

Her dreads wrapped around his only wrist, not unlike snakes. He wasn't going anywhere, even if his legs—demon powered though they might be—could hold him upright. "Yes, people believed in me."

She made a comical "oh" of dawning enlightenment. "That's *why* it terrifies you."

He gave her a squeeze.

"Still," she continued. "I think you did all right. You walked into the jungle, just as you intended, and you converted a bunch of heathens, which was the plan anyway, and you would have died there if you'd had your way. You stayed until the end. Not your end, since that wasn't an option. But your wife's end. That has to count."

"Perhaps. If you have enough fingers to do the counting."

She was silent a moment. "What was her name?"

He didn't pretend not to understand her. "Carine. Her father built the church that sponsored our mission. He didn't want her to go. I wish I'd listened."

"Why? She stayed there her whole life. Wasn't she happy?"

He took a breath. "She stayed there for me. Back home, how would she explain a husband who never aged?"

"So you stayed for her, and she stayed for you. Sounds like love."

With her hand lying on his chest above his heart, she must have felt his heart leap at the word. "It was. Without a doubt. But I think it would have been better if . . ."

Her palm slapped down with a startling sting and then hovered threateningly. "Watch what you say next."

With his hand trapped under her head, he couldn't defend himself. Nor, considering the dark thoughts that circled those long-ago choices, did he have the right to defend himself. "Since when are you a romantic?"

"Just because I've never loved anyone besides Mobi doesn't mean no one else has loved. You love her still, or you wouldn't hurt so much."

For some reason, the accusation—no, it wasn't an accusation; it just felt like one—bit deep. "I'm here, aren't I?"

"Oh, this is just fucking. It doesn't have anything to do with love, no more than my dancing does."

He pulled his arm out from under her, despite her grumble. "Don't call it that."

"Don't get all prim and proper on me now. It's just a word. Like 'mated.' Like 'love.'"

He propped himself up. "Why are you being so dismissive?"

In the dim room, her gaze was murky with shadows. "I'm not. I had a mind-blowing orgasm. I just don't want you to think it's anything more than that."

He stared at her, incredulous. "Are you telling me we should just be friends?"

"Well, I know you married young, and you probably didn't date much before that. And not much since, far as I can tell. We actually call it friends with benefits now."

He gritted his teeth. "So I've heard."

She reached up to touch his jaw. "I just don't want you to think I'm trying to take her place."

"You couldn't." When hurt flared in her eyes—and vanished as quick as a minnow flash on the water—he captured her hand and pressed a kiss into the center. He longed to see that impish smile again. Truly impish, since it contained more than a touch of the devil. "Carine was my sweetheart, my inspiration, my reason to live. Quite literally. But she would not have survived what you did, either before or after the demon."

She softened against him. His elbow slipped across the rumpled covers until he was lying beside her again. The heat of their bodies had cooled, and she reached to flip the edge of the coverlet over their hips.

He touched the wild tangle of her hair. "Do you want to shower again?"

"You're insatiable," she murmured. "Give me a minute."

His cheeks warmed. "I meant . . ." But her breathing deepened. With the slow expansion of her chest, he felt something sink into his. Not love—God, not that again—and not pain. But some awkward mix of the two, tangled, as he'd said earlier, around a core of the desperation they held in common. She'd wanted to get out of her life. Never mind what she claimed—the demon had known. And he'd wanted to get back into the life lost to him along with his arm.

He'd wanted this encounter, too. Had longed for it since he walked into the Shimmy Shack and seen her draped only in a snake and her insolence. She didn't care how exposed she was, how raw. Still, she'd held a piece of herself inviolate and wielded it against the world. He'd feared he'd lost that ability himself, even before he'd lost his hand, but now he knew he could get it back. Through her.

Friends did such things for each other.

When she'd settled into sleep, he eased away, tucking up the blanket to replace his warmth. She sighed and turned on her belly. He echoed the sigh as he eyed the dimples framing the base of her spine. He squelched the temptation to let his tongue travel the path again.

Leaving her side, the room felt colder, darker. Now that his attention widened, he realized it was getting late. The night-roaming talyan would be rising soon. He felt the restlessness gathering around them, one of the reasons most of the men had private retreats elsewhere. The talyan were trained to suspend their emotions, lest their excesses attract dark interests, and the league had invented energy sinks to hold any inadvertent spikes of violent fury. But it couldn't all be held back. Not forever.

Which was why even the best fighters didn't live eternally. Eventually, they all broke. If not physically, then from the weight of their accumulated pain and sorrow.

Evil, of course, lasted longer.

He washed up quietly in the bathroom, then dressed in a fresh T-shirt and jeans and strapped on the hook, and left a similar uniform, minus the hook, at the foot of the bed for when she awoke. He'd have to bother the other women for something better fitting, since he didn't want to visit her apartment when the police might be watching. Although Jilly was too short and Sera too staid to provide anything similar to Nim's usual attire.

For some reason, the thought made him sigh in regret, and he let himself out of the room before he could examine the impulse.

He left his shirt untucked, lest thinking of Nim and her clothes—or lack thereof—betray him.

He found Archer and Ecco in the kitchen. Archer was scowling at a map spread across the table, and Ecco was, inexplicably, at the stove, with a ladle in hand. The fragrance of chicken and herbs wafted from the open stew pot.

When Jonah arched his brow, the big talya shrugged. "Jilly will be hungry later."

Just as well she cooked for the league ahead of time, then, since Jonah knew Ecco couldn't boil water. Malice, yes; water, no. "How is she?"

Without straightening from the map, Archer grunted. "Sera is still with her."

"Did Andre give you anything?"

"A few possibilities. I don't know what your woman

did to him, but he passed out again and his vitals are down in coma range."

Jonah considered. "Do me a favor. Don't mention that to her."

"That she might have killed him?"

"That she didn't get everything we needed first."

Archer gave him a lopsided grin. "Ah, the gentler sex."

"I am reconsidering the illusion, yes," Jonah said. "If Andre regains consciousness, we should let him go."

Ecco rumbled. "Since when are you the forgiving type, missionary man?"

Jonah ignored the other talya. "He'll run back to Corvus, given the chance."

Archer drummed his fingers. "Niall would okay that. He won't kill a child, even one who's sold out to the devil."

"Assuming Nim didn't already kill him." Jonah lifted one of the sticky notes on the map. "Andre said 'flying,' so you're thinking airports."

"Niall said we aren't to make a move without him. So I'm not thinking anything, officially." When Jonah gave him a long look, Archer shrugged. "But since Jilly is down and our fearless leader is distracted, unofficially, I'm thinking a small team on a quick reconnaissance—"

Ecco shook his head. "Better wait for the boss."

"Since when do you obey the rules?" Archer asked.

"Since the girls started coming round and breaking them. Playing with them is more fun. And way scarier." Ecco glowered at Jonah. "The next one was supposed to be mine."

Jonah's hackles rose in atavistic response to the challenge. "They aren't trading cards."

Ecco tapped the spoon against the side of the pot and turned slowly. "They should go to the strongest fighters."

Jonah flexed his fingers. "They did."

"Knock it off, you two," Archer snapped. "We don't

understand the mechanism of the bond, but you can be sure there's more to it than muscle." He gave Ecco a long stare.

The big talya returned the look, and in his hands, the spoon seemed suddenly lethal.

Jonah smoothed his hand down the back of his neck. The short hairs prickled against his palm. What was wrong with him? He wasn't the sort to beat his chest and crow. But the incense scent of Nim was still on his skin. This was why saints renounced the temptations of the flesh.

"I'd join that advance team," he said. "If Nim is in danger from her demon's strength, I want that anklet."

"Not to mention, who knows what havoc Corvus could wreak with the artifact at his disposal." Archer swept his hand over the map again, encompassing the city with his gesture.

Jonah remembered the pull of Nim's allure. "I think the artifact does the djinn-man no good without the matching demon. Which is why Corvus went after Sera last winter." He flattened his palm on the map. "Which is why we'll have no trouble finding him again."

Ecco stirred the soup with unnecessary vigor. "Because he'll be coming for Nim. And you don't seem to care."

Jonah stared at him from beneath lowered brows. "Tell me again how you think you could have her, and I'll show you how much I care."

Archer sighed. "Your mark is on her, Jonah, as surely as the demon's. Ecco is just teasing you about taking her."

"No, he's not," Jonah said, just as Ecco protested, "No, I'm not."

"No one is taking anyone." Sera stood in the kitchen doorway, her voice more threatening than her mate's. She cast an admonitory eye over all of them, lingering on Ecco. "Stop stirring so hard. You're going to puree that chicken. Jilly only broke a few ribs, not her jaw."

Archer went to her side. The tender way he brushed her blond hair behind her ear made Jonah avert his gaze. "How's she doing?"

"Oh, you know how a sucking chest wound sounds worse than it is, at least when the teshuva are involved. All that gasping and bloody foam and turning blue, even though the demon is working its magic. The B team actually took a harder hit than we did. Haji will be down for three days at least with a compound femur fracture. The shattered bone did a lot of damage on the way out. And Nando almost lost an eye, which would have been . . ." Her glance went to his hook, and she stopped herself.

Jonah waited for the gut-curdling shame that usually followed those mortified shifts of gaze. But it seemed carnal relations had an undermining effect on shame. "It's always funny until someone almost loses an eye."

Sera drew her chin back in surprise. "Your mate is rubbing off on you."

"She has made rubbing an art." The words popped off his tongue with Nim-flavored tartness.

Ecco made a pained sound, slammed the spoon into the pot, and stalked out.

Sera watched him go. "What's his problem?"

Jonah grimaced. "Where to start . . . ?" He'd taken his share of needling from the big talya over the decades and rarely found ways to return the favor. Another disreputable Nim skill he'd acquired with their demonic resonance.

He rather liked it.

"Start with the part where you believe Nim is a menace without the anklet," Archer interrupted.

Jonah gestured at the pendant hanging from the cord around Sera's neck. "Did you ever try your tenebraeternum trick without the teshuva's talisman?"

"I never had reason to." Sullen rainbows gleamed under Sera's fingers when she touched the etherically mutated stone. "I've had the necklace ever since the demon first came to me, even before its first ascension."

Archer pulled her under his arm. "We always thought the *desolator numinis* was the weapon and Sera was the trigger. The same with Jilly and her knot-work trap."

"Jilly had her bracelet from the beginning too," Sera said.

Jonah wondered if he should be proud that his demon-matched cohort was the first to pawn her artifact and thus reveal a new facet of the female talyan. "Nim shows every sign of being as dangerously unstable as league records warn about in the few references we have to female talyan." When Archer and Sera stiffened as one, he waved his hand. "Don't bristle. I didn't write those books."

"No," Archer growled. "But your brand of dogma may have lost us our other halves for the last few millennia."

"Not dogma," Jonah said. "Just the truth of what I'm finding. Nim is a lure, just as Jilly makes herself a trap, and Sera is an exit from our realm through demonic emanations. But Nim did it without the anklet. Which makes us stronger than we knew."

"Not if she destroys herself—or us—in the discovery process," Archer said.

"And not if you think of her like that," Sera added.

Jonah scowled. "Like what? A weapon? That's what we all are."

"That's not *all* she is," Sera said. "Not to you." But her tone wavered uncertainly.

Archer completed her unspoken thought. "At least she'd better not be. Or maybe Ecco was right."

Jonah straightened. "I don't have to explain myself to you. You don't know anything more than I do about how this bond works."

"Love," Sera said. Again, her tone lacked conviction.

Jonah shook his head. "They call it the mated-talyan bond. Nothing in there about love." He narrowed his eyes at Archer. "You didn't believe in love."

"No more than I believed in demons. And look where that got me." He unfurled his fingers toward Sera in an oddly courtly gesture, but the smirk he turned on Jonah was decidedly fiendish. "Tell yourself what you will, if it helps seal your bond. But watch your sacrifices don't cut too deep."

He ladled out bowls of soup while Sera rifled through the silverware drawer. Then she whisked herself out of the kitchen with the tray balanced in her arms. Off to feed the invalid and the hovering mate, no doubt.

Caring and cooking pots. Before women had returned to the league, the talyan had been a tribe of taciturn loners, united only by their mission. After Carine was gone and they'd found him, their habitual solitude—bordering on the monkish—had suited him well. The loss of his arm, though . . . that had set him apart in a way he couldn't abide.

And when exactly had his separation—him from his arm, him from the league—ceased to eat at him? He thought he knew.

"Nim is mine," he said. "I won't risk her, even for my own salvation."

Archer lingered, his hip propped against the counter. "Isn't that why you were in Africa? To save others and thus save yourself? The demon lets you make the same mistake over and over. Until you don't."

Having told Nim the story already, Jonah found the admission slipped from him more easily this time. "Actually, I became a missionary for the adventure."

"Well, she'll give you that too." Archer's grin flashed and faded. "We're not perfect, Jonah. In fact, we're as far from it as a mob of selfish, frightened, brutal bastards can be. The sooner you admit that, the sooner you can be something else."

He headed for the door, and Jonah waited until the other talya had gotten halfway out before he spoke. "And what will I be? The man I was?"

Archer didn't look back. "Your list of sins is long enough. Don't add stupidity."

Behind him, a half dozen talyan—looking lethal and hungry and all sleepy-eyed, except for Nando, who was wearing an eye patch and looked only half-sleepy-eyed—filed into the kitchen.

"I smelled soup," Nando said. He squinted around the eye patch, as if somebody might be trying to hide his supper.

Lex jostled him. "Out of my way, pirate boy. You're missing an eye, not a leg." One of the other talyan elbowed him, and he ducked his head with a rueful grunt.

Jonah left them to their dinner and jibes, and took his muddled thoughts with him.

CHAPTER 13

Nim awoke and knew she was alone. She stretched until her spine cracked, then settled on the one pillow.

Not surprisingly, Jonah had sneaked out of their bed. If only she'd gotten around to lashing him to the four posters at the corners. He had too many hang-ups— some might call them morals—to do what he wanted without feeling bad about it. And he had wanted it, she knew, even though she had pushed him a little. Well, pushed him past his hang-ups—okay, morals—which had been a little further than a little.

But she'd made a nice living teasing men out of their morals, so what was this curdling sensation in her chest that made her want to pull the covers up over her head? Did she actually feel guilty?

If Jonah hadn't stopped her, she would have taken Andre's soul. And she hadn't even cared that much for the one she already had. But Jonah *had* stopped her. Still saving souls, Andre's and hers.

And she'd thanked the missionary man by seducing him.

With friends like her, who needed fire and brimstone?

When she shoved the blanket away, the dark lines on

her thighs startled her. Not that she had forgotten the demon's mark. Not exactly. But somehow, her night with Jonah seemed unrelated, which was so completely delusional she almost laughed at herself.

The only thing more pathetic than a john falling for a hooker was a stripper falling for the guy in the back row.

Not that she was falling for Jonah, but she could see how some poor girl might, like the long-dead-and-turned-to-African-worm-food Carine—young, innocent, idealistic. Good thing Nim was none of those things. Only a heart as scarred as the insides of her thighs would keep her safe.

Except the demon had all but erased those. Stupid demon.

She grabbed the T-shirt and sweatpants at the bottom of the bed, refusing to think how sweet he'd been to remember that she didn't have any clean clothes. Most men were thinking of ways to get her out of her clothes.

"He's not most men," she reminded herself. Then she saw her thong neatly draped over the shower-curtain rail. The black cotton was still faintly damp, but the soap had been rinsed out. She shook her head. "He even does laundry. He is definitely *not* most men."

She kicked her sneakers around the bottom of the tub while she showered, knocking most of the muck off. Good thing they were already black. Afterward, she dressed in the clothes he'd laid out. She propped the wet shoes on the windowsill behind the thick curtain that blocked out the heat and light. Then she went snooping through his room.

Or would have. But there wasn't much to snoop. Her earlier impression of simplicity bordering on austerity was unchanged. No pictures on the dresser. No books except a copy of the Bible beside the table, but the binding wasn't even cracked and there was nothing tucked between the pages. She went through the drawers and found only more T-shirts and jeans and briefs, until she yanked open the bottom drawer. She choked and jumped back before she realized the severed hand with forearm was fake.

She poked it. The naturalistic skin was eerily soft and unmarred, quite unlike his calluses. Obviously, Jonah had decided the hook was more serviceable.

Or maybe that was just another example of his painful integrity. Not even a fake hand for him. Thank God she'd never gotten around to buying fake tits.

She slammed the drawer closed and headed for the door. Hand on the knob, she hesitated, took a breath, and pulled it open.

She'd half expected to find Jonah on the other side, glowering. But the hall was empty. For a warehouse full of men, it was surprisingly clean. Maybe Jonah was in charge of housekeeping too. Unlike the basement, where all the haphazard decorations hung, the walls here were as bare as her feet. As if the league had saved all its focus for its mission of fighting evil.

Which made a certain amount of sense, she supposed. But didn't they hold anything back for themselves? Even the fresh-meat stripper knew better than to give it all away, no matter how loudly the crowd clamored for more, or there'd be nothing left at the end of the night. How much worse for the talyan who fought for years and years?

Maybe that was why she was here. . . . No, she shouldn't be thinking she'd somehow been specially chosen to—what?—show the ascetic talyan how to be selfish and extravagant hedonists? She really doubted Jonah would go for that.

Except the missionary's touch had been about more than the mission. She wasn't deluding herself about that.

A door ahead of her opened, and the blond woman, Sera, peered out. "I thought I told you. . . . Oh, Nim, it's you. I figured Liam was still skulking around after I told him to get some rest before the night rush. Come in, will you?"

Nim chewed at the inside of her lip. These girl-on-girl scenes usually made better fantasies than reality, but . . . She stepped inside.

Jilly sat up in bed, her chest swathed in bandages up to her armpits, her jaw set off-kilter in a mutinous slant. She scowled at Sera. "If you think you can keep me quiet by telling bedtime stories to the new kid on the block . . ."

Sera crossed her arms. "Do you want me to call Liam instead?"

Jilly huffed. "He'll wrap the gauze over my head."

"I like the stories where the evil stepsister gets eaten," Nim offered.

Jilly gave her a narrow-eyed stare, as if she suspected who the evil stepsister might be; then she grinned. "Sorry, I don't do well when I'm stuck in bed."

"I do some of my best work there," Nim said. "Maybe I can give you some pointers."

Jilly's grin upended, and Sera laughed. "You fit right in here, Nim."

Nim considered. "Have you ever had someone who didn't?"

Sera shrugged. "From what I've read, the league was never big enough to take its members for granted."

"Except when it decided to evict its female half," Jilly said.

"And yet here we are again," Nim said.

They stared at one another, three women who'd never have found one another in the big city, except for the demons that bound them.

Nim went to grab a chair. The stuffed wingback sprouted a few loose threads, and the desk beside it was missing all its drawers, but the room was cozier than Jonah's, even with the massive hammer hanging beside the door. Nim decided it was the extra pillows that softened all the hard edges. Certainly Jilly was no gentling influence, not with the twin crescent knives hanging next to the hammer.

She dragged the chair closer to the bed to prop her feet on the carved footboard. "So here we are. Sisters in arms."

"Which reminds me," Jilly said. "You need a weapon."

"Besides my apparent ability to dazzle unwary demons and wayward souls?"

"Sometimes it's nice to have a pointy thing too," Sera said. She settled at the foot of the bed and hummed thoughtfully. "Doesn't it seem providential that between us—the lure, the trap, and the end"—she pointed at Nim, then Jilly, then herself in turn—"we are some particularly heavy armament?"

Jilly snorted. "Love the league-speak. Did Archer call us that? But if by 'providential,' you're using the definition 'supplied by God,' then no, I don't think it's providence."

"Considering the whole demon-possession thing," Nim agreed.

"But the teshuva fight evil," Sera said. "Which puts them on God's side. Theoretically, at least."

"And we know how you like your theories." Jilly's teasing tone took the sting out of the words. "But we also know God hasn't claimed the teshuva. That's why they're still fighting."

Nim curled her toes around the plump butt of an ugly winged kewpie carved into the bed. "I figured out a while ago that hanging your self-worth on the approval of a distant father figure is a really bad idea."

Jilly nodded vigorously, but Sera sighed. "Still, it seems to me that us coming together is an opportunity the league hasn't had before."

"The league did have female talyan before," Jilly reminded her. "And kicked us out."

"We won't be letting them do that again," Nim said.

"When I first showed up," Sera said, "Jonah was adamantly against female talyan."

Jilly harrumphed. "Self-righteous bastard. As if the choice was his."

Sera tsked. "It's obviously not conceit. I think he holds women in too high esteem to believe they—we—should be vulnerable to possession."

Nim slouched lower in the chair. "Not a problem with me. The esteem thing, I mean. That's how he ended up with me. To teach him a lesson."

She meant to sound snarky, and Jilly chuckled as intended, but Sera just gave her a long look. "The demons do resonate, with us and with one another, but for once, it's not meant as punishment."

Nim shrugged and held on to her dismissive tone. "You'd have to ask him about that."

This time, Jilly didn't laugh. "Liam said he's never understood how Jonah was possessed. Oh, he's pieced together the spider story over the decades, but it doesn't explain why a demon chose him. He had a job and a wife he loved. He was involved in his community. Such connections usually offer protection against possession."

"Maybe he wasn't as connected as he'd want us to think," Nim said. When the other two women stared at her, she shrugged. "Just a guess."

"You'd know," Sera said.

"No, I wouldn't." Despite her best effort, Nim couldn't bury the bitter note. She'd woken up alone, after all.

"Regardless," Sera said soothingly. "We're all in the same place now."

"Right. Somewhere between doomed and fucked," Jilly mused.

Nim snickered when Sera frowned. "You sound like Archer."

"Your mate's a clever fellow."

"Tell me that again when you find out he masterminded an end run around Liam's decision to wait on finding Corvus."

Jilly shrugged. "They're both big boys. Emphasis on the 'big.'"

"That's what I'm worried about."

"They'll work it out." Jilly shook her finger at Sera. "And I think you're unfair to rat on him. Especially when I suspect you have plans of your own, to go with your theories."

Sera's blush was bright on her pale skin, and Nim murmured, "Busted."

Sera shot her a look and shifted uneasily on the bed. "Well, there's no point in them risking their lives and their souls for no good reason."

"How about an evil reason?" Nim asked.

"I propose a training run before we tangle with Corvus," Sera said. "The three of us and our teshuva, of course. The lure, the trap, the end. Let's give the demons a chance to make us what they intended us to be."

"A weapon," Jilly said.

"An end-of-the-world-as-we-know-it weapon," Sera confirmed. "But we'll start smaller. I know Ecco will help us round up a few malice. We can handle those individually with minimal danger. If together we are something more, it'll be obvious against the poor malice."

Nim snorted. "Poor monsters."

Jilly sighed. "She feels bad because she hears them screaming when she seals them behind the Veil again."

Sera wrinkled her nose. "Will you do it?"

"It gets me out of this bed."

Sera stood. "Tonight, then. When Liam takes his crew out hunting, I'll send Ecco to catch a few malice. One quick and easy test and then we'll take our findings to the males. That's when we'll go after Corvus."

"Set it up," Jilly said. "I'll be done bleeding by then. And Nim will have some clothes that fit."

Nim plucked at the oversized T-shirt. "You're letting me go through your closet? We must be BFFs."

"I just don't think any woman should have to face death and damnation in sweatpants."

Sera headed for the door. "I'll let you know when and where."

Jilly waved her off. "I'll be here," she said sourly. She turned to Nim. "I'm shorter than you and got more bootie, but if you don't mind hip-huggers . . ."

In the end, Nim found everything except shoes. Jilly wore a half size smaller and her tastes ran to thick-soled boots.

"Not sexy to dance in," Nim said as she backed out of the closet.

"But damn good for feralis stomping."

"Ah, a career-minded girl."

Jilly gave her a look in the mirror as Nim zipped her new black capri pants. "In some ways, this was an easy transition, both for me and Sera. We already had a history of helping others."

Nim adjusted the straps on the tank top. No support, really, but she was used to that. On several levels. "Oh, I was in the service industry too." She turned away from the mirror. "Don't worry. I might not have been a do-gooder like you two, but I've always been a survivor. If this is what I have to do to survive, then this is what I'll do."

Jilly's frown didn't abate. "And I thought Jonah's zeal was unnerving."

"It is. That's where we match. Or not so much match as fit together. Missing puzzle pieces." Nim studied the other woman. "Would you have chosen Liam? If the demon hadn't done it for you, I mean."

Twin spots of color flagged Jilly's wan cheeks. "I've never met a better man."

"That wasn't an answer, was it?"

"Then let me be clearer. Yes, I would have chosen

him. It wouldn't have mattered even if my mother had been the one to introduce us. I wanted him. I think I was waiting for him and no other."

Nim shrugged. "Then if it was meant to be, how can we lose?" She waited a moment, knowing Jilly wouldn't speak. "Oh, right," she answered herself softly. "Because love doesn't conquer all. It just seems that way because it's your whole world falling apart. I'm going to go see how my shoes are drying."

"We'll call you when it's time."

As she let herself out of the room, Nim wondered how she'd gotten on board with Team Double X. At least she could be sure Sera and Jilly wouldn't steal her eyeliner.

In the sterile hall, she leaned her back against the wall and sank to her haunches. Who was she kidding? The fantasy had gotten more violent and otherworldly, but still she was just another weapon, to be nailed to the wall when not in use.

She didn't like having nothing to do. Idle hands were the devil's tool, or so she'd heard. Maybe that explained Jonah's excessive goodness; having only one hand kept him too busy for naughtiness. She'd always kept herself busy with stripper intrigues and shopping. Now . . .

Well, she could still go shopping. Jonah had left his wallet in the room. And he owed her for that first lap dance.

". . . But when I woke up, I tried the door, and it was un- locked, so I got the hell out." Andre finished his tale in a rush. One hand clutched his slipping pants; the other he held fisted above his heart, as if only his white-knuckled grip kept him from falling apart.

Behind him, the lake glittered like a broken bottle, the smooth blue-green spiked with light sharp enough to pierce the eyes.

"Just walked out of the league stronghold, eh?" Corvus sprawled in his chair, the hinge of his jaw cradled in his palm as he studied the young man. He tapped one finger thoughtfully against the dent in the back of his skull. "And with your soul. Lucky you."

Lucky too the cloying heat had chased most of the late-afternoon crowds into the air-conditioned comforts of the Navy Pier shops, and only the two of them remained in the overheated wrought-iron tables. Andre's voice had risen exponentially as he'd detailed how the female talya had tried to steal his soul.

Corvus squinted against a closer glare, and he looked down. A glass orb had appeared in his hand while he was distracted; something the djinni had been toying with outside his conscious awareness. He fumbled it in surprise and only djinni reflexes saved him. Fury limned the world in bilious yellow. Was the djinni angry at Andre or at him? "You realize if you didn't tell the talyan what they wanted to know—as you swear you didn't— they'll have you followed."

"I doubled back through a tenebrae infestation like you showed me," Andre said quickly. He leaned away from the glass orb nestled in Corvus's palm. "The demon waste will throw off any teshuva."

"Not forever." When the youth flinched, Corvus waved his hand. "But I can't wait that long."

Andre blinked. "You want them to come?"

Corvus found himself stroking the chain around his wrist. The flesh under the tight links had bruised where the djinni was lax about repairing the damage. The memory of manacles made his skin creep, and a thin stream of demon venom trickled down his arms. His flesh smoldered with an acrid stink that wrung tears from his eyes. From his one eye, anyway. "I need them to finish what they started." Pain laced the words into a long slur.

Andre's gaze flickered over him, and Corvus felt each pause like a thrown stone: the drifting eye, his crushed skull, the filthy sleeves stained in the djinni's poison pus.

But of course the youth could not understand. Corvus didn't blame him. Even the ancient evil inside him failed to grasp the conviction, and they had been bound together for centuries.

As if annoyed at his recriminations, the djinni yanked him to his feet. His voice cleared, his tongue suddenly agile again as he heard himself say, "Not finish. This is only the beginning. Come, Andre. Walk with me down the pier."

His hand tossed the delicate ball into the air. Against the hot sky, movement swirled within the glass, like a frantic wave from the other side of a dirty window. Corvus's focused eye tracked the motion with avaricious delight, but his wayward eye noted Andre's wary, hunched shoulders.

The end of the pier looked scalded in the heat, with the concrete, water, and sky all charred to white ash. Nothing moved except for the endless waves and the frantic churning within the glass.

Andre peered at the globe. "What's in that ball?"

"My freedom," Corvus tried to say, but his tongue tripped as the djinni rose like vomit in his throat. "Our freedom."

The demon rummaged through his pockets, quick as a thief, and withdrew another glass ball. The djinni tossed the clear orb to Andre.

The youth's eyes widened, and the globe fell into his warding hands. His brows furrowed. "It's empty."

The djinni smiled, and when his lips cracked and sulfur stained his breath, Corvus remembered why they weren't doing that anymore. "It's for you."

CHAPTER 14

When Nim stepped out of Water Tower Place, the sun had fallen behind the buildings but heat still shimmered on the concrete. She raised her hand for a cab, and three large shopping bags slipped to the crook of her arm, already sweaty.

The cabbie started the meter. "Where to?"

She thought for a moment. Shopping, done. Couldn't go to the club. Couldn't go to her apartment. Where else did people stay out of trouble? She'd always been curious about those kinds of people. Okay, not always. But lately.

She gave him the address on the outskirts of town.

The lot beside the church was empty except for a staid minivan with the side door standing open. Apparently, the owner expected everyone to stay out of trouble.

Or maybe trouble had already been here.

The cab pulled away, and Nim felt her skin prickle with a sudden chill, despite the humid press of air. She yanked the bags up over her shoulder to free her hands. In case she had to grapple something. Damn it, if she lost another pair of shoes—the cutest Jimmy Choos, on sale too—before she even had a chance to wear them . . .

A woman—her red hair frizzed from its tidy French twist and contrasting unfortunately with her limp orange jumper—backed out of the church doors, leading a vacant-eyed zombie by the hand. "This way," she was saying. "Be careful you don't trip— Oh, my."

The woman stumbled when she saw Nim and had to grab her companion to steady herself. The zombie didn't falter.

"Hi," Nim said. "You must be Nanette. I'm Nim."

"Oh, dear. Another female talya. This is becoming quite the coven."

Nim jerked her chin back with a snort. "Does three even count as a coven? I figured we'd need at least thirteen or some other unholy number."

Nanette smoothed a hand over her hair. "I'm sorry. I didn't mean to say you were a witch. It's not a word I would've chosen."

"I've been called worse. Mostly by your good buddy Jonah."

"He left a message saying he'd been by. Is he here?" Nanette's eyes brightened as she peered past Nim. "I could use his help. I need to move these haints before my husband finishes his sermon and wants his dinner."

Nim shook her head. "I left Jonah at home while I went shopping."

"More tenebrae repellent and Chinese throwing stars? Jilly brought me some a while ago, but I'm almost out."

"Uh, no." Nim tried to imagine what the somewhat plump and obviously uncoordinated preacher's wife did with throwing stars. "But I got sexy sandals and a party pack in black from Frederick's of Hollywood."

Nanette blinked at her.

Nim rattled her shopping bags. "Now you know why I don't object to witch."

The other woman blew out a breath that puffed a wayward strand of red out of her eyes. "Sometimes I understand why the mighty of the angelic host refuse to believe that demons can repent."

Nim almost felt bad for her. No wonder Jonah had taken her under his one wing. He was drawn to women in need.

The thought rankled, and she caught herself up short. She was just being bitchy. That thought stuttered inside her too. Since when had being bitchy become a bad thing? She started to triple-guess herself, and in her distraction realized words were coming out of her mouth. "I'll help you move the zombies out."

"Haints," Nanette said.

"Do they care what I call them?"

"Maybe not, but I do."

Nim gave a mental shrug. The woman had bust out with "witch" quick enough. But she was curious about the life Jonah had abandoned. "Do you want help or not?"

It didn't take long to load up the half dozen passive haints. As Nanette brought them up from the church basement, Nim filled the seats in the minivan, then tucked the remainder into the cargo space in back. The haints listed against one another like pale mannequins. In the thick summer light, solvo glimmered like pearly sweat on their foreheads and in the hollows of their throats. The flecks of soul matter that clung around them were harder to see, even when Nim revved up her demon.

"No seat belts," Nanette fretted.

"No souls," Nim said. "Or at least not much."

Nanette straightened one woman's sharply angled neck. "You're right. It's silly to worry. I'd like to talk more, but I need to get the haints out of town, and since Jonah has been busy ..." She slammed the hatch on whatever else she'd been about to say.

Nim ignored her to study the sky. The sun had dropped out of sight, but it would be hot for hours. "Speaking of

Jonah, can you give me a lift to the warehouse? I spent the last of his money on the cab ride over here."

Nanette pursed her lips. "Maybe you should have passed on the Frederick's party pack."

"Too late now," Nim said with excessive cheer. "You going to make me walk home in this heat?"

Nanette chewed her lower lip pink, clashing even more with her dress and hair. Obviously, she liked to worry. No wonder she got along with Jonah. "I don't think that's a good idea. The angelic host I'm meeting to transport the haints, he's at war with demons."

"Of course, but which ones?"

"All of them."

Nim rolled her eyes. "I'll stay in the van and be quiet."

"I could leave you here and come back for you," Nanette muttered. "But what if Daniel finishes his sermon and comes to church early?"

"Daniel's your husband? Don't worry. I'll keep him busy till you get back." Nim smiled with lots of teeth.

"Oh, please. I don't worry about *him*. I'm worried about you. Do you want to spend an hour as his sermon beta tester?"

Nim shook her head hard enough to make her dreads dance. "For God's sake—no, really, for God's sake— take me with you."

Nanette folded her hands in front of her, upraised thumbs bumping a nervous rhythm. "Okay. My contact has a habit of ignoring anything he considers beneath him."

"Gee, thanks," Nim said.

"Which is pretty much everything," Nanette added. "Just be good." She thought about that, then revised to "Just don't be evil."

Nanette locked up the church and joined Nim in the van. In the close confines, the zombies smelled faintly of falling spring rain, and Nim took a deep breath. "You'd think they'd smell rotten, wouldn't you?"

Nanette checked all her mirrors before starting the vehicle. "It's odd," she agreed. "That's the scent of the solvo coming out through their skin." She hesitated. "Sometimes I think it's the perfume of peace."

Nim swiveled her head toward the other woman in surprise. "Soullessness is peace? Is a preacher's wife allowed to even *think* that?"

Nanette's grip on the steering wheel blanched her knuckles. "I wouldn't say that in front of the other angelic host, of course. But I thought you of all people would understand. They've escaped pain and fear and anger."

You of all people? Nim bit back a sharp retort. But as she swallowed down the words, she thought she got a taste of Nanette's meaning. "Trust me, escape doesn't get you as far as you'd think. Avoiding life isn't peace."

"I realize that. It's just . . . Did you know that some of the scattered soulflies make their way to the haints?"

"Jonah mentioned it. They just look like radioactive dust motes to me."

Nanette grimaced. "They do glow, pure and beautiful. Because they *are* pure. You might not care for the difference because your teshuva can't see it, but the angelic force in me knows only the goodness returned."

Nim twisted in her seat to study the haints. Though one was a man and one a woman, they bore the same glassy stare that made them eerily alike. The woman looked ahead, her hands tucked in her lap, precisely as Nim had arranged her earlier. The man had been heavier and more awkward, and Nim had stuffed him haphazardly into his seat, leaving him crooked, so he appeared to gaze out his window. She doubted he saw the passing city.

She sat back in her seat. "Honestly? If that's the alternative, I'd rather be part evil."

"Of course an exotic dancer would say that," Nanette murmured.

So, Jonah had left more with his message than "I was here," apparently.

"Stripper," Nim corrected archly. "Exotic dancers sometimes forget to take their clothes off. I never do."

Nanette let out a breath that might have been a disdainful huff, but sounded a lot like a laugh. "You aren't what I expected."

Exactly how much had Jonah said in that message? "Well, I don't expect you hang out at many strip clubs."

"Not since the year Daniel and I spent ministering to sex workers." Nanette nodded with satisfaction when Nim choked. "Daniel said they were some of the most sensitive, giving women he'd ever met."

Nim flattened her palms over her thighs. Neither the *reven* nor her old scars were detectable through the thin cotton of her capris, but they burned in her memory. "Yeah, if that's what he said, I can see how I'm not what you expected."

"I noticed they also had the worst self-esteem problems."

"Not an issue with me, I promise you."

Nanette opened her mouth as if she would say something, then just shook her head.

As they crossed into the North Shore neighborhoods, the wider expanse of the estate-sized lots revealed the late sun, but the heavy overhang of old trees and lush green lawns cooled the road. Nim shifted in her seat. If the haints smelled of rain, the neighborhood smelled of old money. "Jonah said you moved the haints down south, where they wouldn't raise awkward questions."

"My warden here has a quiet lake property where he takes the haints."

"Of course he does," Nim muttered.

"Cyril Fane is a powerful man, with an even more powerful angelic force," Nanette warned. "Don't make trouble for yourself, or me, or the talyan."

Nim clenched forefinger to thumb and ran them

across her lips with a zipping sound. She slouched back in her seat as Nanette pulled into the driveway of a particularly Gothic mansion, half-hidden behind massive oaks. The windows were as narrow as pinched lips, and the gables arched like condemning eyebrows. Yeah, she could've guessed an angel lived here.

Nanette idled the van in front of the three extra-tall garage doors. "Wait here."

"Happily," Nim said. When Nanette gave her a sharp look, Nim lifted both hands innocently. "What? Me and the zombies'll be right here."

"I'll have Mr. Fane open the garage. You pull the van inside and start moving the haints to the other vehicle. I'll keep him occupied."

"I thought I was staying in the van."

Nanette gave her a look. "Were you actually going to stay where I told you?"

"Probably not."

"Then just do this." Nanette's tone wavered between threatening and pleading. "I don't want to have to call Jonah."

"Well, I don't want to see him either. At least not before I put his wallet back." Nim huffed out a breath. "I said I'd be good. Okay, not evil."

Nanette gave her one more look and slipped out of the van.

"You'd think somebody possessed by an angel would be kind and sweet and trusting," Nim said to the haints as she shifted into the driver's seat.

They didn't answer.

Nanette knocked at the door and stood waiting a few heartbeats longer than Nim would have before the door opened. She disappeared inside without Nim getting a glimpse of the home's master.

It was another long wait, and Nim was resting her palm on the horn in the middle of the steering wheel when the garage door rumbled upward. She growled something rude, thought about revving the van to give everybody— well, everybody but the haints—a little thrill, thought better of it, and sedately pulled into the garage.

A gleaming silver Lotus took up more than its fair share of the oversized garage. Even in her pique, Nim wouldn't dream of scratching the little beauty, so she maneuvered the minivan carefully as the garage door came down, keeping neighborly nosiness out.

"How come the league doesn't drive high-performance British sports cars? We're fighting evil too."

The only other vehicle in the garage was a compact motor home, shiny new but still dowdy compared to its sleek garage mate. She wished she could indulge the demon in her and stuff the zombies into the tiny Lotus, but her love of overpriced consumer goods—if not Nanette's entreaty to *be* good—constrained her, so she turned off the van and went to the RV instead. The door was unlocked, and she ushered the haints into their new seats, moving them slowly so as not to dislodge their clinging soulflies. She buckled them in and then turned to poke through the drawers of the family mobile. Nothing. Not even a knife in the untouched cutlery organizer.

"Well, I don't suppose an archangel keeps his fiery sword in his motor home."

She took one last breath of the haints' sweet scent and pushed the drawer closed.

"I hope this Fane character doesn't drown you in the lake like a litter of abandoned kittens," she muttered.

"What's your solution?"

At the brisk crack of the baritone voice, Nim straightened abruptly and smacked her head on the corner of the kitchenette cabinetry. "Son of a bitch."

The man in the doorway frowned. Beyond him, Nim could see Nanette wringing her hands.

Nim clutched her skull and scowled at the other woman. "I thought you were keeping him occupied inside."

The man lifted one eyebrow, even higher than his house's gables. "While you rifled my RV?"

"Good God, no. I'd take the Lotus."

In the background, Nanette made frantic lip-zipping motions. Nim rolled her eyes and walked toward the man, forcing him back a step so she could hop down.

He inspected Nanette, who clasped her hands in front of her. "When you said you brought help, I assumed you meant another host of your sphere."

"You know what assuming makes you," Nim said.

"Nim," Nanette snapped. "You are being purposely provoking."

"Yes, provocative is what we strippers do. It comes naturally when we're around rich men." She unleashed a flirtatious grin. "Hi, I'm the Naughty Nymphette, dancing Thursday through Monday at the Shimmy Shack. Until my clientele was brutally murdered by demons. Now I'm fund-raising for a new battle fleet for the Chicago talyan. Care to donate the Lotus? It's going to a good cause. Well, not a good cause, precisely. You got a lock on that, I'm told. But a repentant cause, which, I'm sure you'll agree, is almost the same thing."

That eyebrow lifted another impossible degree. "I always thought the talyan were more taciturn," he mused.

"There are a lot of changes going on," Nim said. "But from what I hear, the angelic possessed aren't really into change."

"I'm so sorry, Mr. Fane." Nanette glowered at Nim. "If he smites you, what am I supposed to tell Jonah?"

"Did I say 'rich men' earlier? I meant 'rich, handsome men.'" Nim widened her smile.

And Cyril Fane was handsome. He was just old enough to look like he'd made his own money, and buff enough to dance under the name Virile Cyril, if he'd been so inclined. Nim decided not to say that aloud.

Fane had turned his sinister eyebrows on Nanette. "I thought the sphericanum had made the demarcation between the blessed host and"—his gaze shifted briefly toward Nim—"the others clear to you."

Nanette's hands clenched but she did not lower her head. "You did."

His voice was mild. "And yet still you seek them out."

"Actually," Nim interrupted. She didn't trust that quiet tone. "I found her."

He whirled to face her. "I will return to you in a moment, *heshuka*," he snapped. Thunder deepened his voice, and sparks, hot and gold, erupted from his glare.

Nim blinked. Ah, right. That was why she didn't trust him. Her muscles tightened and her pulse ramped up as her demon got uppity at his tone.

A low hum echoed from the motor home behind her. The haints had twisted their faces toward the spat. Their blank eyes reflected gold. And violet.

She flexed her hands, and the gloom of the closed garage shifted into the eerie black light of the roused demon. Waves of ether pulsed around them, bouncing off Nanette and the haints in scattering ripples.

"No," Nanette said. "Stop it, both of you." Her voice lacked Fane's celestial boom, but held a mother-hen insistence that required at least nominal obedience. "Our purpose is the same."

"Not so," Fane said. "Theirs is salvation. They fight against the darkness not for the glory of the light, but merely to save themselves."

Nanette set her jaw. "The result is the same."

Fane's expression darkened. Obviously, he wasn't used to being contradicted. "They betrayed us once and embraced the shadows. Would you follow them into the dark?"

"*I* didn't betray you," Nim said. "I don't even know you. Although now that I do . . ."

"Stop." Nanette's voice rose, not quite to a shriek, but getting there. "Before you say something that starts another war."

"Yeah." Nim put both hands on her hips, not to be flirty, but to square herself against Fane. "A war with the bad demons is bad enough."

"I meant another war like the one that fractured the realms at the beginning of the world," Nanette said.

"Oh." Nim thought for a moment. "Well, I don't go back that far either."

Fane's lips twisted in an unkind smile. "And this is the weapon the teshuva think will win them their salvation. You'd be lucky to empty enough half-starved malice to redeem a thimbleful of your soul."

Nim bristled. "Nobody uses thimbles anymore. And we're not stopping with malice anymore either. We're aiming for the djinn this time."

Fane didn't so much as twitch, but the haints groaned at the flare of power that belled through the garage. A faint thump issued from the motor home where one bonked its head against the window, drawn to the swelling energy but trapped by its seat belt.

"Oh, Nim," Nanette whispered.

"Going after the djinn?" Fane's voice wasn't much louder than Nanette's.

There was a saying, Nim remembered, that upon finding oneself at the bottom of a hole, the wisest course was to stop digging. She'd always figured the saying was for people who had another way out.

She propped her hand on her hip. "I think the teshuva got tired of waiting for the Holy Rollers to get rolling and found their own set of wheels. Not as nice as yours, of course. But maybe not so indicative of a tiny penis either."

Nanette took a step back.

The muscle in Fane's jaw ticked in opposition to the vein throbbing at his temple. He'd have to do something soon, Nim mused, or his head would explode.

He laughed.

Nanette took another step back, but Nim just smiled in return.

"You talyan have a death wish," he said. "That's why the teshuva grant you immortality."

"We all have our little flaws," she admitted.

"No," he said. "We all don't." His irises glinted gold. "Shall I drop my pants to prove it to you?"

Nanette took two more steps back and bumped into the stairs that led up to the door of the house. The door that, Nim realized abruptly, was ajar. With Jonah standing there in silence, bound in the absolute stillness that made her think of a peaceful dawn on some gorgeous, remote mountain . . . right before it avalanched.

He steadied Nanette with a hand at her shoulder and she let out a piercing shriek.

Nim winced. This wasn't going to go well. As if the rest of the visit had been so stellar.

The waves of ether had crisscrossed into such confusion she'd missed the demonic aura that must have preceded his arrival. But she couldn't miss the hellish fury that raised the blood to his cheeks and sparked violet along his *reven*.

She considered Fane's challenge. Angels had a sense of humor. Who knew? "Keep your zipper up. I already have too much of a good thing." She met Jonah's glittering stare. "Hey, lover."

CHAPTER 15

She was going to be the death of him. Unlike his wife, with whom he should have grown happily old and who had instead inadvertently fated him to eternal life, Nim—his intended salvation—would be his doom.

Jonah just hadn't thought it would be so soon. And against an angelic host, not even the tenebrae, who were supposed to be his prey.

She sauntered toward him. The snug black pants clung so low, he caught a glimpse of the *reven* gleaming at her hip bone under the hitched-up hem of her skimpy tank top. She stopped in front of him and handed him his wallet.

His pulse spiked, and he tucked the wallet into his back pocket, refusing to wince when the angry thrust yanked his jeans taut across his suddenly attentive shaft. At least he could die happy, his body reminded him.

His tone was harsher than he intended when he asked, "What are you doing here?"

Before she could answer—and he could see her shuffling through the various possibilities in her head—the man across the garage raised his voice. "What are you doing in my house, talya?"

"I knocked," Jonah said. "No one answered. The door was unlocked."

"Because no one else in this neighborhood would have dared test it."

"Just as well you don't live in my neighborhood." Jonah didn't bother mentioning that the door had been unlocked *after* he got through with it. "We lock our doors. We keep our pants on too."

Nanette shuddered. "Jonah, may I introduce you to my warden, Cyril Fane?"

With the tenebraeternum providing entirely enough difficulties, the league kept little more than haphazard records on the angelic host. They were secretive even among their own, and downright hostile toward the talyan. Jonah knew only that the wardens were highly placed among the spheres.

But he recognized a challenge when he saw one. "Nanette, Nim, perhaps you should wait outside."

"Don't presume to order the host from any sphere," Fane growled.

"Or me either," Nim said.

The chill that spread through the garage was tinged with feminine ire . . . and the arid, metallic tang of the demon realm.

Fane stiffened. "Talya, take your feral *symballein* and leave before I'm forced to torch my house to rid the defilement—with you inside."

"Please, Jonah," Nanette whispered. "Mr. Fane has been a friend to the league in ways you can't understand."

"With friends like these . . ." Nim muttered, just loud enough.

"I'd make a worse enemy," Fane said.

Jonah looked at Nanette, who stared back with imploring eyes. She trusted Fane enough to let him minister to the haints she'd taken on. And Jonah trusted her. But Fane . . .

Jonah slapped the hook against the garage door button on the wall beside him with a crack of metal on plastic. The door grumbled up in a wash of late-summer light and heat.

Fane squinted his annoyance. The host, Jonah knew, hated revelation—the public kind, not the end-of-the-Bible kind—almost as much as they hated demons. He could hope that being exposed before the neighborhood Joneses would prevent the angelic possessed from re-creating any scenes from *The Exorcist*.

"Nim." He chucked his car keys. "Back my car out so Nanette can leave too."

She caught the keys. "Trying to get me out of the way?"

He didn't see any need to confirm her words. "Nanette, I'm sorry for the inconvenience."

Nim muttered as she headed out of the garage. "Now I'm an inconvenience."

He didn't respond to that either.

Nanette swallowed. "It's nothing. But I'm not leaving quite yet."

Jonah turned to Fane, whose gold-sparked stare had locked the smaller woman in place. "Why is she frightened of you?"

"Because I am warden and she has transgressed." He waved his hand irritably. "And because I'm terrifying. But I promise I am merely composing a stern lecture in my head, not planning to beat her, so you can stop glowering." The fulminating gilt of his eyes faded, revealing tiny lines at the corners that made him look weary. "I suggest you not be so indulgent with your *symballein*."

That unfamiliar word again. Jonah fixed it in his head. "The teshuva have never been noted for their mercy."

Fane smiled crookedly. "Indeed not."

"Jonah," Nanette protested.

He gave her a look. "Remember who earned you

that stern talking-to. If you wish, say a prayer for her tonight."

She subsided and stood back with Fane as Jonah stalked past them to the open door.

"Talya," Fane called. When Jonah paused, the angelic possessed crossed his arms. "I'll have words with you too about this alleged hunt for the djinn."

"Offering the assistance of the spheres?"

"I think you know better."

Jonah pulled out his wallet—his thin, decimated wallet—and thumbed an @1 business card from one of the inner pockets. He laid the card on the hood of the motor home. "Have your people call my people."

"That would be a good start," Nanette said eagerly.

Fane snorted. "You know better too."

Jonah hesitated another moment, but Nanette gave him a tiny head shake. She looked more forlorn than truly frightened, so he turned away. He wasn't doing her any favors by keeping Nim around to spur the higher angel's temper.

The garage door started creaking down before he'd quite cleared the interior, but he didn't duck.

Nim was in the driver's seat of the well-used hatchback, and he contemplated booting her out. Then he just sighed and slipped into the passenger's seat.

"Where's Nanette?" she asked. "Is he keeping her prisoner? Should I ram the garage?"

He gave her a look.

She put the car into reverse. He didn't speak as they left the curving roads of the ritzy subdivision.

When they merged onto the straight shot back into the city, she finally cleared her throat. "How did you find me?"

"There was a giant, blinking neon sign over the house that said 'Nim is getting into trouble here.'"

"I've been looking for a new place to dance. Maybe Fane will let me keep that sign."

At the thought of the haughty angelic possessed—
and Nim dancing anywhere nearby—Jonah gritted his
teeth. "I'm sure you can just make another one."

Her palm rubbed a quarter circle arc over the steering wheel. "And you'd come for me there too?"

Was that why she'd run off? To see if he'd follow? He
almost snapped. But he hesitated at the odd note in her
voice. If he didn't know better, he'd call it wistfulness. "I
wouldn't be able to stop myself. The bond between us
doesn't care when or where or why. I will come for you."

She didn't turn her gaze from the road, but she
rubbed her palm reflexively down her thigh. The motion
captured his attention until he forced himself to look
away.

"Damn it." She smacked her hand on the steering
wheel again. "I forgot my shopping bags in Nanette's
van. I don't suppose it's a good idea to go back now."

"Why did you go to the church at all?"

"I went shopping."

He shifted in his seat, barely feeling the depleted wallet under his backside. "Can you buy forgiveness?"

"I knew you wouldn't understand. People like you
and Nanette never do."

"People like—"

"Good people," Nim burst out. "You don't understand doing it wrong." She sighed. "I was scared."

"Of coming home with my empty wallet?"

She rolled her eyes at him. "You don't really care
about that."

"Jilly will. Her old life with a nonprofit gave her an
appreciation for making every penny count."

"Yeah, I noticed she doesn't have much use for deadweight." She trailed off.

He frowned. "Did Jilly or Sera say something to scare
you off?"

Still she hesitated. "Oh, it's just . . . everything. I didn't
want to wait around for tonight. I'm scared something

else bad is going to happen because of me. I'm scared I can't even be good at being evil. Repentantly evil. I figured I wouldn't have to think about any of that at the church. And if I had cuter shoes."

"Nim, I'm here, so you don't have to be scared."

"I was scared of that too, facing you after . . ." She regarded him from beneath half-lowered lashes.

They'd stopped at a red light, so he didn't have an excuse to look away. He ran his hand over the back of his neck, flustered. She was a liar when it suited her, a knee-jerk flirt, a thief of convenience, and still she spoke with a painful insight that humbled him.

"Do you hate me for corrupting you?" she pressed. "Am I your bane now?"

Was it too late to return to the angelic possessed and fight him to the death? Another interrealm war would be less fraught than this conversation.

"I could never hate you, Nim."

"Oh, trust me. It's easier than you'd think."

He reached across the space between them and brushed the backs of his fingers against her cheek. In the endlessly lingering summer light, her dusky skin was warm and soft under his touch. She had tempted him, seduced him. But corrupted? "I am not one of those men."

"No," she whispered. "No, you're not."

The light turned green and he released her.

They drove to the warehouse in silence, and she parked inside the barbed-wire lot. The docking bay door was thrown wide-open, and a handful of the talyan had gathered in the twilight.

Liam paced the edge of the concrete dock alone, his mate nowhere in evidence. Jonah felt a twinge of sympathy. Having just suffered through the frantic agony of being unable to locate his other half, he wondered if knowing where she was but that she was injured and there was nothing he could do would be better . . . or worse.

As they got out of the car, he was suddenly, fiercely glad Sera had suggested the women would stay behind tonight in solidarity with the bed-bound Jilly.

Ecco leaned against the wall, rolling a cigarette. In a moment, the scent of cloves drifted across the yard.

Nim nodded at the big talya. "Can I get a drag? Now that I'm immortal and all."

Ecco held on to the blunt. "Immortality won't help me much if your boyfriend rips my lungs out through my nose."

Nim slanted a glance at Jonah, then sighed. "Never mind, then."

Like a pack of hunting dogs, the talyan continued to gather, talking in small groups or lounging near the dock. At some unknown signal Jonah had never identified except by the prickling of his demon, they quieted and came together, senses on alert, the first glimmers of violet in their eyes.

Liam halted off to the side, and as one the talyan faced him. "I have had enough of Corvus Valerius."

A wave of muted laughter rippled through the warriors, but the tension didn't ease. If anything, Jonah's nerves felt strung tighter as the demonic emanations thickened.

"Andre coughed up a hint of a location for us," Liam said.

"With hardly any blood," Archer added.

Liam didn't smile. "He waxed a bit poetical, but we think Corvus is holed up near an airport. We set Andre loose to confirm, hoping he'd go running back, but we lost him when he backtracked through a tenebrae dumping ground outside Englewood. Maybe we'll pick him up again. At least his bones." He shrugged. "Since the djinn are as territorial as the leagues, we doubt Corvus would stray as far as the suburbs. Leaving us two choices: O'Hare and Midway, with the old Meigs Field as a long-shot third choice."

His sharp blue gaze roamed the talyan. "For almost a year now, we've taken hits from the djinn-man, if we can still call him that when the man is almost gone and the djinni runs rogue. According to some interpretations of our mission, confronting him while he still wears the tatters of his human skin is outside our sanction. Maybe we should let the angels and the djinn war over our heads while we and the teshuva are fit only for the shadows. So I'll leave it up to you where to hunt tonight." He paused. "But I do have a half dozen cars that will circle all three locations and end up at the Coil for beer on the league's tab before last call."

From the back of the dock, Nando sent up a little cheer. "I'm ready for a new headache."

This time, Liam gave them a cold smile. "Unless, of course, we find Blackbird, and then I'm calling you all in for the ravaging."

That got a big cheer.

As the talyan divvied up toward the cars, Nim sidled next to Jonah. "Which of the three should we try?"

He jumped down from the loading dock—to get away quicker, not because he wanted to leer at the bounce of her breasts as she followed. "I'm going to Meigs Field. It's not even an airport anymore, and I think Andre was trying to be clever, giving us what we asked for while still protecting his patron. But you aren't going."

She opened her mouth, and he thought she was about to object. He cut her off. "Archer insisted that Sera stay here to keep Jilly from sneaking out. So I volunteered you to stay too."

She bit her lip and slowly shook her head. "Wow, you males really got us figured out."

Something about her tone made him squint, but she looked guileless. Which made him narrow his eyes even more. The bond between them pulled him closer until he stood within the aura of her body, her heat signature, breath, and the incense perfume of her skin all matched to the restless demon in him. The thrum through his bones eased when he was next to her. He wanted to stay there, lost in that solace.

But that was her thrall demon, luring him in again.

He took a step back. "I'll skip the drinking at the Coil."

"But not the ravaging, if you're so lucky."

"That *is* why we're going."

"*I'm* why you're going." She kicked at a patch of gravel. "It's my anklet you're after."

"It's Corvus's head we're after. Everything else is an excuse." He longed to reach out to her, to smooth his thumb over her woeful, outthrust lower lip. "We want so much more than we've had, Nim."

She gazed at him, as if she knew he wasn't talking just about the league. "Come back soon. But not too soon."

She hopped up onto the dock and stood there as they all climbed into their chosen vehicles. She raised one hand to wave. In the last light, with her dreads hanging close around her, she looked like a primitive queen sending her warriors to battle.

Jonah's heart crashed in his chest, as if it wanted to leap past his seat belt and race back to her. He sighed.

Archer slid into the driver's seat. "Yeah, that's love."

Jonah suppressed a curse. "Is it too late for me to pick another car?"

"Yes. We're going to share everything we've learned about the mated-talyan bond on the way to Meigs."

From the backseat, Nando groaned. "Girl talk."

"Shut up," Archer said. "You could be next."

The talya perked up, but Jonah shook his head. "Let me tell you about an angel I met instead."

Nim watched the cars file out past the barbed wire. The crunch of tires on gravel sounded like breaking bones.

She wondered if losing a hand would be as hard as

letting Jonah go. *If thy eye offend thee, pluck it out.* Oh, great. How come she knew only the squicky parts of the Good Book? But the Bible was right; if she couldn't be what Jonah needed to fight his battle, he'd have to cut her off. That was what everyone in her life had figured out long ago.

The scent of cloves teased her, and Ecco stepped out from behind the Dumpster. "I'll go bottle up some malice and meet you back here. Lock up behind me."

She followed him to the chain-link gate. "Do you think they'll find Corvus?"

"No, or I would have gone with them. Blackbird is smarter than us."

She eyed him. "Ever heard of this concept called allegiance?"

The big talya shrugged. "Doesn't get you anywhere. Brutal, but true. Still, now we have the three of you."

Her and Sera and Jilly. And whatever they could become together. "What are we again?"

"I think you're our chance. That's why I didn't go with them, and why I'll risk some serious ass kicking if your boys find out I'm not with any of them."

"What happens if we get in worse trouble than they do?"

Ecco's teeth flashed brighter than his gauntlet blades. "Yeah, that thought had occurred to me."

When he sauntered out the gate, she yanked it shut with more force than was necessary.

He brought his gauntlets down his thigh with a hiss of steel on leather. "What's with the attitude? You like trouble. You got through your old life wrapped in trouble. That's why you didn't need clothes."

"Remember how I gave up my old life?"

"Nobody changes that much." He flicked the stub of his cigarette through the chain link at her feet and walked away.

She waited until he'd disappeared beyond the corner of the warehouse, too far for even a demon to hear, before she answered, "That's what I'm afraid of."

She went to the dock, pulled down the big door, and latched it against the night.

Sera and Jilly weren't waiting for her in the kitchen or in the lobby. She took a breath, closed her eyes, and let her senses flow.

She sensed the deadened zones, where Jonah had talked about energy sinks. And the leftover art no one had claimed from salvage held a sort of brightness from which the teshuva shied away. But a faint track led her to the stairwell and up to the roof.

The two women were sitting on matching bar stools, their feet propped on the low lip of the wall ringing the rooftop. A third stool was pulled up beside them.

Nim dropped onto it with a huff. "Couldn't leave a note?"

"Wondered if your teshuva would sniff us out," Jilly said. "Even without the anklet."

"We already knew the artifacts didn't *give* us our powers," Sera said.

Jilly shrugged. "Tonight we'll find out what they *are* for."

Nim glanced at her. Dressed in cutoffs and a short-sleeved cotton oxford, Jilly didn't look like a woman who'd been nearly gutted earlier in the day. Except for the band of gauze that peeked through at the shirt's unbuttoned neck. "You up for this?"

Jilly gave her a look. "I'm up."

"I already told her we could wait," Sera said. "The female talyan have been MIA for more than two thousand years. Another night wouldn't kill us. Probably. Although weirder things have happened."

Jilly huffed. "With reassurances like that, is it any wonder I got up?"

They sat looking out over the city, peaceful if not exactly companionable as the light faded.

Jilly finally stirred. "What do you think happened to all of us, all the women warriors?"

Sera sighed. "You know the league archives have almost nothing to say."

"Then I'm guessing we all ran away," Nim said. The other two drew identical breaths as preparation to argue, their eyes reflecting their outrage along with the last of the sky glow, but she held up her hand to stop them. "Think about it. A man wins a woman, and he brags out loud to whoever'll listen. He hits her? He's got a long story about how she walked into a door. Hell, he'll kill her and scream about how she had it coming. But if she runs away? Vast, echoing silence."

Sera puffed out her cheeks on a sigh stopped midstream. "That's cynical."

"And believable," Jilly said. "Saw it often enough with the street kids I worked with. Andre told me some of the things his dad used to say to him. . . ." She shook her head.

Nim lifted her eyebrows. "You feel sorry for him?"

"What can I say?" Jilly tugged at the gauze bandage. "I'm a bleeding heart."

"Har har." Sera stood and stretched, blond hair rippling down her back. "Come on. Let's meet Ecco halfway. I don't want to be fighting the league barriers in the warehouse when we try our little trick."

Nim stood, shifting uneasily from one foot to the other. "How will we find him? How will he catch the malice?"

Sera turned away from them, toward the city. Her racerback tank top displayed the traceries of her *reven*. "Ecco has a way with the malice. He flays open his soul, and then they come to feast. Can't you feel it? He's out there now, like he's ringing a bell and singing 'Come and get it.'"

Nim shuddered. "How can he stand to be eaten alive?"

Sera shrugged. "He's come to the same sort of serenity as the dying people I counseled." The violet lights flared higher. "Except he gets to fight back. Unlike our missing sisters, apparently."

"But we're here now," Jilly said. "Let's do it."

CHAPTER 16

They traced Ecco's path to the next industrial park. He'd chosen an empty warehouse, the four stories of brick still standing but every windowpane shattered and the bottom eight feet of the exterior wreathed in layers of garbled graffiti.

Train tracks passed it, but the rails had been partially filled in with asphalt, the line abandoned.

"At least we won't have to explain to Liam how the building got destroyed," Jilly said.

"That does make it easier." Sera kicked open the door.

The interior had been gutted; only broken glass and the support beams that disappeared into the darkness four floors up remained. The darkness was thick with etheric smoke as tangled as the graffiti, and in a strange way, almost as legible.

And the word it pulsed was "doom."

Ecco whirled at the heart of it, gauntlets dulled but his teshuva alight to Nim's demon-amped vision. A dozen forty-ounce liquor bottles surrounded him. Nim realized when he'd said he was bottling malice, he meant actually bottling them. Obviously, he'd had no trouble finding containers in the vacant building.

Not that the malice seemed inclined to participate. A cloud of inky darkness darted around him, staining the air behind it with streamers of demon sign, as the malice tried to avoid the bottles and get to Ecco.

He chanted obscenities, and his eyes blazed. Nim wasn't sure she wanted to get too close either. "What's our move?"

"You're the lure," Sera said. "Call them."

"Me?" Nim stammered the word into multiple syllables.

Jilly wrapped her fingers around her wrist, where her woven metallic bracelet flickered with violet. "Bring them close enough and I'll trap them all."

"And I'll send them to the other side," Sera said.

"Although this is a bigger horde than we've tried before." Did Jilly's voice waver a bit? Her uncertainty was almost lost in the malevolent drone of the malice as they circled.

Nim took a breath. Too late to back down now.

But she wanted Jonah by her side, so badly her knees shook. Or maybe that was fear. Or maybe the *reven* wrapped around her thighs kicking in. She didn't know which. And that was why she wanted him. He'd know. With his steady assurance, his unwavering strength, his devotion. Oh, not devotion to her—she knew that—but to the bond between them, which was almost the same. She wanted it to be the same.

The longing shocked her.

As did the realization that her yearning had distracted the malice.

Their focus weighed on her like a major depression, like the yawning void that before had inspired her to strike entire books of matches. As if those tiny flames could ever light the darkness. The bright flare of pain as she'd extinguished the fire in her skin had been something like light, an illusion of illumination.

But not as bright as the *reven* that flared now to her knees, straightening her stance.

The tornado of malice made a vacuum that sucked at her breath, as if they could stop her heart with their convergence.

"That's it," Jilly whispered. "Lure them in."

The horde wanted her as much as she wanted Jonah. No, they wanted her more. Because all the crazy, luminous, weightless yearning that made her pulse race when she thought of him was not enough to satisfy them.

Because she could not be enough to satisfy Jonah.

"Don't lose them, Nim." Sera's voice came as if from a deep well, distorted and thin. "Nim?"

How could she have spent a lifetime honing herself into a tool of desire, and yet all her hot caresses left him cold, untouched? Not his body, of course; that always rose to her teasing fingers like the teshuva roused to demon sign. But his heart . . . That was locked away where she couldn't ever reach. He didn't want her, not like the malice wanted her.

She straightened and opened her arms. A chill down her spine made the small hairs at her nape prickle.

"Nim, no!" Ecco's shout warped through the black fog. But his wasn't the voice she wanted to hear.

"Come on, then," she whispered. "Is this the darkness you feed on, you sucking little bastards? I'll show you shadows."

They came.

Fast as obsidian wasps, the malice swarmed her. The embers of their eyes burned, and their vicious shrill rose toward a scream.

No, that was Sera, shouting a warning. "Ecco! Coming through the window."

Nim dragged her awareness out of the morass where

she'd gone. The shattered windows at ground level shone red with the last of the setting sun. But the sun had set a half hour ago.

A hot wind spun slivers of glass across her shins. The wind stank of brittle rust. And death.

The red was the glow of salambes.

The malice cloud squealed and spun faster, then rose toward the ceiling. Her pulse, which had faded to a shallow rasp, kicked into the demon's double beat as the sullen gleam climbed to the second set of windows, and then the third. How many of the tenebrae were out there?

Ecco's chanted curses rose to a sharper pitch, which suddenly made her giggle. If the hulking talya was scared, they must be well and truly fucked.

Finally, she was living up to her full potential. And she didn't need any man to do that.

"You wanted to see what we could do," she reminded Jilly, who was standing nearby.

The shorter woman whirled around, her violet eyes widened. "Nim? Are you back with us?"

Nim frowned. "Where else would I be?"

"The Veil was thinning. You must have felt the cold."

"Oh. That."

Jilly grinned. "Yeah. Can you stop with the luring thing now? We're about to be swamped." Her grin faltered. "And there's no way we can take them all."

"I don't think so. I didn't know I'd started."

Sera moved closer to them. "I've always used Ferris to pull myself back."

"Your boyfriends aren't here," Ecco said. "Although it just so happens that I . . ."

He trailed off when Nim gave him a look, and she realized the other two women had leveled identical expressions on him. He shrugged. "Potential hot four-way action. Can't blame a guy for trying."

"Maybe a three-way . . ." Nim hummed to herself.

When the rent check was due, she'd always been willing to do scenarios outside her usual repertoire.

"That'd be fine," Ecco said.

She ignored him and held her hands out to Sera and Jilly. "What makes us different from the guys?"

"Where to start?" Sera mused with a last glare at the grinning Ecco, and took Nim's hand.

"We aren't afraid to look inward, to touch." Nim waggled her fingers, and Jilly finally took her hand and Sera's, completing the small circle.

Nim swallowed hard, hoping she could choke down the lie. She'd *always* been afraid to look inward. And as for touching . . . It could be good. Jonah had showed her it could be good.

Even for repentant evil.

"I think this is weird," Jilly said.

"I think I've died and gone to heaven," Ecco said.

Jilly started to tug away, but Nim tightened her grasp. "No, stay with us. You said we can't take them all. Not alone. I brought them"—boy, had she ever—"just like you told me to. Now you have to trap them."

Jilly swallowed hard and closed her eyes. The *reven* that curled over her breast, barely visible above the band of gauze around her chest, sputtered, then flared again. "This was a bad idea."

Sera tugged at her, lifting their joined hands to rattle the bracelet around Jilly's wrist. "And if you want to live long enough for Liam to tell you that, over and over, you better set that trap."

Jilly cracked one closed eye to peer at Sera. "All right, Miss Know-It-All."

The bracelet glimmered with unnatural lights woven through the dull metal. Nim stared at the knot work, trying to follow even one bead of light sliding through the strands. She startled when Sera tightened her grasp.

"Don't get caught in there," Sera warned. "You won't like where you go when it's my turn to deal with them."

The tenebraeternum. The demon realm.

Sweat beaded on Jilly's brow despite the chill fog that had descended. The malice drifted lower too, their wild churning slowed to a sluggish writhe as they approached. The featureless black haze crystallized into claws and spiked tails and spiteful red eyeballs.

Nim's skin prickled, the demon rising to the menace. She *knew* the little bastards, knew the creak of them that was like a door opening surreptitiously in the night when all should be still, like a cold, groping touch where no one had the right to touch her. *This* was why the demon had chosen her. Because she would fight with everything she had—with everything the teshuva gave her—to never be broken again.

Etheric smoke guttered in oily streamers like a back-firing junker car. But instead of staining the air as it had before, the smoke froze and splintered and fell to the floor. The black residue glazed the sparkling shattered glass until the footing was as treacherous as marbles under heel. Ecco, pacing close, crushed them and coughed at the lung-searing dust.

Nim tightened her grasp on the other two talyan. Beyond the frozen malice, the salambes raged, bigger and stronger. Even in their frenzy, they were better defined than their smaller cousins. Their off-center, upthrust tusks pierced the distorted blur around them. The teeth cast shadows like giants' pike staves three stories up the brick walls.

The salambes circled, seeking a way in, but clearly unwilling to meet the same fate as the malice. Their hot, hungry breath tumbled the malice-encrusted glass shards around Nim's shoes and rattled against the empty forty-ounce bottles. When she tried to kick a clear path around her feet, she almost stumbled on the precarious ground. The other women's grasps on her hands kept her upright.

"Nim," Jilly gasped. "Bring them closer."

"That seems really dumb," Nim said. But since when did dumb stop her? She steeled herself against the trembling in her knees. Not fear this time. Exhaustion. Could she do it again? Did she even understand what she'd done?

She'd been willing to embrace the doom of the malice. All because Jonah wouldn't embrace her. So attractive was her self-destructiveness to the tenebrae, they couldn't help but come closer. And closer. To *their* doom.

Maybe it was just as well she'd frightened Jonah away.

"That's it, Nim," Sera said. "Just a little closer . . ."

The salambes were an encroaching wall of disruptive ether. Inside her, Nim felt the teshuva falter, cutting out like a bad phone connection, overwhelmed by the massive attack.

Oh, they wanted her. Even more than the malice. They would take her and her demon and shred her—body and soul—on an etheric breeze. . . .

But she'd already decided she wasn't giving up body or soul, not anymore, not to anyone else.

Brutally, like a grip on the stripper pole, she clamped down on the demon. "Come here, you. We're in this together, forever. Amen."

Even if becoming what Jonah wanted her to be—a lure to the darkness, her own shadows the bait—meant she would never be what he could love. Every girl who'd ever strapped on eight-inch, clear plastic heels knew where fantasy and reality parted without a last kiss good-bye.

She released the thought like a pheromone of anguish, and the salambes fell on her in a rushing wave.

Ecco shouted as Jilly loosed Sera and flung up her bracelet-clad hand, fingers spread wide and scattering light from the demonic artifact around her wrist. She brought her hand slicing down again. The crystallized malice echoed the motion, tumbling toward the salambes.

And the viscous black wrapped around and through the blistering red. The tangle constricted, flailing tusks and rolling eyeballs drawn tighter and tighter until the congealed mass was only a little larger than the three of them could have encompassed with their outstretched arms. Nim stood equidistant from Jilly and Sera around the noxious snarl.

Caught, the salambes shrieked out one multioctave cry that cracked the bricks. They strained, and little dust devils of unnatural flame skittered across the floor.

"Ah, fuck," Ecco mumbled as he stomped out a blaze. "The teshuva can't hold up walls."

Between the growl of the crumbling bricks, the renewed cries of the tenebrae, and Ecco's next curse, Nim almost missed the low hiss of the rising demon wind.

"My teshuva can break at least one wall." The pendant around Sera's neck gleamed, bright as her eyes. "The Veil to the demon realm."

With a hollow boom, the tangled tenebrae mushroomed up in a cloud of dust, glass, and what else, Nim didn't want to know. Before the pulsation knocked her backward, she caught a glimpse of something in the heart of the tangle. No, not something—some*place*. Then she was skidding across the concrete floor. Her ears rang with the explosion and Ecco's most energetic swearing to date.

She shook her head and levered herself upright on bloody palms, reaching for her demon inside.

To no avail. Could a demon be knocked offline, go into hiding inside her? Seemed so. Sera and Jilly looked equally stunned, Sera with a gash over her eye, as if one of the forty-ouncers had blown upward.

Only Ecco had kept his feet, and he held his gauntlets crossed at the ready, eyes wide and darting, seeking the next threat.

But the tenebrae were gone.

"Well," Jilly said. She gathered her knees under her, but made no attempt to stand.

Sera just blinked. "Very enlightening."

"If by 'enlightening,' you mean 'explosive,' " Nim said.

"I'm always impressed how a little demonic ether, some bad will, and a few good intentions can go so sky-high," Sera admitted.

"Can we go home now?" Ecco asked. "Before what's left of this building collapses on top of us."

Nim, Sera, and Jilly looked at one another, then, with a sigh, pulled themselves upright. Sera touched her forehead and looked down at her bloody fingers.

Jilly bit her lip. "Can you heal before Archer gets back?"

"Or at least come up with a story?" Nim suggested.

"About walking into a door?" Sera gave them a faint grin. "I'll have a few hours."

Ecco cocked his head. "Or maybe less."

Nim stiffened. Had he heard the league's cars returning? Then she heard it too. A rumble and growl.

But it wasn't a league of angry men.

A feralis vaulted into one of the dozen empty windows. From its vantage-point perch, it stretched its naked, birdlike neck toward them and shrieked.

"Bitch, please," Ecco said to it. "You should see what the girls just did to your compadres."

Before his sneer faded, another feralis appeared in the window beside the first. And then, with a flap of wings, the window above held a third feralis. In half a faltering heartbeat, the rest of the windows filled with tenebrae shadows that eclipsed the night outside.

The first feralis tightened its serrated claws on the windowsill, cracking through the last shards of glass, which rained down in a shimming dust. As one, the horde lifted to their haunches and screamed.

Nim winced. "Oh, hell."

CHAPTER 17

The search was a bust. Even O'Hare, with its chronic delays, hadn't produced more than a half dozen nests of malice, grown Cinnabon sleek off the annoyance and desperation of stranded passengers.

Jonah slouched in the passenger's seat beside Liam after the car pulled away from the Mortal Coil, leaving behind a pack of morose talyan to brood in their beer. Liam had handed the @1 credit card to Archer and told him not to let anyone take out their disappointment on innocent bystanders. Their anger might get the best of them, but, conveniently, their demon-fueled metabolism would ensure they burned through the alcohol and were sober before they drove home.

Jonah had never used his teshuva for such a reason, and when Liam announced he was forgoing the antifestivities to check on the wounded Jilly, Jonah jumped on the chance to head to the warehouse.

He wanted to get back. Not to the warehouse. The place didn't matter. Just back to her.

Nando and Haji had elected to skip the club. "Why drink? There's nothing to celebrate until we get Blackbird." Haji stretched his lanky tracker body across the backseat. "And nothing to mourn until he kills me."

"And I already have a headache," Nando said, rubbing at his eye patch.

As he had for Archer, Jonah recounted for Liam the encounter with Cyril Fane, and they tossed around possible outcomes of an alliance—or a war—with the angelic host. Both seemed inadvisable.

As they approached the industrial park, he and Liam fell silent, gazes scanning the dark streets.

"You got that feeling on the back of your neck?" Liam asked quietly.

"No," Nando said.

Jonah tightened his fist. "Yes. Turn here."

But Liam was already turning, apparently drawn on the same garrote tightening around Jonah's chest. The tires rumbled a warning over the abandoned rail line.

Nando slung his arm over Jonah's seat. "Where are we— Oh."

The building at the end of the tracks seemed to twitch. Ferales swarmed in uncountable numbers across its surface, their wings and tails and claws a rattling hiss in the night.

"I never really appreciated the word 'horde' before," Haji said.

Bricks tumbled from the top cornice of the building, as if the structure writhed in pain. Demonic emanations had amassed to such pressure, ether steamed from the upper windows like a kettle about to scream. The same force leapt into Jonah's throat.

"That doesn't look long for this world," Nando commented. "So remind me: Why are we getting out of the car?"

Jonah had fumbled the door open before Liam brought the car to a halt. The other bonded talya was only a half step behind him as he raced for the building.

What could possibly lure this many tenebrae to one place?

As if he even needed to ask.

He hit the first feralis before it knew he was there and easily scaled the eight-foot, sloping spine to bury his hook in its chest. In silence, he wrenched the hook upward. Ichor spilled in a stinking gush.

The demon's frustrated power rebounded through him, and its frenzied craving to be unleashed aligned with his one desire: to be with Nim.

The two nearest ferales cringed away. He ripped through them in one blow and clambered over the husks to boost himself into the open window.

The interior was awash in tenebrae. The sour scent of rot yanked his breath away as effortlessly as he had disemboweled the ferales.

Ecco was a dervish, gauntlets invisible under ichor and feralis chunks. He slashed with deadly grace, but only the sheer mass—the horde getting in its own way—kept him from being overwhelmed. At his back, Sera and Jilly formed the other two points of a triangle, holding back the tide with their small and deadly knives.

Nim stood in the middle, looking lost in the fray.

As Jonah launched himself through the window, he wondered acidly why Jilly—who loved to visit the league's weapons depot—hadn't seen fit to arm Nim before their girls' night out.

Since he'd carelessly not seen to the task himself. He'd kick himself later. If they survived.

He cried out a warning, his throat cracking with the crisscross of human fury and demonic ecstasy. He'd sacrifice the surprise attack to let the defenders know help had arrived. Although only four more talyan against the horde ...

Liam and the other two talyan exploded through the windows on either side of him, and they fell on the rear of the packed ferales.

As if oblivious to the new attack, the ferales continued to press inward. Liam swung his hammer, blasting through three ferales at a time, yet they didn't turn to rend him or try to flee. Instead, they yearned toward Ecco and the women. Toward Nim. They had to get to her and stop the lure, or who knew what else she'd bring down on their heads.

First, though, Jonah had to get through the concentric rings of ferales. And while the tenebrae weren't focused on him, they'd exterminate him if he made it convenient enough.

As he spun past the outer circle, a feralis with spiderlike forelegs reached for him. He ducked, found himself face to ... mandibles with its second, lower head. When he lashed out, it reared back, and he followed, knocking it over. He scrambled across its belly, his boots slipping on the ulcerated gray skin, and then sprang toward the next layer of tenebrae.

Disoriented in the melee, he couldn't see even Ecco's tall form. And yet some awareness drew him irresistibly onward. The bond or Nim's lure? Or were the two the same? Certainly every man in her orbit felt the magnetism, bonded or not. And so, obviously, did every demon.

He had to stop it. Stop her.

The ring of tenebrae drew tighter. He leapt from one gutted feralis corpse to the next—except that one moved. It tossed him off his feet and he sprawled in a pool of ichor. The acidic black burned at his hand as he pushed himself upright.

Inside him, the teshuva reached greedily for the feralis's death throes, matching itself to the resonance and drawing off the emanations to refresh itself. But he didn't have time to indulge its hungers. He tore free, just in time to dodge a winged feralis that dove in and tried to grab his head from his shoulders. He ducked behind another lumbering, roachlike monstrosity.

The flying feralis shrieked and winged backward with

a blast of fouled air. Jonah spun away as the feralis dove at him again.

A wicked whistle of blades cut through the air. And through the feralis's outstretched talons.

It screamed, a piteous sound, but Ecco had zero pity. With a series of blurred punches like a speed-bag boxing workout, he diced the feralis. He reached out with his other hand and pulled Jonah into the inner circle.

"Jonah!" Nim's voice rang with pure elation. She threw herself against his chest.

He grabbed her arm and forced her back a step. "You have to stop calling the tenebrae."

She stared at him. "Didn't you bring the others? Is it just you?"

His jaw worked. She hadn't been waiting for him alone. Wisely. Since there was nothing he could do. No, he couldn't stop the feralis onslaught, but he had to stop Nim's lure. "There's only Liam and two others. Not enough to face what you've brought here."

She winced, and he realized his grip had tightened. "We didn't know this would happen," she said.

"So you waited until the worst possible time, until we'd gone, to take your demon for a spin."

"We knew you'd try to stop us."

"For very good reason, wouldn't you say?" He gave her a shake. "Now you must stop it."

Stop flaunting his orders. Stop calling to the horde. Stop making him want. . . .

"I don't know how." She flinched away from him. "You can't just beat it out of me."

To his horror, he realized he was halfway there. His hand sprang open without his conscious thought to release her. He staggered back, as if there were someplace to go, to escape. Jilly and Sera were occupied with the rising body count, or they probably would've added him to the pile of corpses for grabbing Nim so harshly.

He had never—*never*—handled Carine with such disregard. He'd rather sever his remaining hand than see Nim shrink from him. "Nim . . ."

"I told you, I don't know how—"

How could she know? He hadn't tried to teach her, not even with the same naïve but sincere fervor he'd taken with him to converting all Africa. Or at least the same exhilaration at the adventure. From the first, he'd faced her with his arms crossed, resisting temptation.

"Like you did in the VIP lounge," he said.

She stiffened. "What?"

"Dance. Dance like you did then, just for me." He took a breath, seeking the warm scent of her skin under the miasma of rot and rust and brick dust. And he took a step closer to her, to fill her view. "As if there were just the two of us. Alone."

She gazed up, her eyes glazed in a violet storm. "You don't want this. Don't want me."

"But you know I do." He gathered her close, gently, cursing his lack of poise—he couldn't even blame the unbalance of his missing hand this time—that had made him push her away when she had reached for him with such sweet relief. If she rejected him now, rejected the focus he offered, she'd let the last of the horde close around them. And he'd have only his own ridiculous inhibitions to blame.

"You want to stop me." The demon was in her voice, in the lower octave and an almost inaudible shrill of condemnation.

"I can't stop you," he admitted. He brought her up against his body, let her feel the hard truth in the violent need of his flesh, the pulse that lifted him to her—never mind the constraints of his jeans or the certain death around them. "You danced for me once, and I've wanted you ever since."

The violet in her eyes flared and dimmed.

Somewhere, Jilly called out wordlessly, and Liam answered with her name in a full-throated cry as he broke through to the inner circle. Stronger for being together.

Jonah knew he needed to convince Nim. But how? With his body, with a look, with words? "I have nothing to give you in return," he whispered. "My life is pledged to the league; my soul to the teshuva."

"I didn't ask for either of those."

A heated flush rose in his face. This was the dance, he realized. The back-and-forth of what they could be to each other. For each other. "What's left of my body isn't worth the having."

"You lie," she said. "And anyway, I've had that already."

The blush turned to flame and heated him to the core. "There's nothing more of me."

"The tenebrae know there's always more," she said. "And they want the very last of it. Light and laughter. Hope and peace." She hesitated. "Love."

The word hit him like a tenebrae fang through the belly, ripping upward to lodge in his throat. "I've no more of that either."

She shot him a glare and strained away from him with all her dancer's strength and demon's power. "You lie again."

He struggled to hold her, amping his teshuva against her fury, though his one-handed grip left him precariously unbalanced. "Nim, you ask too much."

In a blink, the violet storm in her eyes vanished, leaving only a deep murk. "And you never asked for anything, except a new right hand. But without the anklet, I can't even be that to you."

"That's not what I—"

The closest feralis fell back on its haunches, pointed its muzzle upward, and let loose a howl of triumph. The rest answered in a cacophony that brought another rain of bricks tumbling down.

Apparently, the tenebrae approved. Always a bad sign.

Nim stood motionless. "If you can't want me, why am I here?"

Behind her, the ferales closed in. Nando stumbled and went to his knees. Jilly leapt forward with a battle cry ... and Liam yanked her back, throwing himself into the fight instead. Ecco howled, trapped across the circle by a quartet of the roach ferales. Sera stood with both hands clamped around the *desolator numinis* around her throat. The chill of the tenebraeternum was a visible swirl of silvery fog, but the ferales marched onward.

Jonah's heart froze. They weren't going to be able to fight off the horde. He couldn't stop Nim's lure. And he couldn't give her what she wanted.

In another second, if that orange-eyed feralis just beyond Nim's shoulder had its way, his other arm would be ripped from him, along with the rest of his soul, and he'd be left with nothing. Truly nothing this time. Oblivion.

Well, fuck that.

In his head, he heard Nim's laugh.

When the orange-eyed feralis jumped, he met its attack halfway. Nim whirled as he arrowed past her, hook extended. The feralis flinched, and he caught it midchest. The hook buried past the thin metal "wrist" and lodged deep inside the feralis.

Intimately close, he stared into its eyes. The dozen orange orbs, arrayed in a ring around its squat head, made the staring contest somewhat inequitable. It clacked its mandibles, and the clatter sounded suspiciously like a snicker. A thin spray of ichor burned on his cheek in a tenebrae kiss.

This was the only sort of relationship remaining to him after he'd doomed himself by saying yes to the demon. Or so he'd come to believe.

But his beliefs had failed him before.

Nim cried out a warning. He yanked the hook free

in a geyser of black rot. His teshuva reached with avid craving for the feralis's faltering emanations. But Nim needed him.

As he jerked around, his vision blurred between the fading tenebrae and Nim as he struggled to focus. His boots slid in the rubbish across the floor, and he windmilled his arms. And smacked a giant feralis in the nose—actually snout, razor fangs bristling—with his hook.

The metal clanged against its teeth and the feralis snapped, faster than any creature of flesh alone, holding him fast.

Nim screamed his name again as a second, winged feralis sprang over the hole in the inner circle to the left, where Liam had gone to Ecco's rescue. The creature unfurled its wings, wide enough to shadow their pitifully small crew. The stink of burnt feathers blew up a with blinding backdraft of dust and glass.

It scrabbled at Nim, and she punched back. Squealing, it dodged her blows. With one lucky snatch, it grabbed her by her hair and lifted off.

She held on to its leg. Blood streamed through her fingers from the sharp quills. If she slipped, the feralis could break her neck with its awkward hold. Still, she batted at the wing nearest her, trying to upset its flight. It spiraled sideways, but steadied with another beat.

In a moment, it would be out of reach.

Jonah broke free of the feralis chewing its way up his arm. And he broke his arm too.

The crack of the upper bone reverberated through his body like a lightning strike. The violence snapped the straps of the prosthetic, and the hook dangled in the feralis's mouth as he launched himself after Nim.

He latched his fingers around her ankle. Before he could hope for any leverage, his boots left the floor. The airborne feralis tilted at the added weight, dipping dangerously over the sea of ferales, before it recovered.

The tenebrae bellowed their excitement, and Jonah had a glimpse of the talyan's pale faces—almost three stories below now—before he looked up at Nim.

How sad. This might be his last sight on earth, and she wasn't wearing a skirt.

"Pull me up," he shouted.

She bent her knees, hauling his deadweight higher. She grabbed his broken arm. Bone grated against bone, and the demon's hunter-light vision sparked with pure, white human pain. He fought it down and hooked his good arm around her waist.

The quills from the beating wings sliced through the meat of his shoulder. Which would have hurt, except for the pain in his arm. And the humiliation of not having a fucking hand to rip the fucking feralis out of the fucking sky.

Ignoring the grind of bone, he looped his broken arm over Nim's shoulder and lifted himself higher. The feralis had gathered the detritus of hundreds of slaughters—avian, insectile, even a hint of humanoid shape to its features swelling around a fleshy beak. Its demonic emanations—twisting and slippery—rivaled his teshuva's.

Which left brute ferocity to determine the winner.

The feralis certainly overwhelmed him in the appendages division, and its underbelly was armored with thick scales. So he reached higher, and punched his fist down its throat.

The sharp beak tore at his forearm, and then up to his elbow. It pierced skin, then muscle, and ground against bone. Ichor burned his hand. His remaining hand . . .

For an instant, he wanted to pull free, fall to the ground. He still had two functioning feet that could carry him away.

But the thought shredded like the wicked soulflies, never to return. He wouldn't let go of Nim.

The feralis choked and spat ichor in black gouts.

Struggling, it ripped at him with seven of its eight feet. Only Nim's grasp on its eighth leg kept her from falling. To his horror, she grabbed at the thrashing wing tip, and the feralis lost altitude.

A mere two stories. A survivable fall. Probably. If they were going to bail out, they had to do so now. Knowing he had mere seconds before the feralis beak would saw through his arm, he reached down inside it.

But a feralis didn't have a heart. Nothing to reach for but the void he'd always feared.

He could do to the feralis what Nim had done to him. He turned it inside out.

His arm went numb as he heaved backward. Boiling ichor and pieces of the decomposing husk erupted from the gaping maw.

The spidery legs spasmed and tossed Nim outward. Her gaze locked on his, silent, and she fell.

Entwined with the feralis, he plummeted on his own painful arc.

In the heartbeat before he hit, lights beamed through the open windows. Car headlights.

With an explosion of feathers and brick dust, he slammed into the ground. The feralis broke his fall, enough that he maintained consciousness.

The cars had to be the other talyan. Archer's bond to Sera must have ignited any alcohol he'd managed to get in his hands. The cavalry had arrived.

Not a moment too soon. Actually, a few moments too late.

All around him, the tenebrae stampeded. Plenty of exits through the broken windows, but talyan—black-clad shadows, fast and furious—poured through the openings in pursuit of the escaping ferales. Who could escape only because . . .

The lure was broken.

The realization sent him reeling upright. "Nim!"

Where was she? The milling claws could easily tear her apart if she lay unconscious.

Or maybe she was already . . .

No. He wouldn't think that. A fleeing feralis knocked him over. He reeled up again. Realized neither arm was working right. Didn't care.

Where was she? He caught a glimpse of scarlet amid the black. Human blood slicked over ichor.

His own blood stopped in his veins. He staggered, slipped again, and went to his knees beside her crumpled body.

He heard Liam's shout, a million miles away, and the answering roar from his warriors. At the talya war cry, the ferales fled in all directions.

Jonah huddled over Nim as claws crushed down on him. His back strained to take the weight off her body, lest some inadvertent pressure sever an artery or pierce a vital organ before the teshuva worked its tricks.

"You fell barely two stories," he murmured. "Anyone who can do splits vertically on a pole while wearing heels as high as you do can survive a little bounce off concrete."

He barely noticed when the last of the ferales had escaped or been dismembered by the talyan. He knew only that the battering had stopped. Externally, at least.

He leaned forward to press a kiss to Nim's lips, but his face was too ichor scorched to feel if she breathed. "Wake up."

"Jonah!" Archer skidded to a stop a yard away. The battle-axe in his hand thumped to the floor, and from the stark widening of his eyes, Jonah wondered how bad they looked.

"She's hurt," he said. He would not allow for anything worse.

Archer opened his mouth, then closed it. "Can you stand?"

They must look bad if he had to ask. "I'm fine." Jonah

gathered his legs under him, hoping he wouldn't tip over and reveal his lie. "We have to get her to the warehouse. The energy sinks will block her lure if she's still broadcasting when she regains her senses." Another hope; maybe another lie. He met Archer's gaze and was horrified to see a spark of pity. He'd rather see fury there at his failure. "I couldn't stop her."

Archer just shook his head. "I couldn't stop Sera either. I'm just sorry it took us so long to get back here. I thought the alarm bells in my head were only about that drinking game. . . ." He rubbed his temple wearily. "Let's get you out of here."

Sera limped up to them. The chill of the tenebraeternum clung to her skin.

Behind her, Jilly was streaked with feralis gore. "We need to set his arms first. If the teshuva heals them in that state, we'll just have to rebreak them."

Archer's eyes blazed violet. "Now you two care about hurting someone?"

"No more fighting," Jonah said. "We need to get Nim out of here. The ferales might circle back if she wakes and casts the lure again."

"We'll rip them apart if they do," Archer snarled. Despite the eddies of teshuva fury, Sera leaned against her mate.

Jilly shook her head. "Now that you're here, Jonah, you'll be able to guide her."

"I couldn't control her before."

"It's not about controlling her." Sera crossed to his side and gave him a few exploratory pokes in the arm that made his vision blur. "Displaced fractures of the humerus in both arms. But they're still attached, obviously. No catastrophic blood loss and no excessive neural severing, which is all the teshuva needs to get to work. You'll be good as . . . before in a couple days." She held out her hand to Jilly, who knelt beside Nim. "Can I have your bandages? I think you need them less than Jonah."

Jilly fumbled down her neckline to unwind a swath of gauze.

"Save it for Nim," Jonah protested.

"She'll be fine," Jilly said. "Her hands are healing already."

Hearing the words sapped what strength was left in his knees. "If she's okay, why hasn't her teshuva brought her around?"

Sera and Jilly exchanged glances. "She'll wake when she's ready," Sera said.

He gritted his teeth. "Is that what you said to your dying patients—'You can go when you're ready'?"

"And it always worked," she said. "So don't worry."

"Let's go," Archer growled. "Maybe you're convinced this will end all right, but there are a half dozen other wounded who'd like to be done with tonight."

Sera's jaw flexed, but she finished wrapping Jonah in silence. She straightened the upper bones, politely ignoring the groan of protest he couldn't hold back, and bound his arms to his chest. Knowing she'd been a thanatologist, ushering out the dying, made him feel as if she were burying him in winding sheets.

Sweat popped out on his forehead. This was how it might feel to have no arms. He'd not been grateful enough for what he still had.

He stood over Nim.

Jilly had straightened his fallen mate so she looked less like a broken doll. He didn't think she'd appreciate a *Sleeping Beauty* reference, not with her skin streaked with blood and ichor thick as war paint. He couldn't even reach down to brush back the tangle of her hair. He'd tip over in his sick fatigue. Oh, and not to forget, he had no hands.

He turned away. "Get us out of here."

Archer tipped his head toward Nim. "May I?"

Jonah nodded sharply. Archer gathered up Nim's limp body, careful to support her head against his chest,

his two strong arms making easy work of her unconscious weight. Jonah stared fixedly away to where a half
dozen talyan, under Liam's watchful eye and ready hammer, were emptying the tenebrae energy from the last
twitching ferales. Swells of demonic emanations swept
the brick dust and crystallized malice remains in eerily
beautiful ribbons of black and red.

A chunk of the ceiling crashed down, bisecting the
patterns.

Jilly ducked her shoulders. "I'll have to remind Liam
to send an anonymous complaint to the city. Make sure
they condemn this place."

"Yeah," Archer drawled. "Wouldn't want anything
bad to happen here."

That kept them silent out to the line of haphazardly
parked cars.

Archer tucked Nim into a backseat of a truck that
had skidded in sideways; then he turned to stab a finger at each of the other women. "You two, separate cars.
And not the one with Ecco."

Sera put her hands on her hips. "We're not criminals."

"Actually, you were once."

"No," Jilly said. "That was me. Sera was a good girl."

Archer shot her an acid look. "*You* meaning female
talyan. The league banished you for a reason. And I
think we're getting a hint why."

Sera's hands fell slowly to her sides. "Don't." There
were no demon harmonics in her voice, just one woman's plea.

Archer scrubbed a hand down his face, over lines of
strain the teshuva had been too busy to erase. "Damn it,
Sera. Can you imagine how that looked, coming through
the window and seeing . . ." A shudder racked him. "Not
the ferales. But you, surrounded."

Jonah bowed his head. The image blistered too fresh
in his mind. "Can we go?"

Archer spun away. "Of course." Sera didn't follow.

Jonah climbed into the backseat with Nim. He couldn't hold her, but he could let her lean against him, though her slack shoulder dug into his broken arm as they jolted over the railroad tracks.

"Not to the warehouse," he told Archer. "Take us to the marina."

"Jonah . . ."

"You saw that horde. If Nim wakes with the lure still engaged, I don't think the energy sinks can contain the emanations. Until we have the anklet back—if the anklet *is* an on-off switch or a padlock or a fail-safe—she's a danger." He gave the other man a hard look in the rearview mirror. "And not an ancient-history, theoretical sort of danger either, as you might have noticed."

"Then you being alone with her—"

"We'll be safe on the boat once we're beyond reach of shore. We won't be carrying any tenebrae evil with us."

Archer's jaw worked. "Still, the isolation . . ."

"I suspect you'll be taking some time with Sera."

The other talya shrugged. "I see your point. But what about your arms?"

"Maybe I won't wring her neck."

With a hint of a smile, Archer said, "Then you're a stronger man than I."

In the pre-predawn stillness, the glassy water reflected the marina lights like a second world—dark and perfect. To sink beneath would upset the flawless skin.

Jonah dragged his gaze off the mysterious depths and gave Archer the code to get through the locked gate. He followed Archer, who held Nim in his arms, to the *Shades of Gray*. As Archer descended into the cabin, Jonah fired up the motors.

Archer returned a moment later. "I put her in the bunk. How are you going to— Oh." He watched Jonah slip out of the bandage around his half arm and work the throttle with the end of his stump. "The teshuva's gotten to work on the bone already?"

"Enough," Jonah answered tersely. He figured the other man would understand what remained unsaid. He tried to force down the heat in his face. He never used the ugly knob of flesh where someone might see. "Although I'd appreciate if you cast off."

"'Go away' is what you mean," Archer said. "Don't worry. No wise-old-man advice before I leave. I obviously suck."

Jonah's lips quirked. "Try that tack with Sera, and she might actually apologize to you."

Archer snorted. "Check in when Nim wakes. When you bring her back, we'll be onshore to make sure it's safe."

And if it wasn't? For the briefest moment, Jonah thought of leaving the city behind, setting south for the Mississippi River and the Gulf of Mexico, or heading north to find the Saint Lawrence Seaway and the Atlantic. A new adventure. One where he never set foot to land again.

Would Nim trade her stilettos for flip-flops?

He waited until Archer recoiled his lines and stood ready to jump to shore.

"Whatever happens," Jonah said, "it's too late to let her go."

The boat was drifting, and he knew the other talya wanted to return to his mate, but Archer hesitated. "Too late for whom?" With the help of his demon, Archer launched himself to the dock. He turned and lifted his hand in a wry salute. Jonah answered with his stump, and Archer shook his head.

Jonah turned away and set his course.

CHAPTER 18

She came awake with her pulse racing in a disorienting double beat. Where was she, with this creak of wood and humid tang? Had she passed out in the bathroom with the sink faucet running again? That time, she'd roused with tap water halfway up her nose, which taught her to always pass out in bed. Now she was naked—that part she was used to—but she was wrapped in a bedsheet with a striped pattern she didn't recognize. She sat up and hit her head on a ceiling that was much too low.

A boat. She took a calming breath and caught the scent that settled her heartbeat into a single, steady beat. Jonah's boat.

She slumped back and hit her head on the wall behind her.

Jonah peered down through the open hatch, silhouetted against the bright sky behind him, his bare toes curled around the upper step. With his appearance, the scent of sun and water strengthened. "I thought I heard you moving around."

"What . . . ?" Her voice cracked.

He stepped down into the cabin, and she forgot for a moment what she was going to ask. Had the missionary man been left behind? Here, instead, was the adventurer. Bare chested, with his sandy hair tousled by the wind, he looked like some dashing, carefree sailor, too cavalier to bother with piracy.

He rummaged through the mini fridge and returned with a can of lemonade. But he couldn't hold it out because his good arm was strapped to his chest.

She sat up again, clutching the sheet to her chest. At least she remembered not to bonk her head this time. "You fell!"

"I got up again." He ducked to sit down on the berth beside her.

"We both did." She took the can, then extended her other hand out in front of her. Narrow white scars crisscrossed her palm, almost invisible except where the light hit just right. "I couldn't make it let go." Her words caught again in her throat.

"Drink. You need the sugar."

"Got vodka to go with it?"

"Your head doesn't hurt enough?"

She grimaced and touched her hair. The dreads were bound into one thick snarl where the feralis had grabbed hold. She popped the tab on the can and took a long swallow. The tart sweetness tasted like heaven. "Why are we out here?"

His hesitation was so minor, she almost missed it. "You need quiet to recover." When she narrowed her eyes, he sighed and added, "By quiet, I mean no more hordes of tenebrae."

Her fingers dented the can. "They're still out there?"

"Maybe. Somewhere." He hesitated again, longer this time. "I tried calling Archer for news, but we're getting some etheric interference." She took a breath, and he interrupted. "Don't worry about the tenebrae. They might be out there, but we're even farther out here."

"If the demons can't get to us, what's interfering with

your cell phone?" He didn't answer, and she said flatly, "Me."

He shrugged, awkward with the bandage.

"God, I almost killed you, Jonah. You should've thrown me over the rail while I was out."

He tugged again at the constricting gauze. "You make it sound so easy with no hands. Plus, you woke up for a bit a while ago. Don't you remember?"

She tipped her head against the wall. As if she'd knocked the memory loose, she vaguely recalled the weight of him beside her on the bed, the whisper of his breath against her cheek. No groping hands, though. Now she knew why. "You said everything was okay."

"Since you weren't unconscious anymore, I even believed it."

How could he say that with even his good arm bound tight? She rolled her head against the wall to look at him. "I don't remember how you got us out alive."

"Don't thank me. Our league brothers arrived to save the day just as we got free from the feralis." He grimaced. "And by 'free,' I mean 'plummeted to our uncertain death.' That was thanks to me."

The note of bitter self-censure in his voice made her wince. "Better a free and uncertain death than what that feralis had planned. I think it wanted my scalp for its collection." She rubbed at her temple. "I remember falling, but not landing."

"No doubt you knocked the teshuva offline for a moment when you hit the ground."

"And now I'm back, broadcasting on all channels, calling all demons," she said. "Maybe if you hit me in the head a few more times, we could change stations."

"From bad to worse. That's what happened to Corvus. We thought he died in a fight last winter, but he came back, his human half crippled and his djinni less inhibited than ever."

She snorted. "Who would've thought humans could have a mitigating influence on evil."

"And on good too." He leaned back next to her. "Cyril Fane's angel would have cast us back from whence we came, with extreme prejudice. Fane himself didn't want to get guts spattered on his pretty car."

Nim looked down at the can in her hand, twisting the tab in a circle until it broke off. "You haven't yelled at me for that yet."

"Hasn't been time. And now, compared to this latest escapade, it hardly seems worth noting." She mimed perking up in relief, but he didn't smile. "Plus, I was just waiting until you were conscious so you could truly appreciate my rage."

She slumped again. "Okay, well, go ahead, then. I can take it."

"I don't think I can. Not anymore."

His words, low and distant, rattled her. "A good screaming match can really clear the air. Maybe a slap or two, to make up for me almost killing everybody in the league." When he didn't respond, she put the lemonade down and touched his leg. "I want to make it up to you, Jonah."

"If you're about to offer a blow job next, don't."

She withdrew her hand, wondering if she was actually on fire from her cheeks all the way down past the sheet around her breasts, or if it only felt that way.

"Your concept of this bond between us is fucked-up," he said bluntly.

For the first time, a curse from him didn't make her want to laugh. That she had pushed him so far beyond his boundaries didn't seem funny anymore. "Jonah—"

But he didn't let her continue. "And so was mine," he admitted. "I wanted you for all the wrong reasons."

"Saving the city from hell is a wrong reason?"

He shook his head. "I wanted you the same way the men at the Shimmy Shack did. For myself."

She stared at him. Was it just another symptom of her fucked-up view of the bond that her heart stuttered in hope when he said that?

"I don't know how," he said, "but if there's a way out of this, I'll let you go."

Her heart lurched to a standstill.

"Let me go?" The words fell from her lips, as cold as a malice sting.

"I'm not going to be another one of those men to you."

"But you're not. You're—"

He waited, but nothing else would come from her mouth. "You wouldn't dance without a bouncer." His hand, trussed against his belly, tightened into a fist. "Without the anklet, I am not enough to be the anchor, the control you need."

Hot denials tried to bubble up past her frozen throat. How could he be so wrong? She surged out of the bed, cracked her head on the low ceiling again, and spun to face him. She had to wait a minute for the spinning room to catch up with her spinning head. "I make one little—okay, one fairly substantial—mistake, but for a good cause—you know, saving the city—and I'm outcast."

He frowned at her—probably because she was naked—and pushed himself upright, grimacing when he jostled his arm. "It's not you—"

"Sure, that's what they said when they caught me with the neighbor man—'It wasn't your fault, Elaine.' And meanwhile, the horror and disgust is all over their faces when they turn away. Or when I took off my clothes for money that first time. 'Oh, she's damaged goods; it's not her fault dollar bills are falling out of her panties.' Hey, at least the lust was an improvement."

"Nim—"

"What else is immortality good for? I get to make mistakes. I don't have to be perfect, I don't even have to be *good*, and I still get to try again. If I'm broken, I get another chance to fix myself." She stopped, aghast at the way her chest was heaving with sobs. *She'd* decide when her chest heaved, thanks anyway, not her stupid hang-up on some holier-than-her jerk. "If you don't want to take that chance, that's your choice. But you can't drag me down with you."

He gave a sharp bark of laughter, but not in amusement. "That's what I did, though, didn't I? Dragged you out of the sky. I almost killed you. Your soul would have been lost at my hand."

She stared at him. Her soul? He was worried about her soul? "That is *so* what I get for falling for a missionary man!" She whirled on her heel and stomped into the tiny bathroom. If only the door was heavier, she could have slammed it.

Splashing water on her face rinsed away any evidence of the sobbing. She stared down at her hands gripping the sink. While she was knocked out, someone—not someone; Jonah—had wiped away the grime. Even her fingernails were clean.

The thought of his handling her unconscious body . . . She wanted to slam *him* for that. But her hands were too clean to get dirty now. Plus, she was returning the favor for him not killing her while he had the chance.

Up on deck, under the high sun, the city was a hazy miniature on the horizon, with no other boats in view. The heat sank into her skin as she settled onto the cushions near the prow. The white vinyl burned the backs of her thighs, but she ignored it. Let the demon earn its keep.

Jonah's steps thudded behind her. "The teshuva's strength won't last all the way to shore, if you were thinking of swimming. And in case you forgot, it can't help you breathe underwater."

"Thanks for the reminder," she said testily. "I'll add that to the list of things I can't do."

Stubbornly, she lounged on the deck cushions, letting the sun soak her skin.

Jonah stomped around somewhere in the middle of the boat, but she refused to look back. He'd made it clear he wanted nothing to do with her, but he'd stranded her out here. Let him deal with her buck-naked ass.

She startled when a long-sleeved oxford sailed over her head and landed in her lap. "I can't get skin cancer anymore," she snapped.

"You can still get arrested for indecent exposure."

"By whom? You nixed the blow job, so what do you care?"

Between one blink and the next, he was looming over her, blocking the sun, his face dark as any cloud. "You are not going to provoke me."

"Looks like I already have." Her gaze drifted deliberately down to where his worn-thin cargo shorts gave him away.

He didn't try to shield himself. "You've already demonstrated your power. And how it can destroy."

Hurt flared like a struck match, still in the book and threatening to inflame the rest. "You still have all your parts after our night together. All the parts you had before it, anyway." Then she winced and rubbed her fingertips over her lips. "You wanted to cast me off. At least I'm giving you good reasons now."

He sank to his knees in front of her. "It's not about what I want, Nim. It's about what's the right thing to do."

When he was this close, the heat of him rivaled the August sun, and the scent of aroused male was spiked with the cool water and sharp diesel. Her wayward emotions tipped overboard, leaving only her desire for him. She trailed her fingers across her thighs where the *reven* curled. "We're possessed by demons. Maybe it's too late to worry about the right thing to do."

His gaze traced the path her hands had led. "I thought you said we had a chance to make up for our mistakes."

"Not till after we make them," she whispered. "I used to do the wrong thing for the wrong reasons. Now I'm doing the wrong thing for the right reasons. That's progress, don't you think?"

He leaned forward. Because she was a lure, after all. Made for sin. Made for him.

She met him halfway, maybe a little more than halfway, and tilted her head to take his kiss. Sun warmed, sweat tinged. A hint of anguish that gave her hope. Maybe he didn't want to cast her off. Not that he wouldn't still do it, of course. The downside of the moral man. But in the meantime . . .

The kiss went on and on until she gasped. She might not have made it to shore on that breath, but she would've been close. Not that she wanted to get away now.

She curled her fingers against his chest where vicious red slashes were smoothing into white scars. "They really got you good."

"That was me. After I made you comfortable below, I didn't want to lie beside you with the ferales' stink still on me. So I cut my shirt off beneath the bandages to wash. Not easy without two hands."

"And I was passed out, useless." She pressed her lips gently to the wounds, as if her touch could speed the demon's healing. As if the wounds hadn't been her fault.

"You're here now." His voice roughened. "The demon removes the scar, but not the pain. Only you do that."

Her fingers tripped up his abs, and his muscles tightened. "Mostly I seem to have made it worse." She pulled herself onto her knees to wrap her hands behind his neck and kiss his throat. "But now's my chance to atone."

She worked her way down his chest again, skimming her fingers over the still, black lines of the *reven* on his back, until she reached his shorts. The snap sprang open under pressure from within. She smiled up at him as his ready erection surged into her hand.

"We should go down," he said huskily.

"I already am." She took him in her mouth.

He jerked so hard, she thought he might come right then. But he steadied himself, his bound hand centered on her skull.

"You don't have to—" He broke off with a groan when she cupped his sack and gave a tug. His fingers tightened in her hair.

The gentlest suction brought him a step closer. A swirl of tongue, and he kicked out of his shorts and put his foot up on the cushion next to her thigh. The conquering-hero pose. She worked the length of him, the fingers of her free hand splayed through the line of hair low on his belly, and when she hummed, he shuddered, not just conquering, but conquered. She snaked her arm up around his leg, dancing her fingers along his inner thigh.

His cock surged in her mouth, and then he was kneeling on the cushion, nudging her back. He spread her thighs with his knee. The August sun heated her—as if she needed it—but not as much as his mouth. *That* she needed, his lips and tongue exploring every nerve, wayward locks of his hair tickling her waxed pubis. Who needed hands?

Which didn't stop her from clutching his head, holding him fast, making sure he touched her there, and there—*ah*—and there.

He whispered something against her flesh, unheard words, hot and wet, that her body knew and tightened around, as if holding them. Another slow rasp of his tongue and another, and then she was coming undone, shivering apart under his touch.

Melted into the cushion, she struggled to help as he tugged her to the edge of the seat and positioned himself between her thighs. His erection slipped into her.

She watched as he tipped his head back and stroked himself in her passage. She drew her legs up so the only point of contact was that wicked thrust, the wet burn of friction. The tremors built again, and she panted his name.

He straightened to look down at her, his eyes as hot blue as the summer sky behind him.

With the merest flex of muscle, he snapped the bandage around his chest. The gauze unraveled in a loose spiral around his hips before he tore it away.

"Your arm—" she started.

"While I can hold you, I will." He raised her legs to his flanks, and she locked her heels behind him, drawing him deep. "Ah, Nim."

He reached down between them to stroke the throbbing flesh of her swollen clitoris.

"Again," she moaned.

With each teasing flick of his fingers, she wound tighter around him, hoping she wasn't hurting him, knowing he wouldn't stop her. Until one more touch tossed her over, and she went ecstatically, in a violent contraction that jackknifed her upward into his arms, just as his own release caught him.

He pumped his body against her a last time, one arm holding her shoulders, his fingers tight on her ass. His heaving breath rocked her against him for a long moment before he lowered her to the cushion and collapsed beside her.

She fitted herself between the hard curve of the hull and his even harder bulk. "Thank God we're immortal."

His breathing broke on what she thought was a laugh.

Her thundering pulse slowed and matched itself to his. Pillowed on his shoulder, she traced a fingertip over the all-but-invisible scars on his chest while he stroked her hair. "Am I forgiven?"

His hand stilled on her head, and abruptly she wished she hadn't asked.

"Because I can do it again," she said quickly.

He wrapped one of her dreads around his finger

and gave it a tug. "What? Get into trouble again?" She huffed into his chest, and he resumed his petting. "I think I'm done passing judgment."

She wished he'd waited until after he'd forgiven her. "If not you, then who?"

"Someone who makes fewer mistakes."

"I thought you'd say God."

"We're here, aren't we? Possessed by demons. Somebody didn't get that right."

"Ooh, heresy." She thought for a moment. "I like it."

"You would." His hand stilled again. "I judged you more harshly than any heathen I'd hoped to convert in Africa."

"It's probably the hair. Maybe I'm more heathen than them."

"Quite likely. But I like your hair."

She laughed, but had to close her eyes against the ridiculous surge of pleasure.

"More to the point," he said, "I think, back then, the concept of converting sinners to save my own soul was somewhat academic. But my fear was no excuse for the way I've treated you. I was braver in the jungle." He sighed. "Carine would have had my head."

"For sleeping with me, definitely."

He didn't laugh. "Last winter, when Sera came to Archer, I realized Carine had been dead for as many years as we'd been together."

Tentatively, Nim offered, "Maybe she'd think it was time for you to move on."

"She said that the first time someone mistook me for her son. And then her grandson. And then, before her death, when she began to slip—or maybe she was just tired of the lie—and called me her husband again, she said I should move on."

"But you didn't. That would have been the sacrilege to you."

He propped himself up on his elbow to look down at her. "And now I find myself reveling in sacrilege. Hungry?"

She blinked at him. "Change the subject much?"

He rolled off the bench and stood. "Those days were long ago, longer with every day that passes. I'm here now, with you. And I'm hungry."

From the tiny galley, he produced tins of tuna fish, a package of crackers, and a can of pineapple rings. She carried the little feast to the deck and pulled on the oxford he'd thrown at her earlier. She rolled up the sleeves while she watched him deftly mix mayo and relish into the tuna, wedging the bowl between his stump and his hip, letting surface tension hold the crackers in place while he spread the salad.

She accepted the mini sandwich and leaned back on the cushions to stretch in the sunshine. "What a glorious day."

His eyes glinted. "Quite."

The heat in his gaze penetrated deeper than any UV, warming her from the inside, microwave style. She decided she liked it, so she stretched her bare legs toward him. "How nice you had a boat to help us escape."

"We discovered our last Bookkeeper—a league posting for a man equal parts librarian, historian, and researcher—was embezzling. One of the few items we recovered was the *Shades of Gray*."

"What happened to the Bookkeeper?"

"He retired." This time, the glitter in his eyes was decidedly toward the cold end of the spectrum. "With Corvus's help, he devised the chemical formula for the *desolator numinis*, what became solvo. Also with Corvus's help, he ultimately lost his soul. Now he's living—if you can call it that—down south with Nanette's haints."

Nim thought about it a moment. "The shades of gray he dabbled in were all rather black, weren't they?"

"Liam would've sold her off, to recoup what money he could, but the market tanked. And then I lost my arm."

She breathed out a sardonic "ah." "Right. Forget about your hand. Look at the pretty boat."

Jonah's lips quirked. "The excuse was the league needed someone to ferry haints out of the city. Spending those hours with the soulless corpses reminded me there are worse fates than mutilation and death."

"That's it. Look at the bright side." She tipped her head to the side, studying him. "And I'm guessing you liked being alone."

Silent a moment, he speared a ring of pineapple on his fork. "After Carine died, I worked a steamship up and down the western coast to earn passage home. The sailors asked about as many questions as the haints, and only slightly fewer than the league, which picked me up within a day of my feet hitting dry land."

"So that was how it started."

"And ended." He ate the pineapple, then stabbed another ring and handed it to her. "All that time in the jungle, then on the water, with tenebrae few and far between, kept me from being overwhelmed with the teshuva's energy early in my possession. The league set me on my new course. Liam sent me back to the water after I lost my weapon hand, with the teshuva misaligned."

She took a bite out of the pineapple. "And then I made it worse."

He reached across the space between them and wrapped his fingers behind her neck, his gaze fierce. "Remember when I said I wanted you? When I was alone, I prayed for you—the notion of you—even though I don't believe anymore. I dreamed of you, even when I was afraid to sleep."

She stared at him, the sweet, sharp tang of the fruit stinging in her throat. Then she kissed him.

Before she could do more, he pulled back. From the lunch tray, he lifted the Swiss Army knife he'd used to open the tins. He poked through the tools and extracted the snips.

He handed her the knife and laid his hand in her lap. "Cut off the ring."

She'd taken jewelry from men before—once or twice when they hadn't even offered it—but watching his thumb worry a circle over the worn gold, the burn in her throat turned to acid. "Why?"

He met her gaze, the eyes so intense she thought his demon was rising, but the blue never phased to violet. "I didn't decide against throwing you overboard just because you'd sleep with me. If we're together, truly, we should do it right."

"Right" as in "good"? She bit her lip. "Oh." And what happened when the lust faded and he remembered, beyond the last shadow of a doubt, that she wasn't good at all?

"I'd cut it off myself, but . . ." He scuffed the stump of his missing hand against his thigh.

She lifted his hand. "Your fingers are still swollen from the break. I don't want to hurt you."

"Nim, I want you to—"

She swept the remains of their meal aside and kissed him again.

This, at least, she knew he wanted.

This, at least, she could give him.

They made love as if they had all the time in the world and no place else to be. Which was pretty much a lie, but the kind that didn't hurt anyone. The sun hovered on the points of distant skyscrapers for the longest time. She made Jonah dance, a naked waltz in the open bow. He pulled her into his arms, and finally, the sun, red as a malice eye, slid behind the city, just as he released himself into her one more time.

She fell back panting. When a cool breeze took the edge from their passion, he pulled the wrinkled oxford over them. "Good thing the teshuva heal us quickly, or you'd be sunburned in interesting places."

She touched his cheek. "Speaking of quickly, we have to go back."

"I know. We have to get your anklet."

"And check on Mobi. He'll have digested his rat by now and wonder where I am."

He kissed her temple. "Save the city from djinni evil. Cuddle snake. Whichever."

"I have a plan for getting the anklet."

He lifted an eyebrow. "Were you planning to tell me about this plan?"

"I'm telling you now," she pointed out. "I thought there should be some mystery. I am a lure, after all."

His other eyebrow rose. "You don't have to be a mystery to me."

It was one thing to be naked and open, but did she want him looking deeper than that? "Right." She eased away from him, avoiding his hand where the gold band gleamed like an unwavering eye.

He pushed up onto his elbow. "We're in this together, remember? Until we get it right, you said. Already we have a better grasp on how your luring works. And how to stop it."

A chill wormed under her skin. "Is that why you fuck me? Easier to get a grasp?"

"Nim." He reached for her, but she dodged him.

"Well, that *is* teamwork. I turn you on. You turn me off."

He drew back. Just as she'd intended. "What are you trying so hard to avoid?"

"Guys who don't listen when I say don't touch." Inside, she cringed. Could she blame the demon for the lies coming out her mouth?

Jonah shook his head. "I'm not the next-door neighbor who raped you, Nim, and I'm not the men who paid for you."

"No, you're worse. They just wanted flesh. Now you want all of me. Like the tenebrae."

"They want your hurt and sadness. That's how the lure draws them to you. I want to give you something else."

Like what? The question churned in her throat.

When she didn't speak, his face stilled, and she realized he wouldn't tell her unless she asked, unless she met him halfway. But there was a reason she'd learned to stand on the stage, out of reach. That way, no one got hurt.

And for once, she wasn't even thinking of herself.

Chapter 19

As Jonah throttled the boat up to speed, his gaze lingered on Nim, sprawled on the prow.

This far out, there was nothing to hit, so he let himself brood over the view in the lingering light. Her hand-washed tank top clung to her breasts, and a spare pair of his shorts rode low on her hips. As if she felt the weight of his stare, she pointed her nose upward.

She was still upset.

She'd stomped away, as far as one could stomp on a small boat, without letting him speak. Don't touch. Don't speak. Now she didn't even want him to look. As mad as she was, she had her teshuva under wraps. Along with the clothes she'd yanked on. He shook his head. He just didn't understand her. Sometimes he angered her and she put clothes on; sometimes it went the other way.

He liked the other way more.

He would've thought she'd be amused that they'd been able to restrain her teshuva's lure with such a simple and satisfying distraction. As he'd pointed out to her, "The teshuva might be repentant, but they are still creatures born of sin."

"So, of course, fucking me was even better than a gag," she finished.

That was when they'd stopped talking.

A dozen boats circled the marina, so he was too busy to talk, anyway, even when the engine noise was reduced enough to not require screaming. He didn't want to encourage screaming. When he edged up to the empty berth, Nim jumped out before he could say a word.

He couldn't leave the boat drifting so he could run after her. It was still registered to Bookie, and the league didn't need anyone looking for him to claim damages. So Jonah moored properly and kept his annoyance in check as he strode up the dock to where she paced the parking lot.

"I don't have any money," she said, as if she'd heard him wondering why she hadn't kept running. "I don't have my house key. And now my demon is gone." She sat abruptly on the curb.

He took her chin in his hand, tipped her face up, and kissed her.

When he stepped back, her eyes sparked violet.

"There's your demon," he said. "And for the rest, you have me."

"Right. I have you to save me. But who's going to save you from me?"

The question was so ludicrous, he could only stand with his mouth open for a moment.

"Never mind. I don't want to talk about it." She stared across the parking lot, as if she could will a prepaid cab out of the evening.

He bit back a curse, not wanting to give her the thrill. "Let's go get your snake."

He finagled the lock on her apartment. Inside, the atmosphere pressed obsessively close, enlivened only by the snake that coiled against the glass as soon as Nim stepped through the door and by the blinking light on her answering machine, which played back a half dozen messages from the police.

"This is Detective Ramirez again," the last message started. "Miss Hamlin, as I said before, we just want to talk to you about . . ." The brisk, masculine voice faltered. "About what happened at the Shimmy Shack. I'm starting to get worried that you didn't make it out alive. Please, Miss Hamlin, call me."

Jonah lifted his brows. "Detective Ramirez is playing good cop and helpless cop, I guess."

"It's nice he worried." Nim opened the tank to let Mobi wind up her arms. "I didn't make it out. Not entirely."

Jonah's fingers twitched, remembering the feel of that silky skin where scales now rested. "You're alive. Despite all your efforts to the contrary."

While she packed a bag—he wondered if she understood she'd never be back, and thought she must when she tossed two overflowing gym bags into the hallway—he called Liam from his cell.

"Nim is still alive," he said. "How about Jilly and Sera?"

The league leader grunted. "If it was a close thing, that was none of my doing or Archer's. I have to admit, Ecco's recounting of the attempt was . . . interesting."

"Define 'interesting.' "

"The three of them—Ecco watched for the most part; imagine that—took on more tenebrae than I would have believed possible. And lived." Liam paused. "If Nim had been able to control her lure, using shorter bursts, maybe, or closer range, they might've systematically cleared the entire district. Without us."

Jonah stared down the hall to where a rolling suitcase hit the opposite wall, trailing lingerie. That had been deliberate, he thought. "Oh, they need us."

"Do they?" Liam sounded thoughtful. "Did the league of yesteryear get rid of the female talyan because they were a menace? Or because they were too good?"

A pair of thigh-high leather boots, stainless steel rivets glaring like accusing eyes, sailed out of the bedroom to land in the suitcase. "Trust me, they are not that good." He turned away. "Besides, if banishing half the teshuva-ridden fighting force for being female was a terrible idea, eighty-sixing the male half is no better."

"Had a come-to-Jesus moment out there on the boat, did you?" Amusement crept into Liam's voice.

"Somebody came," Jonah said. "More than once." He waited while the league leader finished choking. "I—better than any of you—knew what unappreciated power a woman brings to a pairing. I'd been a long time without it, but I never forgot."

Liam was silent a moment. "I understand now," he said finally. "But how can we risk them again?"

Jonah closed his eyes when he heard Nim's steps in the hall. "What makes you think you have a choice?"

"I'm ready," Nim said.

He turned and showed her the phone in his hand. With Mobi coiled tight around her neck, she looked like some exotic queen. She gave him a look quite suited to a queen disgusted with her courtier, then went to the kitchen.

Loading up the dead-rat Lunchables, of course. "We're heading to the warehouse," he told Liam.

"It'll be quiet there," Liam said. "Still have some men down, but the rest will be out on a second sweep of the airports. Andre swore—and I do mean swore—that Corvus has a lair near an airplane, so we're expanding the search to private airfields. I'll check in with you later."

"Yeah." Jonah shut the phone with a snap.

In the kitchen, Nim was standing at the sink with a pair of fat-bladed kitchen shears in her hand. How big were those rats? "Are you sure you— Nim!"

She hacked off a huge handful of her hair.

A second handful of waist-length dreads hit the floor before he could speak. "What on earth are you doing?"

"Making sure nothing not of this earth grabs me by my hair again."

He winced, glad for Mobi's sake the snake was exploring the half tub of standing water in the sink. "Isn't that a little extreme?"

"Extreme?" The next slice left a bare finger's span of stubble at her nape. "Did you see what grabbed me?"

"Then at least let me—" He held up his hand, appeasing, when she turned with the scissors raised.

She lowered them immediately, but ire still snapped in her gaze, disguising some deeper shadow—not the demon—he couldn't quite identify. "I'm not the Naughty Nymphette anymore."

The same shadow was in her voice and twisted her tone upward, almost as if she were asking a question. He struggled to understand, but he was missing something, something as potentially hazardous as a rogue tenebrae.

He hadn't felt this incompetent since he'd learned to brush his teeth left-handed.

"I'm glad you're taking this seriously," he said. "But you don't have to maim yourself."

"It's just hair," she snapped. "It'll grow back." Then she looked aghast, and her gaze slipped to his missing hand. "Won't it?"

He knew he had better not smile. "We're still alive, and human, for the most part." He poked the toe of his boot into the mess she'd made. "That was a lot of weight you were carrying."

Violet arced across the tight crescents of her narrowed eyes. "You said you liked my hair."

"I did. . . . I do," he added quickly as the violet brightened. "I'm not with you because of your hair."

"We're together because you still think you can turn me into a weapon for the light side."

"You are."

"I'm not." The violet drowned in her murky gaze. "If I was good, how could I have been so wrong? The tenebrae I called could have killed everyone in the fight."

"'Good' doesn't always mean 'right,' or 'not dangerous.'"

"I don't want to be dangerous." She let the scissors slip onto the counter. "Not to you."

He stepped into her space, close enough that she'd have to consider the breadth of his shoulders and his hard weight. If she called his manhood into question again, he'd end up flexing for her. "For you, I'm willing to take the risk."

"For the world, you mean. For the sake of goodness and light and kittens and—"

He touched the severed ends of her dreads. "For you."

She swayed toward him until his knuckles bumped her cheek.

Then she closed her eyes, shutting him out, and pulled away. She grabbed an opaque plastic bag from the freezer and tossed the brick labeled RAT JUNE into his hovering hand. "I'll get my bags. You carry Mobi."

Now she was insulting him not by making him a beast of burden, but by burdening him with the beasts. "I can get the bags," he snapped. He looped the gym bags over his shoulders and grabbed the handle of the rolling luggage bag. He tucked the rat brick under his abbreviated arm; it was that or grip the plastic with his teeth. "Anything else?" He thought he managed to ask the question without undue sarcasm.

Nim shook her head, the faintest color on her cheeks. Shame, he hoped. Not that she exhibited much of that. Or maybe she'd just always hidden it under all that hair.

If not for the teshuva's etheric musculature and his own substantial annoyance, he might've made two trips. Nim offered once to help, but backed off with a single look from him.

She wasn't going to redeem herself so easily.

When they got to the warehouse, she reached across the front seat of the cab with money in her fist. He growled under his breath, and she said, "I brought my purse this time."

She was quick to take half the bags through the front door. In the quiet lobby, though, she paused. Without the weight of the dreads, her eyes looked larger. And, if he wasn't lying to himself, more vulnerable.

He paused too, and they stared at each other.

"You're going to make me ask, aren't you?" she murmured. "I thought, in your day, the man made all the moves."

"In my day, we didn't sleep together unless we were married."

She chewed at her lower lip until the flesh burned dusky red. "This is kind of like that. I'm bound to you. Till death do us part, which could be a really long time. We're converting sinners together. By sending them to hell, but I think that counts. And, yeah, I sleep with you. The least you could do is tell me if I'm sharing your room."

"Since you asked so nicely." He started forward again.

As they headed for his room, he wondered at their foolish dance, with him advancing and her retreating, only coming together in the demon realm and in bed—hell and heaven. Was there a middle ground they could share?

After they dropped off her bags, he said, "Come with me. Bring Mobi."

"Kicking us out already?"

He led her to the warehouse top floor and clicked on the lights. Half the bare bulbs came on over the haphazard rows of antiques and junk. The smell of dust and horsehair stuffing thickened the air. The architectural salvage business had been a useful front for an organization that had been around for centuries and had an unfortunate habit of breaking things in the course of their missions.

Nim sneezed. "Is that a real sarcophagus?"

"Solid marble. But I figure Mobi wants a window." He pointed to the far end of the row, just within reach of the functioning lightbulbs. "Would that fit him?"

The curio cabinet had been intricately carved, bottom to top, with sea stars, waving kelp, leaping swordfish, and, finally—as if the woodworker had grown more enthusiastic with his work—bare-breasted mermaids.

Nim trailed her hands over the teak. "Where did this come from?"

"An insane asylum for whittlers? Captain's quarters on a ship bound for madness, maybe."

"Mobi will love it." Then she drew back. "Maybe it's too valuable to toss dead rats in."

"So it turns to sawdust up here? I'll hold Mobi. You grab a hand truck."

The old cabinet was solid and awkward. Even with her demon's help, she was sweaty and smudged by the time she wrestled it onto the wheels. "Do you think this goes with the décor in your room?"

"No."

She looked at him uncertainly, but followed him to his—their—room, lugging the cabinet. "Jonah, I think you should know. I've never been in a relationship that worked out."

Like which one? he wondered. The one with the sly, older rapist? The nightly one with her customers? He held the door open for her. "I've never been in one that didn't."

He showered while she fussed with Mobi. By the time he'd dried and dressed, she'd cleaned the cabinet, oiled the hinges with his prosthetics lubricant, and found a lamp to position over one end and a water bowl wedged with a pile of decorative pebbles for the other. Mobi curled through an African ceremonial mask she must have filched somewhere along her journeys.

They were making it their home. His mate, in his space. With her underthings spilling out of the bags onto his floor. Satisfaction surged through his veins, as elemental as the wood and stone.

Elemental and terrifying.

He shied away from the knowledge it could all end tomorrow. Or in eighty years. Would forever be enough? Could he be enough?

Nim bustled up beside him. "What do you think?"

He straightened, tucking his scarred stump behind him. "I left you a little bit of hot water."

She wrinkled her nose. "Are you saying I'm filthy?"

He touched the smudge of attic dust across her forehead. "You need a shower before you'll even qualify as filthy."

She lowered her lashes. "And once we're both fresh and pure again?"

"Then I have another surprise for you."

She smiled, slow and wide. "I'll just be a minute."

When she emerged, she was naked. Which required another minute, while he indulged in a good, long stare.

The bruises had faded to shadows under her skin. Her butchered hair . . . well, that would take longer to recover. The drastically shortened dreads stuck out in all directions, already fraying into delicate strands, utterly at odds with her hard-set jaw.

She propped her hand on her hip. "You tricked me into asking before if I should stay. You're gonna have to ask this time. Just so I know."

"Know what?" He shook his head. "No, don't distract me again. Get dressed." He tossed her a shirt from her bag. His fingers seemed hypersensitized to the rough caress of the lace around the neckline. Well, of course all the clothes she'd bring would drive him mad. "I think you'll like this."

He took her down to the weapons room.

She gazed around at the walls of bladed and bashing

paraphernalia of paranormal impairment. "Jonah, you have a fucked-up idea of what constitutes foreplay."

He headed toward the closest display. "With the right weapon, you won't be starting anything; you'll be ending it."

"Oh, that is sexy," she said flatly.

He sized her up in a scathing toe-to-clipped-hair sweep. "Not everything is about that."

"More's the pity."

"If you'd had a blade, you could have defended yourself."

"I thought that's why I have you."

With some exasperation, his voice rose. "Remember how you sneaked out in the night to fight on your own? Now you can keep us all at arm's length. No touching."

She scowled. "You never listened."

"I heard you. I just didn't obey. And I'm sorry for that."

She blanched and turned away from him. "Well, I'm sorry it was so awful for you."

In one long step, he confronted her. "You know that's not what I meant. No more twisting my words."

She lifted her chin. "Then say what you mean."

"I don't want you to need me," he said slowly, feeling his way. He lifted his hand to touch her cheek, and the flyaway strands of her hair tickled his knuckles. "I want you to want me."

"Did you miss the part where I tried to get you into bed?"

He shook his head. "I want more than that."

"You said you didn't have any more to give."

His lips quirked. "That's the Naughty Nymphette; always haggling." When she didn't return the smile, he sighed. "I have no doubt many a man spent his entire rent check on a night of watching you. Why shouldn't I mortgage what's left of my soul?"

"And your earnest money is a shiny little knife."

Her lack of enthusiasm made him shift from one foot to the other. "If you see one you like." He heard his voice rising toward a question, and restrained a wince.

Her gaze shuttled from him to the wall and back again. "What would you recommend?"

Relief flooded him. "Perhaps, in antiquity, the female talyan had preferred weaponry. There's no hint in league archives. Jilly and Sera both chose smaller weapons because they have Liam and Archer watching their backs."

She took a step toward the rack of daggers.

He cleared his throat. "But maybe you'd want something bigger."

She looked back with a lifted eyebrow. "You just said—"

"Liam and Archer are prime, unbroken talyan." Heat rose in his face from the lump of charred coal in his chest that had once been his pride. "Their mates can afford to skimp on personal protection."

"And I have you."

"You have half a talya mate."

She scowled. "Three-quarters, at least."

"So you need to replace that missing quarter."

"Why don't you?"

The embarrassed heat evaporated, leaving him as chilled as that night when he'd lain pinned in the wreckage of battle with a guillotine of glass poised above his outstretched arm. "I've told you the teshuva can't regenerate what's gone."

"They don't see fit to give us claws or fangs to fight the ferales either, so we have these." She swept a hand toward the assorted armaments.

This was her payback for making her ask to stay with him. "Perhaps you didn't notice, but I'm missing a hand."

She cast her gaze down the row of weapons. "Aren't at least a few of these intended for one-handed use?"

He gritted his teeth. "You think I haven't considered

that? My balance with the teshuva is shot. I am not that warrior anymore."

She walked away from him.

The abrupt separation almost staggered him.

It was worse than when he'd lost touch with the demon when he lost his hand.

She reached for an elaborate, triple-curved blade. "I saw one of these in a painting next to the mask I found for Mobi. It's African, isn't it?" She unhooked it from the wall and gave it an experimental whirl so the three open arcs of steel sang in harmonious descant.

"Be care—" He bit back the rest of the inadvertent exclamation. She wouldn't be careful. Being careful wasn't in her DNA, or in the etheric mutations the teshuva had given her. But the demon always had a feel for a good blade.

"I like it," she said.

Of course she would. "The design is based on a Congolese executioner's sword."

She took a long step back and extended the arm-length blade. Shaped like three linked sickles, the sword's upper arc came to a point and was sharpened on both sides. The two lower arcs were smaller and sharpened only along the inner edge. She tilted it under the light. "It's beautiful."

Etched lines and indents reflected back the light in baubles that danced along her skin. "Looks good on you."

Abruptly, she reversed her grip. Her fingers pressed precariously around the honed edges, to hand him the blade. "Obviously meant for you."

Dull heat spread through his chest. "Without the demon's balance—"

"I didn't have any teshuva protection when I learned to do a backward walkover pole straddle with no panties."

He choked.

"I mean," she said patiently, "you don't give up just because you can't rely on the demon anymore. If I'd given up every time I was on my own . . ." She shook her head, the blade still held out to him, unwavering. Her stare was equally steady.

He reached out to take the hilt and eased the sharp edges away from her fingers.

With all the elaborate curves, the weight of the weapon seemed to drift, first balancing near his grip, then sidling away, mocking him. Within him, the teshuva shifted with the same restlessness.

She watched him. "So you used that to lop off the heads of marauding cannibal tribes?"

Absently, he frowned. "I've never held one before. I wielded Bible verses in those days."

"What did you use after you joined the league, before your accident?"

In his mind's eye, the guillotine of glass hung above him. He forced away the memory and angled up to the balls of his feet to steady himself, but his palm was slick with sweat. When he tightened his fingers, the strain made his grip even more precarious.

The blade wavered when he pointed across the room. "Like that. A two-handed, double-edged greatsword."

Nim pulled her lips to one side in contemplation. "I see why. It's very straight." Her gaze slid slyly to him. "And big and long too." She shrugged. "Still, I like the one you've got there now. It's kind of . . . kinky."

He almost laughed. In despair at her folly, but still. "You won't let this go, will you?"

"We're bonded, right? That seems to cancel out letting go."

The sword weighed down his left, nondominant arm. The demon energy surged through his bones . . . and buckled to a halt in his missing extremity, just as it always did. His muscles cramped with the urge to toss the blade from one hand to the other.

Which, of course, he couldn't. Bile burned in his throat. Bad enough to have struggled with tooth brushing. What she was asking now . . .

No. She had put her faith in him when he had taken everything else. The least he could do was have some in himself.

He took another step back and stretched, trying to resettle the demon's energy. "This isn't . . ."

Nim stepped into his space, her aura sparking along his skin. She set herself against his back, her breasts soft against his shoulder blades, her hands skimming down his arms to settle at his wrist and stump.

"What if . . ." she mused. The fingers of her left hand brushed the hilt nestled in his palm. "What if the sword was your hand? Like the cup of the spearhead wraps the shaft." She pressed her arms together and transferred the sword from his left hand to her right.

He shifted, unbalanced. She counterweighted, and he settled into his dominant stance. It felt good. She felt good.

"You wouldn't need me as your right hand if you had this," she said.

His pulse thumped with anticipation. "Liam was a blacksmith. He could adapt the haft."

"And we already have the pattern of the prosthetic arm in your room."

"Going through my goods?"

"Naturally," she said.

"Freaked you out, did it?"

"Like you would not believe."

He took a deep breath, indulging in the caress of her flesh. "I thought I was arming you."

She slid around to face him. The blade whispered against his thigh as she dropped it to her side. "Disarming me, you mean."

"If that's what you want." He eased the sword from

her hand and backed her to the wall, where he hung the blade on its hook.

The guilt of making love in the league's weapons room while the rest of the talyan fought for their lives out in the dark city or alone with their wounds might once have given him pause, but Nim of the nimble fingers didn't allow for any pauses. Or guilt.

Still reeling from the possibility of regaining his sword arm—quite literally—he thrilled at the sensation of her, taut under his weight as he pressed her against the wall.

She gazed up at him through half-lidded eyes. "All this time, why did you settle for that silly hook?"

"I was waiting for you."

She lifted her chin. "Don't tease me, missionary man."

He thumped his truncated forearm against the wall beside her head and leaned in to her. One of the small knives jumped off its hook. "I haven't been down here since I was wounded."

She pushed herself up on her toes. "But you like it so much." Her voice was a low growl in his ear as her tongue traced his lobe.

He gasped and spoke the truth. "I didn't think the other talyan would fight with me broken."

"I'll fight with you." She moved down to graze her teeth along his jaw.

Was that a threat or a promise? His head spinning with desire, he hardly cared. Or maybe his head was spinning because she was rolling him across the wall. His shoulder knocked down a scimitar. The glinting blade narrowly missed his foot.

Nim danced over it. "Oh, you really like that idea." Her hand settled on the fly of his jeans. "I can tell."

He spun her again, and a half dozen pikes clattered against one another. The last in the row fell off the wall and clanged into a suit of armor that, as far as he'd known, had never been worn. The polished steel rocked on its stand. He reached out to steady it. "I think the league elders would consider this battle far too kinky."

"Isn't it fun?"

"You are fun." He pushed her wild hair from her face and smiled as the curls fell back over his knuckles. "Every day with you is an adventure."

"Every day that doesn't get you killed," she agreed. "Good thing you love adventure."

"No," he said thoughtfully. "It's you. Nim, I love you."

She froze. Her breasts were tight against his chest. She didn't breathe, but the racing of her heartbeat rattled him.

Maybe she'd misheard him. Although what she might have heard instead . . . "I love you, Nim."

With each frantic pulse of her heart, she shook her head. "You love my body."

"Yes. And your hair. And your wicked smile—"

"You can't. . . . It's the lure."

He scowled, half-amused, half-irate. "It's you."

Her fingers wrapped around his biceps, as if she'd fall without him, and her eyes were wide. "But I'm . . ."

"You're what? You're killing me here."

"Yes," she burst out. She tried to squirm away, but he pinned her with his knee between her legs. "I could do that, kill you. I'm bad that way."

"No, wicked maybe. But wicked isn't anywhere near as bad as I thought." He kissed her, and she moaned. "See? I'm learning." He wedged his thigh a little higher, and she writhed against him. He set his lips against her rushing pulse, then nipped her.

She shivered. "But you don't know—"

"So show me again."

With another moan, she popped his fly. "Oh yes, being good is so hard. Too hard."

The armor crashed to the floor.

He and Nim were a heartbeat behind.

CHAPTER 20

Nim stood in the first light of the rising sun, watching the talyan return on the still-dark street below. From the slump of all those broad shoulders, sagging as if the humidity melted their bones, she knew they'd had no luck again.

"We can't keep sending them out like this," Jilly murmured. "With that black energy they're emoting, they'll spawn as many tenebrae as they destroy."

"At least they are going out," Sera said. "One more night under guard and I was going to have to start my own battle."

The two women turned away from the edge of the roof. Nim lingered a moment until she picked Jonah's blond head from the crowd. She studied his gait. Steady, strong, uninjured. She breathed a silent sigh of relief.

She caught up with the others as they headed inside. "When is Liam going to finish the modifications to the executioner's sword?"

Jilly pulled a face. "Soon. Setting up his forge again was a great idea. He was thrilled. But if I live forever and never work the bellows again, I'll die an ecstatic woman."

"Better than being under computer-lab arrest," Sera said. "Ferris had me downloading every reference to heretical talya women in the league archives. I guess he thought making me write 'I will never crack open the Veil between the realms without broody male talya supervision again' on the chalkboard a hundred times was too juvenile."

"Don't bet on it." Jilly stumped down the stairs, her combat boots unlaced in concession to the heat. "The league adores old school. That's why Liam built a forge like the one his father used two hundred years ago instead of upgrading to something not Jilly powered."

Sera skipped a step ahead of Nim. "How'd Jonah decide to keep you out of trouble?"

Nim struggled to keep the heat out of her cheeks, glad when they exited into the dark main hall. "Oh, I had to straighten up the weapons room."

"Lucky you," Jilly said. "Find anything you like?"

"A couple times. Things, I mean." Nim cleared her throat. "Anyway, it'll be good to join the guys. Maybe we can lure Corvus out."

When the two women straightened in alarm, she clarified, "Not 'lure' as in 'almost get ourselves killed again.' Just tempt him out of hiding with the way he's always been interested in us, ever since Sera's demon first crossed over."

During the two nights of their house arrest, she'd gotten the full stories of Sera's and Jilly's possessions, how Corvus's attempt to break through the Veil had summoned Sera's teshuva, and how he had almost trapped Jilly while trying to circumvent the mated talya bond.

Sera sighed. "It is frustrating how he seems to respect us more than the league ever did."

"He might have been around when the last female talya fell out of the archived records," Jilly said. "Maybe he knows he should be careful. Anyway, the crews have been out every night around the airports and haven't found the tiniest smear of demon sign." She echoed Sera's sigh. "I have to finish breakfast for the guys. I don't want them crashing in and deflating my soufflé."

Nim managed not to snicker as they dropped Jilly off at the kitchen. As if somebody might fight her for the territory she'd claimed, she slipped into an apron that read DON'T FUCK WITH THE COOK over a stenciled cleaver.

Sera waved an absent good-bye as she continued down the hall. "I'd better get back to the computer before Ferris comes looking for me. Maybe I'll find something we can actually use. Like an ancient scroll of easy Crock-Pot recipes for when we're too busy slaughtering demons to sauté."

Nim smiled. "Three hundred and sixty-five centuries of cream of chicken."

Sera shuddered. "That would be hell on earth. Don't let Jonah catch you looking idle."

"Oh, I keep my hands busy." Nim blinked innocently when Sera peered at her. When the other woman had gone, she continued on.

The hiss of water running through the pipes accompanied her down the hall. All the talyan in their rooms, washing the ichor and blood away. She paused outside Jonah's door. Her room too, she supposed.

She'd never lived with someone before. Well, not for longer than a couple weeks. Not that she'd broken that record with Jonah yet. But eternity stretched before them.

Assuming she didn't do anything stupid.

Like believe him when he said he loved her.

She let herself into the room, into the bathroom, into the shower, into his arms.

"I saw you on the roof," he murmured, after he'd finished with a long, lingering kiss that stole her breath and redoubled her pulse.

"I was waiting for you." She worked the bar of soap between her hands and slicked her palms over his chest as the water sluiced around them. Her fingers satisfied her of the truth her eyes had seen from the roof; he was unmarked, other than his quiescent *reven*. Whatever tenebrae the talyan had encountered had gone to their end without excessive fuss. "I missed you."

"I missed the feel of two soapy hands on my skin."

She smacked him, a loud, fishy sound in the confines of the shower, and suds flew. "Naughty boy."

"I was missing your hands. I just didn't know it before."

The murmured words, soft and warm as the touch of the water, carved a little space in her heart. "How could you? You didn't know me then." And if he had, he wouldn't have liked her. She hadn't particularly liked her.

"Maybe my demon knew."

Of course. One creature of shady mortal character to another. She busied herself with a washcloth. "Jilly says Liam is almost done modifying the executioner's sword."

"Well, I still won't be soaping up with that."

She smacked him again.

He caught her against his chest.

"Oh no, you don't," she said. "You need breakfast and then sleep."

He ducked his head down to nuzzle her neck. "Let the demon take care of it."

"Not when I'm here to bedevil you," she said. But she sagged into the caress of his hand down her spine.

A half hour later, he snuck to the kitchen and back, returning with a peanut butter and jelly sandwich. "Everything else was eaten," he said. "Jilly's comfort food always gets to them. Especially when it's frosted comfort studded with mini chocolate chips."

Nim scooted up a pillow for him to lean back on while she nestled against his side. "Sounds like you all needed the caloric encouragement."

"Malice and ferales and even salambes aren't enough anymore. The talyan won't be satisfied until they have Corvus."

She'd been running her fingers down the quiet patterns of the *reven* that curved around his ribs, but she stopped to look up at him. "Because I let Corvus get the anklet?"

He shook his head. "This isn't about you. Or you're just an excuse."

"I'm used to that."

He finished the sandwich and rolled her onto her back. "You're my excuse for not getting enough sleep, for getting worn down to the bone." His mouth pressed softly to hers in a slow kiss, though other parts—seemingly not at all worn-down—were more insistent. "You're my excuse for wondering why I even care about Corvus when you're here waiting for me."

She licked the hint of jelly from his lips. "That's so sweet."

"By the way, I like your hair."

She patted her head and the trimmed curls poked at her fingers. The last weight of the dreads had unraveled, leaving behind a springy mess with pretensions of world domination. "Sera and Jilly evened it up tonight. Said they were sick of looking at it."

He nudged aside her hand and tucked a wayward curl behind her ear. The corners of his half-closed eyes crinkled when it tumbled back again. "Soft," he murmured. "And wild."

She kissed him again, and he was asleep before she lifted her head. Easy for him to be exhausted. He hadn't been sitting around, worrying and twiddling his fingers all night.

With a sigh, she echoed his caress, brushing a blond lock from his forehead. His deep breath never faltered, but he turned to nuzzle her palm. The brush of his lips against her wrist fired her pulse.

God, she couldn't stop touching him, even while knowing he needed to rest, needed to stay focused if he was going to survive the horde. She pulled away and clamped her hand between her knees so she wouldn't reach out to him again. All these years of ruthlessly using her body to get her way and she was betrayed, not by her bones or muscles or nerves, but by a quivering lump of flesh at her center.

And not just her clit either.

Her stupid heart.

What was she doing here? She wasn't just seducing a missionary man. She was luring a damned holy warrior away from his shot at redemption. She had ruined his chances and put him in danger by losing the anklet, and he wouldn't even let her help him get it back. She'd never even wanted to be part of a team—for which everyone was probably eternally grateful, since when she wasn't being useless, she was a downright menace.

Her fingers curled, digging into the flesh of her thighs.

Once upon a time, she would've taken this beautiful moment to burn a hole in her skin. But the demon would laugh at such a wimpy wound.

And this time, she didn't need the outside pain.

She slipped out of the bed and fetched Mobi. She'd forgotten to bring her CDs from her apartment, which was a drag, since the only stereo she'd found in the warehouse didn't have a place to dock her iPod. Another example of the league's slow evolution, Sera had mourned, despite the ever-pressing need for change.

Nim went down through the quiet halls to the dock and pushed up the rolling door. The heat poured in, thick and moist as one of Jilly's soufflés. Nim patted her curls again, feeling them taking on a demonic life of their own from the humidity. Sera and Jilly, with their fine, straight hair, hadn't understood how the dreads weren't a fashion statement, but a life-saving measure.

She plugged in the boom box. It'd be a long time before her hair grew that long. Maybe she shouldn't have been so rash with the scissors. But she'd banished the memory of the feralis's punishing grip with each hack. She couldn't escape the teshuva as easily, of course. Only the soul-cleaving solvo could sever its link, and the soul wouldn't ever grow back.

She dialed through the radio band to the local hip-hop station that promised an uninterrupted marathon, and started to dance.

In the heat, Mobi was lithe and lively, gliding over her arms as if her limbs were obstacles to his hunt. She went into a deep backbend to let him slide up her torso, and then straightened slowly as he climbed to circle her neck. Her hair was definitely a rat's nest now, sweat stiffened and kinked.

Who was she kidding? She hadn't cut her hair to protect her from feralis attacks. She'd done it to sever her old life from the one she wanted now.

She wanted the missionary man. The pure and unholy warrior.

She wanted Jonah, and she didn't see any way on earth—or in the demon realm either, for that matter—that she could ever truly have him.

Sure, he desired her. The Naughty Nymphette didn't give him a choice there. He'd even said "love," but she'd heard that one before. She couldn't hold a man like him. When the desire burned down, he'd see only the darkness in her. No one could love that.

In case she tried to forget again—in case she thought there was something else she could change to capture Jonah's heart—she danced through the songs until her thighs trembled from exertion and Mobi was a limp ribbon in her hands.

When the next set of commercials kicked in, she sank to her knees and pulled the plug.

She knelt, panting in the hot silence, wondering why exactly she'd fallen in love.

She loved Jonah. What a world-ending fuckup to end all fuckups.

Once upon a time, she'd set matches against her skin just to feel anything at all. The holes in her flesh had let out the pain, sorrow, and hatred, like little tears in the Veil around the tenebraeternum. No wonder the demons were drawn to her.

He was a good man who thought he could make her a good woman, but the light Jonah held up only made her shadows deeper.

Sweat stung in her eyes.

A sharp round of applause—three mocking claps—jerked her head up.

"How intriguing," Cyril Fane drawled.

The angelic possessed stood just outside the fence, watching her.

She waited until her breath evened and she could answer with similar nonchalance. "Are you like a vampire, where you can't come in unless invited?"

He shot his cuffs, and the sun gleamed off the pristine starch of his shirt. "It is high daylight, and I'm wearing white."

"I already knew you weren't cool like a vampire." She tucked Mobi around her shoulders, grateful for the scaled armor.

They studied each other through the chain link.

"So, now I've seen the Naughty Nymphette display her charms. But you kept your clothes on. I feel short-changed."

"You didn't pay. And it would've been more than change."

He smiled crookedly. "As delightful as it is to spar with you, *heshuka*, don't you want to know why I'm here?"

"Didn't your mama ever teach you that insults work better when you speak English?"

"How do you know it was an insult? Perhaps *heshuka* is a term of endearment."

She laughed.

He shrugged. "It was the sphericanum—the blessed realm—that christened you 'talyan,' from the Aramaic for 'sacrificial lamb.'"

"See? That's how I knew it was an insult. It came from your mouth."

He crossed his arms in an Old Testament sort of way. "So, you're not going to ask?"

"Most of what I ask for, I don't get. And most of what I get, I didn't ask for." For a heartbeat, she wondered if that mind-set might just be why she was fucking up with Jonah.

But Fane interrupted. "I won't come in because my presence will overwhelm the energy sinks you talyan put in place to swallow your pain and anger and hatred."

"I can only imagine," she mused.

He glowered at her, all pretense of amusement fled. "Really, you can't."

She sighed. "Fine, Angel Boy. What do you want?"

"I want you to come with me."

"After I called you Angel Boy?"

"No worse than me calling you the 'unknown darkness.'"

At least she knew what *heshuka* meant. Swell. Her knowledge of Aramaic had just doubled. "I might not know much, but I'm fairly sure going anywhere with you is a terrible idea."

"Undoubtedly, but it can't be helped."

"Sure it can. By me not going."

His glower deepened. "Elaine, I discover I am finding it less delightful to spar with you."

"Ha, made you lie. Is that going to look bad on your record?" That he had bothered to learn her real name didn't seem like a good sign. Bad enough the devil knew it.

"I know where your anklet is."

A jolt went through her. "So do we. It's with Black-bird."

"And I know how to find Corvus Valerius."

She hesitated and cursed under her breath when Fane smiled, clearly knowing he'd caught her. "I'll go get Jonah." And Liam and Archer and Ecco and, oh, a dozen other snarly, sleepy talyan. They'd want her to tell them. They wouldn't care about the risk, about the fact that it was all her fault. They lived for opportunities like this.

For moments like this, they died.

Liam and Archer and Ecco and the others had their own sins with their demons to match, but this should be her fight. A little voice twisted in her head—too weak and wistful to be a demon's voice; just her voice—and said if she found Corvus and the anklet, that would be good. *She* would be good.

"No league," Fane said. "Only you."

Damn it. This was so obviously the sort of temptation she was supposed to resist. Running off with an angel must look really bad on a talya's record, even if righting her own wrongs was exactly what the preacher man had ordered. So she said, with as much resolve as she could muster, "No."

This time, he laughed.

In her defense, she thought, as the Lotus peeled out of the warehouse district . . . Okay, there was no defense for sneaking out of the league compound without authorization or even leaving a note. Except that she was possessed by a demon, which, by definition, meant she could be unfailingly relied upon to do all sorts of bad things, even when—especially when—she was trying to do good.

"I'm so fucked," she muttered.

"There are certain advantages to the *symballein* bond," Fane agreed.

"The angelic possessed aren't the same? You're not celibate, are you? With a car like this? What a shame."

A smile flickered over his lips, but faded. "As a higher-sphere warden, I am most assuredly not going to share sphericanum secrets with an outcast *heshuka*."

Nim leaned back against the silky leather. "Yeah. You're celibate."

"Can you keep your serpent off the upholstery?"

She frowned at his sharp tone. "I offered to put Mobi back."

"I couldn't trust you not to wake your mate."

"I said I wouldn't."

Fane gave her a look. "Even if you kept your word"—the vanishing space between his furrowed brows calculated the chances of that as slim to none—"your presence, and your withdrawal, could have given you away."

She had to admit he was right. She had already noticed that Jonah in a bed had a gravitational pull she found hard to resist.

"You could just set the serpent loose," Fane suggested.

She gave him a look as disbelieving as the one he'd given her. "God, I hope you're not in charge of any paradises."

His expression turned thunderous again. "Do you even comprehend," he burst out, "how your attachment to the serpent represents your stubborn clinging to the darkness that made you vulnerable to demonic possession?"

She wrinkled her nose. "I had Mobi long before the demon."

"But you permitted the resonance in your soul that matched the teshuva."

"I didn't know that at the time."

"Didn't you?" His fingers tightened on the steering wheel.

"Um, *no.*" She rolled her eyes.

"Emotionally, you must have. Spiritually . . ."

"Like I said before, no. Any particular reason you're looking for validation? Can't you just be holier than me and be happy?"

She was being snide, but at least he shut up.

He'd already told her they were going to the Shimmy Shack, although he wouldn't say why and offered only an annoyingly mysterious "That is why you must come with me. To see."

At the sight of the bright yellow crime-scene tape across the garish red paint, her pulse plummeted and then rocketed with her breath. She got out of the Lotus and wrapped Mobi so tight around her neck he squirmed in protest.

Heat waves shimmered over the asphalt of the empty parking lot, and the crime-scene tape seemed to ripple despite the still, heavy air. Did she just imagine the drifting scent of putrefaction?

Fane yanked aside the tape.

Nim hesitated. The loose yellow plastic licked her ankle like a tongue. "We have to go inside?"

"That's where the people were killed. That's where the souls will be waiting."

He didn't look back, and she hurried to catch up. "You said you'd tell me where Corvus was."

"I will. Right after you find out from the lingering souls." He paused at the front door. After a moment, it yielded to his touch.

For a second, she was impressed at his B&E skills, which seemed inappropriate for an angel. Then she realized he had a key. An angel with a key to a strip club. Even more inappropriate.

She followed him into the stuffy darkness. The newly shortened hairs at the back of her neck would have stood up straight if not for Mobi's comforting presence. Her demon sight flickered into hunting mode as her teshuva caught her mood.

"There are no demons here," Fane said. "Besides yours."

She resisted the urge to sniff, but she was definitely catching a whiff of rot. "How can you be sure?"

He scowled. "Because I am host to an upper-sphere angel that—"

"Okay, no need to preach. You should've let me bring Jonah. You'd like him." Who was she kidding? She was the one who wanted Jonah beside her. But Fane was right; the etheric etchings left by the invading tenebrae had faded until even her teshuva caught the sickening glimmers only from the corners of her eyes. "So what am I supposed to do here?"

"Many who die violently and unexpectedly and brimming with treacherous passions"—he gave her a meaningful look—"are prone to linger at the site of their demise. Bring me their souls."

She squinted at him. "Isn't that what you do?"

His scowl blanked to a mask somehow more unnerving. "If so, would you be here?"

She shifted in her flip-flops, wishing—once again—that she'd worn more substantial footgear. But Jonah had said they looked perfect for some lazy summer afternoon on the boat, and the image had appealed to her, and so here she was, breaking into a demonic murder scene in flip-flops, which were going to sound ridiculous if she had to make a quick getaway.

When he faced her, Fane's eyes were deeper than the shadows of the empty club. "Call the souls."

Nim shook her head. "Bad things happen when I turn up the juice. Besides, the teshuva can't see souls unless they've been shredded out of the body by solvo."

"Not just solvo. Anything demon fouled."

She wrinkled her nose. Charming. Demon fouled, was she? "I know Nanette can see the soulflies, just like me. Why can't you just—?"

"Elaine," he snapped. "Are you always this tiresome?"

"If you'd brought Jonah, you'd know the answer," she snarled back. "And my name is Nim."

"Do you want to find Corvus?"

"Duh."

He gritted out each word. "Then bring me the damned souls."

Wow. Now she was getting actual angels, not just missionary men, to swear. Unless he meant literally damned, and then she supposed it was a technical term and not an expletive. But at least now she was starting to understand. "You don't want to sully your pretty white hands on those nasty, demon-fouled, *damned* souls, do you?"

"It is no business of the league how the heavenly order presides over the war with the tenebraeternum."

She frowned. "I didn't say anything about heaven.... Oh, you mean *you're* not supposed to be here either. And your bosses—how many higher spheres are there anyway?—will notice if you get gunk under your nails. So you brought me to do the dirty work."

He glowered at her.

She shrugged. "I'm not afraid of dirty work."

"We have to stop Corvus."

"What d'you mean 'we,' white man?" She walked into the middle of the room. No one had picked up since the attack, and the tables were still upturned, the chairs broken and strewn across the floor. But the bodies had disappeared. Which, in some ways, was even more eerie, since if she didn't know better, she might have thought the mess was the result of a particularly uproarious bachelor party. But the wrong kind of stains remained, dark and spreading, the source of the lingering stink that had Mobi licking the air. Which made her feel a little nauseated.

She avoided the tainted patches, just as she had walked around the ether signs at the pawnshop all those centuries, years, okay, days ago. She took a breath, then wished she hadn't. "You have to be ready to knock me out if the lure spreads too far."

"Happily," he said.

"You could at least look like you're joking," she said.

But mostly he looked like he had seen a ghost. And she hadn't even started calling yet. The sphericanum must really frown on fraternizing between angels and demons if the mighty Fane was so anxious about what they were doing.

Which, along with actually finding Blackbird, sort of unnerved her now. Based on the name, she'd been picturing something small and fluffy—evil, of course, but fluffily so. But, then, she'd always been one to underestimate wickedness.

Her soul had been invaded and her anklet stolen—well, after she'd sold it—and her life was no longer her own. But if there was one thing she'd always been good at, it was making the best of her own failings. And where better than here, the murky, hell-hot, claustrophobic Shimmy Shack of Lost Souls, with an angel watching over her to revel in her failure . . . and still not let it touch her.

"Here I go." She stepped up onto the unlit stage to gather the energy that would bring down the house.

CHAPTER 21

Throwing Andre off the pier with his spine crushed had been hasty. Corvus lugged the clinking duffel across the rough ground, salty crystals of sweat grating at the corner of his eye when he blinked. Where clumps of grass had poked up, it was hard to see the trash. But breaking bottles had their own special sound underfoot. He winced as he found another and added it to his duffel.

He trudged across the field.

Soul gone. Mind gone. His downtown aerie with its city view gone. His minions gone.

He paused in front of the tower. Nothing else moved in the hot stillness except an eerie, singing hum, like a wet fingertip on crystal. The etheric resonance of amassed tenebrae raised the birnenston-scorched hair on his demon-scarred arms.

Not all gone . . .

Who'd turned the stage lights on? Nim saw the strobe through her closed eyelids.

"Elaine?" The worried voice sounded far away. Much farther than the lights. "Nim, stop now."

She couldn't stop. She had to bring them all. They all wanted her. . . . They all had to want her. . . .

"No," she whispered. The desire was hers to indulge, no one else's. "Don't touch," she hissed. And she opened her eyes.

Cyril Fane stood below her, his hand on the stage as if he were about to boost himself up. Probably to punch her lights out, to stop the call.

But there were already plenty of lights, and she had stopped herself.

They hovered in vaguely human shape, unlike the drifting clouds of soulflies. The brutal terror of the ferales had destroyed their bodies, leaving their blood to soak the floorboards, but their souls were mercifully— maybe "mercifully" wasn't the right word—whole and unbroken.

Not that they seemed reconciled to the distinction.

The souls shifted almost too fast for her demon eye to follow, blinking between the various stains on the floor, then reappearing to hover near the stage, then circling again, with faint etheric contrails connecting the dots. Even when they paused for a moment, they pulsed with an agitation beyond the need for words. Which, now that she thought about it, seemed problematic.

She glared at Fane. "They can't talk."

He looked away. "In stories, they always find a way to tell their secrets."

"Stories?" Her multioctave shriek puffed the souls away like oversized dandelion blooms. "What, like ghost stories?"

He hunched his shoulders. "I don't read much populist fiction. And the upper spheres of the sphericanum haven't bothered with the aftermath before."

"Then why didn't we bring Nanette?"

"She's the one who convinced me we need to get involved."

"But you thought you could handle it. Handle me." In her everyday human derision, the demon overtones melted away, and she shook her head. "Didn't I tell you not to touch?"

She raised her gaze to track the wandering souls. If she was going to talk to any of them . . .

"If only souls kept their fake tits," she muttered. She cleared her throat and called, "Amber?" She thought for a moment. "Myra? Are you here?"

Fane shifted in his loafers. "Maybe choose just one. We don't want them all over us."

Of course not. Who wanted soul smears all over? "Myra picked Amber for her stripper name, even though I told her amber isn't worth shit without a big bug stuck in it. She said Myra sounded like a cow's name. But you should've seen her boob job." Nim kept her gaze out of focus as one of the souls drifted nearer. Maybe Amber, and maybe pissed about the wasted plastic surgery.

How, exactly, was an amorphous column of transparent Christmas lights supposed to pass along a message? And what could a murdered soul know about Corvus, who'd, after all, sent only his human and demonic henchmen? Yet another higher power who didn't want to get his hands dirty.

"Myra . . ." Nim found she had no more words for the dead dancer than she'd had for the live one. "I wish I knew which of us got screwed worse."

The soul strobed between Nim and the stain in the middle of the floor where Amber's leg had lain. The path traced an after-image streak of light through the gloomy club. Abruptly, it added a third point in its rounds.

Fane followed the light to a round table tipped against the bar as if it had had one drink too many. He peered around. When the Amber soul materialized above his head in a silent burst of light, he ducked.

Nim snickered, then noticed the sudden tensing of his shoulders as he swooped down. "What did you find?"

"Demon droppings." He cupped a shard of something in his palm. Glassy glints melded with dull bone.

Nim remembered the decomposing chunk of feralis in the tunnel below the club. "Not as useful as a business card, is it? You lured me here under false pretenses."

From the back hall stepped a man with a shiny badge clipped to his front pocket. "What pretenses would those be?"

Nim winced. Here she'd been thinking the teshuva's senses were warning against calling down a horde of tenebrae on their heads. Sometimes it was hard to remember all the ways she could fuck up.

Fane leaned against the table, as if he hadn't a care in the world—this world, at least. He pocketed the shard so smoothly she wouldn't have noticed if she hadn't been looking for it. "I told her she could get her last paycheck."

The cop came toward them, his right hand hovering in a way that made her think he wasn't as comfortable as Fane and didn't care about revealing his intention to shoot them, should he feel the need. After what he'd seen in the aftermath of the attack, she didn't blame him.

He gave the corner of the stage a wide berth, keeping her and Fane in his sights. "You must be Elaine Hamlin."

"The Naughty Nymphette," Fane supplied helpfully.

Nim shot him a dirty look. But she'd learned a long time ago not to sass in front of cops unless absolutely necessary. "Yes, sir. That's me." Hard to deny with a boa constrictor wrapped around her neck, considering there was a rather lurid *Viva Las Showgirls* promo poster of her and Mobi in the men's toilet.

"I thought I'd see you at your coworker's funeral this morning out at Oak Woods. I've been trying to find you."

She widened her eyes. "You have?" Her other old habit with cops was to lie shamelessly. Asking why he was looking might be a bit hard to swallow, considering she was standing in a murder scene, so she settled for, "I haven't been checking my messages."

The cop's eyes narrowed as much as hers had widened. "So, you didn't know what happened here?"

How to answer in a way he could believe? Answering with the truth was just too unbelievable. "I just can't believe it," she said, interjecting a quaver into her voice. That was true enough.

He sighed. "So after you left here Monday night with the man with the hook— Who was he again?"

"He was my"—she blinked slowly—"date."

"And did your date have a name?"

She blinked even slower. "John." Fane snorted softly, so she ignored him. "I'm sorry I can't help you more, Officer . . ."

"Detective Ramirez. And where is John now?"

She shrugged. "I had another . . . date." And this time she let her gaze slide to Fane, who stiffened in outrage. "Since I'm a little behind on rent, what with missing my paycheck and all."

Ramirez tapped his finger against the gun butt. "Are you two aware that removing police tape to interfere with a crime-scene investigation is a punishable offense?" Frustration echoed in his voice. He wanted to get somebody for something.

"I'm sorry, Detective Ramirez." Fane held out his hands in an innocent gesture. "The insurance company said I could do my estimate for the cleanup." By way of explanation, he added, "Last Call Cleaning, services in decontamination and sterilization. Would you like my card?"

No, obviously, Detective Ramirez would not like it, not unless the card had a murderer's phone number on the back, which, Nim could tell from his even deeper sigh, he'd already decided they weren't.

Well, he was mostly right. They weren't murderers. Not of humans, anyway. Or not directly. Not unless they were possessed.

Fane cleared his throat as Ramirez reluctantly took the biohazard-yellow card. "Detective Ramirez, I was wondering about some of the unusual damage here. Anything I should know?"

The cop gave him another once-over. Maybe it was Fane's angel or the business card, but the wariness faded to weariness. "Your cleanup order should have noted special instructions for a hydrofluoric acid spill. Some of the bodies were ... eaten away." He rubbed his eyes. "The coroner said the acid sinks in without much pain and then dissolves flesh from the inside out. You die before you realize how badly you've been burned. So watch yourself."

"Thank you, Detective. I'll be careful," Fane said humbly, and the humility sounded genuine. Which made Nim narrow her eyes at him. What was he concocting in that angel-addled head of his?

"Miss Hamlin, I'd like to talk to you more about that night. As far as we can tell, you were the last to leave the club before ..." A haunted shadow crossed his face, deepening the lines around his mouth. "Before what happened. Will you come down to the station?"

"Of course," she said, with as much sincerity as Fane. "As soon as I think of something to tell you."

Ramirez looked up at her as if he could hear the echo of the unsaid words. "I'm sure you'll call right away."

"Whatever I can do to help." Really, she was helping him by leaving him out of it. Bad things happened around her. He could just ask Amber.

Ramirez sized up Fane. "If you find anything during the cleanup ..."

"Last Call Cleaning has a long-standing relationship with the Chicago PD," Fane said. "And I have your card."

"Right." Ramirez sighed a third time, and Nim knew he was down for the count.

Out in the parking lot, the detective climbed into his unmarked car and pulled away. After the stinking gloom of the club, the hot glare off bare concrete was almost a relief. Still, Nim hunched against the chill between her shoulder blades as if the Amber soul might be watching her go.

"I'll finish cleaning up," Fane said. "On several levels. Don't be troubled."

Nim followed him to the car. "So, what did you put together in there? I saw something squirming in your brain. I'm assuming that was an idea and not the angel." His gaze slid away, and she snarled, "Whatever it is, I helped you get it. You owe me."

"Deals only work with devils," he snarled back.

They each took a short step to the side, circling each other.

"Don't try me, *heshuka*," he warned.

"Don't tempt me, *gnuna zira*."

He jerked his head back. "What did you just call me?"

"Fucking wanker." She hesitated. "In Aramaic, I think. Maybe Assyrian? I'd have to look it up again." She held out her hand and tapped her fingertips twice against her palm in a give-it-over gesture. "So, what's in your pocket?"

His hand hovered at his hip like one of her former customers running short on singles. "You should leave this alone, for your own good."

"So I can be good?"

"Obviously, I've been led astray." His glower returned. "Which is why the sphericanum commands we stay far away from your kind."

"And yet you brought me here. Which tells me you don't obey commands any better than I do." She pitched her voice toward wheedling. "Come to the dark side, angel."

He arched one eyebrow at her. "Please." But he dug into his pocket. "Corvus Valerius has crossed a line in this battle. He must be stopped. Whatever the cost."

"So where are the choirs of angels?" When he didn't

answer, she cocked an eyebrow at him. "Oh, you meant whatever the cost to us, the league."

He opened his curled fingers and revealed the shard. In the bright sun, the broken edges of the glass glinted like teeth. "As you mentioned before, the angelic forces do not linger forever in their chosen hosts. We aid them in their errands in this realm without the benefit of immortality."

An image of Jonah's grim mouth as he'd spoken of his wife flashed through her mind "There are downsides too. But you get no ninja skills either, huh?"

"Nothing to compare with the meanest teshuva."

She pursed her lips. "That does explain why evil always seems to triumph."

"But if you aren't evil—"

"Some of us aren't," she interrupted.

He ignored her. "Then we should join forces."

"The enemy of my enemy," she murmured. Isn't that the way Jonah felt as well? He had taken her on despite hating everything she was. He had reached out to her despite everything he'd seen. And he'd seen it all. She shook off the thought. "Give me the feralis chunk."

He passed it over with visible reluctance. "What will you do?"

"Take it to Liam Niall."

"And the league leader will be willing to risk all his talyan on this suicidal endeavor?"

She smiled grimly. "It's what they live for."

She made Fane take her to the mall. When he balked, she pointed out, "I can't tell the league I've been hanging out with an angel all day. They'll crucify me. Not for real. But they'll believe I stopped by the club to get my wardrobe. Such as it is."

He wouldn't give her the credit card. "I'm not showing this stop on my expense account."

She sniffed. "Angels have expense accounts? No

wonder we're losing. Everybody else is covering their asses, and only we talyan put ourselves out there."

"You more than most," he said.

"You'll make it all up billing the city for cleaning up the club, thanks to me," she shot back. She wished her voice hadn't wavered at the end.

She bought a bustier—vinyl, not leather, tragically— and matching strappy black sandals with fuck-you heels. She threw in a shiny black, thigh-length trench coat, which was a steal on sale because, after all, it was August in Chicago.

As they left the mall parking lot, she leaned back in the Lotus seat and stroked the leather. This was where she'd been headed: the moneyed men of Vegas and their endless needs. And now she was going to . . . "Take us to the cemetery."

Fane sighed. "There's nothing there."

"Nothing except her body."

He sighed again, gusty enough to blow Amber's soul across the city. If it hadn't been trapped by the horror of its last moments. But he did as he was told.

At the cemetery, she slipped into the black coat.

Fane squinted. "You look like a slutty-hippie-manga Death."

"That's the nicest thing you've said to me yet." She slammed out the door, hoping Mobi got frisky in the hot car with the angel-man.

The new grave had a view of an oak tree. Nim stared down into the open pit. The diggers hadn't backfilled the hole yet, and the top of the casket gleamed like her vinyl trench under a scattering of white rose petals. Another bouquet of white roses drooped in the heat atop the blank granite headstone.

Nim fisted her hands in her pockets, fury coursing through her. Amber or Myra—*something* should've been carved on her rock.

Nim took a breath. Of course, Myra's family, whoever they were, hadn't had time to carve anything, but somebody had cared enough to leave the flowers and the crumpled tissue, white as a wayward rose except for the mascara stains.

Nim pulled her hand from her pocket and opened her fingers. The semifinals ticket wadded in her palm was damp with her sweat. But the gaudy gold imprinted on black and red still glittered in the sunlight: VIVA LAS SHOWGIRLS.

"Not this showgirl," she murmured. "Either one, actually. I guess we skipped straight to the finals."

She stood and tossed the ticket into the grave. She snapped off one of the roses and took a last look back. Her fingers clenched around the stem, but the thorns had been shaved down to nothing.

At the Lotus, she held out the rose to Fane.

He studied her with the same look he gave Mobi. "What? Her gold fillings wouldn't come out?"

She threw the flower at his head. "When you go to clean the club—if that's your euphemism for pretending you're winning this war against evil—take the flower to her. Tell her she's resting in peace. If she can find it."

He dropped her off at the outskirts of the warehouse district, which she thought was cruel, considering the blazing sun, especially since the talyan would still be snoozing off their previous night's adventures and wouldn't notice her return.

"Wouldn't want all your subterfuge to go to waste," he said.

So she trudged the last long blocks to the warehouse. Mobi twined over her shoulders, energized by the heat. "I know; you would've liked Vegas. But the show must go on."

After the heat outside, the cathedral cool of the warehouse interior soothed her skin. She went down to Sera's lab and laid the feralis fragment on the counter. The unnatural mix of muted shell and hazed glass glimmered in the screen-saver light from the computer.

She found a sticky note and scrawled *What is this?* with an arrow pointing toward the shell. She cleared a little space on the cluttered counter so the two items would stand out. Then she went to Jonah's room.

He was still dead to the world, as if she had never gone. She rather wished she hadn't.

She slid Mobi into his cabinet and herself into the shower. Washing off the sweat was easy; the remembered stink of the club . . . not so much. But she scrubbed her skin until the teshuva couldn't keep up with the sting.

When she got out and padded nude into the bedroom, Jonah was propped up on the pillow, arm behind his head. The sheet was crumpled around his waist. The shopping bag lay on the bed where she had tossed it.

He watched her. "A surprise?"

"Oh yeah." She climbed onto the bed and straddled him.

His gaze cut to the bag. "Aren't you going to show me?"

"That's not the surprise. That's the distraction." She leaned down to set her lips under his ears. He shivered at the gentle breath she blew against his skin.

"Probably I should be terrified," he murmured.

"Of the surprise? Or the distraction?"

"Of you."

She circled her hips over his, the sheet scant protection from his heat. "You don't seem terrified."

He settled his hand high on her thigh, his thumb nestled between one of the faint match-head scars and the black tracery of her *reven*. "I'm waiting."

She sighed and sat back. "I went to the club this afternoon."

His fingers closed reflexively, and she winced as his grip drove into a nerve. As her words had, apparently. "There weren't any demons," she said quickly.

"I can't even imagine how you think, after less than a week of possession, you're qualified to make that assessment."

"Nothing killed me, did it?"

He rolled, dumping her off. Not expecting the eviction, she sprawled ungracefully on the sheet. He stood and faced her. His body was hard, his erection straining toward her, but his expression was harder yet and utterly closed. "I can't trust you, can I?"

The accusation stung hotter than the shower. She didn't even have the gnarly dreads to toss back over her shoulder with pointed disdain. "Did I ever give you the impression you should?"

"We're supposed to be together."

"You righteous males left us here while you went out hunting Corvus," she shot back. "You would've locked us in our rooms if you thought the walls would hold us. How is that together?"

"We needed to know you'd be safe—"

"Safe?" she snapped. "You can't save us any more than you could stop time from taking your wife."

He recoiled, not a glimmer of violet in his eyes.

She bit her lip, but it was too late to hold back the words. He'd stayed with Carine despite the demon and the years that had come between them. Had he forgotten what that meant? "We sleep together, we fight together, we *are* together—for all of it. Or what's the point of saying you love me?"

"You could tell me." His eyes glittered now with pure male fury. "But then you might have to say the word back to me."

She took the hit without flinching. She couldn't have hoped he hadn't noticed her lack of response to his declaration. But how could she answer when she knew she wasn't what he'd hoped for?

When once again she didn't answer, his tone dropped coldly. "Then I suppose," he said, "the point is to rip Corvus's djinni from his mummy husk and consign both of them to hell, where his soul is waiting."

Oh, ouch. If only she'd put on the bustier while she'd had the chance. The black leather would have kept her guts from spilling out.

She lifted her chin. "You'll be psyched to know I returned with a little souvenir. A hint to where Corvus is making his monsters. Now, aren't you glad I broke curfew and got you what you really wanted?"

His jaw worked and he clenched the bed post as if he were holding himself back from arguing. She wished he would just let go and shout at her, because then she'd know he didn't care about what she'd found.

Instead, he turned away to jerk on his clothes, not even bothering to tuck in his shirt. "Show me."

A chill spiked inward, like an iron maiden closing around her. She rolled over on the sheet to gather the folds around her. The shopping bag spilled to the floor. "Your surprise is down in the lab. I hope you like it."

He moved so quietly, she didn't hear him leave. Only the quiet click of the door latch and the emptiness of the room told her he'd gone.

Had he noticed how much he'd changed from the awkward, stiff recluse he'd considered himself? She buried her face in the pillow, where the scent of him—salt and sun and maleness—lingered. She thought she would've appreciated it more if he wasn't using his quiet steps to walk out on her.

She'd changed too, unfortunately, or she wouldn't have cried.

CHAPTER 22

Jonah sucked in a long breath and almost gagged on the miasma of hot dust and ancient wood varnish. He'd gone to the stairwell, stomping headlong toward the basement, only to find himself on the top floor amidst the salvaged @1 junk.

That's what he'd been. Junk in the attic. Except he wasn't even useful for spare parts.

With Nim, though, he'd become more than that, just as he'd intended. Even without her twice-damned anklet, she was a force to be reckoned with.

And there was always a reckoning. Apparently, this was it.

He slumped against the window. The smudged panes obscured most of the city beyond, letting in only the white afternoon light that burned his tightly clenched lids when he closed his eyes.

Given the first chance, she'd crept away from him, back to her life of before, even though that life lay in blood-soaked, birnenston-stained ruins. She hadn't seen a reason to take him with her because the bond between them wasn't strong enough. His body and soul weren't enough. As for his heart . . .

His harsh laugh, tinged with demon, cracked the pane.

He was going to lose her. She would find that damned anklet and become twice the warrior he'd ever been. And the loss would hurt worse than his maiming ever had. Not because he'd lost his weapon hand—again—but because this time he'd lost his heart.

But how could he force her to love him back? The demon's unholy power hadn't kept him whole before. Why should that change now?

Reluctantly, he made his way downstairs. At the last minute, he turned aside on the main floor and stepped outside.

At first he thought the clanging was his headache, but he followed the noise to the far docking bay, where Liam had set up his forge.

The league leader had stripped to nothing more than a leather apron over his jeans, but sweat poured down his shoulders as he guided a hammer along the metal cuff he was molding. He nodded at Jonah and continued the rhythmic blows. Ecco worked the bellows. The big talya hadn't deigned to remove his shirt, and he was almost as soaked as Liam.

Jonah went to the doorway to stare blindly out at the chain link, bleached to floss under the sun's glare. At a hiss behind him, he turned to see Liam plunge the cuff into the galvanized-steel washtub beside the anvil.

Liam lifted the cuff, grunted to himself, and dunked his head. He came up sputtering, and joined Jonah in the doorway. "I just need to attach the cuff to the blade you gave me. When I'm done, the only weak spot will be where the weapon attaches to you."

"That's the way it always is," Jonah said.

The league leader stood dripping for a moment, swinging the hammer idly, then hazarded a guess. "Trouble in paradise?"

"Never been there."

Ecco snorted. "Well, then, you gotta get back on the

whore . . . horse," he said hurriedly when the other two talyan rounded on him. "Whoa, take it easy."

"Ecco." Demon harmonics shivered in Liam's voice, and he shoved Jonah back a couple yards. "I thought putting you to slave work down here would remind you why you don't run off with our women."

"I would've brought them back." Ecco hunched his shoulders at the reprimand. "And can I remind you— again—that calling all tenebrae was their idea?"

"I don't care— Damn it, Jonah!" Liam raised the hammer to ward off the downward slice of the executioner's blade aimed at Ecco's head. The big talya yelped and ducked.

Jonah gritted his teeth. Liam had removed the grip from the African blade to ready it for the cuff, so the sword lacked all balance and strength. Not unlike him. But the gleaming edge drew sparks from the hammer as it sheared through the metal.

Jonah pulled up the strike before he hit Liam.

The league leader narrowed his gaze, first on the blade hovering a handsbreadth from his face, then on Jonah. "I'm not done with that yet."

"With the sword or with Ecco?"

"Either."

"It'll be a fine sword once the teshuva's ether sinks in," Jonah said. He cut a glance at Ecco. "I'll wait."

Ecco scowled. "You boys take this chick thing far too seriously." He stalked away.

"Let it go," Liam murmured.

Jonah shrugged. "I don't think I ever have a choice, do I?"

The league leader gave him a look, as if Liam suspected there was more to the comment. And Jonah didn't want the perceptive man to delve any deeper, so he said, "Nim found a clue to Corvus's lair."

Liam stiffened. "Then why are we still standing here? What is it?"

Jonah shrugged again. "She said she left it in Sera's lab."

Instead of racing away, Liam tossed the shattered hammer on the anvil. "Is Nim down there?"

"No."

"Ah." There was weight in the understanding exhalation. "How badly do we want this?"

"Badly." Jonah studied the edge of the blade. Not a nick.

"Then let's go see what she brought us."

Jonah hesitated, the ill-weighted weapon wavering in his hand. He could send Liam alone and go to his room to confront his temptress. But the sword wasn't ready yet.

So he followed the league leader in silence down to the lab.

Liam stopped at the counter and peered down at the shard. "Is it part of a bowl?"

"Nim found it at the Shimmy Shack."

Liam's gaze arrowed to him. "She went back there?"

Jonah gave a sharp nod. "So unless the ferales have retired to pottery . . ."

"Or glassblowing." Liam lifted the piece, and the glass glinted.

"The rest is turtle shell."

Liam grunted. "We didn't have turtles in Ireland."

"We ate them from the jungle rivers." Jonah shook his head. "There's no way any of the people in the club took a chunk from a feralis. The tenebrae must've been on a rampage."

Liam scowled. "Andre blamed them for hurting Jilly."

"That is what they do," Jonah murmured. Which was why he'd wanted to keep Nim safe, leaving her behind while the talyan hunted. How could she not understand that?

"The glass is a strange addition." Liam smoothed his thumb over the etched surface.

"We know Corvus liked glass sculptures," Jonah said. "He had captured the etheric emanations of birds in glass when Archer and Sera tracked him down the first time."

"He already has control—somewhat—of the ferales, so what is he capturing now?" Liam straightened. "I'll wake Archer and Sera, see what else they remember from the glassworks. You get Nim. I want to know what else she found."

Jonah hesitated, and Liam rubbed his temple where the black lines of his *reven* curled around his eye. "Fine. You get Archer and Sera. I'll collect Nim after I get Jilly. She'll be furious if I leave her out."

As they separated to their tasks, Jonah wondered how the league leader had forged such a close bond with a woman as bold and independent as Jilly. The two—like Archer and Sera—were fitted as close as blade to fist.

He and Nim only raised sparks.

His knock at Archer's door went unanswered, so he called the other talya's cell and got a curt message to leave his number. "We have another hint to Corvus's location," he said. "Liam wants you."

Before he'd disconnected, a call was ringing through. He answered with, "Screening your calls?"

"Consider yourself lucky I had to piss, or I wouldn't be up at all."

"Where are you?"

"Had to get away for a day." Archer's voice lowered. "It's easier to keep Sera out of trouble if we're away."

Jonah wondered how far out in the *Shades of Gray* he'd have to take Nim. "Trouble is back."

Archer sighed. "And we will be too. Give us twenty minutes."

"Trouble isn't usually so accommodating."

"We'll be there in fifteen. Hold down the fort." Archer disconnected.

Jonah shook his head. Was that a vote of confidence

from the other talya? Considering they'd always circled each other warily, Archer's nihilism clashing with his own objective moralism, this might very well be the end of the world.

With heavy steps, he made his way to the lab. He slowed when he heard Nim's voice.

The grim and decidedly untrusting Archer trusted him, but his own talya mate did not. She had gone off alone to the tenebrae slaughterhouse rather than seek his help.

Even at half speed, his feet carried him close enough to hear her say, "So, Detective Ramirez said—"

"Wait," Liam interrupted. "There was a cop?"

"But we didn't tell him anything," Nim said quickly.

"We?" Liam's voice rose a notch.

"Me and Cyril Fane, the angel-man."

Jonah closed his eyes. She hadn't come to him, but she'd gone to the angelic possessed. And a cop too, apparently.

He stepped into the lab. Liam and Jilly were shaking their heads in sync, though he doubted they noticed, so aghast were their expressions.

"Nim," Jilly said. "You shouldn't mess with the sphericanum."

"It wasn't my idea," Nim protested. "He came here."

"What?" Liam's voice dropped to a rumble, with demon tones riding the lows. He whirled on Jonah. "Did you know about this?"

Nim took a step forward, bringing Liam back around. "He didn't."

Jonah didn't move, but he gave her a long look. "Do you think that sounds better for me that I didn't know?"

Her cheeks darkened, and she hunched her shoulders. "If you'd let me tell the story in order, it wouldn't sound so bad, because I'd get to the part where now we have a clue how to find Corvus."

Liam said nothing, so Jilly gave a curt, "Fine. Start at the beginning."

"I couldn't sleep," Nim said. "You know, since we haven't been *doing* anything, stuck here at the warehouse. So I got up. . . ."

By the time she'd finished explaining, with only a few more muffled exclamations from Liam, how she'd summoned the lost souls, located the shell fragment, distracted the detective, and taken the angelic possessed to a lingerie store—"So I'm pretty sure we're safe from the sphericanum hearing anything about this"—Archer and Sera had arrived.

The two other bonded pairs stared at her as if she'd sprouted a second head, one that was spouting insanity. Of course, the only reason she didn't have a second head was that she'd left Mobi upstairs. *After* she'd taken the snake on her adventure.

Jonah stiffened against the proof of how much she didn't want him as partner. But with Liam and Jilly and Archer and Sera eyeing her with such consternation, he had no choice but to step up beside her. "Moving on," he said. "What do we really have here?"

Nim murmured an almost inaudible "Thank you." He didn't respond.

Liam set two fingers against the *reven* at his temple and sighed. "I sent a message to the Beijing league. If anyone has archives deep enough to find a reference that might help, it's them. If anyone wants to help, that is."

Archer flipped the shell fragment in his hand. "You're right about it being turtle. I caught them all the time when I was a boy."

"A million years ago," Sera murmured. She tucked herself under his arm to peer at the shard. "When Corvus took me to the lair he was using in his solvo-dealing days, he had the glass bird sculptures, but nothing etched like this. The birds were really quite beautiful. This . . ."

Her finger hovered over the seam between shell and glass. "The way he's melded the demonically mutated husk with the glass is just odd."

"We know art holds the tenebrae at bay," Jilly said. "And we know Corvus wanted to be free of his djinni. Maybe he's building a trap."

Liam wrapped his fingers around the knot-work bracelet at her wrist and pulled her close. "A trick you taught him, perhaps?"

The sight of them, so synchronized, one to the other, stabbed through Jonah. He closed his eyes to focus on the task at hand. "Corvus might have believed tearing through the Veil would set the forces of hell directly against the gates of heaven and free him from his slavery to the djinni. But once he fell out of that high-rise where he took you"—he opened his eyes to look first at Sera, then at Archer—"because you pushed him out the window, the djinni took over what's left of him. And the djinni wouldn't be interested in containing the tenebrae."

"True," Sera said. "Since glass isn't a solid or a liquid, it has crossover properties that might have appealed to Corvus while he was messing with the Veil between the realms. Birnenston is a demonically altered form of hydrofluoric acid, which can etch glass. So maybe the ferales were just adding extra trash to their husks. Maybe it doesn't mean anything."

After a moment of silence, everyone mumbled disagreement.

"Yeah," Sera said. "I don't think that either."

"But it doesn't really matter why," Nim said. "All we care about is where." She glanced at Jonah as if for confirmation, yet her expression was uncertain.

What else was he supposed to care about? He crossed his arm over his chest. He felt like the fragment: half–hollow shell, half–brittle glass. "The djinn-man needs to fall. And stay fallen this time."

"You make it sound so easy," Archer muttered.

Nim dropped her gaze. "How much more do we need? Andre told us Corvus mentioned a float plane. Fane dug up the turtle shell. And Ramirez said the bodies were contaminated with a gnarly acid. How many places could we be talking about?"

Sera gave a wry shrug and tossed the shard toward her computer. Over the discordant clatter and chime as it hit the monitor, she mused, "We live in an industrial city on a lake. Let's see . . ."

"So look it up." Nim pointed her chin at the computer.

"What am I looking up? Demons and esoteric glasswork and apocalypse—oh, hell?"

"I was thinking float planes, turtles, and hydrofluoric acid," Nim said. "But don't exclude demons from the search."

Sera shook her head and crossed to the keyboard. "Right. Because Corvus Valerius is listed on Google. Besides that one Roman general, I mean." She muttered to herself as she typed. "More generic? 'Chicago airport' and 'industrial waste'? 'Turtles' can stay." She sat back abruptly. "I'd forgotten they talked about an airport at Lake Calumet."

"I remember," Jilly said. "I dated an environmental activist for a while who talked about saving the marshes there." She bumped her shoulder into Liam's. "You would've hated him."

"The feeling would've been mutual." The league leader folded his arms over his chest. "The area was used for illegal dumping for decades, and a few rotting ferales' carcasses might've been added to the pile on occasion."

"And now they're coming back to haunt us." Nim gestured at the glass fragment. "Well? Let's go check it out. What've we got to lose?"

Everyone looked at her.

She grimaced. "Oh, other than all that?"

"Tonight," Liam said. "When the others wake."

*   *   *

Under the thick, black sky, the lake was rippled glass. Tar and obsidian, Jonah thought, as he dragged in another humid breath. He let the breath out slowly as he stroked the oar silently through the water. Across the wide deck from him, Lex manned the second oar and matched his paddling. The pontoons weren't made for rowing, but they hadn't wanted to announce themselves with motors.

And, more important, the square, stable craft left room for fighting, should any ferales come winging out of the dark.

Behind him, the second boat they'd "borrowed" was equally silent as they explored the shoreline. Somewhere inland, two other teams poked through the wreckage of industry and the forest that had sprung up around it. But his cell phone, set to vibrate, was as stubbornly still as the woman at his side.

No one had been left behind tonight. He'd understood that to ask her otherwise was pointless. Despite her play at shamelessness, he knew she felt the guilty sting of losing the anklet. But if Corvus had holed up somewhere ahead . . .

The sweat that stained his shirt felt suddenly clammy and chilled.

Kneeling at the prow, Nim turned her head abruptly. Her eyes gleamed violet in the night, and his heart leapt in atavistic delight at the hunter's glow. "There," she whispered. "In that tower."

He followed her gaze. The grain elevator stood abandoned, ringed in a thicket of undergrowth. No terrestrial light shone there, but to his demon's eyes, a flicker of etheric disturbance shot across the single upper-story window and then vanished.

His phone twitched in his pocket. Sera texted from the boat behind them to all the talyan; she'd seen the demon sign too.

Perhaps it was nothing; a lone feralis ghosting through the empty building in pursuit of a sickly bat to add to its corporeal husk. Suddenly, he couldn't say which he wanted more: another false alarm or Corvus's crushed head on a pike.

His phone vibrated again. A call this time, conferenced to the rest of the teams. He tilted the phone so the other talyan could hear.

"We're just outside the fence around the elevator," Liam said. "The ground is littered with bones. And turtle shells. Jonah, you'll have to beach the boats. The dock looks completely rotted out." The league leader's voice deepened with satisfaction. "And if you'll direct your attention to the top floor, you'll notice the rusted-out skeleton of what appears to be a float plane."

Just as Andre had told them.

"Not getting much demon sign." Archer, from the second ground team, sounded disappointed. "If it is Corvus, he's gotten lazy and lonely."

"Then he'll love to see us," Jonah murmured.

Nim's violet gaze fixed on him, then shied away.

Liam's voice crackled. "If there's no etheric interference to distract him, the djinni will know we're coming. Let's move."

The flare of teshuva energy was certainly a giveaway, Jonah thought, but he couldn't contain the surge as he drove the boat through the water. The second boat, with Ecco and Nando at the oars, was right behind him.

The two pontoons hit the brushy shoreline in a burst of mud and murky stink. Jonah jabbed the oar into the muck and heaved the boat another length onto solid ground. The end of the oar clacked against his new cuff as he vaulted over the prow.

Despite his speed, Nim was already ahead of him, half-lost among the rushes. He couldn't call out to her without giving away their location.

As he raced after her, he fumbled over his shoulder

for the executioner's sword strapped against his spine. He hadn't had time to practice the move, to smooth out the reach and grab, much less the twist and latch that locked the blade to his cuff. The metal cuff that Liam had made laced ingeniously up his forearm to his shoulder, like some bizarre cyborg warrior.

He hadn't even swung the sword yet.

Off to his right and a little ahead, Ecco stumbled and swore. Jonah swept past him. Maybe he'd keep the big talya on his right, and if his first practice swing accidentally took off anybody's head . . .

The teshuva rose in him, tightening his muscles, sharpening every hazy, starlit glimmer of grass. He vaulted over a fifty-gallon drum rusting in the weeds and landed with a crunch of old bone. Nim was only a step ahead of him.

From the water, the grain elevator had looked surrounded by overgrowth. But an unnatural clearing spread from the base of the tower to a chain-link fence on the outskirts. The fencing rattled as, somewhere along its length, the first talyan went over.

Nim hit the fence at a dead run. Clad in black from head to foot, she was a shadow against the dark sky. He jumped beside her, hooked the top curve of the sword over the upper rim of the fence, and yanked himself over. To his relief, the blade didn't detach from the cuff, nor the cuff from his arm. And, even more of a relief, now he was ahead of her.

She'd already made it clear she had no qualms about confronting Corvus on her own. He'd make sure she didn't get that chance again.

From the inland side, a dozen talyan converged on the tower, Liam in the lead. He charged across the clearing like a human—human plus demon—battering ram. The hammer shone in a gleaming arc over his head. And he brought it crashing down against the door.

Jonah could've sworn they'd decided on something not quite full frontal, but maybe he'd missed an IM.

With one entrance and the risk of bottlenecking, they had only the element of surprise to get enough of them in the door. So he was right on Liam's heels, with the rest of the talyan breathing down his neck.

Which didn't give any of them a chance to appreciate Corvus's redecorating before the salambes descended in attack, and their flame-bright ether lit the interior like walking into a lava lamp of doom. Nim would appreciate the comparison.

Assuming they survived.

CHAPTER 23

Nim swore as Jonah passed her at the fence. He'd taken the newly adapted sword from Liam earlier in the night and hadn't even acknowledged her when she suggested he give it a whirl before they went out.

He could lose his head with a crappy attitude like that.

What a terrible time to realize she wanted to keep him just the way he was. She was done with dancing alone.

The stream of oversized male talyan flowed into the grain elevator, forcing her to pause as the doorway swallowed him. Her pulse ratcheted to painful intensity. Simply losing sight of him was bad enough.

She stared up. The elevator loomed above her. At the very top, black against the haze of distant city lights, the wings and floats of the half-dismantled plane perched like a weathervane.

Archer rocked to a stop beside her. "Are you armed this time?"

She lifted the African throwing knife she'd picked out. With its uniquely asymmetrical four-pronged design, and every prong sharpened to a wicked edge, she didn't even need to aim.

Archer nodded. "Stay out here with my defensive team."

"Jonah's inside. He needs me." She knew she didn't have to say more.

After a heartbeat, Archer nodded toward the tower. "Go, then. And don't get dead."

She didn't bother rolling her eyes. She just returned the nod and ran for the doorway where the last talyan had disappeared inside. She crossed the threshold, and for a second, her world upended.

Ecco had explained how he neutralized and contained malice in etherically altered glass capped with foil blessed by an angelic possessed. No wonder they hadn't sensed an overwhelming presence of tenebrae; Corvus had made the entire wooden tower into a blessed—or in this case, damned—bottle.

The ravaged interior still showed the bracing structures of the five-story vertical bins where grain had been stored, but the walls had been mostly torn away. What was left was honeycombed but asymmetrical, like a misshapen beehive.

And everything had been sheeted in etched glass.

Nim almost staggered under her teshuva's disorientation against the reflected and distorted emanations of the tenebrae trapped behind glass. This was how Jonah must feel every day with his demon's flow disrupted.

The thought of him straightened her. Where had he gone?

The combined force of the teshuva energy had created a protective no-fly zone over the gathered talyan, but a cloud of salambes hovered just above. Their virulent glow lit the glass as if someone had set the world on fire. And Jonah's blond hair gleamed like gold.

Nim couldn't help but hunch her shoulders as she raced toward him. Good thing she'd worn her sneakers; even the roughly planked flooring underfoot was coated with glass.

She called his name, but the sound was lost in the chime of shattering glass as a feralis—no, not one, but a handful, then dozens—began to break free of the walls.

And the floor. The slick glass heaved under her feet, and she fell to her knees. A half-shelled feralis—she recognized the patterns from the fragment from the club, but the rest was bony protuberances like fish bones—reared up over her. Whatever lock of energies had kept the tenebrae confined had been broken by the teshuva's arrival.

As the other ferales rose, leaving monster-sized graves behind in the glass, she found herself reluctant to actually throw away her throwing knife. Keeping her pointy treasures close seemed suddenly wiser.

From her prone position, she kicked at the feralis. It went down in a tumble, squat legs waving in the air. Ha—certain advantages in fighting a mutated-turtle enemy. Once they were flipped over—

The feralis heaved itself to its spiny side and whirled to slice at her with snapping turtle jaws.

The disadvantages of fighting a mutated half turtle. She lashed out with the knife to force it away. It reared back, exposing the leathery folds of its neck embedded with glass pebbles. . . .

She struck with all the teshuva's force. The knife bit deep, past the first and second prongs, buried to the third. She yanked back and rolled away from the fountain of black ichor. Splinters of glass ground into her palms.

The feralis wasn't going anywhere and she didn't have time to neutralize its emanations. She'd lost Jonah in the melee as the talyan engaged the ferales. The uproar of clashing energies had allowed the salambes to descend, like saber-toothed vultures, and the ruined glass walls glinted crazily.

"Corvus Valerius!"

She heard the shout, though she couldn't see the

shouter. But she felt the surge of demonic energy as the talyan focused.

There was Jonah! He was already running for the stairs, in a pack with five other talyan. Of course, Corvus wouldn't be hanging here with the rabble. If anywhere, he'd be in the cupola at the top of the tower.

She blew past the remaining talyan. Ecco shouted at her, but she didn't hesitate. She tagged behind Haji and hit the stairs with Jonah's group before she thought how this probably wasn't what Archer had meant by "Don't get dead."

Of course, he'd let her go, so he must've known that, dead or deadly, she had to be with Jonah.

The stairs had been built against the exterior wall. With the interior gutted, the steps clung precariously over the open center. A few treads were missing, and she almost plummeted through one gap as Haji, just ahead of her, cleared the opening with typical talya grace.

Locked in the glass prison, the demons had gone mad. The salambes dove at them as they climbed. In their spiraling frenzy, the salambes shredded trailing sparks that rained down on the talyan below like party streamers on fire. Their hunger beat against Nim's awareness and licked in to taste her fear.

She gripped the ichor-stained knife and plunged upward.

Under her hand, braced against the outer wall, the tower quivered. Had the inner coating of glass been the only thing holding up the old wood? A hysterical laugh threatened, and she realized she wasn't much better. A sharp and deadly gleam hiding rot. Jonah should be thankful she hadn't returned his love. At least not aloud.

A stair crumbled under her foot and only a desperate push launched her to the next step. The talyan ahead of her raced on.

If she'd fallen, none would have noticed. Unless, of

course, she landed on someone five stories down. Her
stomach heaved. Been there; done that. Not fun.

A smash from above brought her attention upward.
Jonah had reached the upper landing, just big enough
for one man. The door ran with rippled glass. Corvus obviously hadn't wanted the tenebrae to come knocking.

Unfortunately for him, the teshuva weren't so polite.

With another blow from the sword, Jonah cracked
through the glass. Then he rammed his shoulder against
the door. So much for his lock finessing.

The wood crumbled before him and he disappeared
inside.

"Not again," she muttered.

The other talyan were right behind him, and Nim
sped upward as the stairs behind her flaked away with
the shivering tower.

There was no going back now.

She caromed through the doorway.

Into a seething black wall of malice.

She should've wondered where they all were. No
gathering of tenebrae was complete without festive red
malice eyeballs. Or maybe she meant "festering."

In a way, malice were scarier than ferales. She could
lop off the head of a feralis and disable its corporeal
husk. Malice were cockroach quick, but there was nothing to swing at, just a creeping chill that turned her blood
to ice and her teshuva to frozen Jell-O.

Despite the seeping pain, she struggled forward. The
cupola wasn't that big. The talyan couldn't have gone
too far, although the blinding malice swarm gave her
the eerie sensation that she could step through a hole in
the floor and plummet, sliced and diced by the spears of
glass lining the walls all the way down.

She didn't think that would end as well as the last
time she'd fallen, when she'd ended up in Jonah's arms.

As if her thoughts had conjured them, heavy arms
wrapped around her from behind.

Arms, as in two. Thickly lined with virulent yellow *reven*. Nobody she knew well enough for such a friendly hug.

With a shout, she dropped into a crouch. The abrupt move broke the grasp. She swept one leg out behind her and whirled at the same time, the throwing knife biting through the air.

Air was all she hit as the man who'd grabbed her leapt straight up.

He hovered unnaturally aloft for longer than was possible, and her teshuva-aided vision registered a poison-yellow fog, vaguely human-shaped, around him. The djinni. It had jerked him out of the way of her blow and held him suspended an extra moment, like a toy dangling out of her reach.

Corvus landed lightly on his feet, but his wayward eyeball jolted unpleasantly in his skull, loose as a baby-blue marble. The sulfur gleam in the other eye, though, sent the last erg of her teshuva bravery scuttling for deep cover.

She felt utterly alone.

He waved one hand with obvious irritation, and the malice smog lifted slightly. Around his thick wrist, links of rough chain cut into his skin. A large bead pressed against his pulse point, and the design incised into the dull silver glinted at her.

Her anklet. The key to her teshuva's most potent trick.

"The Naughty Nymphette." His voice rumbled, to match that shaved bullet head and thick features. "Finally."

She braced her fingers against the floor, balancing her weight, and tightened her grip on the knife. All four honed prongs glinted at the corner of her gaze.

And didn't give her any sense of conviction at all. Where were Haji and the other talyan? Where was Jonah?

"If I keep you talking, will you not kill me?" she wondered.

"Why would I kill you, sister mine?"

"I'm an only child. Anyway, I'm fairly certain my mother wouldn't claim you. Sorry." Maybe she shouldn't piss him off. "My dad, though . . ."

Corvus shook his head. The human eye locked on her for a moment before it lost direction again. "Soul siblings." He smiled and held out his hands. His *reven* had cracked and oozed down both arms. The human skin around the tracings blistered and smoked. "I am your brother-in-arms."

"I have all the arms I need," she muttered.

But Jonah might be lying injured only steps away and she wouldn't know. And couldn't do anything. Unless she got that anklet.

"Well," she stalled. She shifted her weight to her thighs. Was she fast enough to spring past him? And could she bring herself to lop off his arm to snag the anklet? She thought yes on the lopping. As for the speed . . . She coughed to disguise a hysterical laugh. "Most of my routines are solo, but if you're interested in the life, I know some male revues."

His jaundice-tinged eye contracted. "No more of your men, Nymphette. I find myself quite tired of them." His voice shifted, lighter than before. "You and I, though, together we could free ourselves of those who have sought to master us all our lives."

Who was talking to her? The djinni escaped from hell? Or the gladiator who'd been tossed from the Colosseum with two broken arms and a demon hunting him? Or had the two joined forces for this rogue rampage against the respectable battle between good and evil?

She kind of understood where he was coming from.

He—whichever he was—must have seen some weakening in her eyes, because he took a step closer.

But, really, just because she knew he was right didn't mean she was going to listen.

Quick as Mobi lashing after a rat, she sprang toward him. The longest prong of the knife scored his chest, but the yellow fog was quicker. The djinni yanked Corvus away, and she flailed past him.

On the plus side, she stumbled into the malice cloud and lost sight of him. On the minus side, she stumbled into the malice cloud and lost sight of him.

The wretched, sucking pain and despair of the engulfing malice was like the worst flu and the worst hangover and the worst night of senseless channel surfing ever. With the teshuva too overwhelmed by the tenebrae energy to fight back, she went to her knees. But she'd spent many a night crawling through bad hangovers, so she wasn't going to give in to a bunch of etheric pests. Below her clenched hands, even the floor—the only malice-free thing she could see—was starting to gray as her vision dimmed. The edges of the knife glimmered and faded.

Was she really going to die for nothing, killed by nothing? Appropriate, when she'd always been nothing.

Wait, she didn't think that. Her rapist had whispered that she had nothing to cry about. Her mother had told her she mustn't speak. Her father had looked away as if she'd disappeared.

But she wasn't nothing. Not anymore.

"Don't touch," she snarled.

She drew herself into a crouch and lashed out with the knife. There was nothing to strike, but the teshuva surged in her muscles, revived now that she was away from the djinni's overwhelming energy. The malice recoiled in a wave, not from the knife, she knew, but from her demon.

She stood, wavered a little, and locked her knees.

"Ah, Nymphette." Corvus's rumbling voice seemed to come from all around, and the malice swirled in agitated funnel clouds. "You wound me. Not literally, of course. You tried to take my arm off."

"I want my anklet back." No point trying to hide from him. He could clear the malice with one burst of djinni power. And clear her teshuva again too.

"And it would look lovely against your tawny hide."

"What? You're going to skin me for a rug?" Could she sneak around through the malice fog, come up behind him, and commence with the aforementioned lopping?

"Don't tease," he chided. "I've no use for those I can walk over. Not anymore. The battle has progressed too far for pawns to carry the banner any farther."

"Good news for the pawns." She crept to her right, toward the voice, knife at the ready.

"It would be, were any still standing. Unlike you."

"I'm not a pawn."

"Not anymore." Between one blink and the next, Corvus emerged from the malice cloud bank, and she bit back a gasp. The knife wavered in her hand. He seemed unfazed by the point aimed at him, skimmed in his still-human blood. "Aren't you tired of dancing for your masters, Nymphette?"

With the teshuva's strength sputtering, the weight of the knife pulled at her arm. "They were never my masters."

Now Corvus was sneering. Jonah had doubted her too. And the teshuva, cowering somewhere behind her navel or something, obviously didn't think she could pull this off.

Like she'd once taunted wallets out of the back pockets of the jaded, cheap bastards at the Shimmy Shack, she focused every nerve and muscle toward a single point. Or four points, in this case. She hauled back and let fly with the knife. The four prongs whirled into one glimmering circle of death.

And sank into Corvus's chest through his raggedy-man clothes, crisscrossing the shallow slash she'd landed earlier.

Both of Corvus's eyes focused on her with malevolent intent.

Empty-handed, she felt way more naked than she'd ever felt with all her clothes off. In retrospect, disarming herself might not have been the smartest move. But since when did she ever look back?

She spun on her heel and fled toward the malice darkness. No quipping now; Corvus's heels on the wooden floor behind her pounded out a rhythm of doom. The fury of the djinni was like an inferno at her spine. She wasn't going to make it.

Through the tenebrae blackness, pockmarked with the stark crimson of malice eyes, a glint of gold shone.

Nim cried out as a blade pierced the shadows; then Jonah emerged a heartbeat behind.

Jonah had heard her voice, and the malice-evoked memories that had paralyzed him—memories where the jungle darkness had never lifted, where he'd never walked out—lifted at the sound.

And he saw her with Corvus Valerius hard on her heels, the djinni's venomous form reaching ahead to snag her.

The teshuva in him hesitated in the face of such unrelenting evil. But he'd stopped relying on the teshuva. So he stepped forward into the fight without a second thought for his doubtful demon.

Nim shouted his name, her eyes bright with fear and, he thought, delight. Well, he'd be glad to see the long reach of the executioner's sword too, if he were empty-handed.

He swung, knowing he wouldn't connect, knowing too that Corvus's djinni would instinctively remove his body from danger, and give Nim a heartbeat to escape.

"Go," he told her.

Of course, she made no such attempt. Instead, she slowed and, incredibly, turned back.

He swung again. He'd already discovered that the sword, cleverly fitted though it was, was no substitute for his arm. The wrist cuff didn't bend, and his entire body was forced to follow through with the blow. A strange dance of power and momentum and vulnerability. A death dance. But who would die?

Nim, the bold and ungrateful wench, darted back in. Even as the djinni was jerking Corvus away from Jonah's third swing, Nim leapt in from the side. She grabbed at the gladiator, and Jonah's heart curdled as he pulled back from another attack. What was she—?

Then the chain looped around the djinn-man's wrist caught a flash of light.

She'd found the anklet.

Corvus lashed out with one birnenston-laced arm. The anklet gleamed. He backhanded Nim and slammed her across the room. She hit the wall in an arc of blood and crumpled.

Corvus's roar tore through the malice cloud and the tower shuddered, sending Jonah to his knees. One of the rotted beams buckled beside his hand, and he rolled away from the sudden fissure that went five stories down.

The malice scattered toward the high corners of the cupola. As they lifted, he caught a glimpse of the other talyan whose teshuva had been overcome by the sheer chaotic energy of the massed tenebrae. Nando pushed upright and gave Lex a hand up, the malice malaise rapidly clearing from their eyes.

Jonah thought that if he could keep the djinni occupied long enough for the other talyan to recover, to take back the anklet, while he went for Nim . . . He lunged at Corvus.

Corvus ducked. As he spun away, he wrenched up

two floorboards, one for each hand. Nails squealed free from the decayed wood. He wielded the two makeshift maces over his head, and the nails glinted like snaggle fangs.

"You talyan should have killed me when you had the chance," he said. "Or, I should say, chances."

"We tried. A good-faith attempt." Jonah circled the hole in the floor, now three boards wide. The glass beneath the open space shimmered in the corner of his eye. Worse, a chill breath circled into the cupola. Somewhere below, the other women were piercing the Veil. And the demon realm was responding with its cold sigh. "Since you ask nicely, we're willing to take another shot."

Corvus tsked and shook his head. His blue eye drifted. "Too late. The djinni has made other plans."

"How is hiding in the top of your pretty tower a plan?"

Corvus spat. Birnenston sizzled on the planks between his feet. "It works for heaven."

Jonah cursed himself for engaging in repartee with a djinni-possessed man who'd left half his gray matter splattered across a sidewalk the first time they'd met. He vaulted across the hole in the floor, the downward whistle of the blade his only response.

Corvus met the blade with his board. The sword sheared through the wood.

Too easily. Jonah stumbled behind the swing, all his weight canted forward.

With a nasty chuckle, Corvus cracked the shortened board upward. He caught Jonah hard under the chin.

Jonah's head snapped back. For an instant, he lost track of up and down as his feet went over his head.

But he'd already seen Lex and Nando right behind Corvus.

He might have felt more gleeful, except he knew the hole was behind him somewhere.

He scrabbled at the rotted wood that crumbled under

his fingers until he finally caught himself. He shoved to his feet, staggered one step as his ringing brain caught up with the new direction.

Lex had Corvus in a half nelson, the anklet-bound arm flailing, while Nando moved in for the kill.

Not that any talya had ever killed a djinn-man before.

Corvus bellowed, but the sound held more fury than fear. The demon marks on his arms wept birnenston, and Lex's face was cramped with the effort of keeping his grip. Jonah knew the other man's teshuva must be faltering from the etheric toxin.

The djinni thinned to a yellow mist that choked the air with the stench of rotting eggs.

Was it trying to escape? Without a soul in Corvus's husk to anchor it, Jonah knew that nothing prevented the demon from leaving. No wonder it had no fear.

The mist unfurled in a graceful, almost lazy spiral. Like when he and Nim had danced on the *Shades of Gray* and he'd spun her out to the length of their extended arms.

And then he'd whirled her back into his grasp, and the shock of her hitting his chest had nearly stopped his heart.

The djinni's outward expansion slowed, stopped. Reversed.

"Nando, Lex, get down," he cried. "Get down!"

The emanations snapped back into Corvus's body, and the sudden compression of demonic energy in a confined space released a detonation of toxic ether. Weakened with age and neglect and the seeping battle stains, the cupola began to buckle.

The wall closest behind the djinn-man exploded in the damp stink of old wood. Malice circled, seeking escape, frenetic streamers of ether staining the air as the night poured in.

At its epicenter, the *reven* on Corvus's arms burst with poison like a backed-up sewer. The beams around

his feet groaned and sagged. His hulking body staggered
but did not fall.

The talyan were not so lucky. Lex and Nando tumbled backward like a pair of dice. Lex went over the
edge where the wall had been, with only Nando's shout
to mark his fall. The talya reached for his disappeared
comrade. And then the malice sprang loose.

The second shock wave hit Nando and knocked him
into the darkness after Lex, a split second before the
force slammed into Jonah.

Again he clutched for some hold as he spun across
the floor. But this time his fingers found only open air.

The hungry tongue of the tenebraeternum wind
swirled up through the riddled floor and sucked him
down.

CHAPTER 24

Nim came to with a hundred malice streaming by, their frenetic screams slicing by her like a thousand paper cuts. The wall beside her was half-gone, and the city on the horizon fuzzed and crackled with bad reception. She blinked hard, and the teshuva snapped everything into focus.

She bolted to her feet and tried to catch her balance. But the tower swayed under her. Not her demon slacking off; the whole thing was going to crumble. "Jonah!"

She was alone.

"Nim!"

Not alone.

Wedged sideways in a gaping hole in the floor, the executioner's sword glinted. Jonah had managed to hook his elbow over the floorboard. Only the oversized length of the sword had kept him from a long plummet down the glass-lined gullet of the abandoned bins.

She ran to him, stepping lightly on the patchwork beams.

He hung suspended. His legs swung above the four-story drop. Below him, the mad swirl of the battle reflected a million times in the facets of shimmering, shattered glass.

She flung herself down beside the hole to hook her elbow under his armpit. "Can you get a grip with your other hand?"

"It's rotting from the inside." He looked up at her. "Get out."

"Do you know me at all?"

Despite his precarious position, he grinned fiercely. "I wanted to make sure you'd stay."

She snorted. "Just reach up on the other side so you don't crack the boards under me."

The wood pulped under his fingers, and the tower seemed to list farther with every handful that tore free. Glass chimed as it fell, and she shuddered at a scream from below. Talyan or tenebrae? She couldn't be sure, but something desperate and hurting.

With her counterweight, he swung one leg up through the hole. Even as the planks disintegrated, he heaved himself toward her. She pulled back, narrowly avoided yanking them both down another fissure opening in the floor, and dragged him away from the gaping center. The flooring around the outer edge seemed sturdier; at least it held their weight for the moment.

"Where are—?" She bit off the rest of the question in horror when Jonah shook his head.

"We have to get out of here." He rose, pulling her to her feet. "If the building comes down with us inside, we'll be minced."

"The stairs peeled off the walls behind me," she said. "We're not getting out that way."

"So where'd Corvus go?"

They both looked up.

Side by side, they raced to the gaping wall of the cupola. Attached to the outside, a ladder went up.

"Not down," Nim noted sadly.

"Climb," Jonah said. He started up.

He'd made it only halfway when dark wings launched over their heads.

It was Corvus, suspended below the wings of the float plane. The skeletonized cockpit was a steel death trap around him, but the wings held just enough glide to descend.

The tower listed again. It was going down. And so were they, one way or another.

Below them, indecipherable figures streamed from the doorway.

"Nim, follow me." Jonah leapt for the fleeing Corvus, the executioner's sword outstretched.

She hesitated for less than a heartbeat, and launched herself after him, thigh muscles screaming, though her throat was locked.

She caught his waist, heard the demonic screech of metal on metal as the blade scraped on the broken tail of the plane.

The blade skittered, then bit deep. Jonah reached for her shoulders to pull her up his body.

"Grab the fucking plane," she shrieked.

"Don't curse," he reminded her. He heaved himself higher on the tail section, dragging her with him.

The plane listed sideways, its glide severely hampered by extra weight.

Behind them, the wood of the tower groaned and snapped. The chime of glass rose above it in crescendoing destruction.

The building gained speed as it collapsed, aiming right at them. They weren't going to get clear of its shadow.

Corvus roared, and his djinni pulsed with a nuclear–mushroom cloud fury. But suspended in the darkness, there was nothing to rage against.

The cupola they'd moments ago escaped raced at them, smashing into the tail section. The planks crashed around Nim, knocking her free. Jonah cried her name, reached back for her. The sword wrenched loose.

And they were falling.

But not far enough even to scream. Nim hit the brush

in a bruising tangle, rolled, slammed into Jonah. He grabbed her close and threw himself over her as the cupola boomed and splintered all around.

They lay in a daze, limbs entwined. Not just their limbs, but tree limbs. Carefully, Nim straightened. Nothing broken. Other than the tree. And the tower. And Corvus?

She stiffened, gaze darting. Even with the teshuva on high alert, she couldn't distinguish the rusted metal outline of the plane. How much farther had it gone?

"Nim?" Jonah's hands were all over her.

She batted him away. "I'm fine. You?"

"There's blood on your face." He cupped her jaw. "It shines to the demon."

She winced as his thumb brushed the cut on her cheek where Corvus had backhanded her. The tenebrae-flustered teshuva had been slow to seal the wound. But she couldn't push Jonah away again. She leaned into his touch. "That was crazy."

"We're down," he pointed out. "And alive."

"And everyone else?"

He didn't answer, but rose and held his hand out to her.

If the wreckage of the industrial site had been Superfund-worthy before, it was positively apocalyptic now. Wood and glass crunched under their steps as they circled the crash site.

In the debris, they found Nando.

His gaze was fixed upward toward the black sky, no demon violet, no human spark. Nim stumbled to her knees in grief. Glass stung her palms in a hot flush of pain.

She flinched from Jonah's hand on her shoulder. "If you say he's in a better place, I'll punch you."

"At least he's not here."

She glared up at him and clenched her fists, driving glass shards deep. At least that explained the tears that clouded her vision.

"Jonah, Nim." With his black clothes, Liam was a shadow in the night, except for the twinkling flecks of glass in his dark hair and the rampant *reven* at his temple. His pupils, blown wide with the teshuva, glowed. "We couldn't come after you. The stairs . . ."

"I know," Jonah said. "Nando . . ."

"I know," Jilly echoed as she walked up beside the league leader.

In silence, they assembled.

"Lex is missing," Sera said. "Also Marc, Argus, and Haji."

"I found Lex," Ecco said. He didn't have to say more.

"Start digging," Archer said. Sera nodded. "Crush injuries or lacerations will be bad enough, but the amount of birnenston that was sealed in the glass chambers will be fatal if we can't find them soon. And the tenebrae could be drawn to the pain."

Someone asked, "Corvus?"

Jonah's voice was monotone, the demon harmonics threaded into one livid tone. "Gone."

They started digging.

With improvised shovels torn from fifty-gallon drums, they managed to keep their fingers attached. Still, blood ran in slick rivulets from Nim's hands and wrists, and her grip on the scoop kept slipping and she kept swearing. Jonah, bent to his own search a few yards away, said nothing and never looked up.

She dug and bled, and the teshuva healed her, slower and slower as the birnenston poison sapped its coherence, and so she bled some more.

They found Marc and Argus, dead. Haji they pulled from the ruins just as dawn's gleam brightened the lake.

The talya was sliced head to foot, his blood a congealed pool brimming the glass depression in the remains of the elevator floor. "I tripped," he mumbled with woozy incoherence. He touched the back of his head where he'd obviously knocked himself unconscious—

and nearly scalped himself—when he fell into the sharp-edged pit. "I never trip."

Sera bumped his hand away. "Don't touch."

The words, the echo of her old life, sent claws down Nim's spine. Her selfish cluelessness had led directly to this moment. She'd sold the anklet, never thinking, never caring.

Not knowing, she tried to remind herself. But in the devastation, the guilt clung dank and thick as river mud.

Four dead, and she'd barely known their names, when the league needed every man and woman it had.

Well, not every woman.

She staggered away from the destruction. Others had taken breaks away from the birnenston to give their teshuva a chance to refresh, so no one paid attention. Thankfully, the tenebrae that had escaped their glass enclosure hadn't returned, though the anguish must have been tempting. Despite their much-vaunted control over their emotions, the talyan almost shimmered with the waves of their fury and grief.

Maybe the pain was so bad even the malice wanted no part of it.

Maybe the malice were smarter than her.

Not far beyond the scattered glass and wood, she found the crumpled remnants of the float-plane wings. She swayed, dripping blood from her fingertips. The divot she and Jonah had kicked up where they hit the ground looked like a shallow grave.

No Corvus, of course. But, really, even if she returned now with her anklet in hand, or around her ankle, actually, could she redeem the talyan sacrifice?

Was this how Jonah had felt when he lost his hand?

To live and fight was to salvage their souls. Anything else—even death itself—was unacceptable. At least she understood him now.

Now that it was too late.

A yellow glimmer caught her gaze, and the first ray

of sunlight filtered through the trees just as Corvus stepped into view.

"Come to me, alone, tonight," he said. "I have no fight with your friends."

Jonah had told her and told her not to scream or swear. So for once, she took his advice and just stared at Corvus with numb fatigue. "Can't you just kill me here?"

His smile was as gentle as sinking into deep water when the last breath was gone. "No."

"Nim!"

She turned her sun-blinded eyes—damn it, were those tears again?—toward Jonah's call.

He bounded out of the woods, someone's borrowed spear half raised in his good hand. Since it was only half raised, he must not have seen Corvus. But his blue eyes were narrowed in suspicion, so she wasn't entirely off the hook.

She smiled grimly to herself. Off the hook? Oh, she so wasn't off the hook.

Jonah was beyond wrecked, she knew, that he took her smile at face value and let the sword drop to his side. "Don't sneak off."

"I didn't get far." She thought she shouldn't bother denying the "sneak" part. "Just wanted to marvel at our miraculous survival."

He prodded the ruined wings with the butt of the spear. "Too bad Corvus survived too."

"Yeah. And took the anklet with him."

"We'll get it back." He wasn't so weary that he didn't recognize the incredulous look she shot him. He shrugged one shoulder. "We must."

No matter what. If she wanted to marvel, here was another opportunity. Not a miracle, but horror. After what had just happened, he was ready to go again. If Corvus walked out from between the trees, Jonah would fight.

She spun on her heel and strode toward the other

talyan. The prickle of tiny hairs rising on the back of her neck spread down both arms. Corvus was watching them go. He wanted her alone.

Well, hadn't she always been that? Until Jonah.

She kept her pace brisk until they cleared the knot of trees, then slowed to match her steps to his. "Thanks for saving my ass."

"Thanks for saving mine."

"Remember you said that," she murmured.

The talyan were draining the last of the ferales they'd incapacitated during the fight. As the orange caution lights went out in the snapping-turtle eyes, the husks clattered apart.

"Ashes to dust to mud." Sera flung down the last husk. It shattered in a spray of shell and bone and glass shards. "And gone."

Archer touched the small of her back, and she whirled with demon speed. Nim took a worried breath, but the other woman threw herself into her mate's arms.

Across the clearing, Ecco ripped apart the chain-link fence. Four white-bound forms lay in the grass, and Nim averted her gaze as the talyan lifted their dead brethren with gentle strength. Haji looked almost as white as they helped him into the truck, their encouraging whispers too soft for her demon to hear.

"Don't," Jonah said softly.

"Don't what?" Don't curse. Don't scream. Don't touch. Don't die.

"You're thinking that it should've been you."

She tried to make her face as smooth as glass, but there wasn't much inspiration in the rubble. Inside, she felt as torn. "You can't read my mind."

"Not even necessary, since everyone here feels the same."

"It wasn't their fuckup, losing the anklet."

"You're part of the league now. Fuckup for one, fuckup for all." His weary smile invited her to tease him.

She couldn't. They had made her one of them—one for all—and look what had happened to them.

Demon possessed they might be, and doomed to fight from the shadows, but they had twisted their darkness into something that looked a helluva lot like light. And love.

If only she could have seen that earlier. If only she could have seen it in herself.

When she didn't answer, Jonah's smile turned brittle, but he reached for her and drew her into his arms. "After I lost my hand, I thought I had nothing more to offer. I thought I'd never be anything but an ugly reminder. But I was wrong." He pulled away a little to look down at her. "I won't say you're my reason for living. I won't burden you with that again. But you make living . . . good." He kissed her temple, and his gentleness—more shattering than anything else that night—made her close her eyes. "We'll get through this."

"I know you will." She'd make damn sure of that.

CHAPTER 25

In the end, she didn't even have to be particularly sneaky.

Jonah, Jilly, and a handful of others had volunteered to take the fallen talyan to the league's burial ground down south.

"It's quiet down there, empty," he told Nim from the shower. "No people means no tenebrae. Just grass and sky."

She sat on the tile floor, her arms wrapped around her knees. She'd lost the impetus to unlace her mud-soaked sneakers. This was the last straw for them, she decided morosely. Even though the canvas was black, the filth was so ingrained, the shoes couldn't be saved. "How long will you be gone?"

"Just for the day. It's a long drive, but we'll come right back. One promise we make is to bury the dead before the decades of immortality catch up with the corpse. And then we carry on the fight."

When she didn't answer, he poked his head out around the curtain. "Get in while the water's hot. I won't bother you."

"I don't mind being hot and bothered." She gave up on the laces and toed off the shoes before stripping. She slid into the shower next to him. "If you're not still mad at me for going with Fane."

"I'm furious." But his hand smoothing lather over her shoulder belied his words. "Just don't do it again."

She rested her forehead against his chest. "I won't go anywhere with the angel-man," she promised. How easy was that?

He took a small step back, as far as the shower allowed, and tipped her head up to stare into her eyes.

Oops, had she sounded too accommodating?

But his gaze was soft. "Are you still mad at me?"

"For what?"

"For being an idiot?"

"Oh. Well, if I held that against every man ..."

"Not every man. Me." He brushed his thumb along her bottom lip. "I want to be your only man."

"You are," she whispered.

"I want you, Nim, as I've never wanted anything. Not for the fight, not for the teshuva or myself. For you. I love you."

Slowly, as if he wanted her to have time to object, he lowered his head to replace the touch of his hand with his lips. He slicked his fingers through her hair and tipped her head back to kiss her neck. "I'd give the rest of myself, all my words of love, everything I am, for you."

She closed her eyes as the water beaded along her lashes.

He knelt, streaming kisses down between her breasts to her belly. He spanned the small of her back, eased her toward his mouth to kiss her navel. "I'd give my other hand, my life, my soul, for you."

"Just give me this."

"Always." He traced the lines of her *reven* with his tongue, and his kiss slipped lower yet.

He brought her to climax against the wall of the shower, eased into her, and rocked her hard until she came again. Then he kissed her gently once more. "I'll see you tonight. Maybe we can go out in the boat. Far out." And he left her standing there.

The water had turned to ice before she stopped crying.

She left a note on Mobi's tank: *Rats are in the fridge. Label says "yogurt" so Ecco won't eat it.* She added a smiley face, which looked really lame, considering he'd be reading the note because she was dead. So she sketched the smiley into a heart. Then she just ripped off that part of the paper and tossed it in the trash.

What he'd said in the shower . . . He knew her in ways no one else ever had. He'd touched her when that had been the one thing she'd forbidden.

Now she remembered why. A touch could hurt. And it hurt worse when the touch was gone.

She left her hopelessly disgusting sneakers in the bathroom, found the strappy new heels she'd bought with an angel's money, and teetered down the silent hall on her toes so the heels wouldn't click.

She'd made it as far as the front door.

"Going somewhere?"

She stopped, pivoted slowly, not to be coy but because the five-inch spikes prevented anything else. "Out."

Ecco appeared from behind one of the columns supporting the inner walls. Walls, she knew, that had been cross-braced the last time the league had confronted Corvus and almost lost. The big talya swept her with a rude gaze. "Nice shoes."

"Thanks. They don't come in a size eleven."

He smiled, sharp as his missing gauntlets. "Size fifteen, sugar."

She didn't think she could take Ecco, even without his gauntlets. She didn't *want* to take him on. If she never saw another single drop of talya blood . . . She tossed her head, wishing she had the dreads to lash around. "I'm meeting Jonah later." There. That would explain the sandals and shut the man up.

She gestured at the box in his arms. "Moving out?" She managed to infuse it with the tone that said, *Running away?* Insults would make him glad to see her go.

"Leftovers from last night," he said. "Sera wanted to run some experiments. She thinks Corvus was up to something superbad."

"No doubt," Nim muttered.

"Worse than usual. Tenebrae, encased in glass . . ." He shook his head. "Strange way to keep them fresh."

"I'm sure Sera will figure it out," Nim said. "If you'd take her the stuff sometime this century."

Ecco's gaze fixed on her again. "We've got forever."

Not necessarily. Corvus had said "tonight." "Trust me, us female talya aren't that patient."

Ecco snorted. "Seems to me you girls put up with far too much."

"Don't worry," she said softly. "Someone will find you one day."

His face tightened. The broken glass chimed in the box under his grip. He turned on his heel and left.

That had been almost too easy. A man rocking gauntlets shouldn't wear his heart on his sleeve.

The heat tried to flatten her as she stepped out onto the street. Luckily, her spiky heels kept her upright. A passing truck driver honked his horn, and she flipped him off. It was good to be out in the city.

She walked the streets like a hooker looking for a trick. And it would be a trick to see how Corvus contacted her. How would he even find her? He couldn't exactly call the @1 number and ask for her.

Somehow, come night, she didn't think he'd have a problem. Which left her with a few hours to kill.

Suddenly, she wished she hadn't used quite that phrase.

She couldn't even shop, since she hadn't taken Jonah's wallet. Well, she'd taken twenty bucks, but only so she could catch a cab to her doom, as soon as she figured out where her doom was.

In the meantime, the new sandals were wearing a blister on her heel. She needed a place to sit while the demon did its patch work. So she walked to the Congolese diner.

The dinner rush was on, but there were still a few open seats at the counter. She slid onto the stool and reached for a menu. Ms. Mbengue had the page in her hand before she could complete the gesture. "Thanks."

The woman nodded. "Coffee?"

Nim hesitated. "Chai, please." She concentrated on the list of odd items so she didn't have to meet the other woman's gaze. "I guess I'll have whatever Jonah ordered before."

"That was breakfast. Would you like to try something more substantial, since it's getting late?"

Nim let the menu drop, wondering at the edge in Ms. Mbengue's voice. Nothing so simple as jealousy; that was easy to recognize. Not pity or disgust either; those were easy to pick out too. The woman was watching her with something like . . . yes, it was kindness.

Nim wrinkled her nose. She had enough kind women in her life now to start her own support group. Somehow she doubted they'd give her a "you go, girl" cheer on her plans for the evening. "Whatever you think is good."

Ms. Mbengue gave another brisk nod. "It's good you trust Mr. Walker. He is a good man."

"Good, good, good," Nim muttered under her breath as the woman bustled away. That's exactly why she had to track down the evil djinn-man on her own. Because the good man had rubbed off on her, got his goods all over her, and see where she was now?

Unfortunately, blaming Jonah for loving her didn't make her feel any better than sitting at his favorite diner without him. Bad enough she had to save his life—a life he was so damned eager to throw away because of her mistake. She also wanted to save him from loving a woman who could never be good enough.

Ms. Mbengue brought a bowl of steaming stew along with the chai, iced this time. The woman hovered, until Nim realized she was supposed to give some indication that the choice was to her liking. She took up her spoon with a silent sigh. Her breath kicked up the scent of potent spices. Oh, so *that* was how kind the lady was.

Nim tweaked her demon to standby and took a sip.

Fires of hell. Tears sprang to her eyes, too quick for the demon's healing.

"Jonah prefers his pepper soup with more chili sprinkles." Ms. Mbengue hefted a small pot of red flakes. "Would you . . . ?"

Nim gestured silently at her bowl, and Ms. Mbengue added a pinch. "He says it brings out the flavor."

"The flavor of hot?" Nim asked hoarsely.

Ms. Mbengue smiled. "Ginger and tamarind."

"Ah yes. I taste it now." She'd never taste anything again, since she'd been told the teshuva couldn't restore what had been permanently removed, like her tongue.

Ms. Mbengue gazed over her head. "Doesn't the day feel cooler now?"

"Pretty much anything would be cooler right about now."

The woman's smile deepened. "Try the tea."

Nim did as ordered. To her surprise, the chai, lightened to the color of Jonah's hair with milk and sugar, took the edge off the burn. "It's very good." Good, good. Just like him. She wished she could kick herself, but she might cause real damage with these heels.

"You'll have to bring him in for a last supper before we close next month. My landlord stopped in, and it seems the end has come at last."

If only she knew. Nim took another sip of soup and wondered if breathing fire might distract the sharp-eyed Ms. Mbengue. "I'm sure Jonah will come by."

"He's a man who deserves to find a light in his life."

The woman hesitated. "You could choose much, much worse."

"I'm about to," Nim assured her.

Someone in the kitchen called urgently.

"We all have fires to put out," Nim said. "Maybe that's what you meant by 'light.' "

Ms. Mbengue gave Nim a sharp look, the kind that reminded her the woman shared her origins with the executioner's sword and the four-pronged throwing knife. "No, I meant the light in his eyes when he looked at you."

Nim stared down at the pepper flakes floating in her bowl like mocking malice eyes. "He was hungry."

"He's in love. Don't you care?"

The rush of heat that went through Nim had nothing to do with the spices. Oh, she cared. For once, she cared so much about being the warrior he needed and the woman he craved.

As always, the only way she knew was to put her body on the line. "Enough chilies will burn it out of him."

Ms. Mbengue said something in a language Nim didn't know, but she wished she could memorize it, since she guessed it'd come in handy next time she wanted to swear around Jonah. Not that there would be a next time. Another call from the kitchen made the woman shake her head. "Fight your own battles, then."

"I will," Nim said softly to the woman's back. Jonah and the league had taught her that.

The dinner rush slowed as she finished her soup, and a few people lingered over their cups. Ms. Mbengue topped off her chai once without another word, and the golden liquid darkened to plain old tea. Nim left a few bills along with an @1 business card she'd snagged from Jonah's wallet. Maybe Ms. Mbengue would check in with Jonah in a few days, out of curiosity, and offer some of her chilies and wisdom.

Nim figured the least she could do was give him his harem back.

Shadows had settled into the cracks of the city, although the sky between the clouds still held streaks of blue. Lighter blue, like Corvus's eyes, to the west. Yellow too, like . . . Wait, the sun was too far down for those fiery streaks.

Heat lightning stitched a ragged line between the clouds, gathering the dark masses closer. The white glare faded, but the streaks in evil's cheap-ass light show remained.

Salambes. In an arrow over the city, pointing east toward the darkest part of the sky.

Good thing she'd always favored the night shift.

CHAPTER 26

Nim avoided a cranky mother wielding a stroller like a war chariot to herd her two kids out of the fountain. "If you don't come out of there right now . . ."

Could the unstated threat possibly be worse than the mass of tenebrae streaking the sky like gangrene? Nim seriously doubted it. Anyway, the kids weren't impressed.

Sera and Jilly had told her that children, crazy people, religious wackos, and sometimes artists might occasionally catch a glimpse of other-realm emanations. So she amped the teshuva, walked past the shrieking girls, and said in her lowest demon harmonics, "Listen to your mother."

The girls spun toward her and froze. She didn't know what they saw; maybe just stranger danger. That was true enough too.

The oblivious woman wrapped them in towels while their teeth chattered, and Nim walked on. That was one little family who wouldn't be caught in the thunderhead of demonic ether building above the pier. She let her fancy heels slow her just a bit, to give them a few extra moments.

More people were coming toward her off the pier. The park was closing; the weather closing in. With luck, no one would be left to suffer her latest—last—mistake.

She might not be as good as Jonah, as crazed as Ecco, as . . . as much of an ass as Archer, but at least she could win the league a smidgen of advantage against the dark. And this time, she wouldn't drag anyone else down, down, down with her.

She wished doing the right thing felt less lonely. But that was what Corvus had demanded.

A cop directing the stream of traffic out of the parking garage and past the entrance gave her a hard look as she passed, bucking the tide of pedestrians. But her heels and short skirt weren't entirely out of the realm of possibility for a nice girl taking a simple stroll on the boardwalk with her beau.

Luckily, he wasn't the fashion police, because the black vinyl trench coat didn't work with the ensemble at all. Except for hiding the throwing knife pinned between her shoulder blades, of course.

And she didn't have a beau either.

She walked past the amusement park, past the mini golf and the shops, past the stained-glass museum and theater, past the grand ballroom where the curved façade reached almost to the water, and stopped at the edge of the pier.

The lake on all three sides was black, the city lights dimmed by the lowering clouds. But to her demon's eyes, the fiery stain of the salambes overhead slicked the water like a burning oil spill. She tried not to hunch her shoulders at the psychic weight of the tenebrae above them. If she hunched, she'd skewer herself on the throwing knife at her back.

"You came."

At Corvus's distinctive slurred voice, she turned with only the faintest wobble. Not from the heels—she was far too professional for that—but from the fear that did unfortunate things to her knees. The thin traceries of the *reven* on her thighs raced like the heat lightning, there and gone again. She faced the gladiator with her teshuva guttering, one tiny match head against the raging flames of hell.

She imagined that match head against her skin, and she stiffened her knees. Yeah, this was going to hurt, but at least it would only be her doing the hurting. "I'm here, just like you asked."

The djinn-man opened his arms in a hallelujah pose, and birnenston spewed from the open sores of his *reven*. The poison hissed on the pavers. "The only one of your kind to listen." He clawed at his arm, and after a moment wrestled off the anklet. Birnenston welled from the gouge the too-tight chain had left in his skin. He held it out. "For you."

She didn't reach for it. She'd have to step too close. Besides, if he wanted her to have it, that couldn't be good.

He twirled the loop around his finger. "You think you can take it from me, as you've taken everything else in your life."

"I always gave a dance in return," she said.

His blue eye twisted toward her. "I know you did more than that for your talya mate. You gave him his soul back. We want ours."

"I don't have your soul. They told me it's woven in to the Veil, until the end of days."

"So end days." His voice thrummed with longing. "You were a slave like me, dancing to the masters' whims. End it."

"I wanted to, every time some wanker undertipped. But I can't." She hesitated. Actually, with Sera and Jilly, she almost had. So she added with reluctant truth, "Not by myself, anyway."

"Even I can't destroy the world alone—though please don't think I haven't tried—which is why you are here. And where are your league sisters?"

She frowned. How extensive was that brain damage? "You told me to come by myself. Remember?"

Both eyes—birnenston yellow and strangely celestial blue—focused on her in disbelief. "And you listened to me?"

Even evil thought she was a fuckup. A dust devil of cotton-candy threads, sulfur stink, and malice whirled around them, caught in the etheric centrifuge. "I couldn't ask them to die."

The djinni's fury reverberated in a language of hatred she couldn't quite make out under Corvus's snarl. "Since when do you care about anyone else in this world?"

"Since I fell in love."

She put her fingertips over her mouth. Her teeth lingered on her lower lip, as if she could bite off the *V* in "love" and stop herself before she said more. Where had that confession come from? And to say it to this monster? How sad.

But with the words said, an emptiness gaped around her. An endless, needy longing to be filled.

For a heartbeat, her knees wavered, and the poisonous darkness spread through her veins. After years of dancing alone, how had she let someone else become her other half? She'd sworn, with each burning match she snuffed on her skin, that no one else would steal her body, her soul, her life.

The stench of sulfur—from those old matches and from the swirling nightmare of tenebrae—sucked tears from her eyes. Around them, the malice hissed, as if sipping her pain.

Not that her petty commitment issues mattered anymore. She would sacrifice any chance of keeping body, soul, or life in order to save the league, the city, and maybe heaven itself.

Slave, he'd called her, and he was right. She had feared all she had left would be stolen. But what he didn't understand, and what she'd finally learned, was that it could still be shared. That knowledge, bittersweet, was all she had now, so she said it again because she always flaunted what she had. "Since I fell in love with Jonah, and he with me."

This time, the words locked her knees where even the teshuva and her years of pole work had failed. She stood so straight, the knife between her shoulder blades never touched her spine.

Corvus's face lit yellow with his djinni. "That is not the force you think it is."

"I know." She rocked up onto her toes until the high heels barely scratched against the pavers. "It's worse."

Despite her warnings, Jonah had touched her, and not just in the ways that made her moan. She was supposed to be the demon lure, and instead he had been the one to tempt her to try living on the light side.

Through the tenuous contact of the stilettos on ground, she sensed the tremor.

Corvus stiffened. "Liar. You aren't alone."

She let the black coat slip down her arms to pool at her feet. The lake breeze teased between the laces of the bustier, and the knife came easily to her hand. "Do I look stupid?"

Corvus scowled and took a menacing step toward her. "With that embarrassment of a weapon? You look suicidal. And your fellow talyan are no better off."

"Then it's a good thing that's not who's coming."

With a shriek and a clatter, the ferales poured over the facade of the ballroom. A crimson-studded tsunami of malice boiled behind.

"You are suicidal *and* stupid." Corvus whirled and spread his arms. But the oncoming horde—drawn irresistibly to the lure of her—was too overwhelming even for his powerful demon. The djinni streamed away from him like a ragged cloak in a hard wind, but the etheric connection never quite severed.

Of course not. The djinni would never believe it could fail.

Well, she knew all about making mistakes.

He spun toward her. "They'll tear us apart. Stop them!"

"Gladly." She leapt forward with a downward slash of the knife at his hand where the anklet still dangled.

He bellowed, and the djinni snatched him away with the careless violence of an angry child with an old toy.

"I can't do it without the anklet," she shouted back.

"Open a path to the Veil first."

She would've stomped her foot, but not in these heels. "That's not my trick."

"You've turned plenty of tricks since the teshuva made you its whore."

Nim wished she had a witty comeback, something about prosti-dudes who lived in glass houses . . . but the ferales were upon them.

Corvus roared again and ripped one of the decorative lampposts out of the concrete. Wires crackled and the two bulbs exploded in a shower of glass. Corvus swept the impromptu weapon in a wide arc and scattered the first line of ferales.

Nim ducked as the arc continued over her head. On the backswing, Corvus took out the next line, knocking a half dozen of the tenebrae monsters into the lake.

Nim straightened slowly and looked askance at her puny knife. Her teshuva needed her to be up close and personal to drain demonic emanations, but right now she needed to be far, far away.

She slid the knife back in its sheath just as a half-human—one arm and one leg anyway—feralis slithered on its other, silverfish legs around Corvus's swing and reared up in front of her. Ratlike jaws opened in its sloped head. Revenge of the Mobi meals.

She grabbed for the nearest lamppost and swung herself around it, one leg at full extension.

Ah, this felt familiar.

The tip of her heel raked through the feralis's throat.

The creature toppled, rat tail lashing, and black ichor spewed in gruesome imitation of the cheerful fountain at the park entrance. But she had already landed safely beyond its reach.

With her demon's strength she grabbed the next lamppost and snapped it off at the base. Electrical sparks burned her ankles. So much for her shiny new sandals.

She bashed the end of the post against the pier railing to crack off the double lanterns at the top. With her newfound spear, she leveled a threesome of rushing ferales. Their attendant malice scattered beyond her reach, but the fiery vortex of salambes kept them from going too far.

No, that wasn't fair to the monsters. The lure that was her only claim to fame was what kept them from going too far. She felt dizzy, stretched outside her skin. Was she glowing like an irresistible bug zapper to tenebrae eyes? She had to get that anklet.

Backed to the end of the pier, at least she and Corvus couldn't be surrounded. Not that the djinn-man counted as an ally, but when ranking all the ways she could die in the next five minutes, fighting beside him seemed pretty low on the list.

At a scream behind her—not human or tenebrae, but mechanical—she moved Corvus even farther down the list.

Because Jonah had just moved to the top.

The *Shades of Gray* was coming in too fast. Jonah was going to hit the pier.

Another pulse of tenebrae energy knocked her back a step as the salambes swirled down and the ferales pressed forward, the malice a frantic presence between them. She was definitely in danger of getting chomped.

A spray of water hit the pier and jetted up as Jonah wheeled the boat sideways. Over the screech of fiberglass on concrete, the engine shrieked.

While she hesitated, her attention torn, Corvus swung

at the closest ferales. Not to batter them. To herd them toward her. He took a step toward the cleared path.

No. He couldn't escape, not again.

"Nim!" Jonah stood on the prow despite the treacherous buck of the boat in the waves he'd kicked up. The wind whipped his hair into a gold corona, as if he'd just risen from a bout of wild lovemaking.

The ridiculous flutter of her heart made her sigh.

He held up his hand, the executioner's sword slung low along his thigh. "Get in."

She glanced back. Corvus had muscled his way into the midst of the tenebrae. Focused on her, on the lure, they didn't care. "Corvus is here," she yelled to Jonah. "I can't let him go."

"Liam is coming from the land side. We have to get you away."

Before the mass of tenebrae slaughtered the last of the league.

This was what Corvus had wanted. For all of them to come, pawns in his attack on the Veil. The teshuva had made that mistake once, in the first battle that had started it all, and they were paying for it with an eternity of penance, along with the men who'd taken a few wrong steps down a dark path and into a demon's possession.

And she had damned them again.

In another heartbeat, Corvus would be clear of the feralis ring. He could slip by the talyan as they rushed to join her.

She took a breath. She couldn't settle the sick waves in her stomach as she took a step toward Jonah.

"Hurry," he urged. "Take my hand. I'll catch you."

She had to jump. Not that she'd ever really been one to keep her feet on the ground.

She took two more steps toward Jonah, opening space between the ferales and herself. She met his gaze; a long look. Or it seemed long to her, although the descending flare of salambes drew no closer, so maybe it wasn't that long at all.

His blue eyes widened, and she had a glimpse of what it would be like to live with someone who knew her better than herself.

It looked maybe a bit like heaven.

"Don't do it, Nim," he said. "Let Corvus go." He clung to the railing with his one hand but didn't pull himself up, unable to tie off the boat in the choppy waves and come after her. If the boat drifted, they'd have no way to escape.

"He's going to cut through the Veil like he cut through you," she told Jonah.

"I don't care, not anymore. Not if it means losing you."

"And now I do care." She smiled. "It's what you wanted, right?"

Stuck between the water and death, he canted toward her, every line of his body straining to reach her. "I want *you*."

"I love you." She whispered the words and trusted the demon lows to carry the truth through the shrill malice cries and the sudden boom of thunder as the clouds cracked and bled rain black as ichor.

Droplets clung to her lashes, lending light-spiked stars to the night.

Then she turned and ran toward the ring of monsters, jammed the broken tip of the lamppost into the concrete, and launched herself into the sky.

CHAPTER 27

Damn her! Jonah vaulted from the boat to the pier railing at her first step away from him and hauled himself over with one wrench of his arm.

Nothing compared to her leap, of course. Adding the teshuva's strength to her own daredevil insanity, she flung herself up into the open layer of night between the ferales roiling across the pier and the flaming cloud of salambes.

For an endless beat that threatened to drag his heart from his chest, she lingered at the top of the arc, a silhouette against the inferno.

The lamppost had no pole-vault flexion, only the demon's power to get her past the tenebrae ring.

It wouldn't be enough.

The sea of tenebrae was already turning to follow her flight, drawn unerringly to her.

Not that he blamed them.

He crashed into their rear guard, the sword a blur even to his teshuva vision. A head, a claw, a wing, a tail yielded to his blows. Ichor flowed below his boots, thin and viscous in the rain.

She was gone. Lost on the other side of the darkness.

And everything that remained of the man he'd been—no, of the man he wanted to be—was gone with her.

But he'd heard her last words. They echoed in his soul, stripped of demon harmonics. From the lips of his twisty, lying Nymphette, words simple and true.

Three quiet words sunk so deep into his heart, no hook would ever fish them out. He wanted her to say it again and again and again, to drown his disbelief forever in her sea-change eyes.

And he needed to say the words to her, to let the cry that echoed out of his soul.

The ferales closed around him. She was tenebrae temptation, no doubt, but he was a force they dare not deny.

The teshuva rose in him, fierce and furious with his desire. Where the loss of his hand had left him unable to balance it, now its havoc matched the tenebrae chaos like the dark water matched the sky. The triplicate edge of the sword and its shining point led him forward, a focus to his yearning for her.

Nothing would keep him from her.

His conviction was nothing mere demons could stand against. Hell itself didn't stand a chance.

He spun and slashed. Every blow was a follow-through that eviscerated another feralis. The teshuva's turbulent ascension spun curls of backwashed energy through the salambes.

A shiver went through the ether, and in mid-dance they paused.

Somewhere, the tenebraeternum was opening.

The league had reached the pier.

"Jonah!"

He looked up through the rain to see Archer beyond the ring of tenebrae. He'd fallen into a nightmare rhythm. Slash. Whirl. Parry. Duck. Slice. Repeat. With his teshuva rising higher, he hadn't realized he had fought almost clear of the ferales.

From the other side of the ring, Archer wielded his battle-axe in an annihilating swing.

Beside him was Fane. To Jonah's teshuva, the angelic host's hand-and-a-half sword did indeed flame, giving the tenebrae one choice: fall back or fall to pieces.

Standing between demon and angel, Sera emptied the husks so thoroughly, no trace of ether remained, banished to hell. The chill of the tenebraeternum hovered over them, as did the cold realization that Nim wasn't with them. They hadn't found her as they fought their way inward.

The four of them circled, back to back.

"Where's Nim?" Sera gasped. "The others are clearing the pier on their way here, but we need her."

"She's gone," Jonah said. It had been so easy to track her here. The thunderhead of demonic emanations rising above the pier had been an unsubtle-as-Nim clue. Now his teshuva senses were muddled with conflicting energies, and he had only his need for her, his desire, to lead him.

"Gone again?" Archer slammed the axe through a particularly insistent feralis. "I'd be starting to get a complex if I were you." He winced when his mate elbowed him. "Sorry. That's right. I *did* get a complex when I was you."

Jonah traced his sword through the last of the oncoming horde and smiled. "Complex? No. It's really quite simple."

"Nothing is simple," Fane growled. "Or I wouldn't be here. Your *symballein* has ruined millennia of perfectly good ignoring each other."

The storm wind yanked at his shirt hem and traced up his skin with wild fingers to unlatch his heart. Jonah was proud. If it was the kind of pride that went before a fall, he already knew who he'd fallen for. "Nim is hard to overlook." The powers of heaven couldn't resist, so what chance had he?

"We'll retrace our steps," Sera said. "She's on this pier somewhere. We'll find her."

Archer put his hand on Jonah's shoulder. "She can't have gone far."

Jonah tipped the blade toward the salambes-laced sky. The tenebrae around them screamed their frustration. Or was it fear? They must feel the conviction that swept through him and aligned every impulse within him. "Not without me."

Nim landed in a crouch and rolled, hoping she didn't impale herself on the throwing knife at her back. She came up running, and the tenebrae didn't follow her. She would have thanked God, but she suspected a much closer, slightly less holy power was fighting on her behalf.

She slowed and came to a stop when she spotted the hulking shape ahead of her on the sidewalk.

"You nearly killed me," Corvus bellowed. He still had his lamppost and he shook it at her.

From the deepened slur, she figured the man was in charge at the moment, since the djinni probably didn't much care about death. Except that it still needed something from the man.

"If you'd given me the anklet—"

"Too late. Your league is here. They'll open the way for me."

"Not on your life."

"That is no longer necessary." Corvus's guttural voice smoothed. The djinni ascended. "And neither are you."

He leapt at her, bashing with the post. She ducked and whirled. The lamppost slammed into the window of the vacant shop front, and glass sprayed.

When she straightened, Corvus was gone.

"No way." She spun. The sidewalk in both directions

was clear. She looked up. Could he have made that three-story vertical leap? She knew she couldn't, even with the teshuva.

She eyed the abandoned lamppost, wedged into the shattered window.

She gritted her teeth against the grind of glass on her palms and climbed through.

Unrelieved darkness, of course. A girl could get tired of never having the spotlight again. She crouched on the table where she'd landed and tweaked the teshuva to survey the interior. The space had obviously been a fast-food joint, and needed only a fresh coat of primary colors and somebody to crank up the deep-fryer to be functional again.

She stared over the counter toward the kitchen area. Toward a glimmer of real-world light.

Nothing to lose. She eased off the table, careful not to crunch on the glass. Tiptoes were good for sneaking.

In the prep area, a wall had been cracked open. The glow came through from the other side. It was a soft, beautiful light, and she found herself drawn forward.

It was the back side of the stained-glass museum.

She'd noticed the sign earlier, though she'd never stopped in on all her trips to the pier. Now didn't really seem the time either, but ...

She ducked through the broken concrete blocks. The vaguely gladiator-sized hole meant she didn't even get any dust on her.

The backlit, colored windows hung on panels throughout the room, seeming to linger suspended in the dark space. She'd come out in a room of eternal spring, with flowers and hummingbirds and sunrises and—oh, look—a cavorting nymph.

She eased her knife from its sheath, wishing she'd thought to pick up Corvus's discarded lamppost. But at least it would be a red flag to the talyan on their way.

"Too late." The voice hissed between panels.

She whirled, trying to target the source. "It's never too late while we still breathe." She thought of Jonah's lips on her. "And sometimes not breathing isn't too late either."

"I wanted to breathe the rarified air, to fly with emperors. But they clipped my wings."

She cocked her head, following the sound. "That was your penance trigger? I think you've paid for your sins by now."

"And now the rest of the world must pay."

"Not our call."

"Who else? We are the only gods that still walk among them."

She slipped around a window that showed a large golden bird feeding a circle of its young. The bird's head was bent to its breast and the droplets suspended from its beak were bloodred. She winced in sympathy and blinked to clear the bright dazzle from her eyes. "I prefer to dance."

"Then we shall."

Corvus stepped out from behind the panel.

She couldn't hold back a squeak of surprise and a startled step away. Her heel hovered over nothingness.

In the least graceful movement of her entire life, she flailed, arms windmilling.

And the knife lashed out and caught Corvus against his knuckles.

He snatched his hand back.

But not his fingers. Three severed digits thunked against the floor, and the anklet he'd clutched flew upward in a glinting arc of silver.

Nim had a split second and a snake-bite reflex to hook the anklet chain with the four-pronged knife.

And then she tumbled backward into the darkness.

It wasn't a long fall. She of all people appreciated the difference.

Nim pushed to her feet, wobbling when her hands

slipped in the shallow water. She must've blacked out for a moment when she hit bottom. How convenient that she'd landed flat on her back and spared her heels.

Best of all, the conk on the head seemed to have shorted out her tenebrae lure, although she vastly preferred Jonah's method of distracting kisses. At least she felt like she fit back inside her skin, and her *reven* wasn't pulsing like other-realm signal fire anymore. Or maybe the slick of slimy water all over her had extinguished the lure.

The lure . . . She fished through the water and winced when she sliced herself on something sharp. She lifted her knife from the muck. How many centuries before she forgot the sound of Corvus's severed fingers pattering against the floor? She turned the knife side to side.

The rough-hewn bead of demon-mutated metal clanked against the upper prong where the chain looped around the blade. "Just as ugly as I remembered."

She fastened the chain around her ankle, then stood to squeegee the front of her bustier. She grimaced up at the hole in the ceiling. No one was ever going to find her down here. How did a pier have a basement, anyway? The stained-glass glow across the opening gave the empty pit an embarrassingly cliché go-toward-the-light motif.

As if she needed inspiration.

The giant, creepy feralis down here with her was motivation enough to get out.

It was vaguely turtle shaped but with tentacles, as if Chihuly had collected an insane number of Japanese glass floats and made an art car out of a Volkswagen Beetle. With tentacles.

At least it was dead. No ether brightened its husk, only the glimmer of the glass orbs embedded in its shell between the limp, fleshy tentacles.

She didn't usually like modern art, and she really didn't like the look of this thing.

Options. Scream? Who knew what she'd bring down on her head. She'd already sworn a couple times, which hadn't done her any good.

She screamed anyway. Her voice, doubled with the demon and her own frustration, shivered the surface of the dank water. The only other effect was that it hurt her throat.

So, not much in the way of options.

She eyed the feralis husk. The uppermost curve of its shell would give her an eight-foot boost toward the ceiling.

With a bit of grunting and more swearing, she centered the carcass below the hole. She scrambled up, cringing at the wet suck of flesh as her heels pierced the tentacles.

The ragged opening was tantalizingly out of reach. Well, what was a demon for if not tempting? She crouched, tightened every muscle, and summoned the teshuva to the forefront. Her vision shifted into the blacklight range.

And she jumped. Her thighs burned as muscles and nerves ripped under the supernatural strain.

Oh, not even close.

She fell back to earth, knees bent to absorb the shock. Her heel punctured one of the orbs in the feralis shell. Glass sliced at her foot and chimed against the anklet chain.

And a geyser of soulflies burst from their prison.

She recoiled at the strange static hiss as they streamed past her skin. To her dismay, her teshuva wavered too, withdrawing from the soul exodus. Her thighs darkened with bruises, and blood from her cut ankle pooled in the empty glass bowl.

The cloud of soulflies dispersed slower. The pale flickers, like ash in the wind, drifted through the chamber.

Nim stared down at the husk where she crouched. She brushed her fingers over another of the orbs. A silvery storm danced across the inner curve of the glass, following her touch.

There were dozens, maybe more than a hundred, of the glass enclosures embedded in the feralis, some the size of her fist, some wider across than her forearm. This was what he'd been perfecting at the grain elevator. He'd learned to capture not just tenebrae, like Ecco bottling malice, but souls. Were all the orbs packed with soulflies? If all that etheric force was released at once . . .

She was standing on a soul bomb.

In the next heartbeat, she found herself standing on the other side of the chamber, her back flattened against the wall. Obviously, the teshuva wasn't keen on sitting on a bomb either. If the teshuva didn't like it, this must be part of Corvus's reason for calling her here, for demanding she and the other talyan open the way to the Veil.

Never mind stopping Corvus. She had to stop Sera and Jilly. If they kept fighting the tenebrae as they always did, defending the league with their *heshuka* tricks, they'd inadvertently help Corvus bomb the hell out of . . . hell.

She had to get out.

Which made her wonder, How had the feralis gotten in?

Since she was already against the wall, she walked the perimeter of the chamber. But touch found nothing that her demon-aided vision hadn't already noticed *wasn't* there—no hidden openings, no trapdoors.

What wasn't she seeing under the scrim of bilge sheeting over the floor? She waded out.

The water never got higher than her knees, but at the lowest point, she took one more step and her foot hovered over nothing.

She yanked herself back. "Great," she whispered. The echo came back even more mocking than she'd said it.

The turtle remains that the ferales at the grain elevator had scavenged must have given Corvus the idea to turn his attention from the skies to the water. It would have been easy enough to haul the huge, soul bomb–embedded husk here where no one would ever find it. Until he was ready for a trio of troublesome female talyan to set off his bomb.

She gave one last longing look at the heavenly gleam of the reflected stained glass above her. She wished Jonah was beside her, so she could make him blush with some crude joke about the pleasures of going down.

Then she dove into the dark.

The divide between the realms stretched thin. Corvus Valerius lifted his head to catch the taste of hell. Thin, dry, and cold, but with a surprising sparkle, like a very drinkable, but regrettably evil, champagne.

He paced the roofline, his wounded hand tucked under his arm. The djinni let the three stumps bleed, focused on the trapped souls far below his feet and the uproar of the tenebrae still battling the talyan. The league would win. They were very good. And Corvus was only one man. Well, one man and one djinni.

But in winning, the talyan and their earnest teshuva would make his dream come true. What he had started, unknowingly, with the first female talya could not be stopped. He had sought a demon to end his pain. And his summoning had possessed Sera Littlejohn. She had stolen his soul to patch a hole in the Veil, but the second female talya had taught him that the bond between souls was stronger even than hell. Jilly Chan's love for her mate had given him the template for the glass traps.

And now the third . . . The Naughty Nymphette had brought them all together at last.

What price, three fingers?

In less time than it would have taken him to finish

a bottle of 1907 Heidsieck, the Veil would be exposed, his missing soul would be reclaimed, and the final battle would light up the world.

Jonah's belief had leached away over every square foot of pier where Nim wasn't.

The talyan were spread out across the pier, slowly but definitively battling back the tenebrae, and the damage was going to make the papers the next day.

Assuming there was a next day.

"Good thing At-One Salvage will have the lowest cleanup bid to the city by nine tomorrow morning," Liam said when Jonah found him. "We'll find your mate too. She's probably trying to keep a low profile while we finish off these ferales."

"Right," Jonah said. "That's Nim; low profile all the way."

Liam gave him a wry look. "Your mate has rubbed off on you. I like it."

She had, Jonah realized. And he liked it too.

No, more than liked it.

The rain had petered out to a mist that starred the lights of the city. His body ached with wounds he'd ignored and left to the demon. But the ache inside sharpened, like a blade whetted on his longing.

Where was she?

He closed his eyes. Even at the Shimmy Shack, when he'd tried to shut out the sight of her naked glory, he'd always known where she was.

He walked away from the knot of talyan. The sound of the skirmish deadened in his ears.

When he looked up, only the dark lake stared back at him, black and restless.

And then the splash and a gasp drew him to the railing.

"Nim!" He clambered over the railing and reached

down to her. "What are you—? Never mind. Will you take my hand this time?"

"Corvus will tell you, that's not a good thing to say to me." She slapped her palm into his, and he hauled her up. "We have to stop them."

"We are. We almost have them contained, and then Sera and Jilly will finish them off, send them to hell."

"No, we can't do that! I think that's what Corvus wants." She dragged her hands through her wet hair so the mismatched locks stood up in wild disarray.

He shook his head, trying to concentrate on her words, not the slick black leather of her bustier. "Corvus wants us to defeat the tenebrae?"

"Because if we use our best weapons—me and Sera and Jilly—we'll open a path to the Veil, Corvus will follow, and then he's going to set off a soul bomb. That much etheric energy will be worse than anything we've faced against the demon realm."

There were all sorts of bombshells, and right then he decided he liked the half-naked kind better.

As she quickly explained the feralis husk she'd found, she dragged him down the boardwalk. She hopped a few steps on one leg to show him the anklet.

He let his gaze linger on her leg. "All this for that?" He traced his way up her exposed thigh, past the black vinyl and lacings, to focus on her wide eyes. And he knew he'd do all this again in a second. Or an eternity.

She thought he was still talking about the anklet. "I told you it was ugly."

As if he cared about the anklet when the woman attached had enthralled him, body, heart, and soul. He wrapped his arm over her shoulder. "You're shivering."

"Gee, I wonder why."

"Because Sera and Jilly are reaching for the tenebraeternum."

Nim strained against him. "We have to get to them."

"We don't have time. The museum is just down there. You can lure the souls to you, keep them from getting through to the Veil."

She shook her head. "I can't. Every attempt has been a disaster."

"You have the anklet now."

"What's this ugly jewelry going to do for me?" Her voice rose, laced with panic. "Trust me, anything I've ever gotten from my admirers has not been good."

"If the teshuva's artifact isn't enough"—he took a breath and looked into her eyes, forcing her to match the steady rhythm of his pulse—"then there's always me."

She stilled. "What are you going to do for me?"

"Be there. Always."

She closed her eyes. "Oh, hell."

He smiled. "Especially there." He tugged her hand. "Come on. It's not too late."

They raced through the abandoned restaurant. In the shadowed museum, the magnificent light of the stained-glass windows cast a halo of color, as if dark clouds has spilled a rainbow across the earth.

"Watch the hole," Nim warned him.

"I see—"

Before he could finish, the temperature had dropped. The water between the laces of Nim's bustier glittered with ice. His vision fogged as the thin layer of moisture over his eyes crystallized before he blinked.

The tenebraeternum swallowed them whole.

Chapter 28

The infinite hues of the glass all drained to icy gray, and Nim's heart withered. Maybe once, she'd imagined setting the world on fire. But all that would remain was ash, and it would look a lot like this. She whirled to run back.

Right into Jonah's arms.

Gold and blue. His hair and eyes held the lingering warmth of summer. "This is the boundary of the demon realm. We have to stop this here."

"It's too late."

"Nim, it's never too late."

How could he say that when he'd spent almost the past hundred years in mourning?

She wanted to call him on it, but he added, "The city and our souls are in your hands."

She scowled. "Oh, no pressure or anything."

He kissed her hard. "At least you have two hands."

The chill settled in her bones. "I can't hold the Veil together, even with two hands."

"You'd be surprised what your touch will make whole and right." He lifted her white-knuckled fist to his lips, and this time his kiss was fleeting.

She had never wanted to fight on the light side. The

stakes were too high. And the darkness never minded a fuckup. But he believed in her. She owed him for more than everything she'd taken from his wallet.

She swallowed. "Where is the Veil?"

"All around us. The boundaries of the no-man's-land between the realms have their own rules."

She turned in his embrace and faced outward. Stirred by her movement, swirls of the gray pulsed outward like a ripple of oil on water, carrying a faint haze of Jonah's gold and blue, as if the demon realm sipped from his warmth. An answering shift in the chill flowed back to her.

Something knew they were here.

Well, it was practically an invasion, after all. Somewhere Sera's calm brilliance and Jilly's quicksilver verve would be lighting the shadows, not realizing their incursion laid a path for the soul bomb straight to the protective Veil between earth and hell.

With Jonah's bulk a comforting heat and heft and *reality* behind her, she closed her eyes and opened her arms. Opened her heart, her soul. *Come.*

In her mind's eye—or maybe to her body's eye, if her body was still standing in a stained-glass museum on a pier in Chicago—a dark hole blossomed with silver as a tornado of soulflies spiraled upward in a spray of glimmering glass shards.

Then the swirl was all around her and Jonah, here in the tenebraeternum. He tightened his grip, his arm warm under her breasts. The soulflies tingled on her skin as she leaned into the strength of his embrace. She could do this; she could save the world. *Touch me. Stay with me.*

"No!"

The scream snapped her upright.

Corvus.

He raced toward them. The djinni loomed above him in a tower of malevolent light, its power unfettered here, so close to its source.

The rage of his coming blew the gray in streaks like storm clouds over a wind-whipped lake. His upraised fist with its missing fingers stained the gray with crimson-black. "The lost souls must take my place in the Veil."

Jonah pointed the executioner's sword at the furious gladiator. "They can't pay for your sins, Corvus. Salvation has never worked that way."

Corvus sneered. With the demon's distortion, his teeth lengthened into fangs. "Not so, if you've read your own scriptures, talya."

Jonah shook his head. "You'll find no saints here to take your place, djinni."

Nim shivered against Jonah's chest. Wasn't that a lie? She knew at least one saint who would do anything to save a sinner.

Her hold on the soulflies wavered. And the Veil began to warp.

Dark pennants unfurled from it like wings and drew the soulflies closer in a fractal whirl.

In the center of the wings, in the maw of the whirlpool, was the tenebraeternum itself.

"Mine," Corvus crooned. He extended his stunted hand, and the wings flexed toward him in answer, as eternally drawn to him as the soulflies were to their haints. "My soul."

The djinni strained in the other direction. What havoc would it wreak unbound from its husk?

"Nim." Jonah's voice broke with urgency. "You can't let the soulflies take his place. Not all of them were meant to be here, and once Sera and Jilly close the path, the souls will go wherever they were bound—heaven or hell. They'll leave a wound in the Veil that will let all of hell through."

"Let them through," Corvus shrieked. "At long last, let them in and set us free."

The ferocity of his scream shredded through the etheric mists, and Nim turned to shelter her face against

Jonah's chest. She couldn't do it. The tear in the Veil that Sera had woven together with the threads of Corvus's soul almost a year ago was too great for any patch of soulflies. Nim wanted to let it go. Throw it all away. As she'd always thrown everything away.

As Jonah would throw her away when the fight ended.

And it would end. Maybe not tonight or in any span of years she'd ever counted, but she'd be there and she'd have to watch him walk away because, in the end, she could never be good enough. She'd never been good enough.

This was why she hadn't wanted to be touched.

She looked up at Jonah and lifted her hands away from his chest. Pulling away from Jonah was like ripping off her own skin. The last hard thud of his heart echoed against her palms and was gone.

He met her gaze. "Nim, no."

"You can't really love me."

"Yes, I do. How can you doubt that?"

Because she'd never known otherwise. But she did know her soul would fit where Corvus's was tearing free. "There's not enough saint in me for you, but the Veil always has room for another sinner."

"No." He reached for her.

The gray chill hardened like ice, like unbreakable glass, between them.

And he kept reaching.

"Don't," she cried. The demon realm closed around her, with knife teeth of cold and dark. He'd already lost so much. Would he sacrifice his other hand, his life?

"I'd give it all for you." His voice whispered through the thickening gray as her vision faded. "And you've already taken my heart."

He stepped through the gray in a searing blast of gold and blue.

The shadows of wings tore loose and flared above her, high and hungry. She could throw herself into the darkness once again, where her only pain was self-inflicted, or she could let life, love, and Jonah do their worst.

She ran for Jonah.

She would've been faster, except for the really ill-considered spiked heels.

He pulled her close. "Dance for me, Nim."

She whirled in his arms to face the Veil. It was all around them now, a coruscating gray nightmare of half-seen shapes. A face, a bowed head, a locked fist—hundreds, thousands, an infinity—all gray as stone, all silent and still. Not tormented by anything she could see, they'd made the hell their own.

The soulflies would be too scattered and shattered to fill the void, for the void was endlessly ravenous.

She stretched out her hand, Jonah's laid atop her own. The ring on his finger glinted.

"Do you trust me?" she murmured.

"With all that I am and more."

"If I call the souls to me now, maybe Sera can guide them and Jilly can contain them. But if I wait until the bomb explodes on its own . . ." She gazed at him. "Under normal circumstances, I wouldn't steal a soul again—I swear."

His lips twitched. "Good girl. Or as good as you need to be."

She sent out her call to the tenebrae as she'd once summoned her own darkness with matches against her skin. The power burned phosphorescent through her body.

Instead of guttering out in a stink of scorched flesh, with no one to notice or care, the etheric call arced between her and Jonah—her power and his focus—and blasted outward from their joined hands.

The shock reverberated through the Veil, and Corvus screamed.

The souls came.

Their white-ash drift coalesced around a million scin-

tillating colored flecks of glass as the soul bomb shattered in the human realm and rode the tide of her call
into the tenebraeternum.

The darkened hole where Corvus's soul had been
inhaled.

Corvus's cry lengthened and rose in pitch. Around
him, the djinni stretched, sucked in toward the demon
realm. It blackened, as if the fires of hell scorched it, but
it would not release the gladiator.

He fell to his knees, and the thick lines of the demon
mark on his arms cracked and bled. The djinni's shadow
mingled with red human blood and darkened the pool.

The rivulets trickled toward the open wound in the
Veil. The glass shards melted in midair and streamed
into the hole.

Still the djinni's hook in the Blackbird held.

Nim looked up, up, and up at the towering cloud of
evil, then down at the gladiator on his knees. "You want
to be free?"

Both his eyes were the pale blue of summer. "So the
demon promised me two thousand years ago."

"About time it paid up, then." She lifted her foot. The
anklet flashed with violet lightning. "Don't touch."

And she brought her heel down on the point where
djinni and blood were one. The Blackbird's soul flew,
loosed from her lure.

Corvus lifted his arms and laughed as the black lines
bled away. This time, the djinni screamed.

Without the soul to root it, separated from the body
it had possessed for two thousand years, the djinni
was sucked through the tear in the Veil. The recoil
blasted through the gray. The molten glass and blood
and the blackened ether streamed inward as the void
hungered.

Nim's fingertips warmed as the first touch of power
returned to her. Jonah thought she was good enough;

maybe that meant her soul wasn't the puzzle piece to fit into the torn Veil.

Who, then, should she sacrifice to keep hell from blowing wide-open? One of the wounded talyan souls she felt toiling at the other end of the no-man's-land? Some other innocent? Or some not-so-innocent who then would never have the chance—as she had—to make amends?

Well, she'd never thought much of sacrifice anyway.

And then someone turned off the lights.

A gentle touch on her eyelids, first one, then the other.

Kisses. She looked up to dark blue sky and dark blue eyes.

"Jonah?" Her voice cracked.

"You're back."

"Hell and back," she whispered.

"Not too often, hopefully." He kissed her again, on the brow this time.

She closed her eyes, just for a moment, reveling in his touch. "How'd we do?"

"You brought down the curtain. But left a chance for an encore."

When she frowned at him, he helped her sit up, though he remained on his knees behind her, cradling her. They were out at the end of the pier. To the east, the first rays of the sun glinted on the horizon.

She stiffened. "An encore? Then we need to get out of here before more people come. We can't let them be caught in this."

He hugged her. "No one will notice. They see what they want to see. And what they'll see is a nice new Congolese diner. I already have a proprietress in mind. What they won't see is the hole to the basement where there's a strange inverted glass sculpture that leads straight into the tenebraeternum."

"Leads into the ..." She winced. "Corvus took his soul, and all I had left to patch the hole were the shards of glass and ether. Nothing else would fit. Nothing else I would give up."

"Keep what's yours. We'll work it out."

"Together? Are we counting that as a win?"

He smiled, and the curve of his lips warmed her more than the sun that now slanted across the water. "We're still breathing."

He led her past the talyan who were hastening to clean up what they could before the morning crowds returned. She paused when they neared Fane. "You were here for the fight?"

Fane lifted one eyebrow. The knee-jerk disdain was tempered by the feralis gore staining him up to the knees. "Dawn of a new day."

She gave an exaggerated sigh of relief. "I work nights."

Jonah tugged her onward. From the museum, they climbed down a ladder someone had found into the chamber below.

Jonah said, "Liam is already drawing up a bid to do the repairs and renovations through At-One Salvage, Sewage & Bistros, Inc."

"Catchy." Nim walked around the old feralis husk. To her human eyes, the cracked-glass orbs looked like a nest of pretty broken eggs, as if—somewhere—birds of every hue were flying free. "Luckily, the museum upstairs only does windows, or they'd want this for their collection."

To her teshuva, the shattered remnants were terrifying. Past the brilliantly colored glass, it saw the void at the bottom of each open orb and the slow, oily churn of the black leading that held the remaining pieces together. Her pulse raced double time with the teshuva's tension. "That blackness ... It's the djinni."

Jonah nodded. "Corvus left the djinni in his place when you freed his soul."

"If by 'free' you mean 'dead.'" She'd seen the clatter of yellow bones half drowned in the shallow pool of the chamber. The dent in the skull and the two broken arms made identification a simple matter.

"Without the djinni to sustain him, he couldn't outrun a couple thousand years."

"I think he met it with open arms." She shivered at the chill that breathed from the exposed void. "Maybe he redeemed himself, but he left us with a hell of a problem. Actually, looks like several hells' worth."

"It just so happens I plan to have much to atone for."

She had leaned closer, despite the teshuva straining away from the hell it had escaped, but some note in Jonah's voice, a light in gloom, made her straighten.

As she did, another glint caught her eye. Threaded through the etherically mutated leading that was the djinni ran a razor-thin strand of gold.

The sudden stutter of her heart rivaled the teshuva for panic. "Your ring." She reached for Jonah's bare hand.

He gave her a smile, pure and simple as the missing band around his finger. "I am free too."

"But . . ." Her gaze slipped past him to the open pathways into hell. "Even possessed by a repentant demon, I'm no good at being good."

"Maybe good isn't what we need anymore. It's definitely not what I want."

He wasn't looking at the hellholes, though. He was looking at her. When she drew a breath to ask him what that shimmer in his eyes meant, he tugged her hand. "Come on."

The storm had passed, and the *Shades of Gray* rocked gently at the railing where he'd left it, with only one rope looped hastily around a cleat.

As they climbed in, she looked over her shoulder at the pier. From this distance, everything looked the same except for a couple missing lampposts. "Shouldn't we stay to help clean up?"

"We saved the day. That's enough for this morning."

He aimed the boat toward the rising sun. She blinked at him when he set the engine on a slow churn and joined her in the prow. "We're just going?"

"For the moment. It's not like we'll hit anything."

"I bet I could find a way," she muttered darkly.

He lifted her chin and kissed her, then settled her in his arm as he leaned back on the cushions and kicked his feet up. "We will find a way."

She'd never seen him so . . . happy. Something loosened in her, and she curled up against him and rested her palm on his chest. She couldn't remember now why she'd thought pulling away made sense.

His elbow was hooked over the side rail, and the cuff caught her eye. She touched the oddly familiar, intricate swirl that ran around it, and a violet spark raced away from her fingertip. She caught her breath and propped her foot on the cushion to look at her anklet.

The bead that had run loose on the thick, rough chain was missing. In its place, tiny glass rivets sparkled among the links.

He shrugged. "Not so ugly now, is it? The backlash of the lure power caught me so hard, it fused the cuff down to the bone." She gasped, but he squeezed her reassuringly. "It doesn't hurt. Not anymore. No straps means whatever weapon I use will fit almost as close as my hand. At least until I take it off." He gave her a wicked grin. "Good demon."

She bit her lip. Any weapon he wanted? "You wanted to be a stronger fighter. Now I guess you are."

He pulled back a little, and she shivered at the breeze that wedged between them.

He stared into her eyes. "I'm stronger with you. Because of you. You made me not the warrior, but the man I wanted to be."

"You were always a good man," she protested. "Too good for me."

He shook his head. "You always knew how to bend without breaking, how to dance even when the world was on fire. If anyone is thrall here . . ." He raised the cuff in a little wave, and the pleasure in him softened the curves of his lips.

She curled into him, and the anklet clicked against his wrist. A single violet spark raced around and through the patterns of his cuff and crossed to the anklet. "Ah, I knew from the start you liked to look. Thank heavens for my newfound ability to prettify hell."

"You've always enthralled me. Stop fishing for compliments."

"I don't fish."

"You caught me." He slipped off the cushions to kneel beside her.

"I guess I'm caught too," she said. "Mated-talyan bond. *Symballein*. Whatever that means."

"Love." He tucked a strand of hair behind her ear and smiled as it sprang loose. "It means 'I love you.' "

"How can you?"

"My body and my sword are yours—were always yours." He rested his forehead on her thigh a moment. "But you didn't just make me fight again. You let me love again."

She buried her fingers in the gilded waves of his hair and closed her eyes to focus on the whisper of his breath across her *reven* and faded scars. The sensation he ignited smoldered in her soul, sweet and everlasting. When he lifted his head, she met his gaze. His eyes reflected the blue of the water and sky, and she felt herself falling.

"But my heart is yours too," he said, "if you want it." He cupped her cheek, and she realized he'd waylaid a tear at the corner of her eye. "You don't believe me?"

"I do. I can't believe I believe you." She knew the wonder in her voice betrayed her. "But I love you."

His smile lit every corner of her heart with a hint of devilish heat. "I have forever to prove myself good and true."

"Start now." She leaned into his hand. "And touch me."

GLOSSARY OF TERMS FROM THE @I ARCHIVES

ascendant: The rise of a demon within a possessed human; refers to the initial incident of possession and subsequent risings.

birnenston: Also, *brimstone*. A sulfuric compound leached from some demonic emanations interacting with the human realm.

***desolator numinis*:** "Soul cleaver"; a demonic weapon.

djinni: djinn (pl.): Upper echelon of demonkind; fallen angels who are content to stay fallen.

djinn-man: A human possessed by a djinni.

ether: The elemental energy of spiritual and demonic emanations.

feralis: ferales (pl.): Lesser demonic emanation encased in a physical shell of mutated human-realm material. Physically strong, but not so impressive in the brains department.

***heshuka*:** The unknown darkness; from Aramaic.

horde-tenebrae: Blanket term for lesser demonic emanations, including malice, ferales, and salambes. Also, *tenebrae*.

ichor: A physical by-product of demonic emanations not compatible with the human realm.

league: Isolated clusters of possessed fighters assigned to high-density human-population areas with the mission of reducing demonic activity.

malice: Incorporeal lesser emanation from the demon realm, typically small and animalistic in shape with protohuman intelligence.

mated-talyan bond: The synergistic combination of male and female possessed powers.

reven: The permanent visible epidermal mark left by an ascended demon.

salambe: Highly emanating demonic form from the same subspecies as malice.

solvo: A chemical version of the *desolator numinis*; produces opiatelike effects in humans while splitting off the soul.

sphericanum: The realm of angels, separated from the human realm by the gates of heaven. Also used in reference to the ruling body of angelic powers.

symballein: A token, such as an engraved metal disk, that is broken into two pieces and used to establish identity when reunited; from Greek.

talya: talyan (pl.): 1. Sacrificial lamb; a young man (Aramaic). 2. A human, typically male, possessed by a repentant demon.

tenebrae: Blanket term for lesser demonic emanations, including malice, ferales, and salambes. Also, *horde-tenebrae*.

tenebraeternum: The demon realm, separated from the human realm by the Veil.

teshuva: A repentant demon seeking to return to a state of grace.

Veil: An etheric barrier between the human and demon realms and composed of captured souls.

From the @1 Handbook of Possession
Excerpted from *Chicago league roll call, Updated 4/11*

Liam Niall: League leader
Possession date: Chicago stockyards, circa 1845
Teshuva subcaste: Ravager
Bonded: Jilly Chan

Ferris Archer: Talya
Possession date: Georgia, circa 1860
Teshuva subcaste: Annihilator
Bonded: Sera Littlejohn

Sera Littlejohn: First confirmed female talya
Possession date: Chicago, 2009
Teshuva subcaste: Enigma
Bonded: Ferris Archer

Handwritten note from interim Chicago
Bookkeeper Sera Littlejohn: *First confirmed? If you
jerks would quit rewriting your history and deleting
the parts you don't like, you might actually learn
something.*

Jilly Chan: Second confirmed female talya

Possession date: Chicago, 2010
Teshuva subcaste: Discord
Bonded: Liam Niall

Jonah Sterling Walker: Talya
Possession date: Congo, circa 1890
Teshuva subcaste: Bane
Bonded: Nimue

Nimue aka Nim, born Elaine Hamlin: Third
confirmed female talya
Possession date: Chicago, 2011
Teshuva subcaste: Thrall
Bonded: Jonah Walker

Ecco (last name unlisted):
Possession date: Redacted
Teshuva subcaste: Chaos (unverified)

Three yellow handwritten notes from interim
Chicago Bookkeeper Sera Littlejohn:
Allies:
Nanette, possessed by lesser-sphere angelic force
Lau-Lau, Jilly's weird old landlady—possibly a witch

Wow, this is a disappointingly short list

Frenemies?
Bella, owner of the Mortal Coil nightclub
Cyril Fane, possessed by upper-sphere angelic force

Definitely enemies:
Bookie, "retired" to soulless summer camp
Corvus Valerius!!!

Fourth note (author presumed to be Ferris Archer):
Finish your notes tomorrow. Come to bed. Now.

From the @1 Handbook of Possession:

Demonic classifications:

Djinn: Upper echelon of demon-realm inhabitants
Subcastes: Unknown
Resonant vulnerability: Evil

Teshuva: Repentant demons
Resonant vulnerability: Penance trigger

Horde-tenebrae:
Known subcastes:
Malice
Ferales
Salambes

Early league writings chronicling the First Battle in-
dicate numerous tenebrae subcastes answered the djinn
rally against the angelic forces. Many subcastes are
thought to have been eradicated at the end of that era,
due to the valiant sacrifice of talyan lives.

Handwritten note from interim Chicago Bookkeeper Sera Littlejohn:

Eradicated, my ass. We haven't seen the worst of it yet.

Continue reading for a preview of
Jessa Slade's next Marked Souls novel,

BY DARKNESS UNDONE

Available soon from Signet Eclipse

The Chicago league of demon-possessed talyan destroyed one enemy . . . and in the process unleashed a horde of new problems. Sidney Westerbrook, the league's interim Bookkeeper, arrived from London less than twenty-four hours ago to sort out the mess and has already had his first encounter with a feralis pack. He'd be dead if not for the unexpected appearance of a rogue female talya. But strange little Alyce might be more dangerous to Sid's mortal human heart than any feralis fang, and rescuing her from the demons of her very distant past could be his ultimate undoing.

Sid kicked off his filthy jeans and eased out of his shirt. He noted the bloodstains from his draining wound, and suddenly had a better understanding of the league's rather shocking clothing allowance. Standing in his boxers, he wrapped his shoulder in gauze, then with a groan crawled into bed. But sleep eluded him, circling him endlessly as his inbound flight to O'Hare had done, so he grabbed his specs and pulled one of his favorite books into his lap. His father hadn't been thrilled to part with the gold-bound and -illuminated texts, but

Sid had convinced him the opportunity to study female talyan with original manuscripts in hand superseded jurisdictional pettiness. Besides, the ancient journal had lots of pretty pictures that weren't done justice in reproduction.

He donned archival gloves in deference to the old man and the old paper and hoped he wouldn't fall asleep and drool on the pages.

Somewhere just beyond the edges of his perception, he sensed the warehouse quieting as the night-fighting talyan rested, secure in their sanctuary. The cinder blocks seemed to breathe out peacefulness that he'd never felt in person among the restless warriors.

Eventually, his eyelids drooped. Through the haze of his eyelashes, the intricately drawn illustrations danced with strange, wild life, a tangle of angels and demons without clear distinction.

He blamed his gritty eyes for making him blink dumbly when he looked up and saw the visitation, as if one of the ethereal figures from the primeval text had stepped off the page, as if a fever dream had come to life. He fumbled in setting his drooping specs higher. "Alyce?"

She ghosted across the room, her bare feet silent on the linoleum. Her pale eyes glittered, amethyst over ice. "Shh. I've come to free you."

A ping raced through his body, from the sudden acceleration of his heartbeat to his extremities, like a warning signal. "Free me?" He sounded as clueless as he no doubt looked. He pushed aside the book, careful not to wrinkle the pages. "Did Liam let you in?"

"There was a devil-man at the gate." She fisted her hands in her skirt. The grandmotherly housedress lacked the ichor stains of her last ensemble, but the powder blue polyester was worn to near transparency in places. And now there were fingerprints of blood in the folds. "I did not stop to ask him his name."

"Oh, Lord." The ping went round his innards a few more times, gaining particle-accelerator speeds. Had she killed Liam or one of the other talyan? That would put a definite wrinkle in his reintroduction strategy.

Alyce shook her head. "These beings are not of the Lord. I see the devils in their eyes."

"They are possessed," he admitted. "But not by devils. Or not evil devils, anyway. Their teshuva—the demons inside them—are like yours."

"Evil," she whispered. "Like me."

"Repentant," he corrected. "Fighting for the light now."

"There is no light for me."

"Not before, maybe. But now that you're here, everything is different."

She pressed her bloody palms together and raised her hands until her fingertips brushed under her chin. Despite the prayerful pose, her gaze speared him without mercy. "Is this where I die?"

He recoiled. "God, no!"

"Lord and God, you say. I thought maybe you would banish the devil from me."

"I can't."

Her hands fell back to her sides, and he was left staring at the *reven* around her neck. The welt briefly shimmered with violet light, then faded to black, as if her teshuva hadn't the strength to maintain its outrage.

But she had incapacitated at least one of the talyan to get this far.

What *was* she?

Slowly, keeping his eye on her, he climbed out of the bed. His navy boxers weren't suitable for an audience with the queen, but he wasn't indecent.

Alyce stood back, showing no sign of bolting. Instead, her gaze flicked over him, touching on the gauze at his shoulder, the bruise on his forehead, and various contusions in between. She never dipped below the belt line. "Were you badly hurt?"

He shrugged the shoulder that wasn't wounded. "They patched me up here, so it can't have been too bad. I've never had to go to the hospital for feralis injuries before."

"Don't. They won't believe you."

His fingers itched to find a recorder, or at least a pencil and paper. "You've tried? When?"

"I don't quite remember." Her wintery gaze darkened. "It did not end well."

Which reminded him about the talya at the gate. "We need to go pick up the pieces of the welcoming party you left in the dust."

"He was rude."

"That happens with talyan. But it's not nice to break them just for that."

She nodded. "I did not understand they were yours."

He halted in the middle of grabbing his jeans. The Chicago talyan? His? Hardly. London had loaned him out because Liam didn't have his own Bookkeeper, but they didn't want him. Hell, *he* didn't want *them* either. He wanted London. Someday. Hopefully a long time in the future, when his father retired to putter around his garden.

Alyce was watching his face, her expression mirroring the furrow of his brow. "I've made you sad. I didn't want to hurt him. But I wanted to come to you."

He smoothed a hand down his face, erasing the quick, helpless calculations of his father's chances of surviving to spring, much less retirement. "You don't make me sad. In fact, I can't possibly explain how happy I am to have you here." He stepped into his jeans, wishing she wasn't watching quite so closely, but intrigued by her empathetic responses. How did a talya—eternally driven by the demon to the furthest reaches of violence and destruction—keep any semblance of softer emotions?

No wonder she was odd.

What a spectacular find. Or, he supposed, how spectacular that she'd found him.

He had a half second to wonder how exactly she'd found him when she reached out and flattened her palm over his belly, just above the unbuttoned fly of his jeans.

Alyce held her hand against Sid's warm skin even when he sucked in a harsh breath to pull away.

She had never of her own will touched a man. She knew she should not touch him now. But the textures of him made her fingers reach out for the smooth planes of his flanks, where hard sheets of muscle wrapped around into his rippled abdomen . . . and the tidy line of hair connected the shadowed indent of his navel to the darker mysteries below the button of his pants.

"You are real," she murmured. He was clean, cared for, wounded but alive. And oh so warm. "Not one of my delusions." She canted her head to gaze up into his brown eyes. "I wasn't sure."

To answer, he had to let out the breath he'd been holding. "I am real. As real as you."

"I haven't been sure of that either."

Slowly, as if she might run—or attack—he lifted her palm from his belly. He tangled his fingers through hers and raised her hand to his chest. Against her knuckles, his heart pounded.

"Real as you," he said.

She nodded.

"Can we go find the other talyan? Don't be afraid. They won't hurt you."

She tensed but released him at once when she saw him wince at the tightening of her grasp. "They'll want to."

"They're just nervous."

"Because of me?"

His lips quirked, and suddenly she wished she'd

touched him there instead, to feel that soft curve. "You are very scary."

She lowered her head, letting the curtain of her hair fall over her eyes.

He closed the distance between them in one step. "Alyce, I was teasing." He hesitated. "Well, exaggerating. Or maybe . . . Never mind."

Thorne had warned her. He'd known she wasn't suited for proper company, even with an unstained frock. She took a sidling step away.

But Sidney followed. "Alyce. Look at me."

She did. Or, she looked at his mouth again. Words came so fast and furious from that mouth, faster and more furious than the devils. And yet she very much liked his mouth even when it confused or teased her.

What did Thorne know—him and his devil's whispers? Well, he had mentioned that one thing, that thing older than evil. That always bought silence.

She jolted up onto her toes and pressed her lips to Sidney's.

So soft . . . His lips were every bit as soft as she'd guessed. And wonderfully warm. And they curved around hers, like a secret smile she couldn't see but could feel. Only for her. She supposed she could get used to being teased.

"My Sidney," she whispered against his mouth. Or she meant to. What came out of her was a moan even softer than his lips.

She reached up to sink her fingers into his hair. The russet locks were just long enough to tickle the backs of her hands and send delightful shivers through her. Then she remembered the rest of his hair, the light patch of curls on his chest, and lower down, and she wondered where else that might tickle her, so she let her fingers trip over his breastbone and down his belly. Ah, this hair was rougher but every bit as pleasing to her touch.

His fingers wrapped around her upper arms. Good, or she might have fallen as her knees weakened. Mouth to mouth, their breath swirled and merged, a close, sultry mingling that promised deeper intimacy if she could just—

He pulled away, and their lips parted. "Wait." He locked his elbows, and his grip on her arms kept her from stepping back into his embrace. "Alyce, wait."

His grasp wasn't really strong enough to stop her—and his hands were shaking slightly, besides—but she waited because he'd asked.

"What are we doing?"

"I know the answer to this one," she said quickly.

He laughed, the sound as unsteady as his grasp. "How did you stay so innocent with a demon inside you?"

She froze. "I am not innocent."

Despite the eerie shiver in her voice, he kissed her again, on the forehead this time. Which was sweet, but not as sweet as on the mouth.

That must be the demon he'd mentioned.

For once, she was rather glad of the devil inside.

ALSO AVAILABLE
from

Jessa Slade

Seduced by Shadows
A Novel of the Marked Souls

When Sera Littlejohn meets a violet-eyed stranger, he reveals a supernatural battle veiled in the shadows, and Sera is tempted to the edge of madness by a dangerous desire. Ferris Archer takes Sera under his wing, now that she is a talya—possessed by a repentant demon with hellish powers. Archer's league of warriors have never fought beside a female before, and never in all his centuries has Archer found a woman who captivates him like Sera.

With the balance shifting between good and evil, passion and possession, Sera and Archer must defy the darkness and dare to embrace a love that will mark them forever.

"Wonderfully addictive."
—*New York Times* bestselling author
Gena Showalter

Available wherever books are sold or at
penguin.com

S0068

ALSO AVAILABLE
from

Jessa Slade

Forged of Shadows
A Novel of the Marked Souls

After surviving the Irish Potato Famine, Liam Niall was possessed by a demon in search of redemption. Now, he heads the Chicago league of taylan in their fight against evil. Jilly Chan is a mentor to the local homeless youth— and warrior against the criminals who prey upon her charges. She's already half-taken by a demon, so Liam reluctantly tries to guide her into full power.

Even as the proudly independent Jilly tries to remain true to her own soul, Liam's fiercely passionate touch leaves a mark on her desirable flesh as enduring as her new demonic tattoo...

"A chilling, complex, and utterly believable world."
—Award-winning author Jeri Smith-Ready

Available wherever books are sold or at
penguin.com